As I fished for my keys, I took a deep breath and froze.

Werewolf.

A moment later, I closed the door behind me and shrugged out of my suit, trying to control the change until I at least had my new skirt off. Less than a minute had passed before I let the urge pulse through me and dropped to all fours, sniffing the trail.

Ears pricked forward, I padded toward the doorway, my mouth coppery with fear and rage at the violation.

I nosed into the bedroom, muscles bunched, prepared to spring. There was no movement, but the smell was much stronger here. I scanned the room; the mattress was upended next to the bed, and the contents of my drawers were strewn everywhere. The closet door was open, the light on. No werewolf. I could tell because my clothes had been torn from the hangers, so there was nowhere to hide.

My eyes flicked to the bathroom. It was the last place in the loft. She had to be there.

I crouched by the door and sprang, teeth bared, re

athroom was gone.

ARK COUNTY
STRICT
AS VEGAS BLVD, N
LAS VEGAS, NEVADA 89101

D0950831

Also by Karen MacInerney

Howling at the Moon

Books published by The Random House Publishing Group
are available at quantity discounts on bulk purchases for
premium, educational, fund-raising, and special sales use.
For details, please call 1-800-733-3000.

On the Prowl

TALES OF AN URBAN WEREWOLF

KAREN MacINERNEY

BALLANTINE BOOKS • NEW YORK

Sale of this book without a front cover may be unauthorized. If this book is coverless, it may have been reported to the publisher as "unsold or destroyed" and neither the author nor the publisher may have received payment for it.

On the Prowl is a work of fiction. Names, characters, places, and incidents are the products of the author's imagination or are used fictitiously. Any resemblance to actual events, locales, or persons, living or dead, is entirely coincidental.

A Ballantine Books Mass Market Original

Copyright © 2008 by Karen MacInerney
Excerpt from *Leader of the Pack* copyright © 2008 by Karen MacInerney

All rights reserved.

Published in the United States by Ballantine Books, an imprint of The Random House Publishing Group, a division of Random House, Inc., New York.

BALLANTINE and colophon are registered trademarks of Random House, Inc.

This book contains an excerpt from the forthcoming book *Leader of the Pack* by Karen MacInerney. This excerpt has been set for this edition only and may not reflect the final content of the forthcoming edition.

ISBN 978-0-345-49626-3

Cover illustration: Gene Mollica

Printed in the United States of America

www.ballantinebooks.com

OPM 9 8 7 6 5 4 3

Dedicated with love to Dorothy and Ed MacInerney,
who have made so many things (including this book)
possible. Thank you . . . for everything!

One

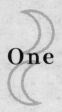

It's always those days when you think to yourself, "Life is just perfect" that life decides to bite you in the ass.

It was a sunny Tuesday morning, and I was sauntering into the office—my new partner office, with a big window, tall ceilings, and a mahogany desk I sometimes just liked to stare at. In one freshly manicured hand was my traditional skinny latte, extra foam. In the other was a little bag with a blueberry muffin in it. (I used Splenda in the latte, which kind of cancelled the calories out.) Tucked under my arm was today's paper, and in my purse—not as yummy as the muffin, but definitely necessary—was a fresh box of wolfsbane tea.

"Good morning, Sally," I trilled to my perpetually spandexed assistant. If she hadn't been hired by my boss, I would have fired her a year ago, but we all have our crosses to bear, I guess. She smiled tightly and adjusted her cleavage, then turned her back on me. We weren't exactly bosom buddies, but ever since I'd discovered a little bag of pot in her desk, at least she was no longer actively trying to get me fired and/or hauled off to jail. Which was progress.

I walked past her to my office, admiring the gold sign next to my door: "Sophie Garou, Partner." Although it had been there for a week now—which was when

Southeast Airlines, the big account I had pitched a few
months ago, decided to hire Withers and Young as their
accounting firm—it still felt like Christmas morning
every time I saw it. I was probably the only werewolf in
the country who was a partner at a Big Four firm, I reflected. Not that anyone at Withers and Young knew I
was a werewolf, of course. That's where the wolfsbane
tea comes in; it helps me keep my animal impulses in
check. Slobbering all over the clients and dashing out
of meetings to howl at the moon isn't great for career
advancement—not to mention client retention.

With the exception of my hairy little secret, I thought
as I tossed the newspaper on the desk and opened my
muffin bag, life was pretty sweet. Withers and Young
was on the fifteenth floor of one of Austin's plushest
buildings, and my new office had a great view of Lady
Bird Lake. Sinking into my cushy leather chair, I took a
bite of muffin and watched a couple of ducks swimming
aimlessly on the glassy surface. The only downside of
the view, really, was that I kept getting distracted by
ducks and squirrels—that whole predator thing. And
now that I was in charge of the humongous Southeast
Airlines account, that could be a problem.

Still, it was a minor concern, all things considered.
Valentine's Day was just over a week away, and since
I'd seen my boyfriend Heath leaving a jewelry store
recently—with a small, ring-sized bag in his hand—I
was, to put it mildly, looking forward to it. My mother,
the semi-psychotic psychic witch, hadn't been indicted
for killing off a right-wing politician in months. And the
equinox was over a month away, which meant there
were no obligatory full-moon transformations in my immediate future.

As I finished my muffin and ran my tongue over my
teeth—I always got crumbs stuck in my canines—the
phone rang.

"Sophie!"

"Hey, Lindsey. What's up?" Lindsey, who was also an auditor at Withers and Young, was my best friend—and a dead ringer for Angelina Jolie, which could have been a problem if she wasn't such a fabulous friend.

"Have you seen the paper?" she asked.

"No. Why?"

"They quoted Heath in one of the big articles. It's on the front page."

"Really? Good for him." I glanced at the front page of the *Austin American-Statesman*. "Three men found dead in Greenbelt: dog pack suspected."

My hand froze halfway to my skinny latte. Heath's pet cause, so to speak, had been eliminating stray dogs in Austin, which he viewed as a "menace." I wasn't too keen on his crusade—needless to say, I wasn't a big fan of dogcatchers—but this would just be fuel on the fire.

"Which article?" I asked Lindsey, even though I already knew.

"The one about the three guys who got murdered by dogs. The quote's on page six. Can you believe it? I always thought Heath was blowing smoke about the dangers of stray dogs, but maybe he was right after all. It gives me the heebie-jeebies. I went hiking there just last week!"

"I haven't read it yet," I said, scanning the text.

"Three guys turned up dead," she said. "Mauled by dogs. And it looks like Heath was one of the first people the reporter called."

I scanned the article. Three unidentified men—two Caucasian, one Hispanic—had been found in the Barton Creek Greenbelt, which was a mere mile from my loft, dead of massive bite wounds. I hoped the reporter was right, and that it was in fact a rogue dog pack attack. But what little hope I had flickered out when I discovered that the victims had been found (a) naked and (b) with fur stuck between their teeth.

"Isn't that great?" Lindsey said.

"That three guys got killed in the Greenbelt?" I asked.

"No, dummy. That Heath got a quote in the *Statesman*."

"Oh. Right. Yeah." I stared at the photo of a black body bag being pulled out of the undergrowth. Unless there was some new group in town whose idea of a good time was stripping down, rubbing ground beef all over themselves, and taunting packs of feral dogs, I had a sinking feeling I was looking at the fallout from a werewolf squabble. Which was more than a little bit disconcerting. I hadn't seen a single werewolf in Austin since last September, and before that, I'd run into a grand total of two in twenty years. The whole dead-in-a-public-park thing was an unpleasant new development, to say the least.

"Sophie? Why are you so quiet?" she asked.

"Sorry," I said, reaching for my latte. "Not enough coffee, I guess. Can I call you later?"

"Sure," she said. "Tell Heath congrats from me when you see him."

After we hung up, I read the article again, feeling a growing sense of dread—and not just because of the extra dogcatchers I was sure Heath was already out recruiting. Ever since I'd moved to Austin at the age of eight, I'd kept my identity secret from the werewolf community at large. So far I'd been successful, but that was largely because there were almost never any werewolves in Austin. If this article was anything to go on, though, that was no longer the case.

My eyes kept returning to the picture on the front page, and I couldn't help imagining what was under the black plastic. Finally I forced myself to turn the paper over and push it away. My eyes drifted to the picture of Heath, which was framed and placed in a prominent position on my desk, and I smiled a little despite the dire news in the paper.

Heath and I had been together for more than a year, and I think we were both considering the possibility of a future together. Aside from the chemistry between us, we had similar goals, and similar family issues. Both of us were hardworking, upwardly mobile professionals trying to distance ourselves from our pasts—I was an auditor with a major firm, and he was one of Texas's rising legal stars. Whereas he had fled to Texas to break free from his uptight New England parents, however, I had spent the last ten years trying to distance myself from my rather unorthodox upbringing as the werewolf daughter of a psychic witch. Okay, so maybe not *similar* circumstances, exactly . . .

But despite a rather annoying—and inexplicable— fondness for the Beastie Boys, Heath had everything going for him. He hadn't run screaming when he met my mother, for starters. Add to that a biting sense of humor, great biceps, dark silky hair, a delightful habit of surprising me with wonderful gifts . . . and major political aspirations. Although that last part wasn't such a great attribute, actually—particularly given his penchant for reining in the feral dog population. Not only had he been working longer hours since he discovered his passion for political advancement, but I still had a scar on my butt from my last dogcatcher run-in.

My thoughts flashed again to that jewelry bag I'd seen Heath with. Could it be that there was an engagement ring in it?

And if there was, how was I going to break the whole *I'm a werewolf* thing to him?

I sighed and sipped my latte, my mind turning back to the werewolves again. No need to be concerned, right? After all, none of them had come knocking at *my* door, so why worry? I'd just stay away from the greenbelt for a while. Right now, I told myself, my first priority was to get cracking on my new account. I shoved the paper into a desk drawer and forced myself to focus on my computer, clicking on e-mail to check for missives from Southeast Airlines. As I scrolled through the spam, my mouse stopped at a weird message titled "Audience required." It was from the Lupine Society. *Maybe it's some kind of society for bluebonnet lovers,* I told myself. Hope springs eternal, I guess.

My latte forgotten, I clicked on the message.

It wasn't about bluebonnets.

In fact, unless I was very much mistaken, it was from the Houston pack.

Crap.

I sucked in my breath and bit my lip, almost puncturing myself with a canine. I had broken twenty years of anonymity a few months ago when I tangled with a few made werewolves. (Made werewolves aren't born werewolves; they've just gotten their paws on enough werewolf blood to join the pack, so to speak.) When I found the three of them harassing a sorority girl in the Sixth Street alley, some deluded hero instinct had made me decide to be Wonder Woman and step in to save her. Even though she *had* been wearing awful shoes. I mean, bad taste isn't enough to die for, is it?

Anyway, the sorority girl got away, but not before the packette (my pet name for the trio) got a good whiff of me. And although they had since been unmade (sort of de-werewolfized), evidently the cat—or in this case, the wolf—was still out of the bag. Either that, I realized with a shiver, or someone connected with the incident on the Greenbelt had sniffed me out.

"Your presence is required by the Houston Lupine Society," read the e-mail. "An audience has been scheduled for Saturday, February seventh at one o'clock p.m. Failure to appear will result in forfeiture of any and all rights."

An *audience*? Forfeiture of any and all rights? Who

did these people think they were? *They aren't people*, I reminded myself. *They're werewolves.*

I cursed whatever werewolf rule it was that made Austin an official part of the Houston pack's territory. I'd recently discovered that my living in Austin made me an intruder.

To make things worse, the date was this coming Saturday—the same day, naturally, as the office retreat my boss had been planning for months. And, of course, the full moon, but with enough wolfsbane, that wouldn't be too much of a problem—thanks to the tea my mom made for me, I'd limited my compulsory transformations to the full moons closest to equinoxes and solstices. Unfortunately, I doubted Adele would be up for rescheduling the retreat—she'd been selecting table centerpieces for a month now. And somehow I doubted the Lupine Society would be willing to compromise.

As if on cue, my phone rang again. It was Adele.

"Sophie, so glad I caught you. I need your help picking tablecloths."

"Tablecloths?"

"For the retreat. I'm thinking suede or gingham. What do you think?"

"Um, about the retreat . . ." I began.

"It's going to be incredible, isn't it? You can't miss a minute of it. So, I'm leaning toward suede. With gingham napkins."

"Sounds fine," I said faintly.

"Great. I'll see you soon; don't forget to pack your boots! There'll be horseback riding—and maybe even a cow patty toss!"

After I hung up, I wiped my sweaty palms on my skirt and tried to focus on work.

But all I could think was, *Crap.*

* * *

I was closing up my office for the day and about to head home for a restorative tumbler of wine when my mother called.

"Sophie, darling! How's my favorite girl?"

"Fine, Mom." Which wasn't strictly true, but I wasn't up for talking about my e-mail from the Lupine Society right now. Or the little issue that had taken place in the Greenbelt. I just hoped my mother's psychic abilities were on the fritz today. "What's up?"

"I was making plans for Valentine's Day, and I wanted your opinion. Do you think I should make reservations at Romeo's, or Chez Nous?" Chez Nous was an intimate little French bistro downtown; Heath had taken me there many times.

"Who are you going with?" I asked, cringing.

"Why, Marvin, of course." Marvin Blechknapp was the pool-ball-shaped attorney who had defended Mom on a murder case recently. I couldn't understand the attraction—he was more Dom DeLuise than Brad Pitt—but my mother was ga-ga over him. As he evidently was for her, even though she was a bit left of center. Okay, so maybe running a magic shop called Sit A Spell and having a werewolf for a daughter was more than a bit left of center. But you get the idea.

"I think either one would be good," I said. "Mom, can I call you back? I'm on my way out the door."

"Sure, honey. But I just had a quick question."

"What?"

"Have you noticed anything unusual lately?"

I sat down. "What do you mean, unusual?" Had she read about the incident in the Greenbelt? I wondered.

"Oh, I don't know. Maybe a chicken head or something."

The hairs on the back of my neck prickled. "A chicken head? Um, no. I'm pretty sure I would have noticed a chicken head."

"No dirt, or anything?"

"Dirt?"

"Oh, you know. Graveyard dirt."

"No, no graveyard dirt that I know of. Although I'm not sure how I'd distinguish graveyard dirt from regular dirt."

She breathed a sigh of relief. "Thank goodness."

"Mom . . ."

"Just keep an eye out, okay?" I heard a bell tinkle in the background. "Whoops—customers. Got to go. Catch you soon. Love you, sweetie!"

She hung up before I could respond.

Chicken heads and graveyard dirt? As I powered the computer down and headed for the door, I found myself—not for the first time—wishing for a mom who did something normal. Like waiting tables, or knitting afghans, or running a corporation or something.

Then again, if I had everything I wanted in life, I wouldn't be addicted to wolfsbane tea and have a Bic razor habit, either. Sometimes I guess you just have to play the hand that's dealt you. Even if they do turn out to be tarot cards.

I drove the five blocks home to my building, said hi to Frank the doorman, and headed up the elevator to my loft.

As my mother requested, I did a quick survey of the hallway. No chicken heads. No graveyard dirt, either, although I did spot a dust bunny in the corner by the stairway.

As I fished for my keys, I took a deep breath and froze.

Werewolf.

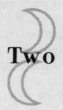

Two

I sniffed again. Bad things seemed to be coming in threes today; whoever was behind my door was definitely a werewolf. And he—or she—was definitely someone I'd never smelled before.

Adrenaline pulsed through me. Was this about to be an instant replay of what had happened in the Greenbelt last night?

I stifled the urge to change right there in the hallway. Even if there was a werewolf in there, I had just bought a new Dolce and Gabbana suit to celebrate making partner, and I didn't want my tail to rip a hole in the back of it. And more important, even if I managed to get the suit off, the last thing I needed was to have a neighbor walk by as I stripped naked and sprouted a fur coat.

I squatted down and sniffed at the edges of the door. Was the intruder still in my loft, or had he or she just left? I got down on my hands and knees—careful not to run my pantyhose—and lowered my nose to the bottom of the doorframe.

"Lose something?"

I jerked upright, almost whacking my head on the doorknob. It was Mrs. Gerschwitz, wearing only one of her customary pink foam curlers today—it was bobbing behind her left ear, evidently forgotten.

"Ummm . . . Yeah. Earring back. I lost an earring

back," I said, hoping the werewolf on the other side of the door was gone. And wondering exactly how he or she had gotten past the doorman. I took a surreptitious sniff. She. Definitely a she.

"Let me help you," Mrs. Gerschwitz said, advancing on spindly legs, which were displayed under a thigh-grazing skirt that matched her curlers. "I can't see a thing up close—getting old's a bitch—but my distance vision is still great. 'Just like a teenager's,' my doctor always says."

I glanced nervously at the door. If the intruder was still in there, I really wanted Mrs. Gerschwitz out of the way. The last thing I needed on my conscience was to have my eighty-year-old widowed neighbor gored by a renegade werewolf. She hobbled toward me on three-inch heels and poked her gold-plated cane at the floor.

Please oh please don't come through the door right now, I thought in the general direction of whatever was in my loft. Then I said brightly, "Oh, look, I found it," as I reached over and picked up a lint ball. I stood up and fumbled for my keys, hoping Mrs. Gerschwitz would take my cue and totter back to the elevator. But she just stood there, smiling at me with lipstick-coated false teeth.

"Weren't you going out for a walk?" I prompted her.

"Oh, yes. I was hoping to see Henry," she said, winking at me.

"Henry. Oh . . . is it a date?" I asked. Mrs. Gerschwitz had recently confided she was interested in the new neighbor on the third floor. Retired actuary, most of his original teeth, recently deceased wife. Hence the miniskirt and high heels.

"Not yet," she said, with something that looked like a leer. "But I know he walks his Bichon Frisé at six every evening, so I was hoping I'd catch him."

"You'd better hurry then," I said. "You've got five minutes."

"Ooh, you're right. I would hate to go to all this effort for nothing," she said. I debated mentioning the curler as she tottered down the hall toward the elevator. If I hadn't been so anxious to get rid of her, I would have told her in a heartbeat. But odds were that Henry's eyesight wasn't so hot anyway—and besides, her skirt was pink enough to grab just about anybody's undivided attention. So instead, I pretended to search for my keys as she punched the button and waited.

And waited.

I had been rifling through my purse for at least five minutes when Mrs. Gerschwitz said, "Is there something wrong, dear?"

"Oh, no," I said, straining my ears for the sound of movement on the other side of the door. Was that a thump I heard? "Just having difficulty finding the key."

"Do you need me to call the super?"

"Thanks, but no. I'm good," I said, just as—finally, thank God—the elevator dinged and the door slid open. Once Mrs. Gerschwitz was safely ensconced in the metal box and on her way to seduce Henry the actuary, I took a deep breath, slid the key into the lock, and stood rooted to the floor.

The place had been ransacked.

Tearing my eyes from my suede couch—were the cushions still intact?—I took a deep breath and tried to focus. The scent was very strong in the loft; much stronger than it had been in the hall.

Which meant whoever had done this was probably still here.

As quietly as possible, I closed the door behind me and shrugged out of my suit, trying to control the change until I at least had my new skirt off. Less than a minute had passed before I let the urge pulse through me and dropped to all fours, sniffing the trail.

It was a female—definitely a female—and she'd been just about everywhere. I scanned the living room and kitchen, trying not to focus on the upended drawers, the shattered CDs, the brand new beaded pillow that was now lodged in the potted plant my mother had given me to "cleanse the space." Which hadn't worked out too well, since there was now dirt all over the place. At least the cushions all seemed intact, except for a bit of potting soil.

I was checking behind the couch when I heard a thump from the bedroom. Ears pricked forward, I padded toward the doorway, my mouth coppery with fear—and rage at the violation.

I turned the corner and nosed into the bedroom, muscles bunched, prepared to spring. There was no movement, but the smell was much stronger here. I scanned the room; the mattress was upended next to the bed, and the contents of my drawers were strewn everywhere. The closet door was open, the light on. No werewolf. I could tell because my clothes had been torn from the hangers, so there was nowhere to hide.

My eyes flicked to the bathroom. It was the last place in the loft. She had to be there.

I crouched by the open door and sprang, teeth bared, ready to attack.

But the bathroom was empty.

An hour later, I was still hanging up clothes and trying to figure out why—and how—someone had trashed my place and vanished into thin air. As far as I could tell, nothing had been taken, so it wasn't a burglary. Still, the fact that my sapphire earrings were still accounted for and that my new couch cushions had escaped perfora-

tion was small consolation for the loss of two of my favorite pairs of shoes, which looked like they'd been used
as chew toys.

When I had cleared enough stuff from the living room
floor so that I could actually find the phone, I picked up
and called the doorman.

"Frank. It's Sophie, up on ten."

"Hiya, Miss Sophie. Mrs. Gerschwitz told me you lost
your keys. You need some help?"

I took a deep breath and said, "No. I'm fine." Which
was far from true—I wasn't fine at all—but if I told him
my place had been vandalized, he'd call the police. And
since the cops would have a hard time tracking down a
female werewolf who was apparently capable of walking through walls, I didn't see the point. So I composed
my voice and said, "Did any visitors come by today?"

"Let's see." I could hear papers rustling. "UPS came
by with a package for the Readings, in unit six-oh-two.
And Mr. Margos had his nurse in. But other than a few
deliveries, it's been pretty quiet."

"Is it possible that someone slipped by you?" Actually, I already knew the answer to that question—with
Frank's HGTV obsession, half the building could col-
lapse and I doubted he'd notice—but I asked anyway.

"Why? Is something wrong? Did you have another
break-in?"

"No, no," I said in a strangled voice. Six months ago,
a trio of werewolves had overpowered him before heading upstairs to visit my loft, and I wasn't sure he'd recovered. Actually, come to think of it, I wasn't sure I had,
either. "Nothing like that," I said. "I was just wondering. . . . Anyway, thanks."

"Anytime, Miss Sophie."

I hung up and walked to the windows, checking to
make sure they weren't open. Of course, since my loft

was on the tenth floor, the odds of someone breaking in and/or exiting through the window and surviving were relatively slim, but you never knew.

Every single one was locked.

A shiver ran through me as I walked back into the bathroom. Where had she come from? What was she looking for?

And most of all, how had she vanished?

After sorting through the rest of the CDs and salvaging what I could, I tiptoed through the mess in the kitchen—my thoughtful visitor had emptied my entire spice rack onto the tile floor—and grabbed a bottle of my favorite white wine from the fridge, which was the only thing in my loft that had escaped the werewolf's attentions. Then I sat down on my recently reassembled couch, sucked down a mouthful of wine, and attempted to regain my equilibrium.

The wine churned as it hit my stomach, but I took another sip anyway. I felt violated and scared. And not just because my feet were coated in cumin and cinnamon.

After a few restorative moments with my wine, I headed to the bathroom to start the tub. As the bath filled, I swept up the spice mess in the kitchen, coughing as the powder formed a cloud that went right up my nose and settled on all available surfaces. After dumping the remains of my spice cabinet into the trash can, I headed back into the bathroom and removed my now very spicy bathrobe. As I dipped my toe into the warm water, an unpleasant thought made me pause. What if whoever it was decided to reappear while I was chin-deep in bubbles?

After a brief internal debate, I decided to go ahead with it. Intruder or no intruder, I couldn't go through the rest of my life without bathing. Besides, my hair was a mess, I smelled like I'd been rolling in a spice bazaar, and I wanted to look somewhat put-together when Heath came to pick me up at seven. (Tonight, I was definitely meeting him in the lobby.) And if I did need to transform suddenly, at least I wouldn't have to worry about clothes getting in the way.

The experience, unfortunately, was less than relaxing. It's hard to do the "Calgon, take me away" thing when you're sitting naked in a bathtub with a razor, expecting a werewolf to pop up next to the john at any moment.

I washed my hair and shaved in record time, then hopped out of the tub and slipped back into my fluffy bathrobe. I had finished blow-drying my hair and was fixing myself a cup of wolfsbane tea when a knock sounded on the door.

My heart rate jumped up. Was it the werewolf again? But that didn't make sense; if she could walk through walls, why bother knocking? She certainly hadn't let an inconvenience like a deadbolted door deter her earlier.

Still, even if it wasn't a werewolf, the last thing I needed was someone in my trashed apartment right now. I was hoping they'd give up and leave, but a moment later, whoever it was knocked again. Probably Mrs. Gerschwitz, I decided, wanting to give me a rundown on her walk with Henry. I glanced at my watch; it was already six-fifteen, and I needed to get dressed and ready before Heath arrived at seven. I'd just pop my head through the door and promise to swing by later.

"Just a minute!" I called, tightening the belt of my robe, grabbing my mug, and hurrying to the door.

It wasn't Mrs. Gerschwitz.

A woman a few years younger than me stood at the door, wearing an ill-fitting charcoal suit and looking nervous. She pushed a strand of her long black hair behind her ear and smiled nervously. Probably selling magazine subscriptions.

"Can I help you?" I asked, making a mental note to

call Frank and complain. Soliciting was off-limits in the building.

"Miss Garou?" she asked.

"That's me," I said, crossing my arms. "How did you get up here?"

"The doorman called you, but you didn't answer. I told him I was a friend, and he let me come up." I hadn't heard him because of the hair dryer, I realized. I took a deep breath to respond.

And that's when I realized she wasn't a magazine saleswoman.

I took an involuntary step back, clutching my tea. "You're a . . ."

"Yes," she said. She tilted her head to the side, and I could see the faint iridescence of her blue eyes. They weren't gold, like mine, but they had the same kind of glow. How had I not spotted it immediately? Was she the one who had been in my apartment? I took another sniff. No; the one who had been in here was much stronger. Smelling, at least.

"Are you from Houston?" I asked.

"Houston?" The young woman looked puzzled, and plucked at her white polyester shell. "No. Texarkana."

That explained the cheap suit. But not what she was doing on my doorstep. Why the heck was Austin—and my loft in particular—suddenly Werewolf Central? "How did you find me?"

"Word gets around," she said, with a small smile that revealed her pointed canines. *Not good news,* I thought. Could she be somehow involved with what happened last night at the Greenbelt?

"May I come in?" she asked.

"Um . . ." I glanced up and down the hall. "My place is a mess, and I don't have a lot of time—I've got to leave at seven—but I think you'd better." This was not a discussion I wanted to have out in the hallway. "What's your name?"

"Teena," she said. "Teena Allen."

"Sophie Garou," I said. "Although evidently you already knew that."

She dipped her head and followed me into the apartment, stopping short just inside the door. "What happened in here?" she asked, staring at the upended tables and the broken CD cases.

"Just doing a little redecorating," I said as Teena perched like a nervous bird on the edge of my couch. Her stockings were too dark for her pale legs—they were the thick, stretchy kind they sold at Wal-Mart, with names like Caribbean Bronze, and her shoes were . . . well, let's just say I finally understood the phrase "down at the heel." She sure had good hair, though—black, long, and glossy, like something out of a Pantene commercial. I reached up to touch my own reddish-brown mop, feeling a twinge of jealousy. Even after about a half gallon of smoothing lotion and an intensive session with the blow dryer, my hair didn't even come close. "Can I get you a drink? Maybe some tea, or a glass of wine?" I asked. My wineglasses were still intact, thankfully.

"Sure," she said, shrugging her narrow shoulders and rearranging her skirt so that it covered another millimeter of her awful stockings.

As I grabbed a glass from the rack and filled it up, I wondered what I had done to deserve this sudden influx of complications. After almost six werewolf-free months, all of a sudden Austin was teeming with them—some of them violent. I sniffed the air again. This one definitely wasn't the one who had torn my loft apart. She was made, not born. And not nearly as powerful as the woman-werewolf who'd played 52-pickup with my loft.

"You said that word gets around," I said lightly as I

handed her a glass and sat down across from her, trying to act as if it was normal to have all of the pictures torn off the walls and bits of glass scattered around the rug. "Could you be a touch more specific?"

She shrugged, her eyes darting around my ruined loft. "I go to a club for our kind up in Texarkana. There were a couple of guys going around saying they'd seen you," she said. "And that a friend of yours had done something to them."

Tom, I thought, my mind flitting back to the handsome Nordic werewolf who'd swept into town last fall, swept my best friend off her feet, and then swept right on out of Austin. Apparently he was an itinerant type: kind of a werewolf-exterminator-for-hire. At least he'd gotten rid of the made werewolves—the architects of my previous break-in—before he hit the road. Too bad he wasn't around to deal with the one who had gotten in today.

"Did one of them have . . . well, a rather strong personal bouquet?" I asked Teena.

She gave me a puzzled look.

"What I mean is, did one of them smell awful?"

She nodded vigorously. "Yeah, he did, now that you mention it. Kind of like skunk cabbage."

Stinky, I thought. One of the packette; the three made werewolves I had dubbed Stinky, Scrawny, and Fluffy. Tom had told me there was a good chance they'd tell others about me. For a moment, I almost regretted he hadn't done something a little more final with them. Okay, so it's not like I wanted them dead or anything— but couldn't he have, like, erased their memories or something?

I took a swig of wine, thinking of the e-mail I'd gotten from the Lupine Society, and gritted my teeth as I swallowed. "Does everyone in Texas know about me, then?"

"I don't know," Teena said, sipping her wine. Her iridescent eyes widened a little. "This is good," she said.

"It's called Conundrum," I said. Which was not just my favorite wine, but seemed to be the prevailing characteristic of my life the past few hours.

"Yum," she said, taking another sip. "Well, anyway, the reason I'm here, Miss Garou . . ."

"Call me Sophie," I said.

"Sophie," she said shyly. "Anyway, the reason I'm here is that I have a few friends, and we were kind of hoping . . ." she trailed off and took another swig of wine.

"Hoping . . ." I prompted, glancing at the clock on the wall. If I was going to be ready by seven, I needed the bulletin, not the extended-play version.

"Well, we were kind of hoping"—she looked down at her scuffed black shoes—"um . . . well . . . hoping that you'd be our Alpha."

I blinked. "Your what?"

"Our Alpha," Teena repeated, sneaking a glance at me before resuming her examination of her shoes. Before I could ask her exactly what she was talking about, she plunged ahead. "There are three of us, and we just transformed recently, and we really need someone to like, you know, guide us and everything. . . ."

"You're not part of a pack?" I asked, thinking that at least I wasn't the only one. "I thought everyone had to be part of a pack."

"That's what we're asking you to help us with," she said breathlessly, looking up at me. "The Texarkana one isn't really an option for us, so we thought we'd start a new one. And . . ." she lowered her eyes and bit her lip, ". . . we'd like you to be our pack leader."

I choked on my wine. "You're kidding me."

"Our pack leader," she said. "Our Alpha." Her blue

eyes shone with hope. "Would you? Please? We've already picked out a name. The Werewolf Grrls."

"The Werewolf Grrls," I repeated slowly.

"But if you don't like it," she said, looking worried, "we can change it. We can make it whatever you want, Miss Garou."

"Sophie," I reminded her. "It's Sophie." I set my wineglass down on my cherrywood coffee table, feeling so discombobulated I didn't even bother with a coaster. I mean, if the entire werewolf community was going to be traipsing in and out of my loft destroying things, what was the point? "Look, Teena," I said. "Until about six months ago, nobody even knew I existed. And to be honest, I'd kind of like to go back to that."

"But . . ."

"Here's the deal. Right now, I'm evidently in the Houston pack's 'territory'." I made the quotation marks in the air with my fingers. "There was a big brouhaha just a mile or so from here last night. I think three werewolves ended up dead."

Her black-ringed eyes got big. "The dog pack killing that was on the news? You think they were werewolves?"

"Why else would the victims be naked with fur between their teeth?"

"Oh," she said. "I didn't think about that." She was quiet for a moment, then turned her blue eyes to me. "Does that mean they're going to come after you, too?"

God. I hoped not. "I don't know," I said, "but the place doesn't look like this because I'm redecorating."

"I thought it looked kind of weird," Teena admitted, glancing at what was left of the potted plant.

"Somebody broke in. Another werewolf."

"Another werewolf?" Her shimmery eyes got even bigger.

"Yes. I don't know if it was the Houston pack, or if it

had something to do with what happened last night, but something called the Lupine Society sent me an e-mail today, telling me to go to Houston to meet with them. I don't think they're crazy about me being here."

"Doesn't look like it," Teena said, eyeing the remains of my CD collection. Poor Christina Aguilera wasn't just "stripped"—she was lying in six pieces on my living room floor.

"I'm hoping to make a case for peaceful coexistence," I said. Which might be an unattainable dream, if the body bag in the paper this morning was anything to go on. I looked at Teena. "In short," I said, "my goal is to stay here and continue my normal, *human* life. I know nothing about other werewolves or packs." Well, maybe not *nothing*, technically, but close enough. "And if the Houston pack thinks I'm trying to form my own little werewolf club, I think that will probably hamper negotiations."

Teena kind of deflated on the couch. If she hadn't already finished her wine, she would have spilled it on my upholstery.

"Sorry to disappoint you," I said. "I'm curious, though. Why do you think you need an Alpha?"

She turned her glass around in her hands. Her fingernails were long—no surprise there, since werewolf nails grow like weeds—and inexpertly painted a rather muddy shade of mauve. If I did take her shopping, I thought idly, it wouldn't hurt to swing by the cosmetics counter at Nordstrom either. Not that I was planning to do any such thing, of course. "The pack in Texarkana is kind of . . . well, not really friendly," she said.

I hoped that wasn't typical of packs, I thought, thinking of my recent summons from the Lupine Society.

"We need help," she said. "We don't know anything, and no one will teach us. We'd stay in Texarkana, but the made wolves are . . . well, they're disappearing." She shivered. "We were hoping you could help."

Disappearing werewolves? "What do you mean, 'disappearing'?"

"Just that. One day they're there, the next . . ." She snapped her fingers. "Gone."

So she didn't mean "disappear" like my magically vanishing werewolf intruder. Still . . . "I can see why you wanted to leave," I said. Unfortunately, however, I wasn't exactly a font of werewolf information, and I certainly didn't have the connections to keep Teena safe. In fact, I was hoping she could tell *me* about the procedure for turning a non-werewolf into a werewolf. Or why you would want to. I mean, sprouting fur and fangs once a month on an involuntary basis isn't exactly my idea of a good time. Sure, wolfsbane tea helped keep things under control, but it wasn't what you'd call a taste sensation. And having to drink it every couple of hours—and shave almost as often—was a real nuisance, particularly during romantic weekend getaways.

Speaking of romantic getaways, it was time to get Teena moving so I could finish getting ready. I did have one more question to ask, though. "How exactly did you . . . transform?" I asked. "I mean, turn into a werewolf?"

"It was my boyfriend's idea," she said.

"Your boyfriend?"

"Yeah. His name is Brett. Well, was, really."

"Did something happen to him?"

Her eyes darted away from me, and I thought I detected a tear. "No. We broke up. And then . . . well, I don't know if he left, or if he's one of the ones who disappeared."

If he left, I thought, it was probably the Caribbean Bronze hose.

"Anyway," Teena continued, dabbing at her eyes.

"He got made about two years ago; he made me just a month or two ago."

"Made," I said. "How do you get 'made'?"

"It's easy, really." She seemed to forget about Brett for a moment. "What you do is you take a syringe, and you fill it with werewolf blood, and then you inject it into yourself."

I took another sip of my tea, suppressing a shudder. I'd always suspected it was something disgusting; now I had confirmation. "Evidently it's not just vampires who have a thing for blood, then," I said. Which, if you asked me, was just gross. Not to mention completely un-hygienic. I didn't know if werewolves could get AIDS or hepatitis, but I didn't want to find out.

"There are vampires, too?" Teena asked, big blue eyes wide.

I sighed. "Yes, there are." Not that I'd ever conversed with one. But I'd smelled them—and I knew they liked to hang out at The Drain, a bar on Sixth Street. Which was right next to the Chuggin' Monkey, where all the co-eds hung out. Hmmm. I'd never really thought about it before, but I was guessing that wasn't a coincidence.

"Cool," she said. "See? There's so much you can teach us."

"Actually, what I don't know about werewolves would fill volumes. Isn't there someone in Texarkana who can help you?"

"Not anymore," she said quietly. "The ones we knew . . . they're gone. That's why we left. We were afraid it would happen to us."

"I'm sorry I can't help you," I said, standing up. I hated to rush her, but Heath would be downstairs at any moment, and I really, really needed Teena to go. "There's really nothing I can do, Teena. I'm sorry."

"Please?" she said, looking a little bit desperate.

"Look," I said, standing up. "Teena, I understand

your . . . well, your desire for leadership, and I hope you find someone. But you're barking up the wrong tree. I know nothing about werewolves. I don't even know the code."

"There's a code?"

"That's the word on the street." Or at least according to Tom—and my mother. "But I don't know anything about it, so I can't help you."

"But . . ."

"Seriously. Teena, it was lovely talking with you, but my boyfriend's going to be here any minute, and I have to get ready." That, I thought, she should understand.

She stood up and set her wineglass down. "Is your boyfriend one of us too?"

I blinked at her. "A werewolf? No." *God, no.*

"But he knows about you, right?"

"No, he doesn't," I said, steering her toward the door. "And I'd like to keep it that way."

"Why?"

I sighed. "Because it's easier." I had to remind myself that she hadn't grown up under the tyranny of the full moon; she'd only been a werewolf for a few months. To her, it was kind of a novelty. To me, it was a big, hairy handicap.

I opened the door. "Teena, I appreciate you coming by." I glanced at my watch. "Good luck with everything, and I hope you find a—a pack leader, or an Alpha. Or whatever you call it. Stay in touch, if you want. But I've got to go get ready for my date. Okay?"

"But . . ."

"Oh, and there's one more thing."

"What?" she said, looking miserable.

I lowered my voice. "I'd appreciate it if you didn't tell anybody else about me. Okay?"

She gave a heavy sigh and slunk toward the elevator with her tail between her legs. Metaphorically speaking.

"Take care," I called to her as she headed down the hallway. The last I saw of her, she was standing at the elevator, shoulders slumped in her ill-fitting suit jacket. I felt a little guilty, somehow. But why? I mean, how was my agreeing to be her Alpha going to help her? Although it was true I could probably lend some assistance in the wardrobe department. Or at least as far as pantyhose was concerned.

I had just closed the door behind her and was heading back to the bathroom when the phone rang. Probably Frank the doorman again.

I grabbed it, prepared to politely tell him not to send any more strange women upstairs without buzzing me first. "Hello?"

"Sophie? It's Heath."

His warm chocolate voice sent little ripples of pleasure through me. Despite the day I'd had, I was looking forward to dinner . . . and dessert, if you know what I mean. I could use a little human distraction right about now. "Hi, sweetheart. I was just getting ready. . . ."

"Um . . . that's what I was calling about, actually." His voice sounded off. Preoccupied, somehow.

I paused at the bathroom door. "What's wrong?"

"Well, something's come up on this case I've been working on, and I'm going to have to stay late tonight."

I blinked. This from the man who, six months ago, had accused *me* of working too hard? "Which case?"

"The case against the city."

"The dogcatcher one." I bit my lip. "I saw your quote in the paper today. Lindsey sends her congratulations," I said, feeling an uncomfortable tightness in my stomach. Heath had his eye on a city council seat and kept taking cases concerning run-ins with Austin's stray dog population, which he viewed as a "growing menace." His current case involved a man who'd been bitten in the butt by a pit bull—he still wasn't able to actually sit down, and had to attend hearings bottoms-up on a gurney—and Heath was hoping to use the case to push through an ordinance on dog regulation.

"Tell Lindsey thanks," Heath replied. "And I know you don't think it's serious, but it's a real problem, Sophie. See what happened last night? It just keeps getting worse."

"I know," I said. "You've talked about it before." At some length, in fact. The last time we'd gone to dinner, we hadn't even made it through the appetizers before he whipped out a chart showing the rise in feral dog attacks, then launched into a passionate speech on the need for more animal control officers. To be honest, as much as I loved Heath, I was getting a little tired of this whole political thing. Not only was it taking up way too much of his time, but when you're a werewolf, it's hard to be intimate with a man whose personal mission is to triple the number of dogcatchers.

"Yeah. That case was a great break for us," Heath said. "Well, not so great for the three guys, of course." It was hard not to agree with him there. "But I think it will really help support our cause."

"So we're not going to dinner," I said.

"Sorry, sweetheart. I think we're just going to order pizza and stay at the office."

The hairs stood up on the back of my neck. "We?"

"Yeah. Miranda and me," he said. Miranda was the new associate at Heath's firm. I'd heard all about her degree from Stanford, and how well she handled herself in the courtroom. What Heath hadn't told me—and what I'd discovered a few days ago, when I swung by his office for lunch—was that she also looked like a life-sized version of Career-Day Barbie.

"Oh," I said coolly. "I see."

"I knew you'd understand," he said. "You're a champ. I'll give you a call tomorrow, okay?"

A *champ*? "Fine," I said. I could hear a woman's low voice in the background: the lovely Miranda, no doubt. I was about to add "I love you," but before I could speak, there was a click.

Heath had already hung up.

Three

After a Tuesday that was chock-full of were-wolves, the next morning was delightfully pedestrian. Heath called, apologizing for the previous night and promising to wine and dine me Friday; there were no more missives from werewolf packs; I slowly got my loft back together; and I heard not another peep from Teena the Texarkana werewolf. Nor had there been any maulings or further break-ins.

The fact that I had a lunch meeting scheduled at Romeo's with the CEO of Southeast Airlines didn't hurt, either. In fact, it was a welcome distraction. Mark Sydney was excellent—if rather flirtatious—company, but more important, I was looking forward to finding out a bit more about what I could do to knock my client's socks off. Plus, my mouth was already watering at the thought of their chicken parmigiana. Yum.

At 11:30 I shaved my legs one last time, checked to make sure that I didn't have poppy seed bagel stuck between my teeth, and headed for Romeo's with a tumbler of wolfsbane tea.

Lindsey called me on my cell as I pulled into a parking space and dug in my purse for a tube of lipstick.

"What's up?" I asked, still searching for my lipstick.

"Wanna have lunch?"

"Actually, I'm on my way to Romeo's right now."

"With Heath?"

"No, with Mark."

"Mark who?"

"Mark Sydney. The CEO of Southeast Airlines."

"Oh yeah, your new star client. Somebody told me he was featured as one of the state's most eligible bachelors in *Texas Monthly* a couple of months ago. I'll have to see if I can track down the issue."

It wouldn't surprise me; being in charge of a multibillion-dollar company at the age of thirty-five was a big selling point. The fact that he rather obviously spent a good bit of time at the gym didn't hurt, either.

"Romeo's, eh? Pretty romantic spot for a business lunch."

I hadn't thought about it, but she was right. Mark had requested the restaurant—said he had a yen for Italian. I closed up the lipstick, zipped my purse, and said, "I've got to run. Maybe lunch tomorrow?"

"I'll pencil you in. That way I can get all the juicy details."

"Don't hold your breath," I said. Then I hung up and prepared myself to meet my biggest client—and, evidently, one of the most eligible bachelors in Texas—for lunch.

The smell of sautéed garlic swept over me as I opened the door, and as my salivary glands went into overtime, I thanked God that if I had to be abnormal, at least I was a werewolf, not a vampire. I might get hairy sometimes, but at least I could enjoy a good loaf of garlic bread— not to mention hold down a day job.

The cavelike bar was decorated liberally with cupids, stars, and grapevines, and I was swallowing back drool and examining a plaster cupid with artfully placed fig leaves when someone touched me on the shoulder.

I whirled around to face my client.

"You're early," I said.

"I'm always early," he said, smiling. His teeth were straight and white, and even though it was early February, he had an even tan. Probably from all the free flights to places like Tahiti and Hawaii, I thought. He had an unusual smell, too, I noticed—a little bit like campfire, and something else . . . cloves?

"Is it just us, then?" I asked, leaning back on my bar stool and surreptitiously checking him for horns. I thought I'd seen them in a meeting once, and now I couldn't help looking for them. Granted, I had been under the influence of a few gallons of wolfsbane tea at the time, and also thought my laptop cord was trying to bite me. But still.

"Everyone else was already booked up," he said. "So I have you all to myself."

I stood up quickly, almost knocking over the plaster cupid. "I'll just go check on the table, then," I said.

I strode over to the hostess stand, conscious of Mark's eyes on me, and smiled at the young woman in—of course—a heart-print dress. She looked to be about twelve, and I found myself wondering about child labor laws. "I have a reservation for twelve o'clock. It should be under the name Sophie Garou."

She flipped through her papers. "I'm sorry. I don't see it."

"Is it under Withers and Young? My assistant made the reservation . . ."

She ran a pink-painted fingernail down the list. "I'm sorry, ma'am."

Ma'am? When did I stop being "Miss"? Then again, I consoled myself, to a twelve-year-old even twenty-year-olds look wizened.

"I don't see it here," the young woman continued. "But I'm sure we'll have a table in the next twenty minutes or so. Name?"

"Sophie Garou," I repeated, and slunk back to my

handsome client. Who was probably worth about $1,000 an hour and would be down a third of that due to my assistant's inability to make a reservation. "I'm sorry . . . They seem to have lost the reservation," I said.

"No problem," he said. "I don't have much on for this afternoon anyway. We'll just get a drink while we're waiting. Double martini for me," he told the bartender, then turned to me. "And how about you?"

"Just an iced tea, please." To be honest, I could have gone for a double martini myself right now. But I had a no-drinking-with-clients policy that wasn't too far behind the no-transforming-into-a-werewolf-with-clients policy. Professional, that's me.

"Oh, come on. Live a little." Mark turned to the bartender, giving me a very nice view of his profile, which bore a remarkable resemblance to George Clooney's. "Why don't you make that a Long Island Iced Tea?" he told the bartender. "Unless you're a Bellini girl?" he asked, grinning at me wickedly.

I shouldn't drink with clients. But he'd just ordered a double martini. Wouldn't he feel uncomfortable if I didn't join him? *When in Rome,* I thought. Or Romeo's, as the case may be. I bit my lip.

The bartender, who had a heart-shaped stud in his lip, said, "Iced tea then, miss?"

"Oh, what the heck," I said. "Make it a Bellini."

The things I do for clients.

Mark leaned back and surveyed the dim room, eyes lingering on the plaster cupid, who looked like he needed to cut down on the Ho-Hos. "This is some place. Cupids everywhere." He nodded toward the bartender. "Even the lip jewelry has a motif. You think that's regulation?"

I pointed to the fig leaves on the chubby plaster statue. "At least Cupid doesn't set the dress code."

As the bartender delivered our drinks—the Bellini

looked delicious, I was happy to see—I heard a familiar laugh from the corner, and a ripple passed through me.

Heath.

I leaned over to get a better look; there he was, with a glass of red wine, next to Career-Day Barbie. *Miranda.* I was surprised I hadn't noticed them earlier; then again, the smell of cooking garlic was so strong it pretty much canceled out every other scent. But what the heck was he doing at Romeo's with her? I mean, this was hardly the place for a business meeting.

"So, what are you doing for Valentine's Day? Got any big plans?"

"What?" I barked, dragging my eyes away from the back of my boyfriend's head to focus on my client.

"Valentine's Day," Mark repeated, swirling his olive around in his martini. "You know, hearts and flowers. Anyone special?"

"Maybe," I said. *Or maybe not,* I added mentally, glowering at the couple in the corner. And why was he asking, anyway?

"What does 'maybe' mean?"

"Just maybe." I grabbed the Bellini and sucked down about a quarter of it. "How about you?" I asked, trying not to stare at the back of Heath's head. As if the arrival of half the world's werewolf population in my hometown wasn't bad enough, now my boyfriend was having lunch at Romeo's with his gorgeous associate. Couldn't they just send out for sandwiches instead? *Focus on business,* I told myself. Castration could come later.

"Maybe," Mark said, taking a long sip of his martini and raising his eyebrows semi-suggestively. Or was I imagining it? My eyes drifted to the corner again. What were Heath and Miranda talking about that their heads needed to be so close?

Business, I reminded myself firmly. "So I wanted to go over our plan of attack," I said, focusing my attention on Mark. He was a good-looking guy; long and lithe, with a shock of dark hair and piercing blue eyes. Good lips, too. "You know," I said, looking into his unsettlingly blue eyes. "Find out what you see as the areas we need to take on first."

"Mmm," he said, taking another swig of his martini and returning the empty glass to the bar. "Drink up," he said, pointing to my Bellini, then called the bartender. "Can we get refills?"

Normally an alcohol-swilling client would give me pause, but today, I decided it might not be so bad. Because I was in desperate need of a drink myself. I glanced at Heath, who was still deep in conversation with Miranda, and sucked down another quarter of my Bellini. Maybe I *could* use a refill. "So as I was saying," I continued. "I'd like to know which areas you're most concerned about."

"Of course we can talk about that," he said. "But I like to get acquainted with the people I work with. We can focus on getting to know the business later. Today," he said, reaching out to touch my shoulder, "let's just get to know each other." The bartender arrived with two more drinks, his lip stud sparkling in the dim light. Mark raised his martini to me. "Bottoms up!"

We touched glasses and I sucked back another slug of Bellini. Mark was saying something about Tahiti, and a golf tournament, but I was having a hard time following him. My eyes kept drifting back to the two heads in the corner—one brown, one blonde—and wondering exactly how much of their lunch was business and how much pleasure.

My mind reviewed the months since Miranda had joined Heath's firm. It was true that Heath had become more absorbed in his work; more long nights, more weekends at the office. But I had assumed that was because of the big case he was working on.

Perhaps I had been a bit naïve.

As I played with my straw, Miranda tipped her head back and laughed. Perfect Barbie-doll profile, little white teeth, like pearls. She had a mystique about her, I'd give her that.

"Do you know her?"

"What?" I let go of the straw, which I had inadvertently twisted into a knot, and focused on Mark.

"That woman over there," he said. "You've been staring at her since we sat down." He grinned. "She's pretty, but I wouldn't have thought she's your type."

"I guess she just looks . . . familiar."

"You want to go over and say hi?"

"No!" I barked, splattering the counter with a bit of Bellini. I swiped at it with my napkin and said, "Why don't I go check on our table?"

Before he could answer, I scooted off the bar stool and headed toward the entry, trying to get my head straight—and trying not to look at Miranda. Or Heath. There were still four couples ahead of us, the juvenile hostess told me with a bubblegum-pink smile, but she would call me as soon as a table came open.

I headed back to the bar and was just sliding onto my stool when the hostess called Heath's name.

As the pair stood up and wove through the tables toward the entrance, I became deeply interested in the contents of my glass, lowering my head as they passed. I glanced up just as Heath brushed by me, and our eyes met.

His eyebrows flew up, but he recovered himself quickly. "Sophie. So good to see you." I breathed in his familiar scent as he reached out to squeeze my hand. "What are you doing here?"

"Business lunch," I said. "Heath, this is Mark Sydney. My new client."

Heath's eyes darted to the drinks on the bar, then to Mark. "Pleased to meet you," he said.

"Likewise," Mark said coolly, studying him—and Miranda. "And who is this lovely lady?" he asked.

"Oh. Miranda, my new associate. Miranda, this is Mark Sydney. CEO of Southeast Airlines, isn't it? Sophie's told me about you."

Mark nodded.

"Miranda," Heath said, turning to his high-heeled associate. "You know Sophie, right?"

She nodded and gave me a little smirk that made me want to smush her dainty ski-slope nose. Instead, I smiled and said, "Nice to see you again. How's that case coming along?"

She blinked fringed lashes. Which were a little heavy on the black mascara when you got close enough to notice. Actually, they looked kind of gloppy. I felt a little ray of hope. So she wasn't totally perfect. "Case?" she purred in a startlingly low voice that was unfortunately more Jessica Rabbit than James Earl Jones. "Oh, you mean the Roberts case. It's pretty smooth sailing, actually. A lot less work than we'd thought."

I turned to Heath and cocked an eyebrow. A lot less work? I thought they'd been burning the midnight oil lately. "Oh?" I said, not trying to keep the chill from my voice.

"I think our table's up," Heath said smoothly. "Would you like to join us? I'm sure we can have them pull up extra chairs."

I was torn. Did I want Heath and Miranda lunching without me? Or did I want to try to choke down my chicken parmigiana without stifling the urge to stick my fork into Miranda's perfect thigh?

Mark solved my dilemma for me. "Oh, no," he said. "We'd just be talking boring old business." He winked at me. "Right?"

"Maybe another time," I said with a tight smile.

"Right," echoed Heath. "Well, I guess I'll see you Friday, then, Sophie." He bent down, and his lips brushed my hair with a kiss. Then he turned to my client and the two men shook hands. "Nice meeting you, Mark."

As they left in a swathe of expensive floral perfume—Miranda's, not Heath's—Mark turned to me. "I thought you weren't sure you knew her."

"Well, I was wrong."

"Who's Heath?"

"My boyfriend," I muttered.

"Ah," Mark said delicately, and took another swig of martini. "Romeo's is a popular place today," he observed. "Must be the cupids."

"Actually, it's probably the chicken parmigiana," I said.

"The perfect complement to my martini," he said with a wicked little grin.

The rest of lunch went by in a blur. Partially because of the Bellinis, of course. And partially because every cell in my body was aware of Heath and Miranda, who were seated four tables away from us and punctuating every other sentence with laughter. Most annoying, really. But every cell in my body was *also* aware of the tall, dark-haired man sitting across the table from me. He downed four double vodka martinis over a two-hour lunch, accompanying it with Romeo's signature dish (the chicken). We finished by splitting a cannoli. Two forks, one plate. Which was also a bit unusual for a business lunch.

We left about twenty minutes after Heath and Miranda, who were presumably returning to their office. While I was feeling a bit wobbly, Mark didn't miss a beat.

"How can you walk straight?" I asked, giggling a bit unprofessionally. If Heath was having such a marvelous time with Miranda, after all, why shouldn't I enjoy a few minutes of my own with one of Texas's most eligible bachelors?

"Years of practice," Mark said, reaching for my arm to steady me. His hand was warm—almost hot, really.

"A man of many vices," I said.

He looked at me with ice-blue eyes, and said lightly, "Is it that obvious?"

A shiver passed through me, and for a moment his smoky smell intensified, kindling a reaction within me that I wasn't sure what to do with. Well, it's not that I didn't know what to do with it. It's just that it wasn't particularly appropriate to do it, given the situation.

"You know that I asked for you to be in charge of the account?" he asked, stepping closer.

"Adele mentioned that," I said, taking an involuntary step back. Adele was my boss, a beaky, ambitious woman with an inexplicable crush on Barry Manilow. She was a good businesswoman, though—a true predator—and, as of the last time I saw her, delirious over landing Southeast Airlines. The account, that is, not the planes.

"There's something special about you, Sophie Garou," he said, eyes lingering on me in a way that made me squirm. "And I intend to find out exactly what it is."

I laughed stiltedly. "Oh, I'm just an ordinary old auditor," I said.

"I can't say I agree," he said. "I sense there's something . . . something *wild* in you," he said.

If you only knew.

"Well, I really enjoyed lunch," I said, "but I've got to get back to the office. I have another meeting."

"We have to do this again."

"Of course," I said. "We need to talk about our game plan."

"Our game plan," he said. "Right." He reached out

to squeeze my arm, and I felt the heat through my jacket. "Today was lovely," he said. "I look forward to doing it again. Soon."

"Sure," I said.

He released me and dug in his pockets for his keys. "I'll have my assistant be in touch. This time, perhaps I can have *him* make the reservation."

I felt myself blush. "Sorry about that."

"Actually, I rather enjoyed having the extra time," he said. "*Arrivaderci,* Signorina Sophie."

"Um. Bye," I said rather inelegantly, and tottered back to my M3.

After my Bellini-studded lunch, the rest of the day was uneventful. I mentioned the lost reservation to Sally, which fazed her not at all—she simply adjusted a fuchsia bra strap and shrugged—and then retreated to my office, where I spent a few hours struggling to make some recalcitrant numbers line up. And to not think about Heath and Miranda. Or my impending trip to Houston. Or Teena. Or the werewolf who had torn up my loft. Or the three guys who had turned up dead in the Greenbelt. Or Mark. Mark the eligible bachelor.

Mark my *client.*

I worked for another hour before giving up and heading home to face my loft. I still had some major salvage work to do, and at least picking the remaining glass shards out of my Kashan rug would keep me busy. I was also toying with the idea of going down to the Greenbelt to see what I could sniff out. It had been a few days since the attack, which wasn't so good for scent retention, but at least it hadn't rained. Besides, waiting a few days had hopefully decreased the odds of my precipitating a second homicide. Or wolficide.

Frank the doorman was engrossed in HGTV when I walked into the lobby of my building. His head was bent over a legal pad, where he was taking copious notes on something they were doing to a bed. Hanging tree branches from it, maybe? Whatever it was, he was so enraptured he hardly noticed me.

A few minutes later, I shouldered my briefcase as the elevator door opened to my floor. Tonight, Mrs. Gerschwitz was nowhere to be seen.

Which was a good thing, really. Because unless my nose was lying, there were three werewolves in my loft waiting for me.

Four

I held my breath and considered my options. It was bad enough having unknown, multiple werewolves waiting for me in my loft. Having unknown, multiple werewolves in my loft two days after a triple werewolf murder a mile away brought things to a whole new level.

I could always run screaming down the hall. But if I did, who was going to help me? Mrs. Gerschwitz and her cane?

Alternatively, I could walk inside and face whatever was in there. And since every werewolf on the planet appeared to know where I lived, unless I wanted to head downstairs, get into my M3 and start driving, I was going to have to deal with it sooner or later.

I dropped my briefcase and took off my jacket, prepared to change at a moment's notice. With the amount of adrenaline pulsing through me right now, it was hard not sprouting a tail right there in the hall. In fact, despite the fact that the hallway was less-than-private, I almost went ahead and transformed outside my door, so that I'd be better prepared to face what was on the other side of it. But that idea kind of fell by the wayside when I realized that I needed opposable thumbs to get the key into the lock.

After a brief pep talk—if I died, I told myself, at least I wouldn't have to drive to Houston and toss cow patties this Saturday—I slid the key into the lock and flung open the door.

The loft looked just the same as it had when I left this morning. Except, that is, for the three fully dressed werewolves lounging on my suede couch. At least they were in human form, not wolf, and none of them was pointing a wooden stake and/or a gun at my heart. However this worked out, I reflected as I reached back for my briefcase and shut the door behind me, I was definitely going to have to have a chat with Frank.

I struggled to calm my shaking body and did a quick visual survey of my living room's lupine population. Except for their eyes—which were golden, like mine—they didn't look like werewolves. In fact, two of them looked like they belonged in a biker gang. The one on the right had a few scratches on his face, and I wondered with a shiver if he'd gotten them while he was ripping somebody's throat out.

One of the two leather-clad werewolves had his feet on my cherry coffee table, which was annoying. The third werewolf had an air of quiet authority about her. She sat with her legs neatly crossed, wearing a nicely tailored beige suit that I would guess cost ten times as much as Teena's charcoal Wal-Mart special. Her hair was shoulder-length and reddish; overall, she kind of looked like an accountant.

In fact, she kind of looked like me.

But she sure didn't smell like an accountant. She smelled like a born werewolf. And if the aroma I was getting off of her was any indication, she was frighteningly strong.

I quelled the urge to change, squared my shoulders, and took a heavily werewolf-scented breath. Then, with my voice shaking only a little bit, I said, "What are you doing in my loft?"

The accountant leaned back into my couch cushions, running her eyes over me like I was a prize steer. "Miss Garou, I presume?"

I swallowed back my fear and said, with only a little hitch in my voice, "How did you find me? And who the hell are you?"

The woman just smiled at me. Despite the fact that I was about to pee in my pants, something about her smug look pissed me off. "And what makes you think you can just waltz into my loft?" I added. My eyes flicked to the bigger of the two biker-werewolves. Fear or no fear, his big muddy boots were on my brand new Crate & Barrel coffee table. It was bad enough that they broke into my place—now they were messing with my stuff. "Would you mind getting your feet off my table?" I addressed him in a chilly voice. "I just bought it last month."

He looked at the accountant; when she gave him a quick nod, he grudgingly removed his feet.

It wasn't much, but it was something.

The woman-werewolf smirked at me and crossed her expensively stockinged legs. Nice shoes, too, I noticed—from the new Prada collection, unless I was mistaken. "I'm Elena Tenorio. Vice President of the Lupine Society of Houston."

"The Lupine Society of Houston," I repeated. "Not familiar with it."

"Also known as the Houston pack."

"Ah." My stomach dropped, but I struggled to keep my voice calm. "That still doesn't explain what the hell you're doing in my loft."

Her eyes bored into me. "Our network informed us that you were on our territory. So we decided to pay you a visit."

"You mean you broke into my loft."

"This loft doesn't belong to you," she said coolly. "It belongs to us."

"I don't remember you chipping in for the down payment," I said. I was scared, but her cool-as-a-cucumber attitude about breaking into my loft was pissing me off. I crossed my arms. "And who's your network?"

"That's classified information. And as for your loft, I'm afraid you'll have to cede ownership of it. All of Austin belongs to Houston, and your presence here has not been authorized by the pack."

What, did she think I was just going to sign everything I owned over to her? Over my dead body. Which was highly likely, I suddenly realized; Elena's sidekicks were eyeing me with an interest that bordered on something like hunger. I ignored them and focused on Elena. "And you're the leader of the pack?" I asked, tightening my arms over my chest. "Like in the song?"

"No," she said curtly. "I am not the leader."

"Then who are you?" I asked. "And how did you get in here?"

Her wide-set gold eyes narrowed just a touch. "The bigger question, I think," she said slowly, "is what are *you* doing in our territory?"

"This is *my* home," I said obstinately. "Not yours." I stared at the scratches on the leather-clad werewolf's cheek. "Are you the ones responsible for the dead werewolves in the Greenbelt?"

"That is not your concern," she said. "You received the e-mail requesting your presence?"

"So you *did* have something to do with the murders." A chill ran through me. There were three of them and one of me; if they wanted to kill me, there was nothing I could do about it. Which made me wonder; if they were so upset that I was here, why bother with the chitchat? Why not just cut to the chase and rip my throat out?

Not that I had a problem with the gentler approach, of course. "Yes, I got the e-mail," I said. "But you still haven't told me what you're doing here. And how you got past the doorman."

"I can be very persuasive," Elena said, smiling and showing a mouthful of pointy little teeth. A jolt of fear passed through me. Had she done something to Frank? Then I realized it was highly unlikely; they'd probably just hit the lobby in the middle of *Trading Spaces*. Besides, he'd certainly looked okay a few minutes ago.

As I perched on the arm of the chair, one of the biker boys adjusted himself in his leather pants. I sniffed. Pleather. Yuck.

"So you had some involvement in the Greenbelt episode," I repeated, anxious to find out more about what had happened. "What was that all about?"

"It's classified." Her lips formed a thin line.

"Were you here the other day, too?" Although I was pretty sure she didn't have the same scent as the vanishing werewolf who'd visited me earlier in the week.

Elena's sculpted eyebrows shot up. "Here?"

"In my loft. A werewolf broke in earlier this week—that's why the place is a wreck."

She glanced at her two Hells-Angels-esque friends, who shrugged. I knew it wasn't them—they were male, and my anonymous visitor had been female. I couldn't help sneaking glances at them, though. My experience with born werewolf males had been limited to Tom and my father, who hadn't stuck around long enough for me to get to know him. These two wouldn't have been bad looking in a fabric other than pleather—they looked like they were in their mid-thirties, and weren't strangers to the gym—but to me, they were about as appealing as three-day-old broccoli casserole. They didn't smell much better, either. Which actually answered a question that had been bugging me. When I first met Tom, I'd been blown away by the sexual energy between us, and I'd wondered if it was just because he was a born were-wolf.

Now, I surveyed the werewolves on the couch, but felt no stirring in response. Although that could be because I was terrified they might rip my throat out at any moment.

"To my knowledge," Elena said, addressing me coldly, "this is our first direct contact with you. But if there is another solo in our territory, I need to know. What is his name?"

"I don't know," I said, wondering if everyone else in the pack spoke lawyerese. I decided not to say a word about the Texarkana werewolves. It was bad enough the Houston creeps had a line on me. No need to get Teena involved, too. "I got here after whoever it was left."

She didn't answer, but I could see the wheels turning behind those golden eyes. Something must be happening in Austin, I thought. I wondered what? "Who are Wolf-gang and Anita?" I asked, remembering the names on the Lupine Society missive.

"Wolfgang is the Alpha male, and Anita is the current Alpha female," Elena said in a way that implied she was hoping Anita's reign would be extremely temporary.

"And what's the meeting supposed to be about?"

"You will find out on Saturday," she said. "I assume you will be in attendance?"

"I'll see what I can do," I said.

Elena rose from the couch. "If you are not there, you can expect another visit," she said. "And next time, my boys will dispense with the formalities." The one with the lacerated cheek leered at me, and I suppressed a shudder.

Her mission evidently accomplished, Elena walked—well, strutted, really—to the door, her two biker-gang werewolves falling in behind her like bridesmaids. As she reached the door, I thought of something else I wanted to add. Maybe it was false bravado, but my instinct told me not to let them know how rattled I was, even though I was sure they could smell my fear. I knew I could. "Elena?" I said.

She turned and fixed me with icy golden eyes. "Yes?"

The male werewolves' shiny pants creaked a little as they turned to look at me.

I swallowed hard and gathered the remains of my courage. "There's just one more thing. Next time you want to see me," I said, staring at her hard. "You and your pals can wait *outside* the door."

She regarded me coldly for a moment. Then she turned and continued her stately procession out my front door, taking the smell of expensive perfume and cheap synthetic textiles with her.

The moment the door clicked shut, I hurried over to lock it, then slumped against the doorframe. Not that locking it made a difference to anyone, but still. Once I'd caught my breath and my legs were capable of carrying me across the room to the phone, I dialed Frank, who once again had no recollection of anybody, human or werewolf, coming up the elevator. As much as I liked Frank, and as glad as I was that he hadn't been maimed or dismembered, he left something to be desired as a doorman.

As I opened the windows and lit an apple-scented candle to clear the reek of werewolf, my own fear, and pleather—and to calm my brain, which was racing about a million miles an hour and coming up with all kinds of unpleasant scenarios—I wondered again why

Elena felt the need to come and visit me in person. After all, I was supposed to be in Houston on Saturday. So why bother to make the trip? It was almost as if she was sussing me out. Did she think I was a threat?

Unfortunately, despite my little touch of bravado, I suspected my presence had been less than commanding. Oh, well. Maybe it would go better with Wolfgang.

When the apartment was mostly clear of the pleather-and-werewolf smell, I closed the windows and blew out the candle. There was no way I was heading to the Greenbelt today; I'd had more than enough werewolf already. Instead, I retreated to the bedroom for some much-needed sleep. Which wasn't too restful, unfortunately, since I kept dreaming about the pleather boys' long yellowed teeth sinking into my neck, and Elena's throaty laugh in the distance.

"Any chance of slipping out of the retreat?" I asked Lindsey in her office the next morning.

"Probably not," she said, brushing back her dark brown hair. "Adele can't stop talking about it."

I sighed and took a sip of my skinny extra-foam latte. How could I manufacture a reason to slip out of the retreat long enough to head down to Houston? I wasn't too optimistic about what would happen at our little meeting, but it would be better to show up than not. Maybe I could offer to throw in a little free tax work in exchange for immunity.

First, though, I had to figure out how to get out of my boss's cowboy-themed retreat.

A few months back, somebody had bought Adele a subscription to *Martha Stewart Living,* with the unfortunate result being that she now called everything "a good thing" and was obsessed with collecting antique pitchers. Which was why the retreat was in Roundtop, a town with a higher population of antique stores than people. The town was picturesque, but unless you enjoyed chasing armadillos in your spare time—which, to be honest, I did, but not during company functions—it was hardly a hotbed of excitement.

It was, however, halfway to Houston.

"Why don't you want to go?" Lindsey asked, peering at me over her cat-eyed glasses. She was wearing a cream silk blouse cut dangerously low, and her long dark hair tumbled over her shoulders.

"Something came up last night," I said vaguely. "Do you think Adele will mind if I slip out of the retreat for a few hours to head to Houston?"

"What's in Houston?"

"Just a meeting I'm invited to," I said airily. "Some . . . Bluebonnet Society thing." Werewolves, bluebonnets. Close enough.

"Bluebonnets?" She raised an arched eyebrow. "Since when are you into gardening?"

"I think it's a fundraiser. Children's cancer, or something. I agreed to go before I realized it was at the same time as the retreat." Time to change the subject again. "Are we still on for lunch?"

"Can't make it after all," she said, sliding her cat-eyed glasses back on. "This report's due by the end of the day. By the way, how did lunch with your new client go?" Her eyes glinted behind the lenses.

"He's fine," I said.

"I know *he's* fine," she said with a bit of a leer. "I'm talking about lunch."

Whoops. "I mean lunch was fine. But Heath was there."

"You brought Heath?"

"Nope." I took a fortifying swig of my skinny latte. "He was there with his 'associate,' Miranda."

Lindsey's arched eyebrow went even higher. "Romeo's is hardly the place for a business lunch."

"I just met my client there," I pointed out.

"And how much business did you discuss?"

"Well, not a lot," I confessed. "He wanted to get to know me."

"Yeah, right. And I'm sure Heath and Miranda got a lot of work done, too." She crossed her legs and looked at me over her glasses. "I'll bet they didn't have any files with them."

No, they hadn't, come to think of it.

She leaned back in her chair. "Well, if Heath doesn't work out, you could do a lot worse than Mark Sydney."

"It's not going to happen. He's a client."

Lindsey slid open her desk drawer and pulled out a dog-eared copy of *Texas Monthly*. "He's also page sixty-six of the November issue."

I turned to an image of Mark, smoldering in an Armani suit that cost as much as my car.

"He's got great eyes, doesn't he?" she said.

"He's off-limits for me. But if you'd like me to introduce you . . ." I said. It would be much better than having her date a werewolf. Although the werewolf in question hadn't been on the scene in six months, so maybe that was a thing of the past.

"I wouldn't object," she said, with a catlike smile.

"I'll see what I can do." Like I said, anyone was better than Tom.

When I got back to my desk, the message light was blinking on my phone. It was Heath.

"Sorry I missed you, Sophie. I know we haven't seen much of each other lately, but I may swing by tonight and see if you're there. Love you."

My place wasn't the ideal spot for a romantic rendezvous—the place still looked like the "before" picture in an episode of *Extreme Makeover*—but at least we had something resembling a date. I decided to call that a good sign.

I checked my schedule for the day; thankfully, it was clear. So at two o'clock, I drank a last mug of wolfsbane tea, closed up shop, and grabbed my spare bag of work-out clothes from my bottom desk drawer.

Because I had one more thing on my agenda—and it didn't involve exercise.

Five

A cold north wind greeted me as I closed the M3's door behind me at Zilker Park, wishing I'd brought a jacket. The playground was sparsely populated today—the thermometer had dipped into the low forties, which in Austin is equivalent to January in the high arctic. One brave young mother with a stroller hurried by; as she headed to a giant green Suburban, I headed toward the entrance to the Greenbelt, wishing it weren't daylight. I could have used a natural fur coat right about now.

It was only a few steps from the parking lot to the bollards that marked the beginning of the trail, and I hadn't even gotten that far before a whiff of werewolf reached my nose. The hairs stood up on the back of my neck; for a moment, I considered turning back to my car and heading home to my comfy suede couch. But I needed to find out what had gone on here; if for no other reason than to find out whether Elena and the pleather boys had been involved. If a murderer had ready access to my loft, I wanted to know.

The afternoon was gray and overcast, and the wind was coming from the wrong direction—north—but I started sniffing the moment I hit the beginning of the trail. Despite the lackluster day, the Greenbelt was still beautiful, with its swathe of bleached gold grass and the still-green live oaks hugging the edge of the meadow. I headed toward the trailhead with a twinge of regret. I was itching to change—nature smelled so much more interesting when I was a wolf—but now just wasn't the time.

As I slipped past the white bollards onto the trail, my hackles rose. Even with the reduced capacity of my human-shaped nose—not to mention the fact that the wind was at my back—I could still smell werewolf here. And blood.

Lots of it.

For about a quarter mile, I trotted across the tree-lined meadow that was the beginning of the trail, searching for the location of the photo with the body bag. Before plunging into the thicket of oaks and cedars, I looked over my shoulder toward downtown—and my building. If I squinted a little, I could make out the window of my loft. A shiver passed through me, and not just because of the cold. Whatever had happened here had taken place—almost literally—right under my nose.

As soon as I trotted out of the meadow and into the woods, the scent of blood and werewolves grew stronger. But it wasn't until the trail veered to the left that the smell hit me full force.

I hurried up the trail. I was getting closer to the source of the scent—much closer. I turned around a bend in the trail and caught a flash of something yellow in the brush off to my right.

Crime scene tape.

I turned off the trail and worked my way through the scrubby brush. A moment later, I emerged from a tangle of thorny branches and stood at the perimeter of a ring of yellow plastic tape.

The grass and brush were trampled, but it was impossible to tell if it was from the fight or the forensics crew that came after it. A reddish-brown streak stained the silvery bark of a sycamore tree. I found myself staring at it, wondering whose blood it was. And how it had gotten there.

Closing my eyes, I pulled a deep breath of air in through my nose. A trace of fear—I could still smell it—and the coppery stench of dried blood. Which wasn't too surprising, because it was rather liberally splashed around. I could smell werewolves, too of course—but it was all such a jumble I couldn't distinguish the individual scents. Not in my human form, anyway.

I looked around furtively. It would be so much more helpful if I had my full capacity. But did I dare change?

I tested the air once again; there wasn't anyone nearby. And I was far enough off the trail that even with the leaves off some of the trees, no one would see me transform. At least I hoped not.

Goosebumps sprang up on my arms and legs as I hid behind a tree and peeled off my workout clothes, then my socks and shoes, hoping no one would report a female flasher on the trail. I didn't bother folding anything; I just closed my eyes and let the impulse that had been tugging at me since I set foot on the trail rip through me.

My skin rippled; I could feel the fur sprouting along my arms and legs as the world around me came into sharp focus. The smell of blood assaulted my nose, and the mingled scents of the werewolves started to separate and become distinct. A wind swept in from the north, and I could hear each leaf scrape against each other, as if whispering to me—*Danger*. A moment later, my eyes snapped open, and I saw the scene with new eyes.

First, I sniffed to make sure I hadn't missed anything—or, to be more specific, anyone. Fortunately, whoever had been here was long gone.

When I was sure the coast was clear, I paced the perimeter, trying to figure out who had been here. I could smell the men and women who had been here, muddling the scents. And the blood—stains of it were everywhere.

Despite the overlay of human scent, I could still smell werewolves. There was no trace of Elena, but I wasn't so sure about the pleather boys—there was something here that reminded me of them. I continued to circle the area, sniffing. As I padded around the dead leaves, I encountered a dark spot on the earth, at the base of the sycamore tree, and froze.

I lowered my nose and sniffed. Blood. Death. And werewolf. I shied away from the spot and padded slowly around the circle, locating two more stained patches of earth. Two more deaths.

Unfortunately, I still had no idea why.

After I'd done a sweep of the trampled circle, I moved out to the other side of the crime scene tape, hoping to find something the police had missed. And it turned out to be one of those rare moments when being a werewolf actually came in handy, because it only took five minutes for me to figure out that a large contingent had come from one particular direction.

Nose to the ground, I followed the trail through a tangle of underbrush, hoping none of it was poison ivy. How had the crime scene team missed this? I wondered. Half the branches were broken off the bushes; it almost looked like a herd of buffalo had come through.

I followed the track along Barton Creek for a while before it turned abruptly toward a limestone cliff. And ended.

I stood at the base of the tall white rock, sniffing. There was smoke here. And something else; something that reminded me of my mother's shop.

Incense.

But where was it coming from?

On the second pass, I found the source: a hole about

eighteen inches wide, hidden behind a spiky agarita bush. I sniffed at it carefully, just to make sure there were no active surprises waiting for me inside. When I was pretty sure the werewolves were long gone, I squeezed my furry body down the hole, hoping the bottom wouldn't be too far down—and that I'd be able to get out again.

The drop was only a few feet, thankfully, and as my eyes adjusted to the dim light, I could see I was in a cave that was about the size of my dorm room freshman year. And it didn't smell much different, either; the dorm room's previous resident had had a thing for pot, and the incense residue had stuck around for months.

This brand, however, had an unfortunate Pine-Sol base note to it. There were other scents here too, though—werewolves, of course. But there was also fire—and the seemingly ever-present aroma of blood. A brief search turned up a blackened area near the door—burned cedar. Little puddles of some ashy, melted goo appeared to be the source of the pine-fresh scent. And a few splatters of something brown.

More blood.

I backed away from the charred, bloodstained limestone. What was with the whole blood thing, anyway? Had these werewolves been hanging out with vampires too much? Or were they making more werewolves here? And if they were, wasn't there a way to do it a tad more hygienically?

I did a circuit of the small cave, but all I turned up was a piece of withered plant that looked like a cactus chunk and a few more lumps of piney incense. I was about to squeeze back out of the cave when I sniffed something different. Something with an animal scent to it. As I padded toward the source of the smell, something round caught my eye. I approached it warily, lowering my nose to sniff it.

It was a leather medallion, attached to a broken leather thong, and something about it made my fur stand on end. I nudged it over with my nose, and the hackles rose even further on the back of my neck.

Because even in the dim light from the cave mouth, I could tell the design burned into the leather was a dead ringer for the amulet I had picked up six months ago at a *yerberia*.

As I pulled at the thong with my teeth, dragging it toward me, a cold breeze swept through the cave opening. *Werewolf.*

I froze and took another deep breath; there it was again. Faint, but definitely there. I flipped the medallion into my mouth and scrabbled through the cave entrance, scanning the underbrush for signs of movement.

Then I bolted toward my stashed clothes.

It took me maybe five minutes to cover what had taken fifteen to uncover originally, and I don't think I've ever transformed and dressed so fast in my life. I slipped the medallion into my pocket and crashed through the underbrush toward the trail, attempting to look like a casual trail jogger who'd been struck by an urgent call of nature. (The ladies' room kind, not the werewolf kind.) The smell of werewolf was stronger as I approached the trailhead—I could see my M3 like a beacon in the distance—and it was all I could do not to break into a mad sprint.

Although it couldn't have been more than a grand total of fifteen minutes, it felt like fifteen years before I was back at the parking lot, pushing the unlock button of my M3 and not daring to look behind me. Only when I was safely ensconced in the front seat with the car in reverse did I risk a glance back at the head of the trail.

A black-haired werewolf stood there, head raised, scanning the parking lot. Trying to look nonchalant, I put the car into drive and glided past him, not daring to turn my head to look. My eyes slid to the rearview mirror as I drove away; his dark eyes were fixed on the back of the M3.

I just hoped he hadn't gotten the license plate number.

As I crossed the Congress Street Bridge over Lady Bird Lake, I touched the little leather disk and shivered. Was the wolf pattern on the medallion a standard pattern? Or was it somehow connected with the amulet I'd picked up at a *yerberia* six months ago? I knew the old Hispanic woman who sold it to me—and whose daughter had tried to off me with a silver bullet—was familiar with werewolves. She'd pegged me for one right off.

Did the medallion come from the *yerberia* too?

What did it mean? And was it connected with the dark-haired werewolf at the trailhead?

I reached down to crank up the heater and reviewed what I'd just seen—and smelled. Evidently the Greenbelt was still occupied—or at least visited—by werewolves. It was possible, from the scents I'd picked up, that one of the wolves involved in the fight was a pleather boy, but I couldn't be sure. I was confident, however, that Elena hadn't been among them.

Which was some comfort, considering I had an upcoming meeting with a hostile Houston pack. Which, if the delightful little bloodstained montage on the Greenbelt was any indication, it would be in my best interest not to miss.

Saturday, I decided as I pulled into my building's parking garage, I would just have to leave Adele and the cowboys high and dry for a few hours. I'd come up with an excuse to leave; then I'd go to Houston and offer free tax work in exchange for immunity. It wasn't a great plan, but it was better than going in with nothing.

Then, if the Houston pack decided against eating and/or imprisoning me, I'd head back to Roundtop and sneak back in before the Hoedown Dinner. At least I think that was what Adele was calling it; she'd had Sally trying to find paper napkins in a bandanna print for a week now.

A few minutes later, I parked the M3 in my favorite spot and headed up the elevator, glad to be out of a blood-spattered cave and back in the world of scented candles and luxury lofts. It was still early, thankfully, which meant I'd have a good bit of time to repair the damage to my place before Heath showed up. Provided, of course, I hadn't had any additional visitors while I was at work. As the elevator crept upward, a nasty little thought crept into my head. Could the werewolf I'd seen today have followed my scent home? I told myself not to be melodramatic. After all, how could a werewolf follow my scent if I was in a closed car? But I couldn't stop thinking about that sense of being tracked—or the medallion. I'd zipped it into the side pocket of my purse, just to make sure I wouldn't lose it. I was dying to compare it with the amulet.

The lobby, at least, didn't smell like werewolf at all, which was encouraging. I stepped out of the elevator and said hi to Frank, who was engrossed in an episode of *Design on a Dime;* he smiled, but barely glanced up from the screen. I liked Frank, but I was beginning to think that from a security standpoint, the television behind the front desk might not be the best idea. The sound of hammers followed me into the second elevator, replaced by a Muzak version of one of Adele's favorite songs: "Copacabana."

It was evidently my lucky day; despite the lingering aroma of Elena and the pleather boys, it smelled like nobody had swung by in my absence. Of course, I checked anyway—you never knew—before heading into my bedroom and pulling out my jewelry box.

I dug through it, searching for the wolf amulet I'd got-

ten last fall. Despite the fact that the woman who sold it
to me was a murderess's mother, I had held on to it,
since it seemed to have some good mojo to it. It made
me feel like someone was protecting me.

Now, though, I wanted to compare it with the medallion I'd found in the cave.

The sapphire earrings were there, as were my pearls,
but the little corner where I kept the amulet was conspicuously empty. Had the little leather pouch somehow
gotten misplaced when I was cleaning up? But I didn't
remember seeing it. I bent down and looked under the
dresser and the bed, then dug through my drawers. It
was no use.

The amulet was gone.

But where? Everything else in the jewelry box was intact. Had the intruder taken it? And if so, why steal the
amulet and leave the sapphire earrings?

I searched through my dresser again, pulling out all
the clothes and shaking them. It was no use; the amulet
was gone.

After the third time through, I gave up and decided it
was time to start cleaning. Heath would be here in a few
short hours, and unless I wanted to explain why I hadn't
called the police about the break-in, I had a lot of work
ahead of me.

I checked again to make sure the medallion was in my
purse—I don't know why, but I felt better knowing it
was there—and for the next hour, distracted myself by
attacking the mess in my living room. And shaving, of
course.

I had just fixed myself a cup of wolfsbane tea and was
about to haul the vacuum out of the closet when the
doorbell rang. The clock on the wall read five, which
was kind of early for Heath. I glanced at the phone;
Frank was supposed to call when I had a visitor.

Since he hadn't, maybe it was Mrs. Gerschwitz, from

down the hall. I slid the vacuum back into the closet and headed for the door.

It wasn't Mrs. Gerschwitz.

It was Teena the Texarkana werewolf.

I stifled a groan and mentally cursed Frank. I mean, what was the point of having a doorman if all he did was channel-surf while entire packs of werewolves cruised by him?

"Teena," I said. She was dressed in the same awful charcoal suit, only this time with a gold shell that did very little for her skin tone. Her eyes were red-rimmed, and her face so white I wondered if she'd just seen the bogeyman.

"What are you doing here?" I asked. "I thought you were going home."

"We can't," she said, glancing down the hall. Two more young women stood by the elevator, wearing tight jeans, heavy makeup, and wary expressions. The leader of this little pack, I decided, must be Teena.

"Well, you can't stay here," I said.

Her face was pale. "Not even for a day or two?"

"I'm sorry," I said. She suddenly looked like someone had let all the air out of her. "Are you sure you can't just go home?"

"I'm afraid they'll kill us," she said miserably.

I glanced at the two girls moping by the elevator and made a decision. Probably a bad one. "Come in for a minute," I said. "You and your friends."

She brightened. "Really?"

"You'd better hurry, before I regain my sanity," I said. Teena waved her friends down the hall, and a few moments later, there we were, in my living room.

I just hoped the Houston pack wouldn't choose this moment to make another appearance.

"Thanks so much for inviting us in," Teena said. "This is my friend Brissa," she said, indicating the shorter of her two friends, a pillowy-looking girl with curly brown hair and a snub nose. Brissa gave me a shy wave. "And this is Lourdes," Teena said. Lourdes had a curtain of black hair that hid her mocha-colored face, and was so skinny I could probably break her over my left knee. Not that I wanted to, of course. "Her place doesn't usually look like this," she explained. "I told you; someone broke in."

They nodded, eyeing me cautiously. All three of them had the iridescent eyes of a werewolf, but none had the gold irises I was coming to think was the hallmark of born werewolves. Teena ran a finger under one eye, checking to make sure her (black, liquid) eyeliner hadn't smudged. They had all ringed their eyes with the stuff; paired with the iridescence of their irises, it created a raccoonlike effect. Was that a Texarkana girl thing, I wondered? Or just a Texarkana werewolf thing?

"What's going on?" I asked as the three of them huddled together on the couch. They all looked to be about the same age, which was not too far out of high school. "Why can't you go back?"

There was an awkward silence as the three of them looked at each other. Then Brissa blurted out, "I think they might kill us. All the made werewolves kept disappearing. Like Brett." She squeezed Teena's hand and whispered, "That's why we had to leave."

The three of them reeked of desperation, with a hefty shot of fear mixed in there, too. Hefty enough that I was thinking about opening the windows. It was still forty degrees outside, though, so I decided against it. "Why do you think they want to kill you?" I asked.

"Because they said Brett shouldn't have made us," Teena said. "It's against the rules. And now, we can't go home, because if they find us . . ."

Teena hadn't told me all of the nasty details. I closed my eyes and massaged my temples. If this was how the

Texarkana pack dealt with unwanted werewolves, it didn't bode well for my upcoming rendezvous in Houston. Maybe if I threw in some free auditing in addition to the tax advice . . .

I opened my eyes. Teena and the Texarkana werewolves were looking at me expectantly. "I wish I could help, but I wouldn't know where to start," I said.

Teena stared at me as if I was a particularly dim child. "What I said the other day. Help us. Lead us. Teach us what you know." She raised a fist into the air, but not very far—the suit was a little tight across the back, evidently. "Grrl Power. You know?"

Grrl Power. I waited for her to tell me she was kidding. When she didn't, I grabbed my mug of tea and finished it in one big gulp, wishing it was pinot grigio. Or maybe a double martini.

"Look," I said. "I'm sorry you're in a bind; I know how hard being a werewolf can be." Did I ever. "But I really can't help you." I glanced up at the clock; I had no idea when Heath would be by, and as much as I pitied the grrls, I really, really didn't want to have to explain the whole werewolves-on-my-couch thing to my boyfriend.

"But you've got to," Teena said, and the smell of fear intensified. "We have nobody else to turn to."

"I wish I knew what to tell you," I said, "but I haven't got a clue."

"But where will we go if we can't go home?" The smell of desperation was so oppressive that I considered slipping into the kitchen to light an apple-scented candle. I felt bad for them—I really did. But I was in hot water with the Houston pack already. And I was pretty sure consorting with "illegal" werewolves would be frowned upon by Elena and the pleather boys.

I had opened my mouth to suggest they try going somewhere else—maybe somewhere like Lubbock, or El

Paso, since Austin didn't appear to be a safe haven at the moment—when somebody knocked.

Four pairs of werewolf eyes swiveled to the door.

Mrs. Gerschwitz?

Heath?

Or—my stomach clenched—another emissary from the Houston pack?

Elena and the pleather boys hadn't felt it necessary to knock last time, so I was betting on Mrs. Gerschwitz. "Hold on a moment," I told the grrls, and headed for the door.

It wasn't Mrs. Gerschwitz.

And it wasn't the Houston pack, either.

It was six-plus feet of hunky werewolf goodness.

Tom.

I cracked the door and peered out at him. "What are you doing here?"

"Hello, Miss Garou," he said, smiling in a toothy way that sent sparks zinging through me. "May I come in?"

"Umm . . ." I glanced over my shoulder at Teena and company. They didn't look like they'd scented Tom yet, but it wouldn't be long.

I turned back to Tom, who was waiting expectantly. I had forgotten how sexy he smelled. Kind of a foresty, musky, primeval thing that didn't just take my breath away—it knocked it clean out of me. And the allure of his aroma wasn't at all diminished by his physical appearance. He wore faded jeans and a black leather jacket, and while I usually go for guys with a more professional look—you know, pinstripes and starched shirts—I could easily make an exception for Tom, who looked like a model from a Calvin Klein underwear ad. Between shoots, of course, and with more clothing. I found myself wondering if he was a boxers guy or a briefs guy before I remembered there were three werewolves in my apartment and I wanted him to leave. For now, anyway. I was dying to interrogate him, but this was not the right moment for that. What with Teena and her friends being on my couch and Heath potentially due to stop by at any time.

"I really need to talk to you," I said in a low voice. "But I've got company, so now's not a good time. Does Lindsey know you're here?"

"Not yet. Is Heap here?" he asked, trying to peer past me.

"Heap?" I looked at him for a moment before it dawned on me what he was talking about. "No, *Heath*'s not here."

He took a deep breath. "No, he's not," he said. "But you're hiding a couple of werewolves in there." He cocked an eyebrow at me. "What happened to Sophie the lone wolf?"

"Trust me," I muttered. "It wasn't my idea."

I glanced behind me as Teena sat up straight, sniffing, and said, "Who *is* that?" And that's when my werewolf compartmentalization strategy went straight to hell.

Tom gave me a big, toothy grin. "Looks like your secret's out."

Six

"You might as well come in," I said, opening the door wider and thinking dark thoughts about Frank the useless doorman.

Three sets of werewolf eyes widened when Tom strode into the living room. I could almost smell the waves of lust emanating from my couch.

"Who's this?" Teena asked breathily, mouth agape. Lourdes brushed her long black hair from her eyes, fluttering her lashes, and Brissa leaned forward, exposing about an inch or two of tightly packed cleavage. They seemed to be recovering from the whole scared-to-death thing pretty darned fast.

"This is Tom," I said. "Tom Fenris."

"You're like . . . wow." Brissa breathed. Teena fiddled with her skirt while Lourdes' dark eyes roamed all over my visitor.

"Tom, this is Teena," I said. "And her friends Brissa and Lourdes. They're from Texarkana, and stopped in for a visit. They were just about to leave."

Teena looked at me open-mouthed for a second, then resumed staring at Tom. "But . . ."

"What are you ladies doing at Sophie's place?" Tom cocked an eyebrow at me, and then the three young werewolves on the couch, who were salivating over him as if he were a T-bone steak. He gestured at the loveseat. "May I?"

I sighed. "Do I have a choice?"

Tom ignored me and sat down. "Tell me about yourselves," he said, leaning forward and focusing his attention on the three young women, who were now all but panting.

I gave them a strained smile and said, "Wolfsbane tea, anyone?" Since we were all going to be here for a while, we might as well be comfortable. Or failing that, at least human.

"Not for me, thanks," Tom said. "But I could go for a beer."

"Me too," Teena said, and Lourdes and Brissa nodded. I was pretty sure they weren't legal drinking age, but serving alcohol to minors was the least of my concerns right now.

"What's wolfsbane tea?" Teena asked.

She hadn't been kidding, I realized. There *was* a lot she didn't know. "You take it to keep from changing," I said. "Didn't anyone tell you?"

"I *knew* you could help us," Teena beamed, sneaking another glance at Tom, who was now sprawled alluringly over my loveseat, his black T-shirt stretched taut over his chest.

"But why wouldn't you want to change?" Teena asked.

I blinked at Teena. Why *would* you want to change seemed like the better question to me, but before I could answer, Tom said, "Who was your sire?" in that sexy, growly voice.

Teena, Brissa, and Lourdes stared moonily at him, and as Teena breathily explained her dilemma, touching her long gleaming hair every ten to twenty seconds, I escaped to the kitchen. *They* might not want wolfsbane tea, but I did. And maybe a few shots of something a little stronger, too.

While the water heated up, I leaned against my Sub-Zero fridge and listened to Teena's lilting voice, interspersed with Tom's occasional rumbly response. Should I call Heath and tell him not to drop by? On the other hand, I really wanted to see him. . . .

Tom's low voice reached me through the door, sending a quiver through me. I couldn't believe there were four werewolves in my living room. All we needed now was another visit from the Houston pack—and maybe that mystery werewolf—and we'd be able to field a fricking baseball team. We could call ourselves the Howlers.

I had just distributed four Heinekens and was settling onto the arm of the loveseat when there was yet another knock at the door.

I raised my finger to my lips and tiptoed to the door. Frank was going to hear about this.

"Who is it?" I called.

"It's me."

Heath.

"Just a minute," I said, whirling around to face the mob of werewolves in my living room. "Hide!" I hissed.

The three women jumped up from the couch. "Where?" Teena asked, looking around the room frantically.

"Balcony, bedroom . . . I don't care. Just get out of my living room!"

The Texarkana trio headed for the balcony. As they pulled the glass door behind them, I yanked the blinds closed. When I turned around, Tom was gone. I didn't have time to wonder where.

Heath had raised his hand to knock a second time when I opened the door. Despite the fact that Tom the über-werewolf was somewhere in my apartment—and despite the fact that the last time I'd seen Heath, he was lunching at Romeo's with Miranda the blonde bombshell—I was still happy to see him. Thick dark hair that gleamed in the light of the hallway, a crisp ivory dress shirt, his tie loosened seductively, and perfectly tailored chocolate-colored dress slacks. I took a deep breath of his human-male-CK1-fresh-laundry scent and felt my body respond. Which admittedly it was already primed to do, since Tom was less than twenty feet away.

"This is a surprise," I said.

"All work and no play makes Jack a dull boy," he said, leaning against the doorframe. "Besides. I missed you."

I was glad to hear it. I just wished he'd decided to swing by and share that with me an hour later. After I'd gotten rid of all the werewolves. "I've missed you too," I said.

Despite Miranda's assertion that things had been smooth sailing at the office, Heath looked tired. I chose to believe it was because he was burning the midnight oil at work rather than working through the Kama Sutra with Miranda, and invited him in. Even with the circles under his eyes, he looked good enough to eat.

"Thanks for stopping by," I said, "Sorry I'm a bit . . . unprepared." I glanced over my shoulder at my messy, recently werewolf-filled loft. "Frank didn't let me know you were here."

"He was taking notes on some TV show," he said. "Something about paint textures. He just waved me on up."

I was definitely going to have to take this up with management.

"Besides," he said, "you know I don't care how your loft looks."

"Come in," I said, wondering what the hell I was going to do about the werewolf in the closet. Assuming he was in the closet. Not to mention the ones on my balcony. Thank God humans couldn't smell worth a darn, because to me, my loft smelled like *Wild Kingdom*.

"God, Sophie. What happened to your place?" he asked, pointing to the stack of broken pictures in the corner that I hadn't gotten around to hiding.

"I'm . . . redecorating."

"Interesting look," he said. "You've got kind of a postapocalyptic thing going here."

"Thanks," I said, sticking my tongue out.

"Fortunately," he said, moving in closer, "I'm not interested in you for your interior decorating skills." He slid an arm around me and pulled me closer to him. "I've missed you so much," he said roughly, burying his face in my hair.

Normally, this would have been just what I needed. I loved spending time with Heath; ever since we'd met, our romance had been a single woman's dream. Heath was funny, smart, successful, thoughtful . . . and, of course, great in bed. We even had similar visions for the future: visions that included his-and-her careers and a nice two-story house in Tarrytown with attractive landscaping and 2.4 kids. (Of course, I hadn't mentioned the fact that our "kids" would likely be "pups," but I was hoping Heath would be okay with it. After all, he had embraced my psychic witch mother, so he must be a little bit open-minded.)

Most important, when I was with him, Heath made me feel special—like I was the only woman in the world.

The problem was, right now, not only was I not the only woman in the world, but I wasn't even the only woman—or werewolf—in my loft.

I glanced at the door to the balcony. The grrls had to be half-frozen by now. "You know," I said, wriggling out of his embrace, "I'm glad you stopped by, but I've got about another hour or so of work to do here. I'm afraid I'd be . . . distracted," I said, shooting him my smokiest look. "Could we maybe catch up later on tonight?"

He licked his lower lip and stared right back. "How about I promise not to pillage you until you're done working?" he asked, lowering himself onto my loveseat. In the exact spot where Tom had been two minutes earlier. *Not good.*

Heath flashed me a smile. "Got any scotch?"

"I'll get you a glass," I said with resignation, and retrieved the Macallan 12 from one of the cabinets. I stocked it just for him—scotch made my nose hairs curl.

"It looks like you've got company," Heath said as I handed him his drink.

The hairs on my arms rose. Was he psychic or something? "What do you mean?"

He pointed to the coffee table. "You've got four open beers here."

"Ah."

His intelligent dark eyes flicked to me. The passion I'd seen a moment earlier was gone, replaced by the same look he had when he was hot on a lead for a case.

"We were, um . . . trying out a drinking game," I babbled.

"Who, you and the potted plants?" He cocked an eyebrow at the shattered pot in the corner that I hadn't gotten around to cleaning up yet. "Or what's left of them?"

"The potted plants?" I forced a chuckle and struggled to come up with a plausible explanation for the four untouched Heinekens. "No, no. It was just . . . Mrs. Gerschwitz and me."

"And who else?" He pointed to the table again. "There are four beers."

"Um . . . Henry. And a friend of his. He lives on the third floor. Mrs. Gerschwitz is kind of interested in him, so I thought I'd see if I could help get things moving." The perfect explanation, I thought, hurrying over to the table and scooping up the beer bottles before he could see that they were all full. "I'll just clear these away," I said, heading into the kitchen.

I set the bottles into the sink and tried to slow my racing heart. Where *had* Tom gone? I snuck a peek into the pantry, but he wasn't hiding behind the beef jerky. "So where's the happy couple now?" Heath asked as I walked back into the living room with a glass of Macallan a moment later.

"They went back to her place," I said, sitting down on the loveseat next to Heath and glancing at the balcony. It was forty degrees out there, and Teena and her pals weren't exactly dressed for the weather. And where *was* Tom? My eyes flicked to the bedroom. My closet?

"Sounds like your plan worked," Heath said, sipping his drink and sliding an arm around me, the beer bottles thankfully forgotten. "Romantic thoughts must be in the air tonight."

He leaned over and kissed me hard, sending little tingles all through my body. *Tom's here,* I reminded myself as Heath slipped a warm hand up my back, under my camisole.

"It's not a good time," I said, but before I could get another word out, he was peeling off my camisole and was sliding the straps of my black lace bra down my shoulders.

"Why not?" he asked, his tongue tracing the edges of my bra, pushing the fabric to the side. He slid the straps down farther, and then my bra was gone, my nipples stiffening as he kissed first one, and then the other. "So beautiful," he murmured, fumbling with the button on my jeans. I caught a strong whiff of Tom just then, and for a moment—just a moment—I imagined it was his mouth on me, his paw warm on my thigh. "Tom . . ." I murmured as Heath's finger brushed aside my lace underwear and slid into me. I pushed against him, gasping.

But the hand stopped, and Heath's head popped up. "Who?"

"What?" I said.

His dark eyes were flat. "Who's Tom?"

Now that the moment was gone, ruined by my stupid subconscious, I realized I was half-naked, with my boyfriend's hand probing my underwear, while Tom himself was in the next room. God. Had *Tom* heard me? Werewolves have fabulous hearing, after all—of that, I was only too aware. My face burned. Not to mention the grrls . . .

"I said *don't stop*," I clarified. "But come to think of it, we probably should," I said, reaching for my camisole. "I'm looking forward to continuing what we just started . . . later. For now, though, I really, *really* have to get some work done." I refastened my bra and slipped back into my camisole, sneaking a surreptitious glance at the door to the bedroom. How much of that little scene had Tom just observed?

"I don't want to think about work right now," Heath said huskily, reaching for me again.

I kissed him, but stopped his hand as it traveled toward my jeans button again. "I'd love to," I said, "but . . . I'm afraid Mrs. Gerschwitz will be back at any minute."

"I thought she and Henry went off for a romantic liaison."

"Oh, you know how we women are. I'm sure she'll be back for a post-mortem any moment."

Heath laughed. "You may be right about the post-mortem. Viagra overdoses can do that to you." He traced the crescent moon on my shoulder. I still wasn't sure how I'd ended up with a moon tattoo on my shoulder—it was the result of a barely remembered evening involving Lindsey, multiple Hurricanes, and several bars on Sixth Street—but even if I hated it, men always seemed to find it interesting. And at least it was only a *crescent* moon. "I have to confess that I'm a bit disappointed, though. I thought you wanted me to come over."

"I did," I said. "But then this thing came up this afternoon. It's really important."

"So important you were playing quarters with Mrs. Gerschwitz and Henry?" He glanced at the coffee table and smoothed his dark hair back. "By the way, what were you playing? I didn't see any coins lying around."

"It was a new game," I said, glancing at the bedroom door again. "Called . . . Hide the Werewolf."

"Hide the Werewolf?"

Shit.

"I'll teach you how to play it sometime. I'll tell you what," I said, glancing at my watch. "Why don't you head home, and I'll swing by after I finish up?"

"Can't I just wait here?" he asked.

"I think it would be too . . .um . . . distracting," I said.

He sighed and ran a finger through his hair, suddenly looking drained. Then again, he had been up several nights in a row working. Or doing other things, a little part of my brain suggested. He and Miranda *had* been pretty close lately.

But I wasn't going to get into that now.

He stroked my arm lightly, and every cell in my body started humming in response again. "Are you sure I can't stay?" he asked, reaching out to touch my cheek.

I wanted him to. God, did I want him to. After the day I'd had, I could use a little pick-me-up. But this was definitely not the time. "Let me finish my work," I murmured as seductively as I could. "I promise I'll come by as soon as I'm done."

He stood up and kissed me again, a slow, lingering

kiss that made my entire insides melt. "I'll be waiting for you," he said.

I walked him to the door, leaning against the frame as he walked down the hall to the elevator. I was blowing him a last kiss when the elevator door opened, and Mrs. Gerschwitz's gold cane emerged, followed by my neighbor, dressed in pink marabou mules and a matching sheath dress. With marabou trim, of course.

"How did things go with Henry?" Heath asked her with a knowing grin.

I cringed.

"Henry? Haven't seen him all night," Mrs. Gerschwitz said, smiling at Heath and then looking down the hall at me.

Heath had turned around and stared at me, lips pressed together in a thin line.

"Wait," I said, starting down the hall after him.

"Don't you have work to do?" he said icily, and stepped into the elevator. By the time I got there, the doors had slid shut.

Seven

"Did I say something wrong?" asked Mrs. Gerschwitz, her powdered face squinched up with worry.

"No, no," I said, feeling my stomach clench. "It was all my fault." I briefly debated getting on the next elevator to chase Heath down. But I couldn't, not with four werewolves hidden in my apartment. I'd have to explain it all later. How, I wasn't sure, but I hoped I'd come up with something.

As Mrs. Gerschwitz hobbled down the hall to her door, I trudged back to my loft to let the Texarkana trio in from the cold. And Siegfried the Viking Werewolf out of my closet.

But there was no need to give them the all clear; by the time I got back to my living room, it was filled with werewolves again. "Hi," I said, but the Texarkana trio barely looked up; they were too busy staring at Tom, who gave me an uncomfortably knowing look.

"Don't mind me," I said sourly, and headed into the kitchen to make myself a fresh cup of wolfsbane tea. And try to figure out what to do about Heath.

Teena launched into telling Tom all her problems as I headed into the kitchen. I returned to the living room a few minutes later with a mug of tea and a very bad attitude. As I sat down on the edge of my armchair, Teena sniffed and wrinkled her nose at the brew in my hands. Which was perfectly understandable; wolfsbane tea was hardly a taste sensation.

"We were out at Big Jake's Smokehouse one night," she continued, as if I wasn't even in the room, staring at Tom with blue puppy-dog eyes. "And suddenly Brett looked real nervous. I don't know who saw him, but he hurried us out to the truck and took us home. And then, the next day, he was gone. He didn't call, didn't leave a note, nothing. He just . . . disappeared."

"Did any of the pack contact you?" Tom asked.

She nodded, then paused and shook her head. "Sort of, I guess. I got home late one night . . . and they'd been there. I could smell them." Her blue eyes teared up, and Lourdes reached over to squeeze her shoulder. "And everything was torn up. Destroyed." Kind of like my place, I realized. Had they followed Teena to my loft? But the break-in had happened before she and I met. Still, the situation was similar enough that it gave me the creeps. "And I'm worried about Brett," Teena was saying. "I don't know what happened to him, or if he's okay." She swallowed hard. "I'm afraid they may have killed him. That's when we left and came here."

Tom glanced at Lourdes and Brissa. "Did the pack visit your friends, as well?"

"We're roommates," Lourdes said.

"We've been friends since high school," Brissa added. "We do *everything* together."

Including, I thought, sharing syringes filled with werewolf blood. Ick.

"How did you know to find Sophie?" Tom asked.

"Some guys were in town—three of them," said Brissa. "They were kind of cute, really."

"Except one of them smelled really bad," Teena added, dabbing at her eyes. The eyeliner was starting to make black tracks down her pale cheeks.

"Stinky," I said to Tom. "One of the packette—the made ones."

Brissa's iridescent blue eyes widened. "How did you know?"

"Anyway," Lourdes said, fluttering her eyelashes at Tom, "they said they used to be werewolves, but they weren't anymore. That some really powerful wolf did something to them, and they didn't change anymore." Lourdes spoke with a faint Spanish accent.

I glanced at Tom, but his chiseled, Nordic face was impassive.

"So they told us about this werewolf named Sophie Garou, and said she was by herself. In Austin," Lourdes continued. "They said she was pretty strong, and was friends with this powerful werewolf, so we decided we'd ask her for help."

Teena glanced at me. "But she says she won't help us."

"*Can't* help you," I corrected.

Teena ignored me and turned back to Tom. "We're desperate," she said. "What do you think we should we do?"

Tom grimaced. "What was the name of the man who made your boyfriend?"

"Carlos," Teena said.

"Last name?"

"I don't remember," Lourdes said, "but I know he's from Mexico City. I met him once; he sounds just like my uncle."

"What is a Mexican werewolf doing in Texarkana?" Tom asked.

Teena shrugged. "I don't know. All I know is what Brett told me. They had him doing something for them, but he wouldn't tell me what. Said it was a secret."

"So they raided your apartment. Did they threaten you directly?"

"No," she said. "But Brett just . . . disappeared. And he didn't want them to know about us. And now I'm afraid . . ." Her shoulders slumped. "I don't know what happened to Brett. And I think they know about us now. I'm sure of it, actually."

Tom sighed. "This is why the making of werewolves is regulated," he said, looking at me.

As if I knew anything about the making of werewolves. Other than that it involved a blood transfusion, which was totally disgusting. Heck, until six months ago, I hadn't even known making werewolves was an option.

Tom turned back to the Texarkana grrls, who were leaning into him like plants toward the sun. "Whatever you do," he said, "I wouldn't return to Texarkana anytime soon. Do any of you have relatives or friends in another city?"

"My mom's in Dallas," Teena said.

"Don't go to Dallas," Tom said quickly.

What was wrong with Dallas? Other than a surfeit of big hair and surgically enhanced anatomies, that was.

"I have family in San Antonio," Lourdes said. "My mother and father are there."

"San Antonio would work," Tom said. "Can you stay with them for a while?"

She shrugged. "For a little while. Probably."

"I would do that, then. But be careful—San Antonio is supposed to be a neutral zone, but that doesn't mean there aren't other werewolves there. And things between packs have been a little . . . well, tense, lately." If the incident on the Greenbelt was any indication, I'd say that was a pretty big understatement.

"What do we do when we get there?" she asked.

"Get jobs, settle in. And stay quiet." He stared at them for another moment, and with the reek of lust in the air, I wouldn't have been shocked if one—maybe even all three—of them just stripped down right there in my living room. "Do you want to remain werewolves?" he asked.

They stared at him. "What do you mean?"

"Do you enjoy being werewolves?" he asked.

"Of course!" Teena said. "I mean, it's so cool. You have this great sense of smell, good hearing, good vision. . . ."

"You don't mind turning into a wolf once a month?" I asked.

Teena shrugged. "It's kind of fun. I like chasing rabbits."

I did too, but not enough to make up for the downside of the whole transformation thing. I perched on the arm of the loveseat and took a sip of tea.

Tom reached into his pocket, pulled out a worn brown wallet, and fished out three business cards. "If I were you, I'd head to San Antonio tonight. If you run into trouble, call me."

"You have a business card?" I asked. What did it say his profession was, I wondered, Werewolf Exterminator?

"See for yourself," he said, handing one up to me. It was a plain white card, with just his name—Tom Fenris—in black block print, and a phone number with an area code I didn't recognize. Not quite what I expected, for some reason. Then again, what was it supposed to have on it? A wolf crest, with his name written in blood?

"Thanks," I said.

Tom smiled at me, exposing a row of gleaming canines, and then looked back at the werewolves on the couch, who were devouring him with their eyes. It was almost like he was granny and they were the big bad wolves; although in truth, it was probably the other way around. Tom might be one hot guy, but there was an undercurrent of danger in him that made him very scary.

Or maybe it's just because I knew what he was capable of doing.

"I wish the three of you luck," he said in a tone that was clearly a dismissal. Despite the fact that they were all in *my* loft. "Go to San Antonio and lie low. If you run into trouble, call me."

"Oh, Mr. Fenris, thank you so much!" Teena gushed. Lourdes brushed her black hair out of her face, and Brissa reached up to adjust her brown curls. Just shameless, I thought as I reached up to make sure my own hair wasn't sticking out.

Thankfully, the Texarkana trio took his cue and traipsed out the door, glancing over their shoulders at him and giggling on their way down the hall to the elevator. Lourdes hung back for a moment, then darted to Tom, stood up on tiptoe and kissed his cheek.

He didn't move a muscle; I suppressed a growl and watched them till they got onto the elevator. Would Frank notice them on the way out, I wondered? Probably not. *Design on a Dime* started at six.

When the door finally closed behind them, Tom turned to me. I was intensely aware that we were now alone. And that I was wearing a rather clingy camisole. Despite my efforts to remain cool and collected, I could feel the heat emanating from him.

"I'm glad you could help them," I said. "I had no idea what to tell them."

"Thank you," he said, staring at me with those deep golden eyes. They seemed to swirl a little in the light and glow from within; although I saw similar eyes in my mirror every morning, his were mesmerizing. "You and your boyfriend seem to be getting along well."

The blood rushed to my cheeks, but I refused to rise to the bait. "Until a few moments ago, we were. He saw Mrs. Gerschwitz in the hall."

Tom's left eyebrow twitched upward. "She didn't mention 'Hide the Werewolf'?"

"Ah, no." I felt my cheeks flush and decided to change the subject. Had he heard me call his name? "What are you doing here? Does Lindsey know you're here?"

"I came to warn you," he said.

Uh-oh. "Warn me about what?" I asked, even though I already had a pretty good idea.

"There's a turf war going on," he said. "The *Norteños* are moving up; they're pushing into Houston's territory. Austin isn't safe right now."

A chill tiptoed down my spine. "Is that what happened on the Greenbelt the other night?"

"I'm not a hundred percent sure, but if I were you, I wouldn't go anywhere near there," he said, giving me a piercing glance.

Of course, I'd already visited, but I decided not to tell Tom that. The downside of not mentioning my Greenbelt visit also meant I couldn't ask about the weird cave and wolf medallion, but I told myself Tom probably wouldn't know anything about it anyway. I looked up as Tom continued. "Several of the *Norteños* have been spotted here, and Houston's sent some pack members to defend Austin." He cocked an eyebrow at me. "There was a rumor that a solo was living in Austin. I suspect it was probably from the made ones."

Tom was referring to the packette—the three made werewolves he had unmade six months ago. "Well, evidently the word is out. The Houston pack sent me an e-mail."

He winced a little. "I was hoping that wouldn't happen, but it was probably inevitable." Then he fixed me with his intense gold eyes. "Sophie. Is there any way you can go to San Antonio for a month or two?"

"I've got a client there, but I can't just pick up stakes for a few months. I just made partner."

"Still, it would be safer if you could find a way to take a trip there. Just until things settle down."

"Why would that be safer than here?"

"Because the Houston pack is focusing on defending their turf, and I'm afraid Austin's where they're going to make their stand. Although they might want to send more scouts out; the *Norteños* are really pushing north, though, if they're all the way up to Texarkana." He grimaced and looked at me. "So the pack finally figured out that you're here. What did they want?"

"They've ordered me to go to Houston this Saturday, and then they sent some . . . well, I guess you could call them emissaries."

"Who?"

"Elena. Tenorio, I think she said her last name was. She was here with two scary guys wearing lots of black pleather."

He grimaced. "Boris and Dudley. They were here? In your loft?"

"They broke in," I said.

Tom glanced around at the mess. "They did this?"

"No—they just came and waited for me. But that's the next question I had. Someone else broke in, too; a female werewolf. She tore the place apart, and then vanished into thin air." I looked up at Tom, whose gold eyes were fixed on me. It had been a long time since I had seen Tom, but despite my general stress level, his effect on me—and on other women, if the panting I'd seen from the Texarkana trio was any indication—hadn't changed a bit. Still, part of me knew that what I was feeling was because of my werewolf genes. And that I wasn't interested in getting involved with a werewolf. Particularly one who was dating—or at least had dated—my best friend.

"What do you mean, vanished?"

"She was here when I got here—I could smell her and hear her. But she vanished."

"Are you sure?" he asked, looking skeptical.

"I'm sure," I said. "Can some werewolves teleport?"

"Teleport?" He cocked a bushy eyebrow at me.

"Like in *Star Trek*. Kind of dematerialize one place and rematerialize somewhere else."

"Not that I know of, no," he said, still not looking entirely convinced that I was sane. And also looking worried, which was a bit unsettling. "Did you recognize her scent?"

"No," I said, "but I know it wasn't Elena. I got a whiff of her—it was definitely someone else."

"Maybe it was a scout," he said. "I'll ask Wolfgang."

I swallowed. "Speaking of Elena, what do you think this meeting will be about?"

"I'm not sure, but I have an idea," he said grimly. "They're probably not too happy that you've been living in their territory all this time."

I closed my eyes. "That's what I was afraid of."

"I've known Wolfgang a long time," he said. "I'll call and see what I can do."

"Thanks. I also figured I'd offer some free tax work in exchange for immunity."

Tom snorted. "Free tax work?"

"You don't think they'll go for it?"

His mouth twitched up into something that looked suspiciously like a smile. "When's your meeting again?"

"This Saturday," I said, crossing my arms.

"And your plan is to offer to fill out their ten-forties in exchange for immunity."

"I might toss in some auditing, too," I said. "Why? Is there a problem with that?"

He sighed. "I'm guessing it'll be the first time they've ever gotten that kind of offer."

Eight

"So you don't think it will work," I said, stomach sinking. Although I really wasn't surprised.

"I wouldn't count on it," Tom said, looking around my loft. "By the way, do you still have that beer?" he asked.

"In the kitchen," I said, and went to grab it. One of the nice things—the very few nice things—about being a werewolf, I thought as I sniffed the bottles until I found Tom's, was that you always knew which drink belonged to whom. It wasn't much, but it was something.

When I got back to my living room, he was sprawled on the loveseat again. I handed him the bottle; our fingertips brushed as he took it from me, sending a zing right down to my . . . well, you know. He patted the cushion next to him and said, in that low, growly voice, "I promise I won't bite."

I was more afraid of what I would do than what he would do. So to be on the safe side, I sat across from him, on my werewolf-scented couch, instead. "So, what should I do when I meet Wolfgang and Anita in Houston?" I asked.

He took a big swig of his Heineken. "Do you know what the protocol is for new pack members?"

I shrugged. "Howl at the moon? Learn the secret

werewolf handshake? Memorize the infamous werewolf code?"

"Evidently the answer is no," he said dryly.

"So fill me in," I said, glad to finally have an opportunity to get some answers, even though Tom didn't believe in my teleporting werewolf.

"Ever heard of a pecking order?" Tom asked.

"I thought that was something chickens did."

He laughed. "It's not restricted to chickens, unfortunately. New pack members always start at the bottom and work their way up."

That didn't sound too appealing. "Define 'start at the bottom.' "

"That means they send you to one of their dens and give you a job."

"They have dens? Like the cub scouts?"

"I wouldn't put it that way in front of Wolfgang," he said, "but yes."

"So if Anita is the female Alpha, what's Elena? A lower-level den mother?"

"In a manner of speaking."

I took a sip of tea. "So what do I do? Is there any way to get them to leave me alone?"

"I don't know," he said, looking grim. "You've got my backing, if you want it. . . ."

"Yes, I want it. Thank you."

He shrugged. "But it really depends on what they decide to do."

"Okay," I said. I didn't have a good feeling about any of this, but it was better to know than not to. Trying to ignore the aphrodisiac effect his presence was having on me, I said, "So what's the most likely scenario?"

He grimaced. "I'm sure you probably know this, since they've been in touch with you, but there are two probable courses of action."

"So I've heard. Join or leave." *Or die.*

"Best-case scenario, they allow you to stay in their territory, but you enter the pack at a low level and cede all authority to them. And probably move to Houston."

"Sounds delightful," I said, feeling my stomach churn. "But the other option appears to be leaving Austin in a pine box," I said. "What if I don't want to do either?"

"You may not have a choice."

I sucked in my breath. "They won't . . . kill me in Houston, or anything. Will they?"

"Not at the meeting, no," he said, in a tone that chilled me.

"But after?"

"Only if you don't work something else out," he said. "But don't worry. Even if they tell you to leave, they'll probably give you a few weeks to get organized. And I'd be happier if you were somewhere else, anyway."

I felt a brief rush of warmth that Tom was concerned for my welfare. But that still didn't change the fact that I wasn't too keen on being ordered out of my home. "Gosh. How generous," I said, reaching blindly for what was left of Heath's Macallan and thinking about my situation. So if I didn't agree to join the ranks, I'd have a few weeks to leave town before they polished up the silver bullets. Or sharpened the wooden stakes, or whatever it was they did. As I held my breath and downed the rest of the scotch, I wondered for the millionth time what I'd done in a previous life to deserve being a werewolf.

"How come you don't have to join the pack?" I asked when I could breathe again. The scotch felt like it was burning a hole in my esophagus.

"We have an arrangement," he said. "And I do not have a residence here."

I digested that for a moment. Maybe I wasn't a werewolf exterminator, but I did have some marketable skills. Maybe there would be some way to bargain. "Are you going to be in town for a while?" I asked. "In case I need advice?"

He stared at me, and once again I found myself very aware that we were alone, and that Tom, despite being a werewolf—or maybe because of it—was intoxicatingly sexy. "I'll be here for a few weeks, probably. Although I could be persuaded to stay longer."

"Where's Hugin?" I asked, referring to the raven that always seemed to be hanging around him. I still wasn't quite sure what the relationship was, but I did know Tom could communicate with it, and evidently the bird did surveillance work for him sometimes. To me, it looked like a gigantic crow on steroids.

"He's nearby," Tom said.

"Are you going to stay with Lindsey?" I asked, taking a deep breath and feeling my hormones buzz in response to Tom's wolfie pheromones.

"Not this time," he said, taking a last swig of beer and setting it down on the table. "I'll talk to Wolfgang, but I'd advise you to go to Houston and be polite. Don't make any snap decisions. Hear what they have to say and then call me; we'll discuss it."

"Can I say we're friends?"

"Of course," he said. "And I'll call Wolfgang tonight, to see what I can do." He gave me a lopsided smile. "Didn't you say you were going to stop by and visit Heap tonight?"

"Heath," I corrected him.

"Right. Heath. He seemed rather anxious to see you," he said, white teeth gleaming as he smiled. "You'll have to teach him 'Hide the Werewolf' sometime. You're very good at it, you know."

"Gee. Thanks."

He walked to the door, then turned and stared at me

with those shimmery golden eyes. "Call me after the meeting. You have my card now."

"I do, yes," I said. He stood at the door for a moment, and I could feel goose bumps rise on my arms from his closeness. "Be careful," he said in a low voice, then leaned forward and kissed my forehead lightly.

My skin burned from the touch of his lips as he walked through the door and headed down the hall, looking every inch the sleek predator he was.

I watched until he got onto the elevator and then slumped against the doorframe, fighting to catch my breath and stem the tide of fear that Tom had done very little to relieve.

And get my animal impulses in check.

Which is tough when you've just spent thirty minutes with a werewolf like Tom.

It was almost seven o'clock by the time I got to Heath's door; werewolf war or no werewolf war, I wasn't going to be able to sleep well until I'd cleared the air with him. When I told the doorman I wanted to surprise my boyfriend, he'd winked at me and let me go on up. Now, as the elevator door slid open, I shrugged off my coat and checked to make sure I hadn't spilled any of my Lean Cuisine on my camisole.

A moment later, I stood outside Heath's door and took a deep breath, feeling a tingle at the residual smell of Tom. Then I knocked. When no one answered, I knocked a second time, resisting the urge to get down on my knees and sniff the bottom of the door to check if he was home.

But I didn't need to. "Just a moment," Heath said.

He opened the door a few seconds later, looking rumpled, and found me standing speechless.

Because there was a woman in the loft with him.

And unless the wolfsbane had completely destroyed my sense of smell, it was Miranda.

"Sophie," he said, looking hurt—and highly uncomfortable.

"Heath."

We stood there for a long, painful moment. Then we both spoke at the same time.

"It looks like now's not a good time—" I said, just as Heath started with "I'm kind of busy right now—"

We were silent again. Then I said, "Maybe we can have lunch this week."

"Sure," he said coolly.

Then a woman—*the* woman, the long-legged Barbie doll I'd love to see on a spit—said, from somewhere in his apartment, "Heath?"

"I see you have company," I said stiffly.

Something flashed over his face, but only for a moment; in a split second, his features shifted into courtroom mode. "I'm not the only one," he shot back.

"Well, then. I guess I'll leave you to it."

He shrugged almost imperceptibly. "Fine."

I turned and headed blindly toward the elevator, feeling like the earth had been yanked out from under me. Heath and Miranda. Handsome, romantic Heath, with that silky brown hair and those amazing kisses. Which were probably now being given to Miranda.

Or was I jumping to conclusions?

Halfway down the hall, I hesitated, and turned back. "Heath . . ." I began.

But the door just shut with a quiet click.

I clenched my fists. Miranda. Stupid Miranda. Part of me wanted to run home and rip Heath's picture in half. Another part of me wanted to press my wolfie ear to the door and listen. Because I might be misreading everything. For all I knew, Miranda could be there to talk about the case they were working on. The fact that she looked like a *Playboy* centerfold could mean absolutely nothing.

Right?

I hit the down button on the elevator, trying to think rationally. So Miranda was at Heath's loft. But that didn't necessarily mean they were getting together . . . er, socially. Besides, I had bigger fish to fry right now— namely my upcoming meeting with a group of were- wolves who might try evicting me from my hometown. Not to mention the dark-haired werewolf who had spot- ted me at Zilker Park today. Overall, boyfriend prob- lems should be pretty low on the list.

The elevator door slid open, and three people stared at me. I hesitated for a moment. Then I said, "I'm wait- ing to go up," and let the doors slide shut again.

As the elevator whirred down toward the lobby, I crept back to Heath's door and pressed my ear to it.

"Where do you think we should go?" Heath was say- ing.

"How about the wine country?" Miranda purred. "It's supposed to be gorgeous this time of year. I've al- ways wanted to do one of those tasting tours, where they drive you from winery to winery, and you stay in romantic little bed and breakfasts. . . ."

As my stomach dropped faster than the elevator, Heath said, "You're right, it's a good idea. I'm just not sure how I feel about it right now. . . ."

Oh, so the fact that he already had a girlfriend was at least a minor consideration?

"Why not?" Miranda said. "It would be so roman- tic!"

I didn't wait to hear Heath's answer; I was afraid they'd hear me snuffling outside the door. Instead, I pulled myself away and stumbled down the hall toward the elevator, which thankfully was empty this time.

Nine

Although there were no more nasty incidents in the newspapers and no one assaulted me on my way to Starbucks, Friday was no better than Thursday—at least from a romantic perspective. I had a hollow feeling in my stomach all day; despite our planned date, I heard nothing from Heath, and after my visit to his loft the previous night, there was no way I was calling *him*. Since Lindsey was in meetings all day, I couldn't call her for a sanity check.

So I dragged through the day and went home early to a loft that was (thankfully) empty of werewolves, but kind of lonely.

To distract myself from my long list of worries, I tried watching some *Sex and the City*. I gave up in the middle of the third episode, though—Carrie was having an affair, which hit uncomfortably close to home—and decided to turn it off and pack for the retreat instead. I tucked a pair of brown leather stilettos—I didn't own any cowboy boots, so it was the best I could do—and a couple of pairs of jeans into my suitcase, then tossed in a fresh bag of wolfsbane tea. Then I went to the kitchen, fixed myself a last mug of tea, and attempted to go to sleep.

As I lay under the covers, staring at the ceiling and wishing I was one of those people who fall asleep the moment their head hits the pillow, I struggled in vain to clear my mind of all the disturbing thoughts. But all I could think about was my upcoming meeting with the Houston pack. And the disturbing break-in, and the murders on the Greenbelt. And Heath and Miranda. And Tom.

I must have fallen asleep at some point, though, because suddenly Mark was in bed beside me, gazing at me from those icy blue eyes, now dark in the dim light of the bedroom. *George Clooney, eat your heart out,* I thought as I caught a whiff of his smoky smell. His fingers were hot on my forehead, on my cheeks. . . . I moved closer to him as they tiptoed further down, caressing the skin of my neck. Mmmm.

His hand pushed aside my nightshirt, grazing my right nipple, then rolling it between his fingers. My body arched in response.

Sophie, he whispered, then covered my mouth with his, and all I could think was, *obviously I need to work things out with Heath quickly if I'm starting to have erotic dreams about my clients.* I reached out to touch the smooth skin of his chest—his skin was so hot it felt like a fire was burning in him. *Nice six-pack,* I noticed as I slid my palm down his chest to his flat abdomen. My fingers paused at a patch of rough skin below his left nipple; it was in the shape of a crescent moon. Weird, how specific dreams are. And then *his* hand slid lower, pushing my legs apart.

As his fingers brushed my clitoris, his tongue lapped at my nipple, alternately flicking the taut tip and circling the areola with wide sweeps. As if of their own accord, my hips rose to meet his touch, and as his fingers caressed my now rather damp folds, my own hand slid down that flat abdomen to encircle his penis.

He groaned as my fingers touched the soft skin of his

cock, the ring he had given me glowing on my finger; in response, he sucked my nipple hard, at the same time plunging his fingers deep into me. I pulled him toward me, spreading my legs, and he pushed against me, sending currents of lust zinging through my body.

I guided him toward me, but he resisted, letting his extremely nimble fingers do some preliminary exploration. As I groaned in pleasure, suddenly the fingers were replaced by his tongue, hot and wet, flicking against me. He lapped at me, teasing me, occasionally darting inside me, until I was on the brink of howling for him. I grasped his cock more firmly, pulling it toward me; finally, he relented, and pushing my legs back, he slid into me, the heat of his penis penetrating me like a molten core. His smoky smell intensified as I pulled him deeper, moaning as he first filled me, then withdrew and thrust again, hard, his teeth grazing my erect nipple. I was on the brink of dissolving into orgasm when he withdrew suddenly and turned me over on the rumpled bed. Grabbing my hips with both hands, he thrust into me from behind, his hands reaching around me to find my naked breasts, and an orgasm swelled in me, rising to an incredible peak before breaking like a tidal wave, leaving me quaking.

A moment later, he was gone, leaving only a trace of smokiness in the air, and a wolf howled somewhere far in the distance. As the dream faded, to be replaced by some disjointed sequence involving tulips and a cheese factory, a stray lucid thought flitted through my mind.

If not seeing Heath meant more dreams like this, I thought hazily, maybe it wasn't such a bad thing after all.

I pulled up outside the Dude Ranch at ten o'clock the next morning, right on schedule, trying to banish all erotic thoughts of Mark from my mind. The dream I'd had had been incredibly realistic—so much so that when I woke up, I was naked. *Was it really only a dream?* I found myself thinking, then shook myself and forced myself back to reality. Which, unfortunately, involved horses and lots of dried cow patties, if the aroma seeping through the BMW's vents was any indication.

Although I wasn't big into cowboy culture, it was a bit of a relief to get out of Austin; it wasn't San Antonio, but at least I wasn't at the epicenter of the War of the Werewolves. And it certainly promised to be a colorful weekend. Adele had gone all out for the Withers and Young retreat; the driveway to the bed and breakfast was flanked with gingham-laced wagon wheels and the entryway looked like something out of a spaghetti Western, right down to the brass spittoon. I half expected John Wayne to swagger through the red-painted saloon doors.

Adele greeted me on the front porch in a flouncy denim skirt paired with a red western-style blouse. I tried not to stare; my boss, the Donna Karan devotee, had been replaced by Dale Evans incarnate—except for the short frosted blond hair and the beaky nose. "Sophie, I'm so glad you made it!" she said. "You're in the Chuckwagon Room."

"The Chuckwagon Room?"

She ran a critical eye over my khaki skirt and white linen blouse. "I'd change out of that skirt before the calf roping, though."

"When's that?" I asked with trepidation.

"Starts at eleven. Team building. If you're hungry, grits and cornbread are in the mess hall."

"Thanks," I said feebly, glancing at my watch. It was ten o'clock now, and I needed to be in Houston by one. How long did calf-roping take? And how hard was it to slip out of?

"I'll just head up to the Chuckwagon Room, then," I said. "Where is it?"

"Upstairs, third room on the right. I'll see you downstairs shortly," Adele said.

"Is Lindsey here yet?" I asked.

"I haven't seen her, but I put her in the room next to yours. The Wrangler Room." Well, that was something, I thought. As I headed for the staircase, Adele greeted the next arrival—Dwayne from accounting, who had donned a belt buckle the size of Oklahoma for the occasion.

"Oooh, are those elephant-skin boots?" I heard Adele ask him as I lugged my suitcase up the stairs to my room.

I changed out of my skirt into a pair of jeans, wishing—for the first time ever—that I owned a pair of cowboy boots. Oh, well. Sneakers were better than nothing.

At 10:45 I moseyed down to the dining room alone—Lindsey either hadn't arrived yet or had gone downstairs already.

Adele had gone for the faux leather tablecloths, adorned with red bandanna-print napkins. She'd evidently found someone to do a cactus centerpiece—the center of each table was prickly with cactus and spurs, liberally festooned with bright red ribbon. Probably to hide the florist's bloodstains.

I snagged a bit of cornbread and some scrambled eggs, then poured myself a cup of hot water and dropped in two wolfsbane teabags from my purse stash. The moon was full this weekend, and even though it wasn't a solstice or equinox, I had brought plenty of extra hits to keep myself from transforming involuntarily. Even with the tea, I still had to do a few extra shaving sessions to get me through the day.

As I added a little bit of Splenda to my cup—I would have liked a skinny latte to go with it, but that didn't appear to be on the menu at the Dude Ranch—Dwayne bellied up to the table, his belt buckle flashing in the morning light.

"How are you, little lady?" He heaved himself into the chair next to mine, smelling strongly of stale beer. And Skoal. Ew. This retreat must be right up his alley, I thought.

"Fine, thank you," I said shortly.

"Looks like it's you and me in the calf roping."

I choked on my tea. "What?"

"Don't you worry, sweetheart. I've roped many a calf in my time. Used to be a bull rider, back in the day."

"How did you go from bull riding to accounting?" I asked.

"Oh, bull riding's fun and all, but it don't pay the bills." He leaned toward me, hitching his belt buckle up over his paunch. I tried not to recoil from the blast of chewing tobacco–scented breath; sometimes having a fabulous sense of smell isn't all it's cracked up to be. "Say," he drawled. "How 'bout you and me grab a couple of drinks tonight, after dinner?"

I blinked at him. "Pardon me?"

"I know we've been kind of exchanging looks, lately." He reached out and patted me on the knee with a big, hot paw. Actually, it was a little farther up than my knee, and it was all I could do not to shoot out of my seat and run for the door. "Don't be shy. I know why you make so many trips to the kitchen. It ain't just the tea, is it?"

Oh. My. God. Did Dwayne really think I was manufacturing reasons to be in his Skoal-and-longneck-scented presence? The reason I made so many trips to the kitchen was to make enough tea to keep me human. If anything, I picked up the pace and held my breath when I got within ten feet of his desk.

"Thank you for the offer," I said, removing his hairy

hand from my leg, "but I already have a boyfriend." Of course, I wasn't entirely sure that was still true, but at that point I would have admitted to dating Chuckles the Clown if it meant getting out of a nightcap with Dwayne.

"No one needs to know," he murmured in a tone that he obviously viewed as manly and seductive. He leaned even closer, with the result being that his belt buckle, huge as it was, was eclipsed by a thick roll of fat.

I glanced around wildly, looking for an escape. Lindsey, thank God, chose that moment to make an entrance.

"Lindsey!" I yelped, bolting out of my seat. My knee banged the table, accidentally spilling my tea on Dwayne. "Come join us!" I said in a strangled voice. "Please!"

Lindsey pegged the situation immediately; I could see her lips twitch into a smile. As she headed in our direction, Dwayne blotted his jeans with a red-and-white napkin, but kept missing, because he was staring at Lindsey's tanned midriff.

Lindsey had abandoned her normal sexy Ann Taylor-by-day, Bébé-by-night wardrobe in favor of a gingham cropped top and boot-cut jeans that clung to her curvy figure. Think Ginger of *Gilligan's Island,* borrowing Maryann's clothes while she waited for her evening wear to make it back from the cleaners.

"Hi, Sophie. Looks like you and Dwayne are all cozied up here," Lindsey said, pulling up a chair on the other side of me and eyeing the buffet table. She managed somehow to ignore Dwayne, whose eyes kept moving from my chest to Lindsey's midriff.

"You two girls are fine-looking women," Dwayne said. "I like a heifer with a little extra padding. Gives a man something to hold onto."

Lindsey glanced at Dwayne. "Thanks for the input,

Dwayne. I think it's every woman's dream to be called a 'heifer'." Dwayne gave her a goofy grin as she grabbed my arm. "Sorry to run, but Sophie was just coming up to my room to talk about an account. Good to see you."

I grabbed my mug and followed Lindsey as she selected a biscuit and a cup of coffee and headed for the door.

"Thank you." I breathed as we climbed the stairs.

"Don't mention it," she said, and a moment later we walked into the Wrangler Room, which was heavily decorated in barbed wire.

"Man, I thought the Chuckwagon Room was bad. Whoever designed your room had some seriously repressed S&M tendencies."

"I'm not so sure they were repressed," Lindsey said, glancing at the yards of barbed wire framing the mirror. "So, how's it going, little heifer?"

"Don't remind me," I groaned, and pointed at her getup. "What's with the Western Girl look?"

"You like it?" She twirled around, fingers in her belt loops. "I figured if I got on board with Adele's little Western fantasy, it might help the whole partner thing. Since not all of us can land Southeast Airlines." She glanced at me sidelong. "Any more lunches at Romeo's, by the way?"

"No," I said, "but things with Heath are sort of on the rocks." Of course, that was the least of my problems, but I couldn't exactly tell her I was at risk of being expelled from Austin or killed in a werewolf territory war. Every once in a while I wished for a friend who understood me—all of me. Someone with whom I could commiserate, or share shaving techniques, even. This was one of those times.

"What happened?" Lindsey asked.

"Miranda was at his loft the other night," I said. I

might not be able to get everything off my shoulders, but at least I could tell her about Heath.

"Ouch. Did you see her?"

"I . . ." I stopped myself from saying *I smelled her* just in time. "I heard her voice."

"Were they . . . well, *together*?"

"No," I said. "I mean, I don't think so. But they *were* planning a little wine country getaway, so I'm guessing it's imminent." I took a deep breath, suddenly realizing that I wasn't just upset. I was pissed.

"Wow," Lindsey said. "So he was planning a getaway with his associate." She shook her head. "That seems totally out of character for Heath. I mean, I thought he was totally ga-ga over you."

I felt a dull pain in my stomach. "Evidently we were both mistaken."

"How do you know about the wine country thing, by the way?"

I shifted from foot to foot. "I kind of overheard it," I said.

"You mean you listened at the door."

"Sort of."

"Don't feel bad," she said. "I would have too. When did all this happen?"

"Thursday night."

"You should have called me!"

"You were in meetings all day."

"So what? Next time, leave me a message. I'll make time."

"Thanks," I said.

"And he hasn't called?"

"Nope."

She let out a long breath. "Well, at least Dwayne's available," she said.

"Thanks for reminding me," I said, and downed the rest of my tea. On the plus side, Lindsey hadn't mentioned Tom, which meant he hadn't gotten in touch with her. And if they weren't dating, my mother wouldn't keep bugging me to tell her about her boyfriend's hairy little alter ego.

At least something was going right.

Ten

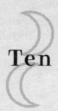

At eleven o'clock, after a little pep talk from Adele, we were all lined up in the barn for the first of the weekend's team-building activities.

Calf roping.

I glanced at my watch for the fortieth time that morning; would I get out of here in time to make it to Houston? Preferably not on a stretcher? I took a deep breath and instantly regretted it, since the barn reeked of hay, horses, and manure that had been lying around for a while. I tried to ignore the buzzing of flies around the stalls and focused on breathing through my mouth.

"Have any of these folks been on a horse before?" I overheard one of the hands ask Adele. He was a good-looking guy in a pair of tight blue jeans that highlighted a rather nice body. If that's what horseback riding did for you, I thought, admiring the fit of the faded denim, maybe I'd have to look into it. And while I wasn't usually a fan of cowboy boots, they worked on him.

"Oh, I'm sure they have." She turned to us, the spurs on her red boots jingling. I blinked; I was still getting used to this new version of Adele. "You all have been on horses, right?" she asked.

A few people said that yes, they had, but once their voices trailed off, there was an uncomfortable silence.

Mr. Blue-jeans looked worried, and I found myself hoping the ranch was up on its liability insurance.

"Well, I'm sure the rest of you will pick it up fast," Adele said, beaming.

"Either that or wind up in the hospital," Lindsey whispered to me.

I glanced warily at Dwayne. He winked and shuffled a little closer to me, bringing a fresh whiff of Skoal and Old Spice.

"Why don't you tell them a little more about how calf roping works?" Adele said to the hand. "In fact, I think a little demonstration might be in order. Don't you think?"

Mr. Blue-jeans nodded uncomfortably to one of the other hands. "Come on, Lenny."

The two of them swung up onto their horses and nodded to a third, who was keeping the calf in check over by the stalls. The whole thing was over in about ten seconds; the little brown animal went bleating into the middle of the ring, and the two cowboys rode over to it, Mr. Blue-jeans lassoed it on the first try, and his partner sprang off his horse and tied the poor animal up before it knew what was happening.

"Think I could convince them to give me some lessons?" Lindsey murmured in my ear. "I wouldn't mind being the calf."

"Lindsey!" I hissed, but she ignored me and headed over to find her own partner. Leaving me with Dwayne, who slapped a meaty paw on my shoulder.

"Ready, little heifer?"

"For your information, Dwayne," I said primly, "most women don't find being called 'heifer' flattering," I said.

His red face grew pensive. "How about little filly?"

Before I could answer, Adele said, "Thank you all for coming. I think this little exercise will help us stretch beyond our comfort zones and also help us learn to trust one another."

Either that or put us all in traction.

I glanced at Sally, who had materialized a few minutes earlier; her jeans were certainly stretched past the comfort zone. As were the buttons of her red-and-blue crop top. I averted my eyes, but unfortunately they landed on Dwayne, who waggled his bushy eyebrows at me. I jerked my eyes away from him and allowed my gaze to drift over to the handsome cowboy, which was much nicer. Although he filled his jeans admirably, I felt a twinge of regret seeing the white circle on the right back pocket. Like Dwayne, he was a Skoal user. Which meant that kissing him would be like licking a spittoon.

I shifted my eyes back to Adele, who was beaming around the room like a deranged extra in a spaghetti Western. "Who's up first?" she said brightly.

"I'll give it a try," said Sally, pulling at her too-tight top and brushing her shellacked hair out of her eyes. Show-off. Or maybe she just wanted to get it over with.

Her partner was a short, squat man with a goatee. Except for the pointy little artist beard, he looked right at home in the whole horse and barn environment. As they mounted their horses, Sally's silver spurs—she and Adele must have shopped at the same store—jingled, and she shifted in the saddle. A few inches of spray-tanned flesh protruded above her tightly cinched waistband—the whole crop-top thing didn't work quite as well on her as it did on Lindsey—and I found myself waiting for a seam to split. When one of the hands tossed her a coil of rope, she grabbed it with a practiced hand. I had a sneaking suspicion she had been working on her form for a while.

The whole thing went surprisingly well. It took the dynamic duo a few tries, but Sally finally got a lasso around the poor little animal—a black-and-white calf

that was bleating for mercy. A moment later, her partner, the short, squat man from the billing department who was gazing at Sally with frank admiration, leaped off his horse and tied the poor animal up with fumbling hands. It had already gotten one leg out of the spaghetti-like mass of ropes when he stood up, face triumphant, to a smattering of applause from the onlookers. Mr. Blue-jeans hurried out to untangle the calf's spindly legs, and as Sally and her helper strode off to the sidelines, Adele smiled big and said, "Who's next?"

Dwayne hitched up his jeans and grabbed my hand. "We'll give it a shot," he said, pulling me forward.

As I stood there, feeling something like a cow—or a heifer—being brought to the slaughter, Mr. Blue-jeans led a horse over to me. "This here is Sparky," he said. "Ever ridden a horse before?"

"Uh, no," I said, reaching out tentatively to touch its velvety nose.

At which point the poor horse's eyes bulged like they were going to pop out of its head, and the animal reared up.

Mr. Blue-jeans grabbed the reins just in time. "I've never seen her so spooked before," he said. "Almost like there was a coyote around or something."

As the horse reared again, I realized with a sinking sensation what the problem was. To other people, I was just a human. But to a horse, I was a wolf in blue jeans.

"Whoa there," the good-looking cowboy said, holding tight to the reins and struggling to keep the horse in check. "If I were you, I'd mount up now," he said. "While she's still."

I eyed the horse, who was sweating hard and staring at me like I was a Frenchwoman with a hankering for a plate of horse-flavored sausage. Maybe if I came down with a sudden case of stomach cramps . . .

"Come on, Sophie," Adele said. Dwayne, who was al-

ready saddled on a horse the size of a Clydesdale, waggled his eyebrows expectantly, and Sally smirked at me, still flushed with pride from her recent show of bovine containment expertise.

Was I really going to let Sally show me up? I took a deep, horse-poop-scented breath and climbed awkwardly into the saddle, trying to send calming thoughts to the big hairy animal beneath me.

The handsome cowboy handed me the reins at the exact same moment that Sparky figured out what was going on. A split second later, I was hurtling across the barn at about a hundred miles an hour, strapped to the back of a gigantic bucking horse who wanted nothing more than to crush me beneath her manure-caked hooves.

"Sparky!" somebody—presumably the cowboy—called from somewhere behind me, but his attempt to call the horse back was spectacularly ineffective. A moment later, the horse, which I was beginning to think was possessed by demons, hurled herself over the gate to the barn entrance and the two of us were hurtling down a dirt road, Sparky running like there was a wolf on her back—which, to give her the benefit of the doubt, there was—and me hanging onto her mane and trying to figure out how to get off without dying.

As I yanked on the reins with one hand and hung onto the horse's stringy mane with the other, we tore past the main building and headed down the driveway for the road. Thank God for the cattle guard, I thought, thinking that at least we wouldn't get beyond the boundaries of the fence. But Sparky just picked up speed and leaped across it like a Suburban negotiating a shopping-center speed bump.

I looked wildly for a place to fall off, but the roadbed was hard-packed dirt punctuated at regular intervals with chunks of limestone. And the shoulder was no bet-

ter, as it was generously decorated with cow patties and huge clumps of Adele's favorite plant—prickly pear cactus. Even if I did manage to get myself off the gigantic animal's back, chances of surviving the landing without ending up in a coffin—or at least a full-body cast—were slim.

While I came up with and discarded a number of escape strategies, Sparky galloped to the end of the inn's driveway and veered to the left. Onto the paved highway. Into the left-hand lane.

Directly into the path of a speeding eighteen-wheeler.

Eleven

As I yanked on the reins in a vain attempt to get Sparky to change course, the eighteen-wheeler let out a huge blast from its horn.

Which had the unfortunate effect of spurring Sparky to gallop faster.

The grille of the truck filled my vision, along with the driver, a tubby man with jowls and a huge mustache, screaming at me through the dirty windshield. *This is it,* I thought. *I'm going to die on the back of a possessed horse, flattened by an eighteen-wheeler.*

And then, suddenly, a violent wave passed through me, and I wasn't holding onto the reins anymore. I was crouched on the horse's back, my paws scrabbling for purchase on the leather saddle. I glanced up one last time; the man's eyes were huge above a massive handlebar mustache. The truck veered to the right. Sparky—a little belatedly, in my opinion—veered left.

But it didn't matter. I had already leaped from the horse's back and was sprinting through the cactus, dragging my DKNY skinny jeans behind me.

I ran for almost a minute before my brain kicked back into gear again. I glanced behind me; the truck had jackknifed across the road, and Sparky was still galloping full tilt toward the horizon.

Unfortunately, three more horses were headed in my direction. Which wouldn't have been a problem, except for the fact that (a) I was a wolf and (b) I was missing half my clothes.

I quickly trotted back the way I had come, grabbing my jeans with my teeth—miraculously, my bikini underwear was still in place, although probably a little worse for wear due to my tail—and hid behind a cactus while I transformed back to my human form. I wriggled into my jeans, adjusted my blouse, and stepped carefully around cactus clumps, collecting my socks and tennis shoes as I went.

The two cowboys were just riding up to the jackknifed truck when I picked my way back to the scene of my almost-death; I could make out Dwayne behind them, puffing heavily on his Clydesdale. Poor horse.

"Are you okay, ma'am?" asked Mr. Blue-jeans. Which was very polite, but I would have preferred "miss."

"I don't know," I said, and as his eyes drifted south, I belatedly glanced down to make sure my shirt was still buttoned. It was. But since there were only three buttons still on it, it didn't cover much. I reached down and pulled the edges of the fabric together. "The horse just took off. She almost ran right into the truck," I said, still panting a bit.

"Looks like she's still going," said cowboy number two, shading his eyes and looking down the road. "I'll see if I can round her up. You'll take care of the lady?"

"Will do," said Mr. Blue-jeans, and I was reaching up to adjust my hair and thinking maybe I could get used to Skoal—at least for the weekend—when the driver staggered around the side of the truck, holding onto the corner of his mustache. His face was gray, and his hand shook as he pointed at me. "You . . . you . . ."

Uh-oh.

"Are you all right, sir?" asked my handsome cowboy friend.

At that moment, Adele trotted up on a fat gray horse, both of them puffing. Her cowgirl hat was almost sideways on her cropped hair. "Are you okay, Sophie?"

"I'm fine," I said.

"She . . ." The trucker looked like he was about to have a cardiac arrest. Which would have been convenient, really. Not that I was wishing it on him or anything; I just didn't want to have to explain to my boss how I'd transformed into a horse-riding wolf a few minutes ago.

"I think he's had a bit of a shock," I said, smiling at Adele and taking a step toward him.

"Don't come any closer!" he yelled, making some kind of evil eye sign and backing into a prickly pear cactus. "You're a demon is what you are," he said, reaching back to brush the spines off his bottom. Ouch. But even being punctured by about three hundred cactus spines wasn't enough to divert his attention. He stared at me, bug-eyed, and pointed a chubby finger at me. "I saw what happened back there," he said, his mustache bouncing up and down as he spoke.

Mr. Blue-jeans glanced at me uncertainly. I glanced at Adele, who was looking startled, and shrugged.

"You . . . you turned into some kind of animal," the trucker continued, little bits of spittle flying out from under the mustache. I took a step back, to stay out of range. Then I raised an eyebrow and turned to Adele, as if to say, "He's deranged."

"I saw it," said the trucker, backing away, thankfully. I surreptitiously wiped a fleck of spit from my arm. "Don't tell me I didn't see it," he screamed. "You're an evil woman. Evil, I say!"

I smiled uneasily at Adele and the cowboy. "I have no idea what his problem is."

"Drugs, maybe," Adele said sagely.

The cowboy stepped between me and the trucker. Evidently chivalry wasn't dead, at least not in Texas. "Why don't you ride back with me?" he asked, glancing back at me.

"She's a demon!" yelled the trucker.

I chose to ignore the driver, focusing instead on Adele—and my cowboy protector. He chewed tobacco, it's true . . . but maybe I could learn to live with it. "I'd love to," I said. And it was true—the idea of riding back with his muscular thighs next to mine, leaning into his strong chest, was more than a little appealing. Then I glanced at his horse, who was eyeing me nervously, and said, "But I think I'd rather walk."

"I understand, ma'am," he said, tipping his hat. He peered down the road. "I'll stick around here, help take care of things," he said, nodding toward the jackknifed truck. "Will you two be okay going back?" he asked.

"Fine," I said. "Why don't you go on ahead, Adele? I don't think I'm up for another ride just now."

"If you're sure," she said.

I held the two halves of my shirt together and started trudging back toward the inn. At least the trucker wasn't shouting at me anymore; he had disappeared back into his little cab-thing. Or whatever it was you called it.

Then the first shotgun blast went off.

I whirled around just in time to see Mr. Handlebar mustache reloading.

"Take cover!" yelled the cowboy.

I threw myself behind a rock just as another round went off, this one zinging by my left shoulder. I waited for a third shot, cringing, but it didn't come; when I was brave enough to peer over the rock, I figured out why. My cowboy hero had hog-tied my mustachioed attacker, and was sitting on top of him, holding the shotgun in his tanned, strong hands. I sank back down on the ground, trying to coax my heart rate back down from the high 200s.

And to think I had been worried about meeting with the Houston pack.

Although I wouldn't usually recommend having an insane trucker shoot at you as a way to get out of a meeting, in this case it worked out pretty well. I'd needed an excuse to skip out of the rest of the calf-roping/team-building activities and head to Houston; now I had it. (Of course, I didn't tell Adele I was meeting with werewolves. I claimed I was going to see a doctor.)

The trucker had been carted off by the police, who were dismissing both his wild allegations and his little shooting spree as a side effect of shock. Sparky, as far as I knew, was still on the loose; I wished her well, but I wasn't about to go out looking for her.

When I finally hobbled back to the main building of the dude ranch, it was coming up on noon. If I was going to make it to Houston by one, I needed to get out of here fast. After a quick shave, I headed downstairs, car keys in hand. I'd miss the pre-campfire cow-patty toss, but—assuming the Houston pack didn't kill me on the spot—I'd probably be back in time for the Hoedown dinner.

"Are you sure you don't want an escort?" Dwayne asked, putting a sweaty, hairy arm around me.

"Um, no. I'll be fine, thanks," I said, shrugging him off and looking around for my cowboy savior. Unfortunately, he had headed back to the barn, taking my Wild West fantasies with him. Oh, well. Maybe the next one wouldn't have a chewing tobacco habit.

"You sure you're okay to drive there?"

Lindsey, thankfully, hurried up to me at this juncture. "Oh my God, Sophie. I can't believe that horse. And someone said you were almost hit by a truck."

"Not to mention shot by the trucker."

"You're kidding me. Are you okay?" she asked, squeezing my arm.

"I'm fine," I said. "A little shaken up, but nothing fatal."

"Come on. I'll drive you to the hospital," Lindsey offered.

"I offered first," Dwayne said, adjusting his belt buckle and putting a possessive paw on my arm. I held my breath and pulled away. "We should stick together, pardner," he drawled.

Lindsey fixed him with a withering glance. "Why don't you go find yourself some other little filly?" Before he could say another word, Lindsey ushered me toward the door. "Are you sure you don't want me to go with you?"

"No, I'm fine," I said, giving her a quick hug and heading to my car. Dwayne stood at the saloon doors watching my M3 as I drove it slowly down the driveway, little rocks twanging off the undercarriage. We were only two hours into the retreat, and already both my BMW and I were significantly worse for wear. I hoped that Martha did a big article on spa retreats before it came time for Adele to plan our next company shindig.

I don't know what I was expecting the Lupine Society to look like, but it turned out to be a sprawling property with a tall stucco wall and a big wooden door, situated smack-dab in the middle of the tony museum district.

After double-checking the slip of paper, I pulled into the short driveway—I was fifteen minutes late, and hoping the pack wouldn't hold it against me. I pulled up short at a big radio-camera contraption, rolled down the window, and smiled up at the lens.

And waited.

There was a little speaker next to the lens—probably an intercom system—but there was no button on it to call anyone.

"Hello!" I called out to it. "Sophie Garou here! I have a meeting!"

Nothing.

What now?

I sat there for another few minutes, trying to come up with a plan. I was considering getting out of the car and trying to push the gate open with my hands—a daunting proposition, since the thing looked to be about two feet thick and was studded with heavy iron brackets—when a buzz sounded, and the massive door slid to one side.

I took a deep, shaky breath and put the car into gear.

Twelve

The heavy door swung shut behind me as I eased the M3 into the compound, trying to quell the adrenaline that was pulsing through my body. Nobody—except Tom—knew I was here, I realized. Which meant if the Houston pack decided I would look good as a wolf-skin rug, there wasn't much I could do about it.

To my surprise, pack life looked to be pretty civilized—even downright plush. And the Lupine Society was a good name for the organization, since its headquarters looked more like the site of a millionaires' garden club than a den of werewolf iniquity.

There were three buildings: a massive Spanish-style house with an orange tile roof, flanked by two smaller structures that looked like guesthouses. I nosed my car into a parking place, next to two Jaguars and pair of Harleys—the pleather boys?—and climbed out of my car. After quickly adjusting my blouse and skirt (I'd changed out of my DKNY jeans), I walked with what I hoped was a purposeful stride up to the gigantic front door.

Then I squared my shoulders and lifted the wrought-iron knocker—which had been forged into the shape of a wolf's head.

A moment later, the door opened, and I was staring into the golden eyes of a werewolf.

"Hi," I said, smiling politely and trying not to stare. Despite his obvious werewolfiness—the eyes, the excess body hair, the smell—he was dressed in the starched black suit of a butler, which was disconcerting. He'd evidently been studying the whole British stiff upper lip thing; his long face was utterly impassive. We stared at each other for a moment or two. When it became obvious that the conversational onus was on me, I took a deep breath and made the first verbal sally. "I think I'm supposed to have a meeting with Wolfgang and Anita," I said. "At one o'clock. Sorry I'm a few minutes late—I got caught up in traffic."

"Enter," he said, sounding a little like Bela Lugosi and pulling the door wide to allow me into the front hall. Which smelled overwhelmingly of werewolf. Then the butler-werewolf pointed me to an uncomfortable red-velvet upholstered chair and disappeared down the hallway, giving me a chance to catch my breath—and to do a little olfactory reconnaissance.

I closed my eyes and took a deep breath. Lots of werewolves were here—at least half a dozen, with the mingled residual scents of several more. Two in particular were very strong—one was male and deliciously reminiscent of Tom. Wolfgang? Despite my fear, I felt a trickle of lust just sniffing him and found myself speculating on his appearance. I was imagining tall and dark-haired, with those intense, werewolf-gold eyes.

I took another long sniff and felt my lust dim a touch, because there was an equally powerful female here. Her scent was different though—it reminded me a bit of the smell I'd picked up in my loft the other night, but it wasn't quite the same. Still, something about it told me I better mind my ps and qs when dealing with Mr. Wolfgang.

Elena was here, too, or had been recently; picking up a whiff of her made my whole body tense up all over again. And although I couldn't smell the pleather boys quite as strongly, I thought I sensed a hint of them, too. Maybe they were in one of the guesthouses. Did all the werewolves in the pack live together? I wondered. Because even though the mansion was big, unless there was an underground warren I didn't know about, it wasn't exactly equipped to handle hundreds of werewolves. In fact, if this was all there was to the Houston pack, you'd think once they got the *Norteños* taken care of, they'd be happy to have a little satellite office in Austin. To help with recruiting and all.

Not that I wanted the job, of course. But if the alternative was winding up with my head on a plaque on the dining room wall, I might be willing to compromise.

When I'd sniffed out everything I could, I opened my eyes, taking in the saltillo tile, the white plaster, the heavy, expensive-looking dark furniture. The walls of the entry were decorated with what looked like old-fashioned European portraits in heavy gilt frames. Whoever decorated the place must have been into the Dutch masters, I thought, until I realized that every single face was staring down at me with golden werewolf eyes.

A finger of ice slid down my spine as I stared at the portrait closest to me—a blond man in a rich dark velvet doublet—or whatever you call those fancy old-fashioned jackets—with a flounce of white at his neck that did nothing to detract from his intense golden stare. His right hand lay on his lap, a heavy ruby ring on the third finger. *Wolfgang Graf,* read the little gold plaque at the base. Must be an ancestor.

An amber-haired woman stared down from the frame next to his, her slim waist cinched into a tight green bodice that made me thankful I lived in a post-corset era. A chill passed through me as I realized that framed in the mullioned window behind her was the broad white face of the moon. And that her smile revealed just a hint of overlong canine, which completely creeped me out. The little plaque read *Astrid Graf*. Old Wolfgang's wife or daughter, probably. But something about her was familiar. Was it the shape of the eyes? Or was it just that they were gold, like mine?

I was staring at the man in the white flouncy collar-thing again, wondering how long ago the portrait had been painted—and how he was related to the current Wolfgang—when Mr. Butler-werewolf stalked back into the entryway and said, in a stiff voice, "Mr. Graf and Ms. Hidalgo will see you now."

Here we go, I thought, standing up to follow the nattily dressed werewolf and wishing I'd worn a suit. He led me down a terra-cotta–tiled hallway filled with yet more golden-eyed portraits, all of which seemed to be staring at me accusingly, to a set of double doors. Adrenaline pumped through me with each step. *Were they going to kill me?*

Probably not, I reasoned; if they were going to kill me, they would have done it when Elena was in my loft.

Or, I thought with a shiver, hired Tom to do it. Not that he would, of course.

As the butler werewolf opened the doors, a blast of male-Alpha-werewolf scent washed over me. Despite the fact that my skin was crawling with fear and adrenaline, I took a deep, appreciative breath before stepping through the doors.

They opened into a sitting room of sorts. I don't know what I was expecting—his and hers werewolf thrones, maybe—but this looked more like a small but posh resort lobby. Three of the walls had floor-to-ceiling mullioned glass windows, with fabulous views of a Spanish-style garden that looked lush even in February. A super-thick wool rug stretched across the tile floor, and the high-ceilinged room was dotted with big, comfy couches, two of which were occupied by werewolves.

Their heads swiveled as I entered, giving me the full benefit of their shimmery gold eyes.

The woman had bobbed black hair, a sharp little nose, coffee-colored skin—and those signature golden eyes. A scar that looked like claw marks ran down the side of her left cheek, white against her smooth dark skin. As I entered, she fixed me with a cool, assessing gaze that sent a shiver through me. There was something about her that would have scared the pants off me, if I weren't wearing a skirt. Which would be the second time in one day, I thought, remembering my little incident with the horse a few hours earlier.

My eyes slid from the woman to her partner, and my breath caught in my throat.

The man was a dead ringer for the werewolf in the portrait.

The velvet and white flounce had been replaced by a toffee-colored button-down shirt that mirrored the gold of his eyes, and his blond hair was now cropped short, but it was the same rich color. Even the ruby ring was the same. And he smelled great—like sex on expensive loafers.

"That portrait in the hall," I said when I was able to speak.

He nodded, a glint of amusement in his eyes.

"It looks just like you."

"It should," he said, with a bit of a smug smile. "Lord knows I paid enough for it."

"Paid for the painting?"

"Paid the painter to paint it," he clarified.

Oh. My. God. Could it be? "Um, when exactly did this whole portrait thing happen?"

The werewolf shrugged, and I could see the muscles rippling under his shirt. "A while ago."

"A while ago like last year? Or a while ago like last century?"

"I think it was sixteen ninety-two," he said lightly, in a European accent. "Or maybe it was the spring of ninety-three. Like I said, it was a while ago."

"Holy shit." I breathed, still staring.

As Wolfgang stared back, obviously amused, the woman beside him said, "You're late." Her accent sounded faintly Mexican, not European.

I suddenly remembered I was here to negotiate with the Houston pack, not stare at antique werewolves. But if he was that old and still looked this good, how old was Tom? Was it possible that I had kissed a five-hundred-year-old werewolf? *Don't think about Tom,* I chided myself, and tore my eyes from the five-hundred-year-old werewolf in front of me to focus on the woman beside him. Who did not look excited to see me. "Sorry I'm a bit late," I said. "Traffic."

"Allow me to introduce myself," the male werewolf said, his golden eyes fixed on me. "I am Wolfgang Graf, and this is my companion, Anita," he said formally, indicating the dark-haired woman beside him.

"Sophie Garou," I replied.

"Please, sit down," he said, pointing to a leather chair.

"Thanks." I crossed the thick carpet and perched on the edge of a massive wing chair. "Nice place you've got here," I said inanely, as if this were a block party and we were making small talk while the burgers cooked. Mmm. Burgers. I swallowed back a rush of saliva and suddenly realized I hadn't had lunch.

"Thank you very much for coming," the male werewolf said stiffly. His accent was German, I decided, and he was very polite. Unlike me, who couldn't help staring at both of them. Wolfgang was a fine specimen of . . . well, I'd guess you could call it animal manliness, dressed for casual Friday. Anita's curvy form was clad in designer jeans and a snug green V-neck sweater. She was toying with a silvery-looking pendant that hung from a thin chain around her neck; there were designs on it, but I couldn't see what they were without looking like I was ogling her chest.

I could think of about a billion questions I wanted to ask—like, how did they find out about me? How had Wolfgang lived since the seventeenth century? Where did they get the money to fund this fancy housing compound? And perhaps most important, had they invited me to Houston to kill me and roast me for dinner? But since I was the guest, I decided to let them set the tone.

"You shield yourself very well," Wolfgang said.

"Pardon me?" I blinked at him.

"You shield your presence unusually well," he said. "I think I'm beginning to understand how you have evaded detection all these years."

"But not anymore," the woman said icily, and I swear the temperature of the room dropped twenty degrees. Which was saying something, since it was already pretty chilly. Must be drafts from the big windows.

"How did you find out I was in Austin?" I asked.

"We have many sources of information," Anita said vaguely.

"Could you be a touch more specific?" I asked.

Her answer was a flat "No."

Anita wasn't exactly rolling out the red carpet for me, so I shifted my focus to Wolfgang, putting on what I hoped was a winning smile. His gold eyes seemed to swirl in the gray afternoon light. "I know—well, I didn't really know, until a few months ago, but I know now—that apparently I've been in your 'territory.'" I unconsciously made the quotation signs in the air with my fingers and immediately regretted it. From the corner of my eye, I could see Anita's eyes grow even stonier.

"Yes," Anita said, squaring her shoulders and staring at me, sharp teeth bared slightly. So much for a one-on-

one with Wolfgang. "You have been in our 'territory.'"
She repeated my little gesture, and I felt my face flush.
"Without permission," she added. "I assume you know
the penalty for your crime?"

"Um, no. I can't say that I do."

"Death," she said shortly. "We do not tolerate out-
siders."

"Ah," I said, the hackles on my neck standing at attention. "That would explain the little incident in the
Austin Greenbelt the other day."

She nodded curtly.

"So those werewolves just happened to be in the
wrong place, and you killed them."

"Yes." Her gold eyes searched mine. "And you, too,
are in our territory illegally."

Jesus. What was this, the Middle Ages? I was getting
the impression that this woman gave the term "bitch" a
whole new meaning. And I hadn't barely survived a run-
in with an eighteen-wheeler and driven an hour and a
half to be verbally abused by a woman who thought she
was Cleopatra reborn.

Still, it would probably be best not to piss her off. "I'm
sorry if I've inadvertently broken a rule," I said stiffly.
"I've been in Austin for almost twenty years; I didn't know
it was considered part of Houston. I mean, I thought the
suburbs kind of stopped at Katy," I joked.

Unfortunately, neither of them chuckled. If anything, the temperature dropped a few more degrees.

"I'm sure we can work something out," I continued,
trying to control the near-panic coursing through me,
urging me to change. The last thing I wanted was for
Anita and Wolfgang to smell that I was uncomfortable.
Okay, terrified. Unfortunately, I was pretty sure I was
broadcasting my fear so loudly that any werewolves in a
five-mile radius would know I was about to pee in my

pants. "I'm a CPA, you know; maybe I could toss in a couple of free tax returns or something."

"I should have known you wouldn't know about the Code." Anita's lips curled back from her white teeth; she stared at me for a long time, then sniffed and turned to Wolfgang, still fingering the pendant at her neck. "I don't know why you wanted to bother. She's a waste of time."

I stood up, my high heels sinking into the thick rug. Terrified or not, I wasn't about to sit here and be abused. "You know, I didn't drive all the way to Houston to be insulted. I'm sorry if my presence offends you, although I can't see how, since for the last two decades you didn't even know I existed."

"Please do not be angry," Wolfgang said quietly, his voice filled with quiet authority. "We invited you here to talk."

I stared at him. "Don't be angry?" And then all common sense flew out the window. "How can I not be angry when you guys send me threatening e-mails and send your henchmen to break into my loft?"

"Henchmen?" Anita's voice was sharp.

"Elena and the pleather boys," I said, moving toward the door. "And the other one, the one who tore up my place and then vanished."

"Pleather boys?" Wolfgang asked.

"Boris and Dudley," I clarified, and Wolfgang shot Anita a questioning look.

"I didn't send Elena," Anita said.

"Nor did I," said Wolfgang, standing up and closing the distance between us. He put a big paw on my shoulder. The touch was electric, somehow. Not pleasant, not unpleasant. But disconcerting. "Please, Miss Garou, sit down. I'm afraid we've gotten off to a bad start."

I glanced back at him, confused. "If you didn't send Elena," I asked, "then who did?"

"I would like to know that myself," he said, with those European-sounding clipped consonants. "Perhaps she was attempting to help, in her own way. May I get you a drink?"

I hesitated for a moment, glancing at Anita, who was staring at me with slitty little eyes. She didn't seem very happy with the way things were going. In which case, why not go along with Wolfgang for a few minutes? At least to see where things were headed—and find out more about what was going on. And about the Code, and Wolfgang's relationship with Tom. Besides, if I left now, I was pretty sure Anita would put a contract out on me before I got back to Roundtop.

I turned back to Wolfgang. "Thank you," I said.

"Tea?" he asked. "We've got wolfsbane, of course. We have it flown in fresh from the Tyrolean Alps; I find the flavor is milder. Or, if you prefer, black tea. Oolong, Earl Grey, or Assam. Unless you'd prefer something a little stronger?"

"Do you have any white wine?" I asked. It was well past noon, after all. And after the day I'd had so far, I could use a little liquid courage.

"Chardonnay?" he asked. "Pinot grigio? Riesling?" Gosh. If the whole Alpha thing didn't work out, he could always pick up a job as a sommelier.

"Chardonnay, please."

"Benny!" he barked. When the butler-werewolf appeared at the door, he said, "A chardonnay for the lady, please."

"Any particular brand, sir?"

Wolfgang turned to me. "Will Cakebread Cellars be acceptable?"

"Whatever you've got is fine," I said, ignoring Anita, whose glare was like two lasers boring into me.

"Cakebread it is, then."

"Yes, sir," Benny the butler said, and shimmered out of the room again.

Wolfgang smiled a tight little smile at me, giving me a view of his sharp white teeth that made me shiver a little. "Now please, Miss Garou. Will you sit down?" He touched my arm again, and once again I got that strange little jolt.

"Call me Sophie," I said as he guided me back to my chair. Benny reappeared a moment later holding a big balloon glass of Chardonnay. I took a sip; it was like nectar. "Wow, this is good. Thanks."

"My pleasure," said Wolfgang, relocating to his chair and leaning forward, staring at me intently. I could feel the blood rising to my cheeks; the intensity of his gaze was uncomfortable. "Now," he said, "as my colleague has mentioned, unfortunately your presence in Austin is in direct violation of the Code."

"Like I said, I'm not really familiar with the Code," I said, taking another sip of the delicious yellow stuff. Mmmm. If being part of the werewolf pack meant ready access to this stuff, maybe I could be persuaded.

As I swirled the liquid around in my mouth, Wolfgang stared at me with a considering look in those shimmery gold eyes. Unnerving, particularly after my encounter with their three-hundred-year-old likeness in the front foyer. And invigorating, somehow. His voice was slow and measured when he spoke. "The punishment, as Anita mentioned, is admittedly a bit draconian."

"I can't disagree with you there."

"Solos are not permitted," Anita said flatly from beside Wolfgang.

Wolfgang shot her a sharp glance but turned back to me and conceded the point. "Unfortunately, Anita is correct. You would either have to agree to relocate to one of our ranches and take a low-ranking position . . ."

"Or be terminated," Anita finished for him, inspecting her nails. I could feel the hairs on the back of my neck prickle.

"But in this situation, there may be extenuating circumstances," Wolfgang said.

Anita grabbed her glass of wine and downed half of it. "I don't see how."

A flicker of irritation passed over Wolfgang's face as he turned to her. "She has evaded our detection for twenty years, Anita. Think of how useful that could be."

Anita glanced at me, then cocked an eyebrow. "San Antonio?"

"Perhaps," he said.

She smiled then, a grin that gave me the willies. "Hmm. That does have possibilities."

"What's in San Antonio?" I asked.

"San Antonio is a neutral territory," Wolfgang said, staring at me with those golden eyes and running a hand through his crew-cut hair. "We've gotten reports of some unusual activity there, though."

"Kind of like what happened in Austin last week? On the Greenbelt?"

"That was a regrettable incident, but necessary, I'm afraid." Wolfgang's eyes gleamed slightly, and for a moment I was reminded exactly how high the stakes were. And that if I wasn't careful, there might be a few of them headed in my direction.

"So the deaths in Austin are related to what's going on in San Antonio?" I asked.

"Perhaps," Wolfgang replied, a bit vaguely, in my opinion. "But our main concern is that one of our most trusted scouts has . . ."

"Disappeared," Anita said in a clipped voice, finishing yet another sentence for him. Annoying habit, really.

"In San Antonio," I said, just to clarify.

Anita nodded.

"So what do you want me to do about it?" I asked,

taking another sip of my delicious wine. Would it be in bad taste to drink the whole glass and ask for another? I wondered. Then I gave myself a little shake. Here I was, negotiating with two werewolves who seemed to think they had the power of life and death over me, worried about scoring a second glass of wine.

"Reconnaissance," Wolfgang said, bringing me back to the subject at hand.

"What?" I asked, mystified.

"Spying," Anita clarified, with a slow smile that gave me the heebie-jeebies.

Thirteen

"Whoa," I said, raising my hands. "I'm an auditor. Not a spy."

"Well, then," Anita said. "Termination it is."

"Anita." Wolfgang's voice was harsh.

"Oh, please, Wolfi," Anita said in a little-girl voice that seemed totally out of character for her. *Wolfi*? "She said she doesn't want to do it." Anita gave me a speculative look. "Although she's got those broad shoulders, wide peasant hips. She might make a good groundskeeper out at Spring."

Wide peasant hips? Alpha or no Alpha, Anita wasn't scoring any points with me. "I'm not a groundskeeper," I said. "Or a spy. But I can save you a lot of money on taxes. Provided we agree I stay in Austin as . . . well, kind of as a friend to the pack," I finished lamely.

"I'm afraid that won't work," Wolfgang said gently.

"You already have a CPA?"

His lips twitched into a smile, and I felt an answering twitch somewhere lower. Were there just an unusual number of attractive men around lately, or were my hormones going into overdrive?

Anita narrowed her dark eyes at me, and I suspected she knew all about my internal twitch.

"It's not about that," Wolfgang said, and I turned to look at him instead. Which was much nicer, even though

there was still something kind of disturbing about him.
Maybe it was just because I knew he was older than dirt.
"You can't just be a 'friend' of the pack. You have to
join."

"Or leave," Anita added. I shot her a look.

"What about Tom?" I asked. "Tom Fenris is around,
but he's not a member."

Wolfgang's blond eyebrows rose a fraction. "You are
a friend of Tom's?"

I nodded, feeling my face heat up as I thought of the
last time we'd met. Were we friends? More than friends?
More than friends only when Lindsey wasn't around? "I
thought he was going to call you," I said.

"Perhaps he has. I'll ask."

"But why is it okay for him to be here, and not me?"
I asked.

"Tom visits with our permission," Wolfgang said
coolly. "He has not established a residence in our territory. He performs services for the pack, and as such is
permitted to occupy pack territory."

"Exactly," I said. "That's just what I'm proposing.
Filing returns. Even a bit of auditing. It's a win-win
situation," I babbled. "You didn't even know I was in
Austin; now, I'll keep staying out of the way, but you'll
get your taxes filed for free."

I knew it wasn't working before Wolfgang shook his
head.

"It is not enough," he said. "And normally, to join,
you would have to start as the Omega." As he said the
word, Anita's lips curved into a wicked smile.

"At the very bottom," I clarified. I remembered that
much from my reading, at least.

"She's smarter than she looks," Anita said.

I ignored her. "So my options are to leave Austin, or
join the pack and scoop wolf poop or something," I
said, focusing my attention on Wolfgang.

Wolfgang looked startled. "Scoop wolf poop?"

"You know what I mean. Do grunt work."

He nodded, and a hint of a smile tugged at his mouth. "I'm happy to tell you that 'poop scooping' is not one of the tasks we ask lower ranks to perform—most of us are familiar with modern facilities. However, being assigned to 'grunt work,' as you call it, is the general procedure. You do have special talents, though."

Somehow I didn't think he meant my facility with numbers.

"And if you are willing to do some work for us in San Antonio," he continued, "we might be willing to make . . . shall we say, a special dispensation for you."

"Would I have to join the pack?"

"Is that so unappealing?" he asked, looking a little bit hurt.

"Not necessarily," I said, hurriedly. "I think I'm just used to operating alone."

"We might be able to make an exception," he said. Anita's lips, I couldn't help noticing, were a thin line, and the white of her scars stood out starkly against her skin. I glanced around at the lush surroundings; you'd think with all this money, Anita would have sprung for plastic surgery. Then again, with hospitals come tests, and with tests come all kinds of questions . . . particularly if the patient transforms while under sedation. Lord knew I'd done my best to avoid doctor's visits over the years.

Speaking of doctors, I thought, glancing at my watch, it was time to get this over with and get back to the Dude Ranch retreat. Wouldn't want to miss the Hoedown dance.

I looked at Wolfgang and considered his offer. I had no desire to go to San Antonio to do spy work. On the other hand, Southeast Airlines was based in San Antonio, so I'd be there a lot anyway. And if it meant not having to move out of Austin, and maybe creating a bit of goodwill with the Houston pack's head honchos, maybe I should at least hear them out.

"Okay," I said. "Before I make any decisions, though, at least tell me what it is you want me to do."

It was almost five o'clock by the time I drove out of the werewolf compound, wondering exactly what it was I'd agreed to. And whether drinking four glasses of yummy wine during the negotiation phase had been a good idea.

The plan sounded simple enough. They'd given me a San Antonio address and asked me to see what I could find out about who was there—and what they were talking about. Evidently the missing bigwig was a guy named Hubert (they showed me his portrait, and he looked a lot like Wolfgang, only less handsome and with a rather bright red velvet jacket). He'd disappeared a few weeks ago, while on some kind of assignment in San Antonio.

"I thought San Antonio was neutral," I'd said to Wolfgang over a plate of filet mignon. (He'd insisted I stay for a late lunch, and I'm a sucker for a good steak.)

"It's supposed to be," he said, after a sip of wine. I had to give the Houston pack credit for their taste in liquor, I thought, reaching for my own glass. Benny had poured a grand cru burgundy, and it was delicious.

Wolfgang swirled the dark liquid in his glass and sniffed deeply. "But *Los Norteños*—the North Mexican pack—are starting to push past their borders. We've even seen a few of them in Houston, which is highly unusual."

I thought about Teena; she'd mentioned meeting a Mexico City werewolf in Texarkana, which was a lot further north than Houston. It was on the tip of my tongue to mention it until I realized I hadn't mentioned

Teena to Wolfgang. Instead of saying something, I stuffed another chunk of rare steak into my mouth, accessorizing it with a delicious sautéed mushroom.

When I'd swallowed, I asked, "What happened to Hubert?"

Anita speared a bite of steak and stared at me. "He disappeared."

"Just disappeared?"

Anita glanced quickly at Wolfgang, and a shiver of apprehension crept down my back. "He was in San Antonio on business," she said.

"You mean spying business," I said, putting my fork down. "If he disappeared, what's stopping the same thing from happening to me?"

"Sophie," Wolfgang said, reaching across the table to place his hand over mine. The hairs were gold, like his hair, and I found myself wondering what he would look like as a wolf. "When you arrived at the compound, until Benny introduced you, I didn't know you were here. Which has never happened before. It's an unusual talent. I've met very few *lupins* with your . . . ability."

"Until now, I didn't even know I had it," I said.

"But you do," he said, in a voice that made me feel all soft and warm inside. Or maybe it was just the three glasses of wine. "And trust me. With your shielding abilities, you'll be quite safe."

Anita shrugged. "Besides, you don't really have a lot of alternatives, do you?" Compared with Wolfgang's warm tones, her voice was like an ice pick. How had the two of them gotten together? I wondered. *Were* they together? They seemed like an odd couple. I mean, they were both Alphas, but did that mean they were . . . well, you know. *Together?*

I ignored her and took another sip of burgundy. Wolfgang's hand was still hot on mine, and I was trying hard to dampen the response it was igniting in me. Even though he wasn't nearly as attractive as Tom. Or Mark, actually. *Or your boyfriend Heath,* I reminded myself. I kept my voice as steady as possible. "So, if I go down and see what I can find out, you'll leave me alone?"

"Do you really want to be left alone?" Wolfgang asked, his voice low. "You must miss your own kind."

I took another sip of wine and eased my hand out from under Wolfgang's. "Actually, no," I said. "I like my life just fine."

He continued to stare at me, as if considering something. After a long moment, he said, "You know, we'll be heading out to one of our ranches tonight. Would you care to join us? It can be quite exhilarating to run with the pack."

It took me a moment to realize what he was offering. Then I remembered; it was the full moon tonight. What would it be like, I wondered, to run with other wolves?

Then I shook myself. This was not a part of my personality—if that's what you wanted to call it—I had any interest in encouraging. "Thank you," I said, smiling tightly. "But I think I'll pass." I reached for my wine, then reconsidered. With the full moon rising in a couple of hours, I needed to take preventive measures. "And if I could have a cup of wolfsbane tea, come to think of it . . ."

Wolfgang held my gaze for a moment, then nodded and picked up his fork. "As you wish," he said. As Benny the butler hurried from the room to get me a cup of wolfsbane, Anita sat back in her chair and smiled.

It hadn't been a very nice smile, I reflected now as I turned off Highway 71 onto the little road that led to the Dude Ranch. And since Anita didn't seem to be overly fond of me, her apparent pleasure at my assignment was a tad worrisome.

At the time, of course, after several glasses of fabulous wine and a big, rare steak, the job had seemed relatively reasonable. To hear Wolfgang tell it, all I had to do was hang out outside a house and report back on what I heard. Which sounded like a far better alternative to leaving town. Now, though, as I headed up the road to Roundtop, I was wondering if there was more to this little assignment than Wolfgang and Anita had mentioned. The Houston pack's reason for not sending one of their own seemed on the up-and-up. If none of them had this supposed shielding talent, then of course it would be tough to spy on other werewolves. Even though the two of them seemed powerful enough to take down anyone who got in their way.

But who had collared Hubert? Were they connected with the murders on the Greenbelt? And was my so-called talent enough to keep me from meeting the same fate?

I was still worrying about what I'd just agreed to do—and about the fact that the moon was due to rise any minute and I hadn't had wolfsbane in almost two hours—when I bumped up the long driveway to the Dude Ranch. According to the clock on the dashboard, it was almost seven o'clock. Lucky me; I'd be just in time for the end of the chuckwagon dinner.

I'd stopped at a gas station for a touch-up shave; I was low on wolfsbane, and the moon would be full in a matter of hours. I did a quick check in the rearview mirror, searching for excess fur. So far, so good, but if I didn't get another cup of tea soon, things would start getting hairy fast.

The smell of barbecue greeted me as I opened the front door, and despite the late lunch, my mouth started watering. A moment later, I walked into the dining room—the prickly pear cactus had been augmented by an ice sculpture of a longhorn, complete with a cowbell—and faced an onslaught of concerned coworkers.

Including Dwayne, who hurried over to me as fast as

his substantial girth allowed and slung a smelly arm around my shoulders.

"How are you, darlin'?"

"Fine, Dwayne," I said, wincing. "I'm fine."

"Nothin' broke?"

"No," I said, attempting to extricate myself. "Just a little banged up."

"Well, then," he said, leering at me—his nose was covered with clogged pores, and I had to resist the urge to recommend a good exfoliating lotion—"since the calf ropin' didn't work out, I was hopin' you'd accompany me to the ballroom for some square dancing. . . ."

I shuddered at a brief vision of being hurled around the dance floor, swathed in a cloud of Skoal-scented breath, semi-impaled on Dwayne's enormous belt buckle. "I'm not sure I'm up to it, thanks."

"You can't miss the square dancing!" he said, massaging my shoulder with swollen, sausagelike fingers. Just then, Adele swept up to me in a pinafore—a pinafore!—and a little white cowgirl hat.

"I'm so glad you're back, Sophie. Better go get your boots on—you don't want miss the dance!"

Honestly, I couldn't think of many things I'd rather miss—including major surgery *sans* sedation—but for the sake of being political, I kept my thoughts to myself. "Actually," I said, prying Dwayne's hand off my shoulder and affecting a limp, "the doctor said I should probably avoid too much physical activity. . . ."

"Are you sure?"

"She said it would be risky," I said. "Very risky. In fact, if you don't mind, I think I'll just fix myself a plate and head upstairs."

"If you think that's best," Adele said, pursing her thin, red-glossed lips. But after almost getting flattened by a runaway horse and an eighteen-wheeler—not to mention meeting with two scary, potentially murderous

werewolves and agreeing to spy on another bunch of
scary, potentially murderous werewolves—there was no
way I was going to help fulfill Adele's Martha Stewart–
inspired dude ranch fantasies tonight. And not just
because I'd rather have my bikini line tweezed than be
anywhere near a dance floor with Dwayne and his six-
pound belt buckle. It might not be the equinox, but it
was still a full moon, and if I didn't get some wolfsbane
tea down me soon, the whole office would be in for a bit
of a surprise.

She sighed heavily. Thank God I'd already made partner, I thought, or I'd be sweating it. "I'll see you later
then," she said. "If you change your mind, you know
where to find us!"

I glanced over at the expensively booted country
band. There were four of them, all well past their spring-
chicken years, and from the volume of the strangled-
turkey sounds coming from the amps, I was guessing I'd
be able to find the dance if I were anywhere within a ten-
mile radius. Blindfolded.

As Adele and her pinafore bustled over to the band-
stand, I limped over to the table and filled a plate with
brisket and potato salad. Then I grabbed a mug of hot
water and a fork and headed up to the Chuckwagon
Room, assuring a number of concerned coworkers that
I was fine, just in need of some rest. It felt good to finally
close the door of my room behind me, even if the walls
still vibrated slightly to the strains of the C&W band
downstairs. Not country and western, exactly—more
like cacophonous & wrinkly.

I had filled the bath (which was actually a cattle
trough), opened a fresh bag of wolfsbane and dropped
two teabags into a mug of hot water when somebody
knocked.

My first impulse was not to answer—I was more than
ready for a soak in the tub, and the last person I wanted

to see was Dwayne. Or any other nosy coworkers. On the other hand, a visit from Lindsey would be most welcome. After the day I'd had, I was in the mood for some normal—human—company. It was the full moon, but once I got a cup of wolfsbane tea in me, I should be safe. It was only the full moons that fell near solstices and equinoxes that made my little transformational issues unavoidable, and the vernal equinox was still almost two months away.

"Who is it?" I called, wrapping a towel tight around me.

"It's Heath."

Heath?

What was he doing here?

My heart pounded as I opened the door to my attorney boyfriend, who stood there in jeans and a red polo shirt, looking good enough to eat.

But I still hadn't forgotten the Miranda incident. Or the whole "Hide the Werewolf" fiasco. "What a surprise," I said. "I didn't expect to see you here."

"I had to see you," he said, eyes filled with longing. My hopes rose, then deflated as I gave him a surreptitious sniff. Miranda. Definitely Miranda. "Can I come in?" he asked.

"Of course," I said, letting him in and closing the door behind him. "You're not working the weekend with Miranda?" I asked, trying not to sound snippy and failing abysmally.

"Not today, no." He surveyed the room. "Nice décor," he said, fingering the chambray bedspread. "Very John Wayne."

I groaned. "Adele's on a Martha Stewart chuckwagon binge. There's a cow patty toss tomorrow, if you're interested."

"I think I'll pass," he said, with a grin that for a moment, made it feel like Miranda and the whole episode in my loft had never taken place.

But of course, they had. And Heath hadn't forgotten about them, either. His smile dimmed a little bit. "No drinking games tonight?" he asked dryly, nodding toward my mug of tea. Of which I hadn't had a drop.

And which I'd better start drinking soon, unless I wanted Heath to be in for a real surprise. "No, not tonight," I said, picking up the mug and downing half of it. Blech. Whatever my mother had done to "improve" the flavor wasn't working.

Of course, what I wanted to ask in response was, *No romantic wine country getaways this weekend?* But I didn't. I wasn't about to admit that I'd been eavesdropping. So instead, I said, "Actually, I was about to take a bath."

"You're not going down to dinner?" he asked.

"No," I said. "I've had . . . well, kind of a rough day."

"I ran into Lindsey. She said you had a bit of an accident with a horse," he said.

Not to mention a trucker with a shotgun and a nasty werewolf named Anita.

He drew closer to me; I could feel his concern. "Are you okay?"

"I'm fine," I said. "The doctor said I just need rest. You're welcome to go down to dinner . . . either that, or you can have my brisket."

"No, that's for you," he said. "Why don't you hop in the tub and relax? I'll just head downstairs and see what I can rustle up; when I get back, we can talk."

Rustle up? I shook my head, thinking it must be the influence of the décor. Next thing you know, Mr. Armani the transplanted Yankee would be dipping snuff and trying on spurs. I adjusted my towel and wondered how the evening would play out. "Are you staying the night?" I asked cautiously.

"That depends," he said, looking at me with those big brown eyes. Miranda or no Miranda, I could feel myself melting and looked away.

"Why don't you take your bath," he said, "and I'll be back up in a bit."

"Okay," I said. "See you soon." He walked over and gave me a little kiss. On the forehead. Which wasn't exactly what I was hoping for.

As the door shut behind him, I took a sip of wolfsbane tea and wished it were something a little stronger. I still hadn't come up with a viable explanation for "Hide the Werewolf." And I'd better start thinking fast, because Heath was going to be back before I knew it, and it was a good bet that conversation topic would be pretty high on the list.

On the other hand, I wasn't the only one with some explaining to do. I might have had unexplained beers in my loft, but he'd been talking weekend getaways with Career-Day Barbie.

I hung the towel on the hitching post next to the trough and lowered myself into the bath, which thanks to its sheet metal construction, was already cold. Still, it felt good to wash away the scent of werewolves—not to mention the traces of dirt I'd picked up during my little fracas with Sparky that morning.

I grabbed a razor, took a big swig of wolfsbane tea, and swished the stuff around in my mouth. I was going to have to tell my mom to go back to her original recipe, because this batch tasted more like lawn clippings than peppermint. After forcing down another sip, I attacked my legs. I was glad Heath had gone downstairs; my calves were looking rather Yeti-esque.

Twenty minutes later, I'd done a thorough de-furring, the tub had progressed from cold to downright frigid, and my mug was empty, but Heath still hadn't come back upstairs.

As I climbed out of the trough and pulled the drain plug, I felt a wave of nausea. God. How long had the brisket been sitting out before I got to it? Or had it been the potato salad?

I wrapped a towel around myself and found myself grabbing at the wall to fend off a sudden dizzy spell. My stomach churned ominously. And urgently.

I dashed the two yards to the toilet and was still clutching it when Heath returned a few minutes later with a plate of pork ribs.

"Sophie, are you okay?"

I didn't have time to answer before the heaves started again.

Fourteen

"Let's get you into bed," Heath said, helping me from the bathroom floor over to the patchwork-covered bed. So much for my hopes for a nice, romantic reconciliation. As I climbed between the covers, my stomach did a flip-flop, and the sound of twanging guitars from downstairs made my head throb. Wouldn't they ever stop? It was nice to have Heath here, though. I took a deep breath of his familiar clean aroma, comforted by the scent.

Until I caught a glimpse of the full moon out the double-hung window.

Shit.

My stomach turned over again as I realized I had just thrown up the full dose of wolfsbane. And there was no way I was going to be able to keep more down.

I stared at my hand, waiting for the fur to start growing, and then at Heath. I needed him to leave. Now. Before I started sprouting a natural fur coat and a full set of canines.

"Heath," I said in a voice that was entirely too growly for my comfort. "I know we need to talk . . . but I think I need to just be alone for a while." Like twelve hours, really.

"I can't leave you like this," he said firmly, eyes dark

with concern. He grabbed my hand and squeezed it. "Not when you're sick. I'll stay with you."

Under any other circumstances, those words would have been delightful to hear. Right now, though, they made me want to scream.

"Please," I said, racking my brain for a way to get one of the two of us out of here. If only I could keep the tea down. Should I try brewing another cup? But just the thought of sucking down more grassy sludge made my stomach threaten to turn itself inside out again. I squeezed my eyes shut and made a mental note to ask my mom to come up with something I could inject instead of drink. But that wasn't going to help me now. "I need to be alone," I said. "Just for a little bit."

"But . . ."

"I'm not going to go anywhere," I said, pulling my hand away—was it already changing?—and tucking it under the covers.

"Sophie . . ."

"Ice water," I croaked. "Could you get me some ice water?"

"Ice water," he said slowly.

"Ice water," I repeated, resisting the urge to scream.

He put a hand on my arm, and it was all I could do not to flinch. I could tell the hair was growing. And so could he, because he looked a little startled.

"Wow. I didn't realize you had so much hair on your arms."

Stick around for another few minutes, I thought, *and you'll be in for a* real *surprise.*

"Drink," I reminded him.

He withdrew his hand. "You sure you'll be okay?"

Although my stomach was doing its own version of the square dance—something with lots of ups and downs, like the Schottische—I gritted my teeth and nodded.

"I'll be right back," he said. "Don't go anywhere."

Yeah, right. I just smiled weakly in lieu of responding.

And then, thankfully, he was gone, leaving the scent of CK1 and laundry starch in his wake.

As soon as the door clicked shut, I struggled out of bed. I had to get out of here before he saw what I really was. I had no idea how I was going to explain my disappearance, but it was better than trying to explain my (extremely imminent) transformation into a four-legged fairy-tale creature.

I staggered toward the door and had my hand on the doorknob when I realized I was naked. I doubled back for my robe, fighting through waves of dizziness to get it on. Unfortunately, the whole process had deleterious effects on my stomach lining, which sent me back to the bathroom. A moment later, I tied the robe as best I could, slipped through the door, and staggered toward the back stairway, praying that I wouldn't run into Heath. Or Dwayne. Or Adele, come to think of it.

I didn't. Instead, as I turned the corner to go down the second set of stairs, I smacked right into Lindsey.

"Sophie," she said. "I was hoping I'd see you. You wouldn't believe the rumors about this morning. . . ." She peered at me. "Are you okay? How did your trip to the doctor go?"

"Sick," I said.

"I can tell. Jeez, you look awful. Shouldn't you be in bed?"

"Heath." It came out like a growl. Not good.

Her gray eyes got big. "Heath? He's here? You guys are talking?"

I nodded.

"When did this happen?"

"Ten minutes ago."

"But . . . where are you going?"

"Out."

"Why?" She peered at me. "Is that hair growing on your face?"

I nodded, heart sinking.

"Oh, I see," she said. "This is that medical issue you were telling me about."

I nodded again. Last fall, I'd told her I had a recurrent condition—one that involved excessive hair growth. I hadn't explained about the tooth and snout development, though, and unless I got out of here pronto, Lindsey would soon know the full extent of my little "disorder."

I could almost see the wheels turning in her head as she stared at my rapidly furring cheek. "You don't want Heath to see you right now."

Bingo.

"Do you want to come to my room?"

"But Heath . . ." I croaked.

"Come on," she said, grabbing my arm and pulling me after her. "I'll just tell him you're with me."

"Lindsey," I said, pulling away and marshalling the tattered remains of my human resources. "Tell him I'm with you," I said, in a voice so low Barry White would have been jealous. "But I have to go now."

"What? But Sophie, you're ill. And your voice . . ."

"I know. Trust me."

"Sophie . . ." she called after me as I stumbled down the stairway. The moon was rising higher every second; I could feel it on my skin. I pushed through the door and out into the back, away from the awful guitar music, away from Heath, away from Lindsey, who stood in the doorway, silhouetted against the light.

My stomach heaved again as I plunged through a prickly stand of agarita (ouch) and stumbled blindly into the undergrowth.

Lindsey called me one more time, but it was too late; there was no way I could answer. I shrugged off the robe as I ran, feeling the moonlight course through me like a drug.

And then, for the second time that day, I was down on all fours, running. Only a little ways, though; I stopped at the first big bush, startling a sleeping cow, who mooed and broke into a frightened trot as I crawled under the branches. My stomach was clenched in a constant cramp by now, and the world was spinning around me.

As the band played on, I curled up shivering in a pile of sharp leaves, struggling to settle my churning stomach. The moon sailed high in the sky, and the temperature was dropping by the minute; even with a fur coat, I was freezing. Why had I not taken the robe with me? I thought in a moment of clarity.

Finally, the twanging, thrumming noise stopped, and I drifted into queasy dreams. That piney smell again, the one I'd smelled in the cave, seemed to settle over me, making my stomach churn. Then it faded, and a pack of coyotes yipped and howled somewhere in the distance, followed by a long, doleful sound that sent shivers down my spine.

Unless I was hallucinating—which was entirely possible—it was the cry of a werewolf.

I woke to the grayish light of dawn, shivering violently and feeling like I had the worst hangover ever. I shifted and groaned, making my stomach flip over again—and causing all the little sticks I was lying on to dig into my skin. My naked, frozen, human skin.

Oh, God.

I did a mental review of the previous evening, which was admittedly sketchy. I'd puked my guts out, of course, more than once, and remembered kind of sliding in and out of some sort of greasy consciousness as I curled up under the bush. What had caused me to get so sick? Was it the new batch of tea? Or just bad potato salad? My stomach churned just thinking about the brew I'd sucked down last night; it had tasted awful.

Had my mother gotten the ingredients wrong somehow?

I took a shaky breath and caught a faint hint of a now-familiar smell.

Werewolves.

Even with the goosebumps, my skin prickled as I recalled the howling I'd heard. I took another deep sniff, just to make sure it wasn't a dream.

It wasn't.

I closed my eyes, trying to get a better read on the smell. It had rained at some time during the night, so the scents weren't as clear as they could have been, but there had definitely been werewolves nearby. I sniffed again. A lot of them, in fact.

Weird. Had the Houston pack tracked me back to Roundtop? And if so, why?

Not that I was in any condition to worry about that now. If I didn't get warm fast, I'd be dead of hypothermia. With an effort, I disentangled myself from the bush and stumbled toward the main building, not really caring who saw me. Fortunately, the only eyes I encountered were white-rimmed and bovine, and all of them were keeping a very safe distance from me.

The tin roof of the guesthouse gleamed in the gray light—it wasn't too far off, thankfully. I stumbled from bush to bush in the building's general direction, shivering uncontrollably in the damp cold and keeping a sharp eye out for cow patties—and for my robe.

I found it a few minutes later, half-draped over a prickly pear. It would help ward off a bit of the chill, but the prickly pear spines were a bit of a drawback, since several hundred of them were embedded in the fabric and they were all at least half an inch long. I put the robe on anyway—it was better than being naked, if only slightly—and it was a very sorry Sophie who knocked at Lindsey's door a few minutes later.

She answered the door and squinted at me, pulling her satin robe tight around her. "Sophie?"

"It's me," I said, my teeth chattering.

She opened the door to admit me, still rubbing the sleep out of her eyes. "What the hell happened last night? Where did you go?"

"I just needed to be away," I said.

"You must be half frozen. I'll start a hot bath for you. God—did you sleep under a bush or something?"

"Is it that obvious?"

"You've got leaves in your hair," she said. I reached up to finger comb them out with quaking fingers as Lindsey hurried into the bathroom to turn on the bath. As the heat started to penetrate my numb skin, I flexed my toes experimentally. The feeling was coming back to them, with the unfortunate side effect that it felt like someone was holding hot pincers to them.

"Can you get frostbite if the temperature's above freezing?" I asked.

"I don't know," Lindsey said, coming back into the room and perching on the edge of her rumpled bed.

"Watch out for the barbed wire," I warned her, pointing to the spiky footboard. The movement drove another couple of spines into my arm, and I winced. Stupid cactus.

"No kidding," she said, raising her arm to show me a hole in the sleeve of her satin robe. "I just about killed myself on the dresser last night." She scooted away from the barbed-wire-festooned headboard. "The bath'll be ready in a minute. But I still don't get it. Why did you leave? Why didn't you just stay with me?" she asked.

"It's not just that I get a *little* hairy," I said. "I look like I'm wearing a fur coat."

Lindsey's eyes darted to my now relatively normal arms, parts of which were peeking out of the robe's sleeves. I still looked kind of like the 'before' picture in an electrolysis ad. But at least I was no longer sporting pointy ears and a tail. "So, what happened?" she asked. "Did you take Nair along with you?"

"It . . . fades," I said vaguely.

"That makes no sense at all," Lindsey said. "How does hair ungrow?"

I shrugged. "Like I said. It's a weird condition." Time to change the subject. "What about you? Where were you last night?"

"Wondering what happened to you," she said sarcastically. "And trying to keep Heath out of my room."

My stomach clenched, which wasn't good—I still hadn't recovered from last night's retching episode. Heath. I'd almost forgotten he was here. "What did he say?"

"He's not happy."

My stomach clenched again, and I swallowed hard. "No?"

"It's not the first time this has happened. Remember last fall, when you disappeared without even taking your car?"

I did remember. I had transformed on our anniversary and stood him up on our big date.

Why *had* I gotten so sick last night? I was almost never ill; I'd always figured it was a side effect of being a hybrid of sorts. I'd read somewhere that half-breeds were supposed to be stronger, or something. "Did anyone else get sick last night? You know, like food poisoning?"

Lindsey shook her head. "Not that I know of."

"What did you eat?"

"Brisket, potato salad. The pecan pie was to die for."

Just the mention of food made me queasy again.

"I think the bath's done," Lindsey said. "Why don't you go warm up, and we'll talk when you're feeling human again."

I looked at her, startled, and examined her face. Worry, yes, and a touch of irritation, but I didn't think she knew. Not yet, anyway. Unfortunately, the way things were going lately, half the state would soon be aware of my little "condition."

A moment later, I sank into a tubful of hot water, wincing at the heat on my half-frozen skin. Once the initial pain went away, though, it was wonderful. So wonderful, in fact, that I would have preferred to stay there the rest of the day. Maybe even the rest of the month.

"Are you doing okay?" Lindsey called through the door.

"Fine," I said, lathering up with Lindsey's lemon verbena soap.

"We've got breakfast in half an hour," she said. "Then there's the cow patty toss, and the hay maze."

And somewhere in there, I'd have to explain last night's disappearing act to my boyfriend. I groaned. A full-day bath was starting to sound better and better.

I stayed in as long as I could—which with Lindsey hammering on the door every fifteen minutes was not nearly as long as I would have liked—and reluctantly emerged from the bathroom wrapped in a gingham towel. I still had a few red welts from the cactus, but for the most part, the bath had restored me to my pre-werewolf appearance. (Particularly since I had taken the liberty of borrowing Lindsey's razor.)

"You want to wear some of my clothes?" Lindsey asked, opening a drawer and pulling out a top that looked more like denim macramé than actual clothing.

"You do realize it's February?"

She shrugged. "I'm just hot-blooded, I guess."

"Thanks, but I think I'll head back to the room like

this," I said, shucking off the gingham and pulling my prickly, mud-smeared robe around me. If I got dirty again, it would be a good excuse to take another bath.

"What are you going to tell Heath?"

"That I had a virus, and I didn't want him to see me look so awful."

She bit her lip. "Good luck with that. Any word on the little bag from the jeweler, by the way?"

"No," I said, thinking of Miranda. Maybe it had been for her the whole time.

Stop jumping to conclusions, I told myself. Just because they'd had lunch at Romeo's and had been discussing a wine-country getaway in Heath's apartment—at night—didn't mean anything at all. I was sure there was a logical explanation for it.

"Go see what you can do to fix it," she said. "After all, Valentine's Day is less than a week away."

She was right. I sighed, wrapped my still slightly prickly robe around me, and headed back to the Chuckwagon Room.

And Heath.

Fifteen

I stood outside the door, brushing the dirt off my robe and marshalling my thoughts for a couple of minutes before taking the plunge.

I knocked.

No answer.

Then I opened the door—it was unlocked, for some reason—and hoped for the best.

But Heath wasn't there. And by the faintness of his scent, he hadn't been there for a long time. Since last night, in fact.

Crap.

Where could he be? Maybe he'd spent the night downstairs somewhere, or checked into a Days Inn or some hotel that had an actual bathtub, rather than modified farm equipment.

I shucked my robe, then tugged on jeans and a sweater and headed down to the dining room. The smell of bacon, usually enough to get my salivary glands working overtime, had the opposite effect on me this morning. Heath was nowhere to be seen, but Adele was directing a harried-looking young woman on napkin placement. Today's ensemble included spurs, purple boots, and a matching suede fringed skirt.

I stared in morbid fascination as she jingled over to me. "Good morning, cowgirl," she said in what I think was supposed to be a drawl. "Feeling better this morning?"

"Not a hundred percent, no," I said, tearing my eyes away from Adele's dangly silver longhorn earrings and scanning the room for signs of my boyfriend. "Have you seen Heath this morning?"

"Nope," she said, shaking her head. "I didn't know he was here. But you're just in time for breakfast. Lucky us—grits!"

"Great," I said, eyeing the pan of white mush with a wave of rising nausea. "I think I'll just stick with a biscuit instead. My stomach's a bit off."

"Want some cream gravy with that?" she asked, pointing to another pan of whitish, congealed goo.

"Oh, no thank you," I said. "I'll just stick with a biscuit."

"Glad you're doing better," she said. "Wouldn't want you to miss the cow-patty toss."

I smiled and escaped back upstairs, where I banged on Lindsey's door.

She opened the door almost immediately. "What happened?"

"Nothing. Heath's gone."

She sighed and let me into the room. "I'm not surprised. He wasn't buying the whole vomiting thing last night."

"What did you tell him?"

"Just what you said. That you didn't want him to see you looking so awful."

"And he wouldn't take no for an answer." Just like Heath.

"He insisted on coming in and seeing you, but I wouldn't let him, of course. When he stopped knocking, I figured he might have left in a huff. Did he leave a note?"

I bit my lip. "Nope."

Lindsey let out a big sigh. "Sophie, I've been thinking about it. If Heath did buy an engagement ring the other day, you're going to have to tell him about this little hair condition of yours sometime. When you're living together, it's going to be tough to hide."

No kidding. Particularly when we started having kids—or should I say, pups. "I guess I'll cross that bridge when I get to it," I said. "But now what?"

Lindsey reached over and squeezed my hand. "Talk to him."

"He's never going to believe me," I groaned. "Besides, I'm still pissed about the whole weekend-in-the-wine-country thing."

"I'm sure there's a logical explanation."

I snorted. "I seriously doubt it."

"You're probably right," she said. "But what else are you going to do?"

By the time I made it back to my car that evening, I was convinced I was going to smell like cow poop for the rest of my life. Not only had there been a cow-patty throw, which involved hurling chunks of inadequately dried manure across a field of bluebonnets—not recommended, incidentally, for those with a touchy stomach—but there had been another team-building activity, in which someone led you blindfolded through a hay bale maze. Unfortunately, Dwayne glommed onto me like a flea on a dog. Equally unfortunately, the cows had discovered the maze at some point during the night, and had left a number of offerings in their wake. Dwayne of course, managed to get me to step in each and every one of them. The net result being that as much as I loved my Louis Vuitton mules, I would never be able to wear them again.

All in all, it hadn't been the best of days, I reflected as

I nosed the M3 out of the pitted driveway and in the direction of Austin. But at least it was over.

I'd only driven a few miles when I realized that despite the fact that I'd triple-wrapped my shoes—if I couldn't wear them, at least I could give them to Goodwill, so someone with a less active nose could enjoy them—the smell of cow was still rather strong. I reached over and cracked the window, shivering at the blast of February air.

It was cold, but it wasn't unpleasant; the world outside smelled fresh, like rain, and green plants.

And werewolf.

I pulled the car over with a squeal of tires and opened the window wider.

It wasn't just one werewolf, actually. It was a lot of werewolves. I gazed at the rather imposing barbed wire fence flanking the road. This must be the source of the wolfie aroma I had caught early this morning. Was it one of the Houston clan's outposts?

I inched along the shoulder in my little BMW, and the smell intensified. About fifty yards down the highway, there was a dirt driveway with a massive gate, crisscrossed with what looked like an entire network of electrical wiring. No name, unlike the other gates I'd seen, most of which were emblazoned with clever sobriquets like "Tres Amigos" and "Bum Steer Ranch." This one bore only a number, in peeling white decals. Which was surprising; from what I'd seen of the pack's main digs in Houston, I would have expected something a bit grander, maybe with six-foot gold letters. And if not gold, at least handpainted Mexican tiles, with some professional landscaping for show.

I took another sniff—I could make out the mingled smells of dozens of werewolves, none of whom were familiar—and thought of the howl I had heard last night. Had it come from here? Tempted as I was to investigate a little further—after all, the Houston pack's downtown mansion was the only other werewolf enclave I'd encountered—I decided it was best to keep moving. The fewer werewolves who knew about me, the better.

So after one last sniff, I closed up the windows and put the car into gear. Maybe I'd ask Wolfgang about it next time I saw him. Or Tom, I thought with a delicious little involuntary shiver. After all, if things with Heath really were on the rocks . . .

No, no, no. For so many reasons, no. It took a bit of effort, but I blocked Tom out of my mind and concentrated on the road in front of me. A few minutes later, the last whiff of the strange little werewolf ranch was far behind me, and I was struggling to figure out what I was going to do about Heath.

It was almost eight o'clock by the time I got myself cleaned up and headed over to Heath's building. I'd called several times, but when no one answered, I figured it was time to show up in person.

"Heath Thompson?" the doorman asked me. Usually the normal guy, Evan, let me go right up, but this was a new employee. "I'll buzz him and let him know you're here. Is he expecting you?"

"I'm sure he is. I'll just go up and check, if you don't mind," I said.

"No, ma'am, I'll call for you."

As I stood there in my red suede Jimmy Choos and tight jeans—looking confident and sexy, or at least I hoped so—he buzzed up to Heath's apartment.

"Yes, sir, there's a lady here to see you." He glanced up at me. "No, sir, she says her name is Sophie. Sophie Galou."

"Garou," I corrected.

"Garou," he said, then listened for a moment or two. "Okay, sir. I'll tell her."

I smiled as he hung up the phone. "Great. I'll just head up, then."

The young man looked pained. "Actually, ma'am, he says he's not taking visitors right now."

I blinked. "But I'm his girlfriend. I'm sure there's just a mistake. . . ."

He shrugged. "I'm sorry, but I can't let you up."

"You're kidding me."

"I'm sorry," he repeated.

As my face turned the same color as my Jimmy Choos, I whipped out my phone. First I called Heath's loft. Then I called his cell phone. When he didn't answer either of them, I jammed the phone back into my purse. "Thanks," I muttered, then headed for the door, feeling the spotty doorman's eyes on my back all the way.

I hadn't been so humiliated since my mother donated herbal aphrodisiacs to the school raffle in the third grade.

Sixteen

Monday morning found me stuck on IH-35 headed toward San Antonio to meet with my biggest client. And my first spying gig.

As I sat in traffic, inhaling the fumes of a couple of thousand cars and trucks, I picked up the phone and called my mom. I still didn't know whether it was bad potato salad or the tea that had made me so sick the other night, but I hadn't been able to stomach a cup of it since then, so I was in desperate need of a new batch. Without the secret ingredient this time.

"Sophie!" my mother said as soon as she picked up the phone. "How's my favorite girl?"

"I'm your *only* girl, Mom."

"That doesn't change the fact that you're my favorite," she said. "I sense a bit of stress in your phone aura, dear. How is everything?"

"Not too bad," I lied, thinking, *A bit of stress?* My boyfriend had just dissed me, werewolves kept popping in and out of my loft, there had been a trio of grisly werewolf murders a mile from my house, and I had been drafted to spy on scary werewolves—or face potential execution. Plus, I'd just ruined an expensive pair of mules. But there was no point telling any of this to my mother, who would simply tell me my spirit guides were "testing" me. Instead I said, "I was just wondering;

what did you put in that last batch of tea you made for me?"

"A little bit of peppermint, and some wintergreen. To help mask the taste. Why?"

"Are you sure you didn't add anything else?"

"Nope."

"I think there's something wrong with it," I said as I shifted lanes in an attempt to raise my speed from fifteen miles an hour to twenty. It was a good thing Mark had scheduled a late lunch. At the rate I was going, I wouldn't get there until tomorrow.

"Hmm," my mother said. "Maybe I put in too much wintergreen?"

"It didn't taste like wintergreen to me," I said. "It was more like grass. I was sick as a dog this weekend, and I don't know if it was because of the tea, but now I can't keep the stuff down."

"Oh, poor you. I'm so sorry, sweetheart. I was only trying to help."

"I know, Mom. And I appreciate it. But can you whip up another batch for me? The normal kind?"

"Are you going to swing by and pick it up today?" she asked. "I'd love to catch up. We've been so busy at the store lately, you wouldn't believe it. Some strange things going on—if I didn't know better, I'd think someone was trying to hex the shop."

"Chicken heads and graveyard dirt?" I asked.

"Exactly. Somebody's been sprinkling goofer dust all around the doors, and I've spent all my time doing counter hexes."

"Goofer dust?"

"Graveyard dirt," she clarified.

Ah, yes. She'd told me to be on the lookout for that myself. And chicken heads, of course, which were a bit more easily identified. "How can you tell graveyard dirt from regular dirt?" I asked.

"It just looks different," she said, which was no help at all. "But enough about hexes. Come by the shop, sweetheart; I'd love to see you. Besides, I have a few ideas I'd like to run by you."

Since tax time was coming up, I hoped those ideas involved better bookkeeping strategies, but I wasn't optimistic. "I'm on my way to San Antonio, actually, so I won't be back until late."

I could hear her gasp. "Oh my goodness. I almost forgot. How did your meeting with the Houston pack go?"

"All right, I guess."

"Just all right?"

"Well, they didn't turn me into a wolf-skin rug," I said, "so that's something."

She sucked in her breath. "What did they say? How was it meeting with your own kind? Did they tell you to leave? Or are they going to ask you to join?"

There were so many questions I decided to just answer the last one. "I'm not exactly sure, actually." Then I told her about my little "assignment."

"Why do they want you to do it?" my mother asked.

"Because I supposedly have this weird shielding ability," I said. "Other werewolves don't know I'm there. Apparently that's why I've been in Austin so long without anyone figuring it out."

"Interesting," she said. "I think it's wonderful that you're finally in touch with your own kind. It's so good for you."

I didn't share her rosy assessment, but I kept my mouth shut. Which was fine, because she just kept on talking.

"But I have to tell you, something about this plan gives me a bad feeling. I don't like you sticking your neck out. Still," she mused, with a hint of pride, "I always knew you had a lot of your father in you, but maybe you got a little bit of me after all."

"What do you mean?" I asked, swerving to avoid a chicken truck.

"You can hide yourself," my mother said. "Keep yourself from being known."

"How does that relate to telling the future?" I asked. "Or calling up ghosts, or knowing who's on the phone before you pick up?"

"You're shielding your aura, honey. It's a hard thing to do; I'm surprised you picked it up without training." She sighed. "I probably should have pushed harder when you were little; I always suspected you had talents. . . ."

"Whoa," I said. "Just because other werewolves don't know I'm there doesn't mean I'm about to start doing séances or anything."

"The talent comes through in different ways. Just because you're not a student of the Tarot doesn't mean you don't have skills. Maybe it's a little different in you because you're part werewolf."

"Please tell me you're alone," I said, cringing at the thought of a store full of people, listening in on my mom's conversation.

"Sweetie, it's just me. We don't open for another hour. But what do you get in return for this spying business?"

"I think they're talking about letting me stay in Austin."

"Without joining the pack?"

"We weren't really clear on that," I said. "I think the spy work was a kind of payment."

"You should probably see if you can get clear on that, my dear. Just to protect yourself. Have you talked to Tom about it?"

"How did you know he was back?"

"He stopped in for some wolfsbane," she said.

Of course. I thought of Tom's card, which was still tucked into my purse. Between the deranged trucker, the whole food-poisoning incident, and the Heath fiasco, I'd forgotten I had it. "Maybe I should call him."

"Oh, you've exchanged numbers now?"

I groaned. "Mom."

"Sorry, sweetheart. You know I want the best for you."

"I know, but you keep forgetting I've already got a boyfriend." Or had one, anyway. "Besides, Tom is seeing Lindsey."

"They're still together, hmm?"

"I'm not sure, but I think so."

"Does she know about the two of you yet?"

I assumed she meant our shared animal instincts—not our illicit little smooch. "The werewolf issue hasn't come up in casual conversation, no."

"You're going to have to tell her sometime, you know."

"I know."

"And Heath."

I was *so* not up for this conversation right now. "Look, Mom, my battery's running down."

"No it's not."

Why did my mother have to be psychic?

"I've got to go," I repeated, hoping to get off the phone. "I'll drop by tonight."

"Be careful!" she warned me. "Keep an eye out for strange things in your loft—although the doorman might be a deterrent."

As if, I thought. Besides, I already had plenty of strange things turning up in my loft.

"Even so, I'm going to see if I can drum up some magical protection for you this morning."

Since the last spell she'd cast on me was intended to make me fall in love with a werewolf, I wasn't sure how jazzed I was about the offer of supernatural assistance. "Please, don't go to any trouble," I said quickly. "I know you must be busy, with tax time coming up. Are you getting your papers together?"

"Oh, April is still months away, Sophie!"

"Actually, it's only two months," I reminded her.

"Oops! I've got a customer. I'll see you tonight!"

I smiled as I hung up the phone. The tax topic worked every time. I just hoped my mother was sufficiently preoccupied with her dire bookkeeping to forget about the protection spell.

Despite the gazillion huge trucks driving thirty miles per hour down IH-35, I got to Southeast Airlines a half hour early.

The building was a massive tan concrete box located not far from the San Antonio airport. It was utterly unremarkable—except for its size. I had no idea it took so much room to run an airline. Heck, you could store planes in the thing.

After a quick shave and a makeup refresher, I grabbed my briefcase and headed for the door, bracing myself for a security check. I was half-expecting to be asked to take off my shoes and surrender my laptop, but after telling me to sign in and making a quick call upstairs, the smiling front-desk folks simply sent me on my way. If only Heath's doorman had been so accommodating, I thought darkly.

Something like anticipation welled up in me as the elevator doors slid closed and I pressed the button. I was about to meet with an extremely handsome CEO—one who had been sending me flirtatious e-mails at least five times a day for a week. Now that we were about to meet in person, though, I began second-guessing myself. Had my instincts been wrong? Had I read too much into his e-mails? Then again, he *had* scheduled a business lunch at Romeo's. Besides, regardless of my personal feelings—not that I had any, of course—this was a business meeting, and Mark was my client. I'd be cool and professional.

I did a quick check to make sure my blouse was tucked in and I hadn't developed a run in my hose—not that there was anything I could do about it at this point, of course. I plucked a few stray hairs from my suit jacket and had twisted around to inspect the back of my skirt for lint when the elevator door opened.

I brushed a piece of fuzz off my bottom, then stepped off the elevator—and right into Mark.

His eyes twinkled, and my face flushed as I wondered exactly how long he'd been watching me brush fuzz balls off my butt. Strike one for professional.

The CEO of Southeast Airlines was dressed in a crisp blue shirt that I was sure cost at least as much as my new Prada purse. As the elevator door closed behind me, he made a point of glancing at the back of my skirt. "Looks good to me," he said.

I decided to pretend I was deaf.

His mouth twitched into a hint of a smile, and he placed a warm hand on my arm; the man seemed to be running a perpetual fever. Despite the fact that I felt like a total idiot, I felt a little stirring at his touch—and at his slightly smoky, totally masculine aroma. "Sorry to surprise you," he said. "They told me you were on your way up. How was traffic?"

"Not too bad, once I got out of Austin," I said, trying to regain what was left of my composure. At least we were off the topic of my skirt.

"I've been looking forward to this," he said in a low voice that sent a shiver through me. "Let me just introduce you around, and then we'll go to lunch," he said, steering me down the hall. "But first, can I get you a cup of coffee?"

"Sure," I said, as he guided me down the hall to his office.

And what an office it was. The industrial carpet ended at the doorway, transitioning into smooth dark hardwoods and expensive-looking Oriental rugs. The antique desk—with claw feet—was so big it could have been used as a runway.

"Nice digs," I said, blinking.

"Thanks," he said, motioning me toward what looked like the living room annex. Which was about ten times the size of what I had—up until now, anyway—considered my rather spacious new partner office. It's good to be king, I suppose.

"Have a seat," he said, sinking into the cushions of one of the plush leather couches and patting the cushion next to him. A silver coffee set and a plate of croissants lay on the mahogany coffee table. "Tea?" he asked. "To help keep you human?"

I froze halfway to the couch. "What?"

"Remember?" he said, fixing me with those unsettling blue eyes. "At the interview? You told me it kept you human."

"Oh, yeah." He was right; at the big pitch meeting, I'd been guzzling gallons of wolfsbane tea to stave off an inadvertent transformation.

As I settled myself on the couch, I looked around at my surroundings. I had been expecting pictures of airplanes; instead, there were a bunch of what looked like original paintings from the middle ages. "Interesting artwork," I said. "I didn't know you were into medieval stuff."

"Certain subjects have a fascination for me," he said.

Particularly women in fancy headgear, I thought, my eyes drifting over the assortment on the wall. Lots of pasty-faced females in heavy cloaks, with Gothic-looking lettering around them. It wouldn't be my choice, but there's no accounting for taste.

"Cream and sugar?" Mark asked as my eyes drifted

from a crumbly-looking picture of a woman in a funky blue headdress to the handsome man across from me. Gosh. Even if medieval art wasn't my thing, it was interesting. Certainly more interesting than the pictures of airplanes covering the rest of the building's walls. Good-looking, wealthy, and cultured to boot. Toss an Armani suit in there, and it was easy to see why *Texas Monthly* had listed him as a major catch.

"Splenda, actually," I said. "And skim milk if you've got it."

"Of course," he said, filling a china cup of coffee and adding a dash of milk and some Splenda.

"Wait a minute," I said, reaching for the mug. "I'm supposed to fix *you* coffee. You're the client, remember?"

"But I want to," he said in a husky voice. "And since I'm the client, you're supposed to give me what I want, right?" he added teasingly, fixing me with those deep blue eyes.

I swallowed hard. There were limits on that, of course. Or were there?

"Now," he said, saving me from answering by handing me my cup. "Shall we go and meet the troops?"

"Sure," I said, standing up. I felt a tingle as his hand brushed my arm. Perhaps I needed to make the trek to San Antonio more often.

Two hours and about fifty brief introductions later, Mark and I were sitting on the River Walk, drinking margaritas and watching the ducks bob by on the dark water. As Mark tossed tortilla chips to them, I alternated between worrying about the hair on my legs, trying not to think lustful thoughts about my client, and resisting the urge to jump into the lake and grab the fattest duck with my teeth. Not only had I not eaten for several hours, but my tea consumption was way down, so I was feeling a little more animal than usual; it was also close enough to the full moon that my predatory instincts were in full swing.

It was typical Texas weather; yesterday's frosty cold front had been replaced by mild southerly breezes. It was almost warm, in fact. Or maybe that was just the heat emanating from the man across the table from me.

"Want to share fajitas with me?" asked my lunch companion, folding up his menu and leaning toward me.

I tore my attention from the ducks—which wasn't that hard, really, since Mark was far more intriguing than the waterfowl—and surreptitiously checked the hair growth on my legs. Not too bad, but I would need to shave soon. For some reason—maybe because I was half human—the growth on my legs was the worst. Which was fortunate, really, because the last thing I needed to deal with was hairy forearms and a full beard. "As long as we do half chicken," I said, even though what I really wanted was steak. Rare, red steak. "And you can have my sour cream," I added.

"I love a girl who will give me her sour cream," he drawled. "Although with your figure, I think you could stand the calories."

I took another sip of my margarita. Here I was, sitting on the River Walk on a Monday afternoon, drinking a frozen strawberry margarita with one of Texas's most eligible bachelors. *My client*, I reminded myself. It would have been a pretty fabulous day—if it weren't for that pesky little job I had in mind for later on. The one that involved spying on foreign werewolves. Foreign, potentially murderous werewolves.

I shook myself. *Don't think about that right now, Sophie.* Now, I was supposed to be giving my new client lots of TLC. And finding out what he needed us to do on the account. "So, about the auditing work," I said, reaching for a chip and banishing thoughts of Anita and Hubert the missing werewolf. "Where do you think we should begin?"

Mark took another sip of his fishbowl margarita. "I think we should begin by enjoying each other's company on this gorgeous February day. I mean, could you ask for better weather than this?"

He had a point. I toyed with my straw as a gaggle of pale-skinned tourists wandered by. They sounded like they were from Tennessee. Which would be a more appropriate place for Southeast Airlines's headquarters, now that I thought of it.

I looked back at Mark. "I've been meaning to ask, by the way. How come headquarters is in San Antonio?"

He looked around. "With a day like this, you have to ask?"

I laughed. "I see your point. But last time I checked, Texas was in the Southwest, not the Southeast. Is it a fabulous airport or something?"

"Actually, it's a dump," he said, grinning. "But I've got a great house in Alamo Heights, and the rent on the building's cheap."

"Aha."

"But enough about the company. Let's talk more about you."

"Me? Well," I began, "I got my degree from the University of Texas, and I've been a CPA for seven years . . ."

He stared at me. "I don't care about your resume."

I swallowed hard. "Well, what *do* you want to know?"

His mouth turned up at one side in a grin. He pointed to the ring finger of my left hand. "You're single."

I felt the color creep to my cheeks. "To the best of my knowledge, yes."

"But you have a boyfriend. I believe we met."

"Yes," I said. Then I remembered being dissed by Heath's doorman. "Well, I think so, anyway."

"You *think* you have a boyfriend?"

"Yes. Maybe. I mean, we haven't broken up or anything, so I guess so." I grabbed my drink and took another big swig. *God.* Could I sound any more like a babbling idiot? And couldn't we talk about something else? *Anything* else? Well, other than werewolves, anyway.

He cocked a dark eyebrow. "Care to elaborate?"

I took a fortifying swig of margarita. "Things are . . . well, up in the air right now."

"I see," he said, running a finger around the rim of his glass and staring at me with a look that made my insides quiver. "So you aren't officially . . . taken."

He was nothing if not direct. I closed my eyes—largely so I wouldn't stare back into Mark's—and thought about Heath. At the rate things were going, I wasn't even going to have a date on Valentine's Day. What kind of date would Mark plan for Valentine's Day?

No, no, no, Sophie.

Mark started to say something.

But I didn't hear a word of it. Because at that moment, I got a whiff of something that made every hair on my body stand up straight.

Werewolf.

Seventeen

I put down my margarita so hard half of it sloshed onto the table. "I'll be back in a minute," I said, interrupting whatever it was Mark was saying.

He looked mildly surprised. "What's wrong?"

"Nothing," I said. "I just . . ." *Werewolf*. Where? Had he—or she—spotted me? ". . . have to go to the bathroom," I blurted. "Be right back." Before he could say anything else, I pushed back my chair, hurried across the footpath, and rushed into the restaurant.

Which wasn't the best evasive action, as it turns out. Because that's where the werewolf was.

It was one I'd never seen or smelled before—a big hairy one with a ponytail, sitting alone at a corner table. A big, creepy, hairy one, who looked capable of ripping other werewolves' throats out and leaving them in pieces in the grass. I shuddered and prayed he wouldn't catch my scent.

Since he hadn't turned around, I was guessing that meant he hadn't—at least not yet.

I glanced back at the front door. I could go back outside, but our table was ten feet from the entrance; the moment Mr. Hairy Werewolf stepped out of the restaurant, he would spot me. San Antonio was supposedly "neutral" territory, but for some reason, I really wasn't up for another werewolf encounter just now—particularly with one who made my skin crawl.

After weighing my limited options, I conjured up every shield-y thought I could and barreled toward the ladies' room, where I planned to stay until the coast was clear. It wasn't ideal, and I wasn't sure how I was going to explain to Mark that my urgent call of nature required thirty minutes or more to attend to—but a closed door between Mr. Hairy Werewolf and me would help mask my scent. I hoped.

And if nothing else, I doubted he'd follow me into *Las Senoritas'* room.

I scurried through the swinging door and took a deep breath.

Which was unfortunate, since the little room smelled like gastrointestinal issues, Lysol . . . and werewolf.

Again.

Shit.

I backed toward the door, hoping my mystical shielding abilities were working. Then I took another sniff and stopped mid-skulk.

The werewolf in here already knew about me. Because it was one of the Texarkana Trio.

A moment later, she popped out of the nearest stall, looking like a refugee from Disneyland's Little Mexico.

"Miss Garou!" she said, shimmery brown eyes open wide. Even her hair had been done up in a little bun, with dark tendrils escaping around her face and accenting her dark, glowing eyes. The peasant skirt and blouse might seem hokey on someone else, but on Lourdes, it was a good look. "What are you doing here?"

"Lourdes!" I hissed, glancing under the next stall to make sure we were alone. At the rate my day was going, I wouldn't be surprised if a werewolf popped out of the ceiling next. "What are *you* doing here?"

Lourdes jutted her chin at her outfit. "Working. At

least until twenty minutes ago. Now I'm hiding from
that big hairy guy out there. There's something really
creepy about him."

"I thought so, too."

"I hate to bail on my shift, but I don't want to go anywhere near him. It's a good thing my aunt owns the
place, or I'd probably be out of a job."

"You don't know him?"

She shook her head. "No. And so far, anyway, I don't
think he knows I'm here."

"He didn't scent you?"

"I'm not sure; I didn't get too close." She shrugged.
"Maybe he's got allergies."

Good point. Cedar pollen was high right now; if it
weren't for Claritin, I'd have a hard time even picking
up the odors in the bathroom. Which, come to think of
it, was an argument for going through allergy season
drug-free.

"Why are you in San Antonio?" Lourdes asked. Then
her face brightened. "Did you change your mind about
being our Alpha?"

"No!"

She looked a little hurt. "Oh."

"I'm here on business," I said. "Working."

"Pack business?"

"Business business," I said. And pack business, too,
but that was my business. Not hers.

"Is that tall guy with you?"

"What tall guy?" Did she mean Mark?

"You know. The cute one." She simpered. Just a little
bit, but it was definitely a simper. "From your apartment."

"You mean Tom."

"Tom," she repeated, a dreamy look on her face.

"No," I said tersely.

"Oh," she said, looking disappointed. "He was so

helpful. What a great guy. But the only thing is, I thought he said San Antonio was neutral territory. I think he got it wrong; this place is just *crawling* with *lobos*," Lourdes said.

A little shiver crept down my spine. "Really?" Lots of werewolves weren't necessarily good news for me, if I wanted to stay out of trouble. On the other hand, it could be that Hubert was one of them. Maybe all I had to do was walk around town and sniff till I found someone who smelled like Wolfgang. Provided, of course, I was able to get out of the *Senoritas'* room.

"How long has that werewolf been out there?" I asked.

"Like I said, about twenty minutes. He should have his food soon, though, so he'll probably be gone in another twenty. Unless he was meeting someone."

I groaned. It looked like we'd be here for a while. I'd have plenty of time to come up with a story to tell Mark. Although I think even with a few weeks to put it together, I still might have a hard time coming up with something plausible. I reached down and touched my leg; the bristles were already a quarter inch long. "I guess I might as well shave." I took a deep breath, preparing to sigh, and almost choked. "You guys need to work on the whole bathroom cleaning thing. It smells like a water treatment plant in here."

"I know," she said. "I keep complaining, but they keep not doing anything about it." Lourdes pulled up her poofy red skirt and examined her slender legs. "I should probably shave, too." She was right; her coffee-colored skin was heavily laced with black bristles. "Too bad my razor's in my locker."

"I've got a spare if you need it."

She dropped the hem of her skirt and looked up at me. "Really?"

"Of course." I never traveled without a spare. Then

again, I theoretically never traveled without wolfsbane tea, either. But I'd used up the rest of my purse stash in Roundtop, and wasn't about to risk another teabag from the new package. I dug out a Lady Bic and tossed it to Lourdes.

"Thanks!"

"No problem."

"The whole werewolf thing is pretty cool," Lourdes said, "but I get so tired of having to shave every two hours. I tried Nair, but . . ."

"I know," I said. I'd tried it too. Once. It had burned half of my nose hairs to a crisp and knocked out my sense of smell for a week.

"Have you tried waxing?" she asked.

"It works, but only if you switch salons a lot," I answered as I headed for the nearest stall. "Otherwise they start asking questions. It's expensive, though—and it hurts like hell. Especially when you do it twice a week."

"What about those do-it-yourself kits?"

"Trust me. Leave it to the professionals." I shuddered, remembering my first at-home waxing attempt. By the time it was over, I'd stuck myself to the shower curtain, a roll of toilet paper, and the bathroom rug. I was missing a good three layers of skin, but I still had every last one of my hairs.

Locking the stall door behind me, I peeled off my pantyhose and said, "I'm glad you and the other girls made it down here okay. Where are you staying?"

"We're all at my aunt's house for now," she answered from the neighboring stall. "Once we've saved up a little, we're going to rent an apartment."

"Any more threats from Texarkana?"

"Not that I know of."

"Good," I said, and turned my leg so that I could reach the back of my knee. It was actually kind of companionable, I realized, shaving with a buddy. It made it somehow less—I don't know. Weird? "So your aunt owns the restaurant?" I asked.

"She and a couple of my cousins. Yeah."

"Great. I'm glad things are working out for you."

"I still want to go back to Texarkana, though."

I resisted the urge to ask why. "San Antonio's pretty nice." Nicer than Texarkana, anyway.

"Unless you grew up here. Too much family."

"I know what you mean," I said, thinking of my mom. As much as I loved her, life would be easier if she didn't live five minutes away.

Despite the fact that a hairy unknown werewolf was lurking in the restaurant and both Lourdes and I were AWOL from our respective jobs, we spent a rather chummy twenty minutes together, hanging out by the sinks. Finally, when I couldn't stand waiting anymore, I headed for the door. "I've got to go back outside," I said. "I'm having lunch with a client."

"But what if he's still out there?"

"I'll just have to take my chances," I said.

As I steeled myself for a potential encounter with the big creepy werewolf, Lourdes thrust a restaurant check into my hand.

"What's this?"

"My phone number," she said. She'd scrawled it down next to her address.

"Thanks," I said, stuffing it into my purse.

She gave me a shy smile. "It was nice to see you. Give us a call next time you're in town."

"I may do that," I said. And to my surprise, I actually meant it.

A moment later, I inched out of the bathroom and crept to the end of the little hallway, then peered around the corner.

I could still smell Mr. Big and Hairy.

But he wasn't at the table anymore.

I doubled back and cracked the door of the ladies' room. "I can smell him, but I can't see him," I told Lourdes. "I think maybe he just left."

"Thanks," she said, and scuttled out of the bathroom behind me. We parted ways in the dining room—she to return to a surly-looking man glowering near the kitchen door, me to see if my client was still waiting for me. There was no sign of the creepy werewolf, thank God, and my client was still sitting at the table, in front of a now-cold platter of fajitas.

"I was about to send in a search party," he said as I slid into my chair and reclaimed my margarita. He had a fresh one lined up for me, even though by now it was half-melted, and had started a new drink of his own. "Was the nearest restroom in San Marcos or something?"

"There was a line," I lied.

"A line?" He cocked an eyebrow at me.

"And I got a phone call," I stammered. "From the office. Thought I should take it. Sorry about that."

"Well, I'm glad you made it out," he said with a look on his face that told me he wasn't entirely convinced. But he didn't pursue it any further. "Anyway, now that you're back," he added languorously, studying me in a way that made me tingle, "you can help yourself to the fajitas. And we can pick up our conversation. Where were we, again?"

I cleared my throat and adopted a businesslike tone as I helped myself to a flour tortilla. "Actually, I was about to ask you which departments you felt needed attention first," I said.

"I thought we were talking about your boyfriend," he said teasingly.

I busied myself stuffing my tortilla with strips of steak and a big green glob of guacamole. It was going to be celery for dinner, but it would be worth it; I was starving. "I think we pretty much exhausted that subject."

"I don't know about that," he said, reaching out for a tortilla of his own. "I do have one more question about him."

"What?" I asked.

"How would he feel about it if you accompanied me to the ballet this Friday night?"

I paused with my fajita halfway to my open mouth. "The ballet?"

"I've got front row seats to the show in Austin—Southeast is a big arts supporter—and it's supposed to be fabulous." He glanced up as he speared a piece of meat. "If you don't join me, I'll have to go alone. Consider it an act of mercy."

My pulse raced. "Let me check my schedule," I said.

"There's a restaurant downtown I'd like to try, too. Flemings."

Flemings. Ummm. "I don't know," I said.

"They've got great steak," he said, leaning forward. "And prime rib, too." How did he know I liked steak so much? I wondered. He grinned. "My treat."

"Isn't this backwards? Shouldn't I be taking *you* out to dinner?"

He shrugged. "I enjoy your company, and I don't know that many people in Austin. Besides, I already have the tickets."

I thought about Heath, and his little rendezvous with Miranda. His wine country getaway.

"It's a long drive back to San Antonio," I said half-heartedly.

"A friend of mine owns the Driskill," he said. "I'll get a room."

"Gosh. Isn't that kind of expensive?"

"He'll comp me," Mark said with a shrug. "He owes me a few favors."

"I don't know," I said, taking another sip of my margarita.

"Your client's offering to wine and dine you in your home city, and you're declining?"

He had a point. After all, Adele had told me to give the client what he wanted. And it wasn't like I had a hot date planned or anything. Let's see: free steak dinner and ballet with handsome eligible bachelor, or an evening with my television and a bag of microwave popcorn. "You've talked me into it," I said.

"Good," he said, reaching for his fajita again. "And I think this calls for another margarita."

"I'm fine, thanks," I said, covering my glass with one hand as he ordered a fourth—or was it a fifth?—drink for himself. And wondering if there was some way to call a cab after lunch without mortally offending my client.

Eighteen

It was almost seven-thirty, and all that was left of the sun was a faint glow in the western sky, when I slowed the M3 outside a dumpy fifties split-level. I'd gotten out of Southeast Airlines late that afternoon and spent the last three hours in a coffee shop, trying to get some work done. Unfortunately, all I could think about was my upcoming spying expedition. And the number of potential things that could go wrong.

The house I had been assigned to check out reminded me of *The Brady Bunch* house, only much smaller, and with a Mexican flair. Well, not flair, exactly. It had a crumbling stucco exterior and an orange tile roof, but other than that, it looked like a smaller version of Casa Brady. After Mike had lost his job and Carol had started consoling herself with nips of Alice's cooking wine stash, that is. It was certainly a far cry from Houston's five-star digs.

An ancient El Camino hunkered in the front yard, liberally dinged, with each door a different color and a shattered back window; overall, it looked like it was only a few miles away from the automobile graveyard.

Although the homeowners' association probably wasn't too keen on the crumbling stucco and weedy front yard—the other houses, while not candidates for *House Beautiful*, all sported fresh coats of paint and mowed lawns—the neglect was a big benefit for me. The bushes were overgrown enough that it should be easy to station myself outside a window without being seen from the street.

Not that being seen from the street was my primary concern. Avoiding detection by werewolves was much higher on the list. But I figured the evening would probably go more smoothly if it didn't involve sirens and handcuffs.

As I eased the M3 past the house, I unrolled the window and took a quick sniff. Unless my nose was terribly wrong, someone was home. And whoever it was was not entirely human.

I parked the car about a block away and tried unsuccessfully to calm my nerves, wishing I had another strawberry margarita with me. Or maybe just a bottle of tequila.

A few minutes later, I trotted up the sidewalk, attempting to look nonchalant. When I was halfway between the deteriorating house and its neighbor—a nice little brick colonial with geraniums flanking the front door—I left the sidewalk and scuttled across the yard, the high heels of my Manolos sinking into the ground.

I hurried through the dead weeds, putting most of my weight on the balls of my feet (I'd already ruined one pair of shoes this week) and headed for one of the windows on the side of the house.

A few moments later, I pressed myself against the crumbly stucco wall, heart racing. What was I doing here? Would my so-called "shielding" thing work well enough to hide me?

As I stood there, attempting to avoid being impaled by a wax leaf ligustrum and trying to calm my nerves, I picked up the thread of a voice. Two voices, in fact.

But they weren't coming from inside the house. They were coming from somewhere in the backyard.

I tiptoed around the house, thinking lots of shield-y thoughts and wondering who the heck would be sitting in a dark backyard in the middle of February, and came nose-to-nose with a wood privacy fence.

Fortunately, the less-than-stellar upkeep of the house had extended to the fence, and it didn't take long to slip through the gate, which was held up with chicken wire and a dangling nail; I discovered the latter when it snagged my jacket. Designer clothes are not meant for active werewolves, unfortunately.

A moment later, I crept into the backyard, ears pricked. It didn't take long to figure out that the voices were coming from a shed in the back corner of the yard; light spilled from its single grimy window. I sniffed before approaching it; there were at least two werewolves, I decided, neither of which I recognized. Others had been here, too, but none that I knew.

As I approached the ramshackle little building, I focused on listening, trying to ignore the sound of the breeze through the live oaks. The voices were becoming excited now, and louder—which was quite helpful. What were they talking about? I strained my ears, hoping to hear something like, "Hubert's in the front bedroom of the house, watching *Diary of a Teenage Werewolf*." Which would be just perfect; if I could knock this out tonight and report back to Houston with Hubert in tow, I might be able resume my normal life without any further werewolf intrusions.

After what felt like hours but must only have been a minute, I was outside the shed, peering through the cloudy glass. It appeared to be a cluttered shed, with two werewolves moving boxes of something around. Neither of them was Hubert—they both had black hair, not blond. But a thrill of excitement—and fear—passed through me when I realized I was close enough to make out what they were saying, and they didn't know I was there. I was just like James Bond! Well, if James Bond was a female American werewolf/auditor, that was. I pushed aside a weed and took a step closer, ready to memorize everything I heard.

There was only one problem. They were speaking Spanish.

I swore—mentally, of course—and listened for a few minutes more, shivering in the cold breeze and hoping they might at some point transition to a language I could understand. Or at least say something slowly enough that I might be able to figure it out.

If I were James Bond, of course, I'd understand every word they said and be able to converse in Spanish like a native—either that, or they'd switch conveniently to English. Of course, I wasn't, and of course, they didn't.

After twenty minutes of shivering, watching two rather husky werewolves sort through things in boxes, and listening to a spirited conversation that I had no hope of comprehending, I gave up. Why had I taken French instead of Spanish in college? And how was I supposed to spy on these guys if I couldn't understand what they were talking about?

Maybe I'd just have to go and tell Wolfgang it was tax advice or nothing. He'd been right about my spying ability; as far as the werewolves in the shed were concerned, I blended right in with the shrubbery. But unless there was an incredible crash Berlitz class available, my amazing ability to conduct clandestine observations wasn't worth squat.

I took a step away from the shed, feeling defeated.

And that's when things went horribly wrong.

It all started when my brand new Manolo Blahnik pump caught on a wayward root, snapping the heel clean off and sending me barreling—with a rather unlady-like grunt—into a prickly holly bush.

Which kind of blew the whole "Super Spy Sophie"

thing, unfortunately, because a moment later, a howl went up inside the shed.

I scrambled to my feet, cursing silently. Not that it mattered anymore; I might as well have used a bullhorn.

Although my instinctive reaction was to search for my heel—they were expensive shoes, and it was painful just to think of giving them up—the clamor of approaching voices quickly convinced me that it might be time to retire this particular pair.

I abandoned the search and rescue operation, squeezed through the fence, and raced across the yard, plunging my right hand into my purse and praying it would come up with the car keys.

Fast.

Because two big werewolves (in human form, thankfully) were loping across the grass after me.

They yelled something incomprehensible as I put on an extra burst of speed—which, in case you were wondering, can be challenging when you're only wearing one-and-a-half shoes. The urge to change was overwhelming, but I fought it; I needed my opposable thumbs to get into the car. My hand was jammed into my purse, searching for the keys—lipstick, tampons, aspirin, tissues, more tissues, another lipstick—everything, in short, but keys. I risked a backward glance. I was closing the distance to the car, but the werewolves hadn't bothered to stay human and were gaining on me. They were only twenty feet away now, and unless I could find a way to start the car with a Bic razor and a tampon, I was screwed.

As I ran on my toes and dug in my purse, searching in vain for my stupid keys, I realized it was time to abandon the shoes. They were holding me up.

I tried not to think too much about them—the supple leather, the gorgeous wooden heels (well, heel, anyway), the cute pointy toes—as first one, then the other, thudded to the pavement behind me. Maybe it was because of my supreme sacrifice, but at the exact instant my second gorgeous, heel-less pump hit the ground, I found my keys.

The next few seconds went by in a blur. I punched the unlock button on my key chain. My M3 blinked welcomingly, a beacon in the night. And from somewhere behind me came a low, menacing growl.

I risked another backward glance. My poor, abused shoe was still working for me. It had tripped one of the werewolves.

Which just goes to show that quality shoes are *always* a good investment.

In record time, I wrenched the door open, jammed the key into the ignition, and hit the accelerator. My trusty BMW peeled out seconds later, leaving two rather chunky black wolves stranded on the street behind me, one of them favoring his right paw. The blood thundered in my ears as I stepped on the gas and drove blindly ahead.

I was almost halfway to Austin before I realized I hadn't taken off the emergency brake.

When the alarm clock buzzed the next morning, I was right in the middle of a nice, comfortable dream involving a five-star hotel, eggs benedict, and Heath. It took me a few moments to realize that the eggs benedict were a figment of my imagination, and that a harsh, room-service-less reality was lying in wait for me like a recurrent nightmare.

My stomach twisted at the thought of the man I hoped I could still call my boyfriend. Odds were good that there weren't any five-star hotels in our immediate future. Unfortunately, I couldn't say the same for Tom and Lindsey. Or Heath and Miranda. And then there was the whole Houston pack problem, including but not limited to last night's werewolf spying fiasco. Not to mention the loss of yet another pair of shoes.

I gave the alarm clock a hefty whack and stumbled to the bathroom, where I hit the lights and was immediately reminded of my other problem.

I'd forgotten to drop by Sit a Spell and pick up my tea last night. Which meant the face that greeted me in the mirror bore more than a passing resemblance to Wolfman Jack.

I decided on a pants suit—for leg coverage—and after an extended session with my safety razor and judicious application of pancake makeup, I hit the front door.

As I closed it behind me, my hand hit something sticky.

Blood.

I jerked my hand away; there, on my stained oak door, was a track of blood; the coppery smell stung my nostrils, and unless I was mistaken, there was a definite aroma of werewolf about it. But what was worse was that above it, embedded into the door, was a knife.

The hairs prickled on my neck, and the urge to change swept through me. I jerked my head around, on high alert, but whoever had left it here was gone. It wasn't graveyard dirt or a chicken head, but it sure wasn't what I wanted to find on my front doorstep first thing in the morning. Did this have something to do with my crappy surveillance session last night? Was it some kind of warning? Or was it connected to the hex my mother was convinced someone was putting on the shop?

I worked the blade out and pushed back through the door, feeling very, very, unsettled. First I wrapped the knife—which was made of some kind of shiny metallic stone—in a paper towel and tucked it into my purse to show my mother. Then I did a quick rubdown to clean the blood off my door, grabbed my coffee cup, and hurried down to my car. If I drove fast enough, I could swing by Sit A Spell, pick up my tea, ask my mother about the knife, and still make it in to work on time.

Of course, I'd forgotten about the City of Austin's obsession with scheduling construction on as many north-south roads as possible—simultaneously. Which meant I had a lot of time sitting in traffic to think about the knife in my purse and my growing sideburns. And my problem vis-à-vis the Houston pack.

I was hoping my mother could help me figure out the knife, but as far as the werewolves were concerned, I knew I was on my own. As traffic crawled down South Congress, I drummed my fingers on the steering wheel and considered my options. I could always tell the Houston pack that the spying thing wasn't working out and re-offer my tax assistance services. But I had a feeling that would result in Anita writing me a one-way ticket out of Austin. Either that or putting a contract out on me.

Was there a way to get around the language barrier? I could try a tape recorder, but I wasn't sure it would be able to pick up voices well enough to hear later. It was incredibly frustrating that I couldn't just take Lourdes with me to translate.

As the M3 crawled past a taxidermy studio ("WE MOUNT DEAD ANIMALS!"), I stared at a poorly rendered montage of three squat hunters in camouflage, stalking a buck with an improbable set of antlers.

And that's when I got an idea.

Sit A Spell was closed when I got there, but my mother was at the door waiting for me.

"Sophie!" she said, enfolding me in a big, patchouli-scented hug. Today she wore a gauzy pink sari; as always, a brace of bangles clanked on her arms as she moved. "How are you?" she asked, her dark brown eyes searching my face.

"Fine," I said.

"Looks like you've got a bit of stubble, dear." As I raised my hand to check my cheek, she said, "Let me get you that tea you asked for. Did you bring the other back?"

"It's right here," I said, handing her the bag. "I wouldn't try to sell it, though. It tastes like grass, and it made me really sick."

"Strange," she said, opening the bag and sniffing it. "It *does* smell like a freshly mown lawn. But I don't think it's grass. And it doesn't look like the tea I usually send you." As she took a spoonful and spread it on her worktable, inspecting the leafy substance, she said, "How did that invisibility spell work out?"

I thought of my hasty exit from Casa Brady the night before—and the little present on my door this morning—and said, "Not too well, actually." I pulled the wrapped knife out of my purse. "I found this in my door this morning, with a lot of blood."

My mother took it from me and frowned. "Bad vibrations," she said. "Whoever left this meant you ill."

"I kind of gathered that."

She gingerly removed the paper towel and stared down at the knife. "Obsidian."

"What?"

"It's made of obsidian. The Aztecs used obsidian knives when they . . ."

"When they what?"

"Made sacrifices," she said, and I shivered.

"Do you think it's related to what's been going on at the shop?"

She shook her head. "We haven't had any blood-stained obsidian knives left around, if that's what you're asking. I'm going to hold on to this," she said, wrapping it up and tucking it into a drawer, touching it with only her fingertips. "The less contact you have with it, the better."

No kidding, I thought.

"Are you sure you don't want to stay with me? Just for a bit?"

"Aren't you having hex problems, too?"

"Good point," she said. "Maybe we should both check into a hotel." Then she sighed. "Let's take a look at this tea."

As I watched, my mother picked up a bit of a leaf with tweezers. "This isn't grass, Sophie. It's too fleshy—almost leathery."

"What is it, then?"

She took the little piece of leaf and raised it to her lips. "Oh, Sophie," she said. "It's a good thing you didn't drink more."

"Why?"

"Because this is mistletoe." When I raised a questioning eyebrow—I wasn't quite as up on the herbs and spices as my mother was—she replaced the leaf on the board and said, "It's deadly."

"Really?" I'd always thought of it as a romantic kind of plant—you know, the whole stand under a sprig of it and get kissed thing. On the other hand, considering the state of my love life, having a poisonous plant represent romance might be spot on. Still, that didn't mean I wanted to drink it. "How the heck did mistletoe end up in my tea? And if it's poisonous, why do you carry it?"

"Wolfsbane's poisonous, too," she reminded me. "But the druids considered it a sacred plant. Some people hang it to ward off evil. Or to invite . . . amorous intentions."

"So you *do* carry it. How did it get mixed in with the tea?"

"Sophie," she said. "I haven't had a shipment of

mistletoe in over a year." Something about her tone of voice sent a chill up my spine. My mom reached over the counter and took my hand in hers. "Somebody doctored your tea, sweetheart. And whoever it was knows what they're doing."

"What do you mean?"

"Mistletoe isn't just poisonous. It's got a specific use."

"I know. You hang it up to ward off evil."

"But that's not the only application." She squeezed my hand and said quietly, "Mistletoe has been used for centuries to kill werewolves."

Nineteen

Well, crap.

I stared at the green stuff on the board, and my mind turned over what my mother had just told me. "You mean . . ."

"I mean that it's highly likely that someone who knows what you are wants you . . . well, out of the picture."

A shiver passed through me as I let this piece of information sink in. As if the bloody knife in my door wasn't bad enough. Who had managed to poison my tea?

"Did anyone here handle the bag before you gave it to me?" I asked.

She shook her head. "Just me. And I was by myself that night." She bustled over to her canister of wolfsbane, opened it, and took a sniff. "This is pure." As she screwed the lid back on, she asked, "Where did you keep the bag?"

"At my loft," I said. "Then I took it with me to Roundtop."

"So it was somebody at one of those two places, probably."

But who? The only ones who knew I was a werewolf were werewolves themselves. Tom had been in my apartment, along with Teena and the Texarkana werewolves, and then there was the Houston pack—although since they had me doing spy work, it seemed unlikely. Had Tom or Teena tried to poison me? It didn't seem likely—Tom had saved me once or twice already, and if the Texarkana girls didn't know about wolfsbane, what were the odds they'd know about mistletoe? Even *I* didn't know about mistletoe.

But I was betting Elena and the pleather boys did. And there had been another werewolf in my loft, too. The magically vanishing one.

"Sophie?" my mother asked.

My mother's voice jerked me back to the here and now. And speaking of the here and now, I'd better get cracking if I was going to get to work on time. Or at least within an hour of on time. The rest of my life might be a mess, but I wanted to at least keep my reputation at work. Still, before I left, I definitely needed an infusion of wolfsbane.

"Could you whip up another quick batch of tea for me? And do you have any hot water?" I asked.

"A little," she said. "I'll get you a fresh bag and fix you a quick travel mug."

"That would be great," I said.

"And I'll cast another protection spell, too," she said.

"Oh, no need to go to all that trouble," I said, although to be honest, I wasn't sure I believed myself.

"Honey, you're going to need all the help you can get right now," my mother said, filling a travel mug and handing it to me.

She was probably right. But I wasn't sure the kind of help she was offering was going to do me any good.

By the time I got to the office, I could feel the wolfsbane kicking in already; the sideburn growth had slowed down significantly. Even so, I took the time to brew up a second cup before closing my office door and pulling the restaurant receipt with Lourdes's number on it out of my purse.

I took another sip of my tea and picked up the phone. I might not be able to salvage my love life this morning, but perhaps I could make a little bit of headway in earning my green card—so to speak—from the Houston pack.

I'd just dialed the number when there was a knock at my office door, and Tom walked in.

" 'Allo?" came a voice from the receiver.

"Sorry," I mumbled. "Wrong number." And hung up. With Tom ten feet away, I wouldn't have been very coherent anyway.

"Sophie," Tom said in his low, sexy, rumbly voice.

I took a deep, werewolf-scented breath, with the result being that I felt like an electrical charge had passed through me. "Tom. What are you doing here?"

He closed the door behind him, and I couldn't help notice that his faded jeans fit just perfectly. "Thought I'd stop by and see how your meeting went," he said, turning around and giving me the benefit of his shimmery golden eyes.

"It was two days ago," I said.

"I'm sorry for the delay. You weren't here yesterday."

"You stopped by?"

He nodded. "I would have called," he said, "but I didn't have your direct line."

"Oh." That's right. I had his card, but I hadn't given him mine. "Well, it wasn't awful, but it wasn't great, either."

"That's encouraging," he said, pointing to my visitor's chair. "May I?"

"Of course." Now he was closer. Just five feet away.

"What did they want from you?" he asked in a soft voice.

"How did you know they wanted something?" I said,

struggling not to be distracted by his presence. His gold hair gleamed in the light, and his smell—if someone figured out how to bottle it they would make millions—made me want to pant. His strong chin, with just a hint of golden stubble, the way his eyes probed me, as if they could see through me . . . or at least through my blouse . . .

"They always want something," he said grimly.

I shook myself a little, trying to dispel my lustful thoughts. *This is important, Sophie.* "I have to spy on a house in San Antonio," I said, perhaps a bit breathily.

"Why?"

"They're missing someone. A guy named Hubert."

His eyes flickered a little, and he nodded. "Yes. They have been concerned about him for some time now."

"You know about Hubert?"

"I know Hubert, yes. And I know about his disappearance. He was their specialist on the Northern Mexican packs." He stared at me, and a quiver ran through me. "So when Wolfgang and Anita realized you have a special ability, they asked you to use your shielding talent to find Hubert."

"Pretty much. But there's a problem."

"Other than the fact that it's a very dangerous proposition?"

I swallowed hard. "Yeah. There is that. But the other problem is, that I don't speak Spanish."

"Why is this a problem?"

"Because I dropped by the address they gave me—the one in San Antonio—yesterday. And everything the werewolves there said was in Spanish."

His gold eyes sparked a little bit. "Did they know you were there?"

"Not at first, no. But . . ."

He leaned forward in his chair, and I felt my breath

catch. *If I did kiss him, what would be the harm?* I thought. We were both consenting werewolves. . . .

"But what?" he asked, breaking up my romantic reverie.

"I kind of . . . well, I tripped."

He drew a breath in through his sharp teeth. "You tripped. And then what happened?"

My lustful thoughts were dampened a bit by embarrassment. "Well, I ran to my car, but I lost my shoes."

"They discovered you were there. And you left your shoes behind."

When I nodded, he winced.

"What's wrong?" I asked, not sure I really wanted to know.

"If you left your shoes," he said softly, "you left your scent."

"Oh." I drew a sharp breath in. "Somebody left a knife stuck in my door last night. Do you think they tracked me back?"

He raised an eyebrow. "What kind of knife?"

"It was obsidian, my mom said."

A flash of something—like fear, almost—crossed his face. "Anything else?"

"Blood. There was blood."

"Sophie," he said, closing his eyes for a moment. "That is a very, very bad sign."

A finger of ice crept down my back. "What does it mean?"

"It's a warning. I know you want to stay in Austin, and remain . . . unaffiliated. But this surveillance is not the right assignment for you."

"I totally agree with you. I tried to offer them free tax work. . . ."

"I'm guessing they didn't jump on your proposal," he said dryly.

"Nope. How did they make all their money, anyway? They've got a pretty posh place."

"Cattle rustling," he said.

"Cattle rustling? You've got to be joking."

"They made a lot of money back in the 1900s and invested it well. Werewolves have rather longer time horizons when it comes to the stock market."

"Do they all live in that compound? It doesn't seem big enough—and I didn't smell that many werewolves."

He shook his head. "They have several locations in the Houston area, including a few ranches."

"I think I may have seen one near Roundtop. I know I heard one; and then on the way home, I saw the gate to the . . . enclosure. Ranch. Whatever you call it."

"Den, actually. You may be right," he said, shrugging a little bit. I tried not to watch the play of muscles under his T-shirt. "I don't know the locations of all of their dens."

As I stared helplessly at Tom's broad chest, I put all of this together. So they made their money cattle rustling. And their leader was—based on the name and the accent—originally from Europe. "How long has Wolfgang been here?" I asked.

"He came over with the German settlers."

"You mean like in the 1800s?"

Tom nodded. "The packs were getting pretty crowded, back in the old country. Which was part of the reason for the breeding regulations."

"So exactly how long do werewolves live?" I asked, thinking of the portraits in the Houston pack's compound.

His gaze was level. "A very long time."

"Like, more than five hundred years?"

He nodded.

"How old are you?" I asked tentatively.

"Older than you," he said.

"Could you be a bit more specific?"

"What do I do if you don't like older men?" he said, grinning.

I pretended to ignore his comment, even though it sent my pulse rate up a few ticks. "What about—well, half-breeds?"

"What about them?" he asked in a playful tone of voice.

"I'm talking longevity. Are you saying that I could live to be several hundred years old?"

"It varies," he said. "But yes. You will probably have centuries ahead of you." Then his face got serious again. "Presuming you don't manage to kill yourself in San Antonio."

"And aging?"

"Very slow," he said.

I felt a thrill of excitement—I was semi-immortal, or at least had the potential to be extremely well-preserved. Which was good news for my skin care budget. But might cause some trouble with Heath as time went on; after all, there was only so long I could claim plastic surgery. Speaking of plastic surgery, I realized Tom might be able to fill me in on Scarface. "What about Anita?" I asked Tom. "How long has she been here?"

I thought I saw a shadow flit over his face. "She came more recently. From one of the Mexican packs."

"The *Norteños.*"

He nodded.

"I thought the packs didn't mix?"

"It's a long story," he said. "With a lot of history. But that doesn't concern us right now. I'm much more worried about keeping you alive."

"Thanks for your concern," I said. Despite Tom's aphrodisiac effect on me, the prospect of my potentially imminent death put a damper on my thoughts. "I'm not exactly thrilled with the situation, either. But what am I going to do? I don't want to leave my life behind. Besides, if most of the country already belongs to packs, I'll run into the same problem wherever I go."

"True. But there are neutral zones."

"Like San Antonio? I've got news for you. I was there the other day, and it's not exactly werewolf-free." I thought of the creepy werewolf I'd seen at the restaurant. "It may be neutral, but I'm not sure how safe it is."

"There has been a lot of disruption along the border lately. I'll talk with Wolfgang," he said. "Convince him that this assignment is too dangerous. See if I can bring you into the pack at a somewhat higher level. I have some other contacts, too," he said vaguely.

"Wolfgang might be willing to cut me some slack, but I doubt Anita is going to go for it."

"Before you go back to San Antonio, let me see what I can do," he said. "I'm serious. The knife was a serious threat. You are in mortal danger right now."

I swallowed hard. I knew that already, of course, but somehow hearing it from Tom made it that much more real. Still, as much as I appreciated his willingness to go to bat for me, I had a hunch my negotiating position would improve if I could manage to get the Houston pack a little bit of information on my own.

"I will call Wolfgang today," he said, fixing me with those shimmery gold eyes. "Please. Do not return to San Antonio. If you can leave Austin for a while, it would be good."

"Thank you," I said. Unfortunately, there was no way on God's green earth Anita was going to grant me clemency that easily, and I knew it. But I didn't want Tom to know I was going to continue with my plan. So I decided to change the subject. "By the way, I've been meaning to ask. What are you doing in town?"

He shrugged. "I like it here."

"So you're here on vacation?"

"Sort of."

"No you're not." I narrowed my eyes at him. "You're here on a job."

He shrugged again, doing interesting things to his rather snug-fitting T-shirt. "Perhaps."

"Another werewolf extermination contract? Not me, I hope?"

He sighed. "I am on assignment, yes. But you are not my assignment. And even if you were, it looks like all I'd have to do would be to sit back and watch you take care of my job for me." He glanced at his watch. "I didn't realize what time it is; I'm going to be late for Lindsey." He looked up at me, and something about the look in his eyes made my stomach catch a bit. "Please stay in Austin, and let me try to handle it."

I swallowed hard and tried to sound nonchalant. "You're seeing Lindsey again?"

"Yes," he said, rising to his feet in one smooth movement. Even when he was in human form, I could see the sleek predator in him. I stood up and rounded the desk, feeling the temperature increase with each step I took. When I was a few feet away, he reached out to touch my chin; the heat of him radiated down my body. "I'm worried about you," he said quietly.

I crossed my arms and tried to banish the welling emotion—lust? Or something more?—inside me. I could smell his scent—masculine, and spicy, and deeply erotic—as he said, "Find a way to leave town if you can."

"But I can't," I protested.

He sighed. "Then I'll speak with Wolfgang. Hopefully tonight."

"Let me give you my number," I said, reaching back to pluck a business card from the holder on my desk. Our fingers grazed each other as I handed him the card, and I took a deep breath at the tiny shock that went through me. "Does Lindsey know?" I asked.

"Know what?" he said, cocking a blond eyebrow.

"You know," I said, trying to ignore the fantasies that had started reeling through my mind. All of which, unfortunately, involved sexy werewolves. A very specific sexy werewolf, in fact.

"You mean, does she know what I am?" he asked, with a wry grin that exposed his sharp teeth and made my heart do strange things in my chest. He was a werewolf, all right. God, was he ever. "What do *you* think?"

"That's what I figured." I bit my lip. "Are you planning on telling her?"

"I don't know," he said, taking a deep breath. His body tensed suddenly. "You smell . . . different." He sniffed again, and his pupils dilated. "Smoky."

"Maybe it's the new tea," I said. "Someone poisoned my last batch with mistletoe."

"Mistletoe? That's serious business." The wry grin was gone; his mouth was a thin line. "Why didn't you tell me?"

"I guess I forgot."

His gold eyes hardened.

"You think it's the Houston pack?" I asked.

"I don't know," he said. "But I plan to find out." He took another deep breath, trying to catch my new smoky scent, presumably, and even though he was only a few feet away, I could feel the heat rolling off of him in waves.

He closed his eyes and said, "The smoky smell . . . it is familiar, somehow. I wish I could place it." He stepped closer to sniff again. So close I could kiss him. Wanted to kiss him. Was dying to kiss him.

But that was a very bad idea, particularly with Lindsey just down the hall.

Which he must have thought of, too, because he said,

in a strangely formal voice, "It's good seeing you again, Sophie." Then he looked down on me in a way that was tender, almost, and held up the card I'd given him. "I'll call you as soon as I've spoken with Wolfgang," he continued in a low voice that sent a tendril of lust snaking through me.

"Okay," I said again, perhaps just a touch breathily.

And a moment later, he was gone, leaving only a trace of his intoxicating scent behind.

I retreated to my desk, turning over all this new information in my head. Tom was incredibly sexy—not that that was new information, but it certainly was something I had a hard time not thinking about. After a brief fantasy involving a five-star hotel and hot oil massage, I forced myself to put my misplaced lust aside and focus on the situation.

Tom thought my spying on the San Antonio werewolves was dangerous, and that the knife might be a death threat. He was going to see if he could intercede on my behalf. And I was evidently, if not semi-immortal, at least extremely long-lived.

Unless, of course, I managed to get myself killed.

Twenty

When I'd recovered from Tom's surprise visit, I picked up the phone again and called Lourdes. Tom might not think my plan was too hot, but I thought it was clever enough to deserve a shot. If I could win myself a Stay-in-Austin-Free Card with a few hours of surveillance, it was well worth it.

As long as I didn't end up dead, that was. I pushed that thought aside and focused on dialing.

The woman who answered the phone was not exactly proficient in English. I must have managed to communicate that I was looking for Lourdes, though, because a moment later she was on the line.

"Miss Garou!"

"Sophie," I said.

"Miss Sophie. I'm so glad you called. Are you in San Antonio again?"

"Not at the moment. But I wanted to ask: do you speak Spanish?"

"Of course. Why?"

I took a deep breath and said, "I may be in need of your translation services."

"What did you have in mind?"

When I told her my plan, she was quiet for a moment. I started to get nervous. Particularly when she said, "Do you really think it will work?"

"I have no idea. But I only want you to do this if you're comfortable," I added. "It could be dangerous."

"So's waiting tables," she replied. "Particularly if Mr. Creepy Werewolf keeps dropping in for tamales. At least this will be exciting. "

That's one word for it, I thought.

"I'll see you tonight, then? Seven o'clock?"

"Great. Meet you out front," she said.

I hung up the phone a moment later, wondering if I was a total idiot for putting both of us in jeopardy.

On the other hand, I told myself, nothing ventured, nothing gained.

I just hoped I was right.

At 6:45 that evening, I pulled up outside Cabela's, a gigantic hunting store just south of Austin, with serious misgivings. What if my plan didn't work, and Lourdes and I ended up sporting obsidian knives? Or steeping in big vats of mistletoe tea? Maybe, I thought, I should bag the whole idea and just see if Tom could work something out with Wolfgang.

The problem was, from what I'd seen in Houston, there was no way Anita was going to let that happen. In any case, I told myself, it might not be as dangerous as Tom was making out. I'd gotten away clean last time, and Lourdes looked pretty light on her feet. If worse came to worst, we could just run for the car and hope for the best.

By 7:05, I still hadn't seen hide nor hair of Lourdes, and I was starting to get jittery. As I scanned the parking lot for the fifteenth time I heard a bright voice behind me. "Miss Sophie!"

I turned to face Lourdes, who had exchanged her frilly Small World Mexico dress for tight jeans and a midriff-baring top. "I'm glad you made it," I said.

"Me too," she said. "Teena and Brissa said hi. They

wanted to come too, but I told them you just needed the translation thing, and that too many of us would probably be risky."

"How are they doing?"

"Teena's still mooning around over Brett, but she and Brissa both got jobs. We're all staying at my aunt's, but we're going to start looking for an apartment."

"Seen a lot of werewolves?" I asked.

"Yeah," she said. "And they're all from Mexico, based on their accents." Drat. That meant no Hubert—unless he was from south of the border and Wolfgang hadn't told me. "I thought Mr. Fenris said San Antonio was neutral, but it doesn't look like it."

What was going on? I wondered. Was the San Antonio pack trying to move north? Was that part of the reason Houston wanted me to find out what was going on?

"Ready?" Lourdes asked, reminding me that if I was going to find anything out, we'd have to figure out a way to spy unobserved.

"Let's go," I said, and we walked through the big sliding glass doors into hunter's mecca.

As we walked past a gigantic display bristling with rifles and guns, Lourdes looked at me and murmured, "Is the thing about silver bullets true?"

"I think so," I said.

"Do they sell them here?"

I stared at the boxes and boxes of live ammunition and said, "I hope not. But since they've got everything else, it wouldn't surprise me."

We passed the gun section and came face-to-face with a stuffed wolf that looked entirely real, except for the glass eyes. I stopped to stare at it, feeling a pang of empathy, and realized it was part of a much larger montage; a kind of *Wild Kingdom* under glass. The exhibit—labeled "Conservation Mountain"—featured a number of other large animals, too, none of which were likely to coexist in nature. There was a moose (that's right, a moose, in Buda, Texas) and farther down the fake hill was a whole pack—if pack's the word I want—of deer. All of which had evidently merited preservation rather than conservation.

"This place is *espeluznante*, isn't it?"

"*Espeluznante?*"

"I think the word in English is strange. Creepy."

I nodded. "I think that's definitely the word." I scanned the area, passing over the racks of guns, searching for what we'd come here for. I'd called earlier about it, and evidently they had an entire section of products to choose from. "So, the guns and the trophies are here. Where's the gear?"

"I think it's over there," she said, pointing at an area rife with olive drab camouflage fabric. "Scent control."

"That's what we're looking for," I said. Unfortunately, I wouldn't be caught dead in any of it.

At least I hoped not.

As we wandered through a sea of green and brown overalls and jackets, Lourdes turned to me. "How do we do this?" she asked.

"What size are you?" I asked, flipping through the racks.

"Zero," she said, "although sometimes those are a little big on me."

I resisted the urge to say something crass—I mean, really. Size zero?—and handed her an extra-small jumpsuit-looking thing just as a pimply young man with a shock of red hair wandered up. "Can I help you ladies?"

"Actually, yes," I said, pleased that we'd have some expert advice. "We're going to go hunting this weekend, and we're looking for something to wear that will kind of mask our scents."

"Really?" His eyes roamed over us, and he looked a

bit dubious. I guess most of his clientele didn't come to the store clad in Dolce and Gabbana suits. Or midriff-baring T-shirts, either, I thought, glancing at Lourdes. "What are you going to hunt?" he asked.

Hmm. Hadn't thought about that one. I glanced at the animal montage, and the first thing that looked back at me was a spotted fawn. "Deer," I blurted.

"Better not," he said.

"Why?"

"Deer season closed last week."

Nice going, Sophie. "Well, we'll go for whatever's in season, then."

The clerk smirked at me. "Not much, I'm afraid. There's always quail, and turkey season's coming up. And mallards are in season."

"Great. I've always been a fan of ducks." It was true; they gave big, satisfying quacks when you snuck up on them. Which I'd only ever done to pass the time when in wolf form, of course. "We'll do mallards, then."

"But only if you're using falconry," he added unhelpfully.

"Falconry?"

"Birds of prey. No guns."

"Okay. What about quail? Can we use guns on quail?"

"Sure."

"Great. Quail it is. But the main thing is, like I said, we want clothes that are going to mask our scent."

"In February, that shouldn't be too much of a problem, ma'am. If you just wear your regular clothes and wash them in scent-free detergent—as long as you shower first—you should be just fine."

This young man was turning out to be not so helpful after all. I didn't want cheap. I wanted effective. Unfortunately, I couldn't exactly tell him that my prey was not in fact a small, brown bird, but a potentially large pack of dangerous urban werewolves. I glanced at Lourdes, then lowered my voice. "I tend to have a little problem with excess perspiration," I said to the hunting clerk. "I don't want to scare off the ducks."

"Quail," he said shortly, then jerked a thumb toward my companion. "Then why is *she* trying on the clothes?"

"Look," I said in my bitchiest voice. What, did you need to ace an asshole test to get a job here? "I told you what I need. Now, can you help us, or not?"

"Just trying to get enough information to help you, that's all," he said, raising his hands in a patronizing gesture that made me want to bite him.

"Okay," I said. "So now you have all the information you need. We're going hunting, and we need to have the smell issue taken care of. Will this thing work?" I said, pointing at something like an oversized jumpsuit.

"It should, but you'll want to shower and dust yourself with baking soda first."

Lourdes blinked at him. "Seriously?"

He nodded, looking pleased to be the keeper of this bizarre information. "Yup."

"So we shower and roll around in baking soda. Any other tips?" I asked.

"Well, you'll want rubber boots and gloves, of course."

"Rubber boots?" I had never in my life owned a pair of rubber boots. "Like waders? What colors do they come in?"

"You'll probably want something to match your suit," he said, smirking just a little bit.

I cringed. "Olive drab." I looked awful in olive. Just awful. Then again, since my goal was not to be seen at all, I reminded myself, I hoped it wouldn't be an issue.

He nodded. "And you might want to pick up a scent spray, just in case."

"How much is all of this going to cost?"

"A couple hundred, maybe."

A couple hundred? I could buy at least one new pair of Jimmy Choos for that. I sighed, then handed the jumpsuit to Lourdes. "Go try this on," I said. "We'll see how well it works."

Fortunately, when Lourdes disappeared, our helpful hunting clerk wandered off in search of other prey. A few minutes later, Lourdes emerged from the dressing room looking like she was ready to storm Baghdad.

"Can you smell me?" she asked.

I closed my eyes and sniffed. Nothing. "Come nearer," I said. I could hear her shuffling, but I couldn't smell a thing. Could it be that this was going to work?

"Keep coming," I said, taking deep breaths, trying to get a fix on Lourdes' scent—corn tortillas, a spiciness, kind of like jalapeños, and a warm, friendly, animal aroma.

By the time I finally caught a whiff of her, she was five feet away.

I opened my eyes and said, "Now I smell you." And then noticed that the happy hunter was back in the vicinity.

"Did you just say that you can smell her?" he asked, brown eyes wide.

"We'll take the suit," I said, trying to gloss over the whole smelling thing. "And one in my size, while you're at it." An eight, as it turned out. I was nowhere near a size zero, and never would be.

"How could you smell her? I mean, that's impossible."

I ignored the question—I mean, what was I supposed to tell him?—and gave him a tight smile. "Could you show us those boots you were talking about?"

About twenty minutes later, we traipsed out of Cabela's with two giant bags of hunting gear—including, God help me, two pairs of green rubber boots—and a credit card receipt for almost $500. Still, I thought, if the San Antonio werewolves couldn't smell us, it would be worth every penny. Provided I avoided tripping over any tree roots.

I could only hope the werewolves I'd heard the other night were still in residence.

Three hours later we were back outside Casa Brady, wearing our new gear and feeling like military Michelin women. (I'd bought my suit, just in case—after all, I'd left my shoes behind a couple of days ago, so odds were good that they were pretty familiar with my scent now. And I was only willing to trust this special shielding talent so far.) After a little bit of experimentation, we decided the baking soda dusting was overkill; after all, there would be a wall between the werewolves and us, and from what I could smell (or couldn't), the clothing was pretty darned effective.

"Just one more thing," I said as we trundled out of the car and zipped up our jackets.

Lourdes wrinkled her nose as I pulled out a black spray bottle of something called Carbon Blast. "Do you think we need it?"

"Better safe than sorry," I said. "Besides, it's better than rolling around in baking soda." I sprayed us both head to foot. When I'd emptied half the bottle, I shoved it back into my car and said, "Ready?"

"Whenever you are."

Casa Brady was dark tonight, and I worried that we'd made the trip for nothing. Still, to be on the safe side, I parked the M3 two streets away. As we waddled toward the house, I noticed a squeaky sound.

"What's that?" I asked.

"I think it's the boots," Lourdes said.

I took another two steps. She was right. "Aren't these supposed to be hunting boots?" I asked. "I mean, it's bad enough that I had to spend money on the stupid things. And now I find out they squeak?"

"Maybe if we walk on tiptoe," she suggested.

For some reason, the tiptoeing thing seemed to minimize the squeakage, and we managed to make it the two blocks to Casa Brady in relative silence. The problem was, Casa Brady seemed to be pretty silent, too; the dumpy El Camino was no longer in the driveway, and although the lights were on inside the house, the smell of werewolf was very weak.

"The car's not in the driveway," I whispered to Lourdes. "I hope that doesn't mean they're gone."

We positioned ourselves outside the window, sniffing and listening, just in case we were wrong. I could smell werewolves, but only faintly. Had they abandoned the house after my amateur surveillance attempt?

"They were in the backyard last time," I whispered, and together we crept to the fence.

They'd beefed up the fence since my last visit—a few bright new nails gleamed in the moonlight, and a padlock now graced the gate—but with the help of a nearby tree, we managed to make it over the fence.

Tonight, the shed was dark. My thoughts kept going back to the boxes the werewolves had been working on. "Let's see if we can get in," I said, but the door was locked. We peered through the window, which didn't help much, since I'd forgotten a flashlight.

"What now?" Lourdes asked as I stepped away from the window.

"I guess we see if they show up," I said, feeling defeated. Had I scared them off? Probably not, I reasoned; or else, why put in a new padlock?

We retreated behind a bush and waited for almost an hour, shifting from foot to foot in our bulky camo gear. The waning moon was high in the clear sky, making the dirty panes of the shed window look almost silvery in the cold night air.

What if they'd decided to leave town? I wondered. Had I spent $450 on ugly clothing for nothing? "I guess they're not coming back," I finally whispered to Lourdes.

She nodded grimly. "Doesn't look that way."

"I'm sorry to drag you out here. Maybe we could try another night?"

"We could. Or maybe we could just break into the shed tonight."

I stared at her. "Through the window?"

"Why not? You said yourself they're not here. And if we find something, it would save you the trip back."

"I don't know," I said. "It just seems kind of . . . well, risky."

"You're already standing outside a werewolf den in rubber boots and a scentproof jumpsuit," Lourdes reminded me.

She did have a point. I was about to agree—reluctantly—when the question of whether or not to break in was answered by the sputter of the ancient El Camino pulling into the driveway.

The car engine cut out, and as we huddled in the bushes, hearts pounding, we heard voices and caught the faint scent of three werewolves. Including Mr. Big and Hairy, the creepy guy from the restaurant on the River Walk.

Twenty-one

We crouched down even lower, and I thought every shield-y thought I could come up with. The big guy gave me the creeps; the hairs were standing up on my arms even from this distance, and a glance at Lourdes indicated that she was feeling the same way. If the happy hunter at Cabela's was wrong about the scent-proof spray, I decided, I was going to drive back to Buda and stuff my forty-dollar rubber boots down his throat. Provided, that was, I got the chance.

I heard a door open and close, and the scent of werewolves—overlaid with the aroma of tequila and beer—faded. Should we creep up to the house and eavesdrop? Or would they come back to the shed?

There wasn't too much time to debate it, as it turned out, because a few minutes later, a sliding door squealed slightly as it opened, and two of the werewolves stepped out of the back of the house. Lourdes and I clutched each other, praying that the guy at Cabela's knew his stuff. Fortunately, either the gear was working as advertised or the wind was in our favor, because they—it was Mr. Big and Hairy and one of his pals, each carrying a big box—walked by not ten feet away from us. I heard the jingle of keys, and then the shed door creaked open, and a second later the shed light flicked on.

Their voices were boisterous tonight, and although I

couldn't understand a word, I could hear them clearly. Lourdes was listening intently; she gave me a quick gloved thumbs-up, and I felt a surge of hope.

We stood there listening for about twenty minutes. I was massaging a cramp in my calf and imagining my triumphant return to the Houston pack—the details on Hubert's location (which I hoped Lourdes had heard by now), the surprised look on Anita's face when I divulged juicy details (which I also hoped Lourdes had picked up) about the San Antonio werewolves—when Lourdes tugged at my sleeve and pointed to the shed window.

She wanted to move closer.

Before I could answer, she had crept out of the bushes and was advancing on the little building.

I wanted to scream "Where are you going?" But I didn't; I just trailed behind her, high-stepping to avoid wayward roots.

She was at the window now—I could see the silhouette of her dark head—and I was two steps behind her. She peered in, and then waved me over.

I stepped up next to her and peeked through the corner of the glass.

The two big boxes were open on the floor; they were filled with piñatas. And as I watched, the two men—correction, werewolves—were pushing something into them.

"What is it?" I asked Lourdes.

The werewolves' heads whipped up; one of them dropped his piñata. Dora the Explorer, I think. He'd been filling up her backpack.

"Shit," I said. Which also probably wasn't a good idea.

But Lourdes didn't hear me, because she was already galloping toward the fence, boots squeaking with every step.

A split second later, I fell in behind her, just as the door of the shed slammed open behind me.

They were on us.

Despite the extra forty pounds of hunting gear, Lourdes slipped through the fence and took off like a track star, cutting across the grass and loping in the direction of the M3. I followed her as best I could, shooting a glance over my shoulder in hopes the tequila and beer would slow our pursuers down.

The werewolves were a little wobbly, but the alcohol unfortunately hadn't hampered their speed. They had transformed in a flash, and they were fast. Certainly faster than I was as a lumbering human in ugly rubber boots. Which were squeaking so much I felt like an oversized chew toy. Which is not how you want to feel when there are two werewolves on your tail.

When I turned back, Lourdes had almost made it to the car, still human, still clad in ugly camo. I fumbled in my pocket for the keys, which I'd had the foresight to put in an easily accessible place this time.

"Sophie!" Lourdes screamed, and just as my hand closed on the keys, a massive, beery-smelling paw closed on my shoulder.

"Take the car and go!" I yelled, hurling the keychain in Lourdes' general direction. She ran toward me, reaching down to swipe the keys off the sidewalk.

"I can't leave without you!" she yelled back. Then a barrel-shaped werewolf started leaping after her. Evidently she reconsidered her options, because a split second later she was sprinting for the car.

The hand on my shoulder had tightened and slammed me flat on my back on the grass, knocking the wind out of me. I looked up at the clear starry night for a moment, thinking *Where's the Big Dipper?* And then thinking how stupid it was to be searching for constellations when you were about to be mauled by a hairy werewolf.

As it turned out, I didn't have a whole lot more time for deep thought, because a moment later the Milky Way was blotted out by a big, hairy head and the stench of garlic, tequila, and Lone Star beer. My adrenaline kicked into high gear; it was the creepy werewolf.

Mr. Big and Hairy said something to me that I didn't understand. Because it was in Spanish, of course.

I yelled the first Spanish word that popped into my head, which happened to be "Burrito!" Which must have surprised the werewolf, because his grip loosened just a hair. And then something big and feathery dove down and slammed into his head.

Mr. Big and Hairy let go of me and snapped his huge jaws at the thing. Bird. *Hugin.* I took the opportunity to scrabble out from underneath him and crawl away. *Tom,* I thought wildly. As the raven dive-bombed him a second time, I got to my feet and staggered to the car, which Lourdes—blessed girl—had already started, but not driven away.

I wrenched open the door and threw myself into the passenger seat as Lourdes gunned the engine. A moment later, we tore down the quiet residential street, leaving Casa Brady and the werewolves far, far behind.

"Man, that was close," I said as soon as I had my breath back enough to speak. We were headed toward the Wal-Mart parking lot where Lourdes had left her Celica. Lourdes was still driving; neither of us had wanted to stop.

"No kidding," she said. "I thought you were toast. How did you get him off of you?"

"I didn't," I said. "Something attacked him." Hugin. But what was Tom's raven doing outside Casa Brady? Had Tom asked Hugin to keep an eye on me? Or was Tom staking out the house, too?

Speaking of Casa Brady, I was dying to find out what

Lourdes had found out. "So what did you hear?" I asked.

"They really like tequila," she said. "And they talked a lot about *lobos*. Wolves—coming over the border."

"Did they say anything about Hubert?"

She shook her head. "Not a word. I think there is some big ceremony coming up, though; they said a weird name a lot, Tezco-something. Sounded kind of . . . what do you call it? Like one of the old Aztec words."

Aztec? A shiver crept down my spine. According to my mother, the Aztecs had a thing for obsidian knives, too. Was there a connection? I sincerely hoped not.

"What kind of ceremony?" I asked, thinking of the weird scene I'd come across in the Greenbelt, with the incense and the blood. "And did they say where it's supposed to happen?"

"At some cave, I think. It sounded almost like it's a religious thing; and they kept talking about someone they just called 'She'."

Anita, maybe? I wondered. But she was with the Houston pack, not the *Norteños*.

"They said something about a jaguar, too; almost as if the jaguar and the woman were the same thing."

Interesting, to be sure, but since it got me no closer to finding Hubert, pretty much useless. "Anything else?" I asked.

"Not really," she said, shaking her head. "Wait . . . when they were talking about the ceremony thing—it's got some long name I can't remember—they started talking about someplace called Clumpers."

"Maybe that's where they're holding the ceremony," I said, getting excited. "Maybe if we can figure out where it is, we'll find Hubert."

Lourdes gave me a funny look.

"What?"

"I hate to disappoint you, but I think it's a restaurant. They thought the steaks were overdone."

"Crap."

"They said something about expecting a new shipment sometime next week, though," Lourdes said hopefully. "That could be important, couldn't it?"

"What kind of shipment?"

She pursed her lips. "I don't know."

"Maybe it was more piñatas," I said gloomily.

I sighed. So much for bargaining power.

Thirty minutes later, after parting ways with Lourdes and promising to be in touch soon, I was in a Taco Cabana, smelling the comforting aromas of rotisserie chicken, borracho beans, and tortillas. I'd just placed an order for a Burrito Ultimo (I'd skipped dinner, and ever since my run-in with Mr. Big and Hairy, burritos were all I could think about) and was ducking into the bathroom when someone touched my shoulder.

I knew who it was before I turned around; even the smell of roasting garlic from the rotisserie chickens couldn't erase the Southeast Airlines CEO's signature smoky scent.

Twenty-two

"Fancy meeting you here," Mark said in a throaty, sexy voice.

I turned to face him, cringing. Why, oh, why hadn't I changed back into my Dolce and Gabbana in the car? I looked like I was equipped for an episode of *Survivor: Backwoods Minnesota*. Mark, on the other hand, looked like he was ready for luncheon at the yacht club. Docksiders, khakis, and a blue oxford shirt that brought out the blue of his eyes. Eyes that roved up and down me while I stood there dressed in perhaps the most unflattering clothing I had ever worn. "Nice outfit," he said.

I glanced down at my bulky jumpsuit and considered pretending I had no idea who he was. Unfortunately, it was a little late for that, so I smiled feebly. "Thanks."

"I didn't realize you had such an interesting after-hours wardrobe," he said. "I learn something new every time I see you. And running into you here is such an amazing coincidence. Here I am, strolling in for a taco, and I find my favorite auditor." He touched my arm with a hot finger, and I repressed a shiver. His voice was low, teasing. "What brings you to San Antonio? I had no idea you were into hunting. Although I always suspected you had a hidden predatory side." His finger tiptoed up my camo-clad arm.

I tried to ignore his touch, which was a challenge.

Partially because even through the canvas, his fingertips made my body feel like it was set on smolder. And partially since I was struggling to come up with a reasonable cover story. "Actually, I was at . . ." *At what?* A house full of werewolves? A rifle range? A lunatic asylum? ". . . a costume party," I babbled. "For Women in Accounting. Kind of a . . . well, a Mardi Gras thing."

"I thought Mardi Gras was in March," Mark said, fingers lingering on my shoulder.

Damn. He was right. But wait . . . I'd said it was a group of accountants. "It's because of tax season," I improvised, feeling slightly more confident about my implausible cover story. "We celebrate it early." Fortunately, at that moment, the large woman behind the counter shouted "Seventy-three!" into the microphone. "Whoops! My order's up," I said, sidling away from Mark and toward the counter.

"Mind if I join you?" he asked, which under normal circumstances would have been delightful. But wolfing down a messy burrito with your star client—your very handsome and available star client—while dressed like GI Jane was not too high on my list of fantasy evenings.

Still, what was I going to say? No? "Sure," I said, grabbing my order and trundling to the nearest pink Formica booth with Mr. Eligible Bachelor in my wake.

We slid into the booth facing each other, and I was aware once again—even over the smell of rotisserie chicken and burrito—how tantalizing his aroma was, and how blue his eyes were. Caribbean, almost. My mind flashed back to that dream I'd had—the one where he had taken me in my bed—and I looked down, afraid I'd say something totally inappropriate. Something like, "Forget the burrito. Let's go back to your place."

But instead, I decided to shift the topic from my faux Mardi Gras party to his unexplained presence at a fast-food restaurant. "What are you doing here?" I asked. "I didn't peg you for a Taco Cabana kind of guy. Particularly not at eleven o'clock on a weeknight," I said, unwrapping my burrito as he watched.

"I just had a hankering for Mexican," he said, eyes twinkling.

Yeah, right. "But you haven't ordered anything," I pointed out.

"Huh," he said. "I guess I was distracted by your sexy outfit."

I rolled my eyes and bit into my burrito, surreptitiously watching him as he walked up to the counter and placed his order. He was asking for two margaritas when another familiar scent wafted over me.

It was Tom.

I almost dropped my burrito as he sauntered over to my booth. "What are you doing here?" I hissed, glancing over at Mark, who was studying the menu. Tom was dressed in faded jeans and a black leather jacket, and maybe it's just because I was primed by being next to Mark, but I could have jumped him right there in the Taco Cabana. Of course, since Mark was a mere thirty feet away—not to mention the employees and diners—I restrained myself.

As always, he smelled—and looked—like something out of one of your best fantasies. Unlike me, unfortunately. I knew I should have gone through the drive-through and waited till I got home to use the bathroom.

"That's what I was going to ask you," he said, sniffing the air. I couldn't help but admire the way his eyes caught the light—almost kaleidoscopic, in a way. Then his body tensed, and his eyes narrowed. "That smoky smell. It's here."

"Maybe it's the rotisserie chickens," I suggested, trying to figure out how to get rid of Tom before Mark, who appeared to be flirting with the young woman behind the counter, got back to the table.

Tom turned and looked at me hard. "What were you doing outside that house?" he asked. "And why did you bring Lourdes into this?"

"So it *was* Hugin who helped out with Mr. Big and Hairy," I said, grabbing a napkin and wiping a glob of guacamole off my chin. "Thanks for getting rid of him," I said. "But is there any way we could talk about this in a half an hour? I've got your number now; can I call you? I want to hear what Wolfgang said." I didn't know why, but I had a feeling that introducing Tom and Mark would be a very bad idea. And not just because I'd be tempted to jump both of them at once.

Tom ignored me and slid into the booth across from me. "It's a good thing Hugin was there, too, or you would have been . . . what do you Americans call it? Toast."

"So is Hubert your assignment, too?"

"Yes. And no," he said. But before I could ask him anything else, he raised his head again, for all the world like a bloodhound on a particularly intriguing scent. At the same moment, Mark handed the woman behind the counter a twenty and glanced back at the table. His blue eyes quickly shifted from me to Tom. There was a flicker of recognition, and he nodded politely, a strange smile on his face.

"You know him?" I asked Tom.

"There's something . . . wrong about him," he said. "How do you know him?"

Hmmm. Jealousy? I wondered. "He's my client," I said, watching as Mark grabbed two margaritas and headed toward the table. "He's CEO of Southeast Airlines," I said quickly. "That's the account that got me my partnership."

"CEO of Southeast Airlines," Tom repeated. "Your client."

"Yup."

Tom cocked a blond eyebrow. "Then what are you doing having dinner with him at eleven p.m. in a Taco Cabana in San Antonio?"

"Coincidence," I said, just as Mark arrived at the booth. I thought I heard Tom snort, but I couldn't be sure.

"Hi," Mark said, extending a hand toward Tom and smiling. "I'm Mark Sydney."

"Tom Fenris," Tom said shortly, grasping Mark's hand like a prizefighter about to enter the ring.

"Interesting last name," Mark said. "Historical significance?"

"Perhaps," Tom said in an extremely chilly tone of voice. "And yours?"

A smile played over Mark's lips. "Just a garden-variety name."

"Tom is a friend of mine who just happened to be in the neighborhood," I interjected, trying to smooth things over. "What a coincidence; I don't even live here, and I run into two people I know!"

"You live in San Antonio?" Mark asked Tom.

"No," Tom said shortly. "You?"

"Yes," Mark said. "For the last couple of years, anyway."

"And before that?" Tom asked in a steely tone of voice I'd never heard before. What was going on here?

"Here and there," Mark said, still wearing that smirky little smile. "I'm sure you understand."

"So you're just Sophie's client," Tom said, and I shot him a warning look. *Just* my client? Tom might not be Mark's biggest fan—in fact, he looked like he couldn't stand being in the same room with him—but he could at least be polite.

"Yup. Lucky me." Mark's grin widened.

"I'm glad to hear it's a strictly professional relationship," Tom said.

"Oh, it's professional, all right," Mark said, nodding at me. As I sat clutching my burrito, he said, "Sophie's professional through and through. I mean, look at what she'll wear just for the sake of networking!"

Stupid scentproof clothing.

The air was bristling with tension, and finally I couldn't take it anymore. I wasn't sure what kind of macho thing was going on here, but I wasn't going to jeopardize the Southeast Airlines account just because Tom hadn't taken a shine to my client contact. I turned and smiled at Tom, wishing yet again that I were a tad more fashionably dressed. Or at least not looking like I was AWOL from the National Guard. "Thanks again for swinging by. Can I call you later?"

Tom's eyes bored into Mark, who somehow, despite the intensity of those gold irises, didn't seem at all perturbed. "Of course," Tom said. Then he looked at me, hard. "Call me when you leave. We have more to discuss."

"Sure," I said. "Thanks for stopping by."

After one last searing look at Mark, Tom turned and strode to the door, taking his delicious werewolf scent with him.

"What was all that about?" Mark asked as the door swung shut behind Tom. Which one was more attractive? I found myself wondering. Then I stopped myself, since both men were strictly off-limits.

"I was going to ask you the same thing," I said. "It was almost like you knew each other or something."

He shrugged, his blue eyes twinkling. "I was just being friendly. How do you know Mr. Fenris?"

"He's a friend," I said, wrapping up the remains of my burrito. "Look, Mark, I'd love to stay and chat, but it's late, and I've got to get back to Austin."

"Are you sure you won't have a margarita?" he

asked, pushing a glass in my direction. "I got one, just in case. It's not Cuervo, but it's pretty tasty."

"I'd love to," I said, sliding out from the booth. "But since I'm driving back to Austin, I'll have to take a rain check."

"We're still on for Friday though, right?"

I paused, crumpling the burrito wrapper in hand. "Friday?"

"The ballet. Remember?"

"Oh. Yes. Right."

"I'll pick you up at your place at six, then."

"Sure," I said. "See you there." *It's not a date, Sophie,* I told myself. *It's just a business dinner. Right?*

Unfortunately, I wasn't quite sure.

I waited until I got onto 410 West before grabbing the phone and calling Tom. Who, despite all his urgency about talking to me, didn't pick up. I hit End and tossed the phone back into my purse, not bothering to leave a message.

Typical werewolf.

Twenty-three

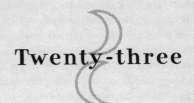

When I got into the office the next morning, Adele was at Sally's desk, showing my assistant an antique pitcher she had picked up the previous weekend at the Roundtop Dude Ranch fiasco. "Hi, Sophie," Adele said, acknowledging me briefly before turning back to her conversation with Sally. "Now, I know Martha says solids are in vogue right now," she said, "but I just thought the rosebud pattern was so dear I couldn't pass it up. Don't you?"

"You've got such great taste," Sally said in a voice so sugary it could have sent a diabetic into insulin shock.

Adele beamed at her. "That cute little shop from downtown Roundtop called today, actually; they've got a matching sugar and creamer that just came in. I think I may head out there tonight and pick it up." She brushed an imaginary spot off the handle of the teapot, which looked to me like something I'd pass up at a yard sale. "There's a great little German restaurant out there. Maybe I'll stop by for some bratwurst before heading back to Austin."

I excused myself, leaving the two of them to their discussion of overpriced antique china, and headed toward my office, taking a big swig of my skinny latte. I hadn't gotten home until after one the night before, and although I was technically conscious, it would require a whole lot of caffeine to get me to what I would term functional. Things were looking up, though; there hadn't been a single bloodstained knife embedded in my door this morning, and unless my nose was lying to me, my loft had been werewolf-free the whole night.

After checking my cell phone for messages one last time—Tom hadn't called back, of course—I decided it was probably time to get in touch with Wolfgang and Anita. And since they hadn't given me a phone number, it looked like e-mail was my only option.

I opened the Houston pack's original missive to me, hit Reply, and typed, *Dear Wolfgang and Anita.* Which was a lovely salutation. The problem was, what should come after it? I took another sip of coffee and thought about what to write next. Which shouldn't have been that hard, because there wasn't all that much.

Per your request, I finally typed, *I undertook the assignment you recommended. While I have been unable to find the individual you described, I have acquired some information that may be of interest to your organization.* The "information" was rather limited, unfortunately, and would look even sketchier on paper. It would be better to lay it out in person, I decided—or at least on the phone. Particularly if it was Wolfgang, not Anita, who called. *Please call me at your earliest convenience,* I typed, along with my cell number, and hit Send.

With that out of the way, I positioned my cell phone in a prominent spot on my desk and forced myself to focus on the Southeast Airlines account. Mark might not be interested in the nuts and bolts of the audit, but I was determined to do a bang-up job. I pulled a stack of files over and focused on the work at hand. Which actually worked, surprisingly. I was starting to get my arms around the scope of the project when Lindsey walked into my office, wearing a form-fitting cashmere dress and an irritated look.

"What's wrong?" I asked.

"I'm sure it's nothing," she said, flopping down on my visitor's chair, "but I haven't heard from Tom."

I was about to say "Me neither," but stopped myself just in time. Lindsey had no idea Tom and I were in contact—or at least had each other's numbers—and it was probably for the best. "Was he supposed to call?" I asked, glancing at my cell phone. He'd never called me back after our run-in at Taco Cabana, either. Then again, since I hadn't left him a message last night, he could still be waiting for *me* to call *him*.

"We were going to have an early lunch at Mongolian Grille," she said, biting her pillowy lower lip. "This is the first time he's been late."

"What time was he supposed to meet you?" I asked.

"Eleven-fifteen."

I glanced down at my watch. "He really is late. Over half an hour." For a second there, I was actually a little bit worried. Which was ridiculous, really. I mean, was there anyone who could take care of himself better than Tom? He was probably just letting his true werewolf colors shine through.

"What do I do?" she asked. "I called him, but he didn't pick up."

"He's got your cell number, right?"

"Of course. And I've had my phone with me the whole time."

"Then he knows how to get in touch with you. Why don't we just head down there now?" I asked. "I don't have any lunch plans, and I'm sure it's just that something came up. Heck, maybe he's already there." Although something told me he wasn't.

"Maybe you're right," she said, brightening for a moment. Then she bit her lip again. "Still. I don't like being stood up."

"I can't imagine it happens all that often," I observed.

"It doesn't," she said flatly. "And if Tom doesn't have an excellent explanation, there may not be any more opportunities."

Good, I thought, closing up my files and following her out my office door. If Tom and Lindsey broke up, that would be one less thing to worry about. And lunch with Lindsey would be a welcome diversion; I could use some normal, non-werewolf conversation for a change. Maybe she'd even have some tips for going forward with Heath.

Besides, I'd been craving Chinese food for a week.

There were a lot of people who evidently shared my yen for Chinese food, because the line at Mongolian Grille was almost out the door. Unfortunately for Lindsey, Tom didn't appear to be among them.

Which kind of confirmed my suspicions regarding the constancy of werewolves.

As I stood at the end of the line, trying not to think of all the complications in my life and salivating over the intoxicating aroma of stir-fried meat and vegetables, Lindsey crossed her arms over her cashmere-covered chest and said, "I can't believe it. He stood me up."

I took a deep, beef-scented breath and said, "Maybe he got his wires crossed. Or maybe he got here on time and thinks you stood him up."

"But he didn't call!"

"Did you call him?"

"No," she admitted, pushing out her plump lower lip. "And I'm not going to. Now, let's decide what we want to eat."

I was already working on that—definitely beef, I decided, with lots of vegetables to go with it. Green onions, some carrots, and some of that spicy sauce . . . mmmm.

I was debating whether or not to add Chinese cabbage when Lindsey said, "Look who's here."

I looked up from the menu, my heart picking up the pace a little bit. "Tom?"

"Nope. It's Miranda."

I followed Lindsey's gray eyes to the blond head at the front of the line. It was Career-Day Barbie, all right, in a trim navy suit that clung to her like Velcro.

"What's she ordering?" I asked.

Lindsey craned her neck. "Looks like all veggies. No oil."

Of course.

"At least Heath's not with her," Lindsey said.

I thought a few dark thoughts about Heath. And Miranda. "Not at the moment, anyway. She's probably on the phone with a travel agent, trying to decide between Napa and Sonoma."

"What's going on with you and Heath, anyway?"

"I don't know. He told the doorman not to let me go up to his loft the other day."

Lindsey grabbed my arm. "Get out."

"Yeah, that was pretty much the message."

"That's not what I meant."

I closed my eyes and sighed. "I did stop by his office yesterday, to try to talk things out, but it wasn't one of my best moments. And Mark asked me to go to the ballet with him."

"Wow. Does Heath know about that?"

"What do you think?"

"So you have a date with Mr. *Texas Monthly*? Not bad."

"It's not a date," I said. "It's just dinner and a ballet."

"*Just* dinner and a ballet? And somehow you forgot to tell Heath?"

I had to admit she had a point.

"Sounds a whole lot like a date," Lindsey said.

"It's not a date," I repeated.

"Whatever, Sophie. Sometimes I think that tea you drink has side effects. Like delusional thinking. Still, if things with Heath don't work out, you could do worse." Lindsey glanced up toward the front of the line and hissed, "Here she comes." As Miranda tip-tapped past us in a pair of killer slingbacks, Lindsey touched her arm. "Miranda, isn't it?"

Miranda turned and blinked at Lindsey, and I caught a strong whiff of her scent. Euphoria perfume, and—strangely—a hint of that smoky smell I associated with Mark. I sniffed again. Was it coming from Miranda? Or was someone burning something in the kitchen? As I snuffled the air, Miranda smiled at Lindsey and said, "I'm sorry. Have we met?"

Lindsey nodded. "At a party, once. But I think you know my friend. She's your colleague's girlfriend," Lindsey said, with emphasis on the last word. "I'm sure you'll remember her. Sophie Garou?"

Miranda's eyes darted to me, flickering a little—in recognition, maybe? Or because she knew that Heath and I were on less-than-fabulous terms? "Of course. Heath has told me *so* much about you."

"How's the case coming?" I asked, sniffing surreptitiously. The smoky smell *did* seem to be coming from her. It was faint, but definitely there. Weird. Did she know Mark somehow? That couldn't be it; when they'd seen each other at Romeo's, they hadn't seemed to recognize each other.

"The case? It's coming along just fine," Miranda said, shifting her plate of vegetables from dainty hand to dainty hand and smiling a perfect cupid's bow smile. "Anyway, it's nice seeing you both, but I've got to eat and run. Big client meeting this afternoon; I'm sure you understand."

"Of course," I said, resisting the urge to growl at her.

"She sure was in a hurry," Lindsey said as she trotted off to a table by the window.

"I'd like to think it's because she feels guilty for planning to whisk my boyfriend off to Napa, but I doubt that's it."

Lindsey glanced at her watch. "And Tom's still not here."

I scanned the room again, my eyes skipping over Miranda's bright blond hair. Lindsey was right; he wasn't there. "I'm sure something came up."

"It better be something major," she said. "Like traction."

At least there was some good news today, I thought, trying not to stare at Miranda, who was daintily nibbling on something that looked like celery. As I ordered my beef and vegetables—double the beef, hold the celery—I tried to look on the bright side of things. My relationship with Heath might be on the skids, but at least it looked like I no longer had to worry about explaining the whole werewolf thing to Lindsey.

And at least I'd have a yummy lunch.

An hour later, I was back in my office, regretting the choice of cabbage—I felt a bit like a helium balloon—and trying not to think about Miranda when my cell phone rang.

Heath? Tom? I grabbed it and looked at the number.

It wasn't Heath. Or Tom. It was an unfamiliar number, but I recognized the area code.

Houston.

I took a deep breath before hitting Talk. "Sophie Garou," I said briskly.

"We received your message." It was Anita, of course. Just my luck. "What information did you uncover?" she asked. Something about her voice made the hairs stand up on the back of my neck.

"Is Wolfgang there?" I asked.

"He is indisposed."

"I'd really rather talk to Wolfgang."

"You will talk to me," she said coldly. It was funny; her accent was stronger on the phone than it was in person.

"I want a guarantee that I'll be allowed to stay in Austin," I said.

"That will depend on the nature of your information," she said. "Did you find anything out about Hubert?"

"Not exactly."

"Then why are you wasting my time?" she asked.

"The Mexican packs are moving north," I said. "They're transporting werewolves over the border."

"We are already aware of that," she said.

"And they said something about a restaurant named Clumpers," I said.

"Clumpers?"

"Yes. Clumpers."

"So you want amnesty for telling us what we already know and naming a restaurant."

Put that way, it did seem a bit far-fetched. "There was something about a shipment, too," I said hurriedly.

"A shipment? What about it?"

"Um . . . Just that there would be one, actually."

"You don't know what it is? Or when it will come through?"

"Ah, next week sometime. And they're having some kind of ceremony, soon, and there may be a were-jaguar. . . ."

Anita's voice was chilly. Okay, it was a little more than chilly. It was downright polar. "Miss Garou, you have seven days to find out something useful, or your time will be up."

"But . . ."

And then she hung up on me.

I sat there staring at the phone. What was I going to do now? There was no way I was going to be able to spy on that house again—not unless I had a death wish. Was there some bit of information I had somehow missed? If only they'd said something about Hubert. Had Lourdes somehow missed something I might be able to uncover if I asked her about it again?

I scrolled through the outgoing calls and dialed Lourdes, but the woman who answered the phone told me she was at work. Then I scrolled through until I got to Tom's number. After a moment's hesitation, I hit Talk. I didn't know what I expected him to say, but I needed to talk to someone about Anita—and find out if there was some way I could get around her to Wolfgang.

My stomach clenched as the phone rang. *Please, please pick up, Tom.*

Of course he didn't.

As I put down the phone, a tendril of fear slithered through me. He might be a werewolf, but Tom had never disappeared like this before.

Was he just being a typical werewolf?

Or was there another reason he'd fallen off the face of the planet?

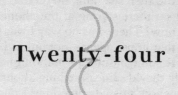

Twenty-four

Fortunately—or unfortunately—I didn't have a lot of time to worry about werewolves. Because I had enough on my plate worrying about my upcoming not-date with Mark.

At three o'clock, another missive appeared in my inbox. *Leaving now. See you at your loft at six.* XO *Mark*

P.S. Hoping for something a little slinkier than camo.

Slinkier? My mind flashed back to the hot dream I'd had the other night, and a little tingle of anticipation coursed through me.

It's not a date, Sophie.

But Adele had told me to keep him happy. And right now, I could use a little diversion. What was the harm in an evening out with a client, after all?

I made a pretense of working until about 4:30, at which point I closed up shop and headed for the elevator, shouldering my purse.

As I stood at the door, tapping my toe, a whiff of B.O. and Skoal drifted to my nostrils.

Dwayne.

"Where are you off to so early, darlin'?"

"Client meeting," I said.

"Hope he doesn't have a shotgun," he said.

"Pardon me?"

"You seem to have that effect on men," Dwayne said. "Five minutes with that trucker and he was after you hell-for-leather." He edged closer. "A little heifer like you needs a cowboy to look after her."

I bit back a snarl. "If I ever need one, I'll let you know." The elevator dinged. "Now, if you'll excuse me . . ."

"I'm going down too," he said.

We stepped onto the elevator together; I stood in the corner with my arms crossed, trying to look cold and forbidding. Either I was spectacularly unsuccessful, or it was totally lost on Dwayne, because he just kept leering at me. Of course the elevator stopped at every floor. And of course, with every person that got on, Dwayne and his polyester pants—he reserved the belt buckle for casual Fridays—edged closer to me, until I was smashed up against the wood paneling and considering clawing my way through the roof.

When we reached the lobby, I escaped as fast as I could, taking in a deep, non-Skoal-scented breath of air.

And froze.

Dwayne stopped next to me and said, "What's wrong?" With the unfortunate result being that his personal bouquet completely obliterated the elusive scent I was trying to nail down.

"Nothing," I said, taking a few brisk steps away from him and trying to find the scent again. I was sure there was a werewolf somewhere here. And it wasn't Tom. Unless I was very much mistaken, it was one of the werewolves from San Antonio.

"Are you sure you're okay?" Dwayne asked, shuffling closer yet again.

"Good-bye, Dwayne," I said, starting toward the door. With a hurt look on his doughy features, he hitched up his pants and drifted toward the Sweetish

Hill bakery in the corner of the lobby. Probably hoping to stock up on half-priced cookies.

While he glowered at me through the glass window of the bakery, I criss-crossed the lobby, trying to look casual, and struggled to track down the scent. But it was hopeless; what little had been there was gone.

After a few minutes of hopeless sniffing, I gave up and headed for the parking garage elevator. This time, thankfully, I rode down unencumbered by cowboys, and ten minutes later I was home.

By five-thirty, I had done my hair and makeup, but still hadn't decided on a dress. I had a slinky black silk number that dipped down my back, but it was a bit on the sexy side for a purported client meeting. Besides, it was one of Heath's favorites. My other non-summer options included a kind of high-necked cashmere one that kind of bunched up near my hips, and a short red cocktail dress that just felt too . . . well, too flashy.

I finally decided on the black dress; if I threw a coat over it, maybe it wouldn't look so suggestive. And it was certainly slinkier than my camo get-up.

I had just slipped it on and was touching up my lipstick when the intercom buzzed.

"Miss Garou?"

"Yes?"

"A Mark Sydney here to see you."

"Tell him I'll be right down."

"Will do," he said, and buzzed off. I hurried to the bathroom, spritzed on a little bit of Euphoria, and gave myself a quick once-over. My hair, for once, had cooperated, and instead of clinging to my head, actually kind of cascaded over my shoulders, almost, but not quite, covering up the crescent moon tattoo on my shoulder. As much as I regretted having it done—not that I remembered having it done—I had to admit it did give me a certain sexy *je ne sais quoi*. My red lipstick contrasted perfectly with the darkness of the silk, and charcoal eyeliner made my eyes look even more shimmery than usual. All in all, I looked pretty damned good, I decided. After one last lipstick touch-up, I took a deep breath and hurried to the door, steeling myself to meet Mark in the lobby.

Only he wasn't in the lobby.

He was standing outside my door, wearing a killer Armani suit and holding a long white box. His blue eyes raked over me, and I felt almost naked in my black silk dress. Which was a bit discomfiting—and more than a little bit erotic. "Much better than camo," he said. "I heartily approve."

"Thank you," I said, trying not to blush. "But I thought I told Frank I was coming down to meet you."

He opened the white box; inside, wrapped in red silk ribbon, were a dozen red roses. "I thought you might want to put these in water," he said.

A dozen red roses? Perhaps Lindsey was right about the whole date thing. "They're beautiful," I said. "Wow. You shouldn't have."

"Why not?"

I could think of about a billion reasons why not—number one being that he was my client, and number two being that I at least theoretically still had a boyfriend—but instead of listing them, I just said, "Let me get a vase."

As Mark followed me into my living room, I was glad I had done a quick tidy the day before. "Nice place," he said, fingering the leather couch appreciatively.

"Thanks," I said.

"I'd love to linger," he said, shooting me a smoldering glance, "but we've got dinner reservations at six-thirty."

"Where?"

"I was going to get reservations at Vin, but something told me you'd prefer Ruth's Chris."

I had to agree with him. "Sounds fabulous," I said, reaching for my coat.

Mark closed the distance between us in a heartbeat, and I took a deep breath of his erotic, smoky smell. "Allow me," he said, brushing my naked arm, tracing with one hot finger the outline of the little moon. I shivered.

By the time he'd buttoned me into my coat, my breath was coming in short bursts, and I was imagining what his touch would feel like in other places. Lots of other places. "Ready?" he asked.

Yes, yes, yes, I thought, and managed to nod.

"Your chariot awaits."

I followed him out of my loft and toward the elevator. It dinged almost immediately, and the doors slid open to reveal Mrs. Gerschwitz. Today's ensemble featured pink marabou mules and a sheath dress with marabou trim.

"Hi, Mrs. Gerschwitz."

"Hello there," she said, addressing Mark. Her eyes roved up and down him. "You've got fabulous taste in men, dear. And so many to choose from!"

Oh, God. "This is my client, Mark Sydney," I said stiffly.

"Delighted to meet you, Mrs. Gerschwitz," he said, taking her bony hand and raising it to his lips. "And I'm glad to know I meet your rigorous standards."

"Helluva client," Mrs. Gerschwitz said, winking at me broadly. "You've got that handsome lawyer man, and then that gorgeous blond guy who was here the other day."

Mark raised an eyebrow. "I had no idea you had such an active . . . social life, Sophie."

"Anyway, good to see you," I said to Mrs. Gerschwitz, face burning. "I'd love to stop and chat, but we've got dinner reservations at six-thirty."

"Well then, don't let me keep you. I need to pretty myself for Henry, anyway. Did you know he's taking me to Luby's?"

"Can't wait to hear all about it," I said, hustling onto the elevator. "Bye, now!"

I let the air hiss out of my lungs as the door slid shut behind us. I loved Mrs. Gerschwitz, but her timing sure was lousy.

"You sound like a very busy girl. So, how many men *are* you dating?"

"I have a boyfriend," I said stolidly.

"And what about that man—was his name Tom?—we met in San Antonio the other night?"

"He's a friend," I said.

"Mmm," he said, sounding unconvinced.

"He's actually dating a friend of mine. But enough about me," I said, anxious to change the subject. "How's business?"

"We're opening up a new route to the Virgin Islands," he said. "I was thinking of checking it out myself. Do you have any vacation time coming up?"

The Virgin Islands? I thought of Miranda, planning her little wine country getaway with Heath, and almost said, *Why not?*

But until Heath and I officially broke up, we were still a couple—and I, at least, was determined to act that way. Besides, even if we weren't, a trip to the Caribbean would definitely be crossing the line between business and pleasure. Heck—the man had just given me a dozen red roses and was taking me to dinner, so we were pushing things already. And if things went sour with Mark, the account would likely follow suit.

Then again, if the Houston pack was about to send me to werewolf Siberia, what would it matter if I lost the

Southeast Airlines account? *Was there a pack in Tahiti?* I wondered.

I shrugged. "Things are kind of hectic now, but I'll think about it."

"I'm glad to hear it," he said as the elevator door slid open and we emerged into the lobby. A moment later, he held the door open for me and we emerged into a chilly February night. A black stretch limo was parked at the curb. I blinked at it, then looked back at Mark, who was grinning at me. "Your chariot awaits."

"What happened to the Mercedes?"

"I left it home," he said, motioning toward the door the driver held open for me. "After you."

I hadn't been in a limo since prom night, and this one was a lot nicer than the one I'd shared with Eddie Marks. I'd barely settled into the beige leather seat before Mark poured two glasses of champagne. He handed one to me and held the second up. "To a successful partnership," he said, his dark blue eyes steady on mine.

I clinked the rim of my flute to Mark's, breathing in the scent of expensive leather, Veuve Clicquot, and Mark's smoky, sexy aroma.

The line between business and pleasure was getting very fuzzy very fast.

Twenty-five

We emerged from the limo a scant five minutes later at Ruth's Chris and were soon ensconced at an intimate corner table. Mark ordered a bottle of expensive wine and then smiled across the white tablecloth at me. The flickering candlelight made his blue eyes even darker and more mysterious.

"Tell me about yourself," he said, leaning in as if he couldn't bear to miss a single syllable I said. Which, after Heath's refusal to let me up to his loft the other night, was a refreshing change of pace. "Did you grow up in Austin?" he asked.

"We moved around a lot when I was little," I said vaguely, "but we've been in Austin since I was about eight."

"Why did you move around so much at first?"

Uh-oh. We were definitely venturing into unsafe territory. "Oh, my mother was just trying to find the right place to settle in, I suppose." Which meant one not already inhabited by a pack of werewolves. Of course, there was also the problem of my unfortunate tendency to sprout teeth and fur in day care, which necessitated more than a few hasty relocations, but I felt that fell into the category of too much information for a first date. Not, of course, that this was a date.

"What about your father?"

"He, um, wasn't around much." Which was true. He'd stuck it out for the first six months of my life, when my mother was in Paris, but had wasted little time shipping the two of us off to the States "for our protection." Personally, I thought our relocation had a lot more to do with his desire to "protect" his free and easy single werewolf lifestyle, but whatever. "How about you?" I asked, anxious to get off the topic of my early childhood.

"Oh, I've lived lots of places," he said, eyes flickering in the candlelight. His smoky smell seemed to intensify— or maybe it was just the smell of browning butter from the kitchen. I swallowed back a mouthful of drool. "Sometimes I feel like I've been around since the dawn of time. I don't know if there's anywhere I haven't been."

"One of the benefits of running an airline, I suppose."

"I suppose," he said. "What about your mom?"

"What about her?" I asked guardedly. What was with the twenty questions? I didn't know how comfortable I was sharing my mother's somewhat unusual profession with my clients. Heck—other than Lindsey, no one at Withers and Young even knew about my mother's occult occupation.

"Is she in Austin?"

"Uh-huh," I said, lifting my glass to take a sip of wine—a Cabernet like liquid velvet—and wishing we could talk about something else. Anything else, really. "How about you?" I asked again. "Where did you grow up?"

His blue eyes were steady on mine. "A long way from here," he said.

"Where?"

"I guess you could say Persia," he said. "Which has had many names. These days, it's Iran."

I blinked at him; with his blue eyes and dark hair, he

looked anything but Middle Eastern. "Really? But your parents weren't originally from there, were they?"

"Good guess," he said. At that moment, the waiter appeared. Mark smiled at me. "Do you know what you want?"

No, I didn't, I realized. I loved Heath. But I was having a hard time keeping my thoughts about Mark platonic. Of course, the roses, the limo, and the champagne didn't hurt, but even without the trimmings, he was very intriguing.

And then there was Tom, and his mesmerizing golden eyes. Who had vanished yet again. Was it just his werewolf nature? Or had something happened to him?

Mark touched my hand, and a shudder ran through me. "Sophie?"

"Sorry," I said, looking up at his flickering blue eyes.

"Do you know what you want?" he repeated slowly. And something in his voice told me he wasn't referring to the merits of sirloin vs. rib eye.

No, I thought. *Not at all.* "I think so," I said, and ordered the filet. Medium-rare, with sautéed mushrooms on the side.

At least I was clear about something.

A north wind was howling down Sixth Street by the time we left Ruth's Chris, and even with my coat on, it was nice to have a warm limo right there waiting for us.

I'd barely gotten myself situated before Mark handed me a glass of something brown and highly alcoholic. Too alcoholic for me, actually—I don't know if it was because of my wolfie senses, but hard liquor had always been about as appealing as battery acid to me. Too strong.

I sniffed it from a distance. "What is it?"

"Cognac," he said.

Like I needed more alcohol. As attractive as Mark

was, I was starting to wonder if he had a drinking problem; he'd kept the wine flowing through dinner and was at it again already. I'd stopped at the third glass and was still feeling tipsy, but he'd gone through at least an entire bottle. At least he wasn't driving.

Now, as the limo pulled away from the curb, he poured himself a glass and settled in next to me. His nearness made me almost dizzy.

"So, what are we seeing at the ballet tonight?" I said, trying to make light conversation. *It's not a date, Sophie. Not, not, not a date.*

"It's a Valentine's Day performance," Mark said, his fingers caressing my arm. Even through the heavy wool, his touch felt like fire, and his eyes were dark with barely restrained lust. I totally got the whole Eligible Bachelor thing, and I was deeply, deeply curious about what it would be like to well . . . you know.

I was eyeing the partition between the driver and the back part of the limousine and toying with the idea of temporarily suspending my better judgment when Mark turned to me and fixed me with those fiery blue eyes.

"Sophie," he said in a voice rough with lust. And before I could answer, he kissed me.

His mouth was hard on mine, probing me urgently. And he was hot—so hot—he even tasted smoky, like he was on fire from the inside. His warm fingers slid down my cheekbone, caressed my ear, sent tongues of heat rippling across my skin.

"So beautiful," he murmured, his fingers trailing down my neck, tracing the plunging neckline of my dress, touching the space between my breasts with the tips of his fingers. I leaned into him, and he crushed me to him suddenly. "I want you so badly," he whispered, his body taut with longing. "Since the first time I saw you, I wanted you for my own." His hand slid through the folds of silk, traced the line of my lace bra. When his finger grazed my nipple, I gasped.

I was about to throw all caution to the wind when the door opened, letting in a gust of icy wind. I jerked away, embarrassed.

"Well, that's unfortunate timing," Mark said, grinning at me. "I guess we're here." I glanced up at the driver, who was politely staring at some point in the middle distance as I adjusted my dress. "Are you sure you want to go?" Mark asked in a low voice, adjusting his tie.

"I thought you had to. Aren't you one of the big donors?"

"Yes, and you're probably right," he said with a rueful grin. "But I hope we can continue our mutual exploration later. . . ." He leaned over and kissed me once more.

Maybe we *could* bag the ballet, I thought, until my brain reminded me that I was still officially with Heath, and that leaving the ballet early to go have some quality time with Mark could be termed cheating. Actually, so could my decision to let him kiss me a few moments ago. Although it really felt more like a biological imperative than a decision. Besides, who knew what Heath and Miranda were up to?

Still.

I pulled away. "Ready?" I said brightly.

Mark stepped out of the limo and held a hand out to me as I climbed out after him.

"I'll wait for you here, sir," said the liveried driver.

"Thanks, Ben. It'll probably be nine-thirty or ten." As the driver closed the door, Mark slid an arm around me and ushered me up the steps to the glowing entryway of Bass Concert Hall. "This better be short," he said, his lips grazing my earlobe, and then he swept me through the doors into the concert hall.

He had front-row seats, of course. "I like to watch the piccolo player sometimes," he admitted as we settled in together. I lay my jacket across my lap, and Mark slipped his hand under it, onto my thigh. Near the knee, at least, and not so that anybody could see. Still, shouldn't I tell him to move it? Of course I should. I even briefly considered asking him.

But then the lights dimmed, and the first set of dancers—a man and a woman, both wearing what looked like strapless one-piece bathing suits covered with feathers—took to the stage and started moving around artfully.

I'm sure whatever they were doing was amazing. But I wasn't paying a tremendous amount of attention. Because Mark's hand was stroking my thigh, moving upwards, edging my dress up farther and farther. And I didn't want him to stop.

By the time we were into the second set of dancers, his finger was grazing the crease between my thighs, and I could feel my breath coming in short bursts. I vaguely remember something flowy and green, with lots of soulful music, but the whole of my being was focused on what Mark was doing beneath my coat. He leaned over, his lips grazing my ear. "Are you sure you want to stay?"

I nodded, and he squeezed my thigh gently.

A squeak escaped me, attracting the attention of the blue-haired matron next to me. I smiled at her and pretended to watch the dancers while Mark's hot fingertips worked themselves farther north.

And all of a sudden the lights were up, and it was intermission.

Mark withdrew his hand from my lap, and I blinked in the bright light.

"What did you think?" he asked as I surreptitiously

adjusted the hemline of my skirt and tried to catch my breath.

"Amazing," I said, standing up and smoothing down my dress. "Um, I mean, those dancers in the first act were great."

"The ones in the bathing suits?"

"Yeah. What were they doing?"

"I don't know," he said, putting his hand on the small of my back and guiding me down the aisle. "I'm afraid my attention was elsewhere."

We edged past the people in their seats, including the blue-haired matron, who gave me a disapproving sniff, and out into the lobby. "Drink?" Mark asked.

"No, thanks." I said.

"Probably for the best," he said. "It's usually jug wine anyway." He slipped an arm around me, his fingers sliding up and down my side, pausing at the thin strap of my bikini underwear. He leaned down and murmured into my ear. "Do you really want to go back in there?"

I hesitated. No, I didn't. Not at all. But if I didn't . . . "Well," I began . . .

"Let's get out of here," he said.

"But don't you need to stay?"

"I've put in an appearance," he said. "Besides, it probably won't look too good if I start kissing you in the middle of the second half. And I'm not sure I can hold out that long."

"I don't have my coat," I said.

He gave me a squeeze. "I'll be right back. Don't go anywhere."

I watched as Mark strode off toward the auditorium, feeling a rush of anticipation. His kisses were amazing, and his hands . . .

I wandered toward the doors, struggling to regain control of myself. I was about to leave the ballet with a man with whom I was dying to have sex—and who had spent most of the last hour caressing me in a way that could only be termed extremely intimate. Which was a very, very, very bad idea.

I touched the cold glass of the door, and on an impulse, pushed it open and stepped outside.

The icy air buffeted me, sending a shock through me. I closed my eyes and sucked in my breath, trying to cool my heels, so to speak. My eyes flew open a split second later.

I wasn't the only werewolf out here.

And the other two didn't look very friendly.

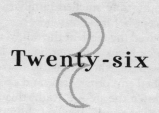

Twenty-six

They were about twenty feet away, dressed
in leather jackets and jeans, with short black hair and
coffee-colored skin. They had the golden eyes of born
werewolves. Menacing golden eyes. And they were loping toward me.

Crap. As they advanced, I whirled around and yanked
at the door. Which of course was locked.

My enchanted evening was turning into a nightmare
pretty damned fast.

I pounded at the glass, but before I could catch anyone's attention—the nearest group of people, an elderly
trio of women in feathers and sequins, had evidently
turned down their hearing aids—a hairy hand closed on
my naked arm.

If you thought a cold shower was an effective lust deterrent, try being manhandled by two werewolves when
it's thirty degrees and you're wearing about six ounces
of silk. My fantasies involving a little quality time in the
back of Mark's limo were quickly replaced by fantasies
involving not being killed and left in a roadside ditch.

"Nice dress," the hand's owner said. With a jolt, I
realized I recognized his scent: he was one of the two
werewolves from Casa Brady. But there was something
different about his smell tonight. Something sharp. And

the other one smelled familiar; I knew I'd encountered his scent before. But where?

I bared my teeth at the tall werewolf, who had a shock of thick black hair, but he just laughed. A second werewolf—a bit shorter, with a strong aroma of cumin—grabbed my other arm, and the two of them propelled me down the steps. "Right this way, miss."

"Let me go!" I yelled, hoping someone would hear me. The urge to change was overpowering; I could feel it rippling under my skin. But I couldn't; not in the middle of Austin. "Help!" I yelled. But everyone was inside, and Mark's limo was nowhere to be seen.

"Shut up," the shorter one growled at me. Evidently they'd decided to drop the niceties.

"Who the hell are you?" I demanded. They didn't answer; the hands just tightened on my arms and pushed me forward faster. "Where are you taking me?"

"We have some questions," the one on my right said. As he spoke, an old woman in a wool hat toddled over. Not exactly my fantasy version of a rescuer, but if she could operate a cell phone and call 911, I'd take it.

"Help me," I cried. "These people are kidnapping me! Call the police! Please!"

Unfortunately, either English wasn't her first language or she was on the side of the nasty werewolves, because instead of pulling a phone out of her voluminous black purse, the old woman's dark eyes raked over me. A second later she nodded briskly, then issued a few sharp Spanish words to the werewolves that were holding me.

"I know you," I hissed, and I did. But from where? Her scent was familiar, and those eyes . . . but before I could do or say anything else, the werewolves started hauling me away again, and the woman tottered off.

I turned my attention to the werewolves who were trying to pull my arms from my sockets. "Are you with the Houston pack?"

One of them snorted and muttered something in Spanish. I took a deep shaky breath and glanced around, looking for Hugin, Tom's raven. Or Tom, which would also be nice. Unfortunately, it appeared I was no longer under avian surveillance. Were Tom and Hugin just AWOL? Or had these werewolves gotten their hands on them, too?

They were pushing me toward a dark SUV when I realized with a sick sense of dread that I was totally on my own. There would be no rescue this time; it was up to me.

As the two werewolves shoved me forward, I took a deep breath, stifled a twinge of regret over my silk dress—not to mention yet another pair of shoes—and let nature take its course.

"Cuidado!" one of them yelled as my furry foreleg slipped from his grasp. I yanked backward, trying to free myself from the tangle of my dress and underwear, and ducked away from them. A moment later, I was galloping shoeless toward the LBJ Library, wincing at the sound of tearing silk. I glanced back a moment later; the two werewolves had transformed and were almost out of their leather jackets. Their gold eyes looked angry—and all four of them were trained on me.

A shiver ran through my limbs, and I ran harder, hoping that the cumin smell meant they'd had a heavy Mexican dinner. And that neither of my pursuers did a lot of recreational running.

As I loped up the white terrazzo steps toward the library, I struggled to think. Where would I be safe? They'd be able to track my scent wherever I went, so it was going to be hard to hide. Ideally, I would change back to my human form and join a crowd of people, but without any clothes, that was going to be tough. And what was Mark going to think when he walked out of

Bass Concert Hall to find nothing but a pair of Jimmy Choos and the remains of my dress?

I rounded the corner into one of the big, open plazas of the LBJ Library, still trying to come up with a plan. As it turned out, though, I didn't need one. Because a moment later, I barreled right into a large black wolf.

God, he was huge. We tumbled into a heap, and as I struggled to right myself, I realized he wasn't alone. Because the second one was coming up behind me, gray fur bristling. Fear snaked through me—how had the black one gotten here before me?

When I managed to get back on my paws, I backed away from them, baring my own teeth and trying—unsuccessfully—to come up with an exit strategy. As I struggled to find an escape route, the two of them advanced toward me, smelling like cumin, and animal—and that weird sharp smell. And, I suddenly realized, Tom. One of them had been near Tom.

I hesitated for a moment, confused. Did that mean Tom was working with them? Or had they somehow managed to capture him?

Not that this was the time to worry about it. I kept my eyes trained on my two opponents, waiting for them to pounce. The muscles bunched in the gray werewolf, and my body tensed, ready to spring away from him.

He leaped, and I darted to the side. Which unfortunately brought me muzzle-to-muzzle with the second, much larger werewolf. My eyes fixed for a moment on the leather medallion tied around his neck—twin to the one I'd found at the Greenbelt. Then I saw his mouth open, revealing gums spiked with long white teeth. Pain seared me as his jaws clamped down on my neck. *This is it, Sophie,* I thought. As his teeth punched through the skin, tearing at my throat, I wondered if I would revert to human form before I died, like the werewolves at the Greenbelt.

The world started to spin, and pain lanced through me like an arrow. Couldn't breathe, couldn't scream . . . *Will my mother ever find out what happened to me?* My legs were giving way, the blue-green floodlights dwindling down to a small, single point, when suddenly the pressure lifted. I gasped for breath; the cold February air smelled like a bonfire. And under it was the black wolf's sharp smell, and the shorter werewolf's elusive, familiar scent. Ah! Now I remembered where I'd smelled it before . . .

"Leave," someone said in the distance. "Now." There was a growl, then something like a whimper, and then everything went dead.

"Sophie."

The bonfire/werewolf smell was gone, replaced by leather, and ashes, and cognac. I opened my eyes with a start. I was somewhere warm and soft, staring into Mark's dark blue eyes. I looked around—I seemed to be in bed, in a fancy hotel suite—and then glanced down at myself. I was wearing my coat. How had I gotten here? How was I not dead?

"Where did they go?" I asked. "What happened?" I touched my throat, which was throbbing from where I'd been bitten; I had some pretty bad puncture wounds, but they felt like they were starting to close up already.

Mark's eyes were still trained on me. "I picked up your coat for you. And your shoes," he added, nodding toward my red Jimmy Choo slingbacks. "I'm afraid the dress was beyond repair."

"I loved that dress," I croaked.

"You look better without it," he replied, and I realized that if I was now wearing my coat, he must have put it on me. I could feel the blush rising to my face. He'd obviously seen me *au naturel.* But had he seen me in my natural fur coat as well?

"How did you find me?" I asked cautiously. My voice was husky; my windpipe must be bruised. At least it wasn't punctured.

"Well, I came out to find you, but there was nothing but a heap of clothing. It didn't take me long to figure out what had happened."

That three people had transformed into werewolves and gone galloping up toward the LBJ Library? How had he figured *that* out?

"I tracked you down just in time," he said.

I felt my body tense. Had he seen the werewolves? Was it his voice I'd heard? More important, had he seen *me* as a werewolf? "What exactly did you find when you tracked me down?"

His lips twitched into a grin. "I think you know the answer to that question. But they're gone now."

I closed my eyes, thinking, *Oh, God.* The CEO of Southeast Airlines—my biggest client—had seen me as a werewolf. But why wasn't he surprised? And how had he gotten rid of the other two? My eyes snapped open. "Was that you I heard? Telling them to leave?"

He nodded.

I blinked at him. "You told them to leave and they just did?"

"Well, there was a little more to it than that," he admitted.

"And that bonfire smell. That was you, wasn't it?" As I stared at him, his blue eyes flickered just a bit, sending a chill down my spine. I pulled my coat tighter. "What are you, Mark? What did you do to them?"

"You're not the only one with a secret, Sophie," he said.

I swallowed hard. Mark had unplumbed depths, apparently. Which was more than a little scary. On the other hand, since he had such a way with werewolves, perhaps I should take him with me next time I visited the

Houston pack. "So now that you know . . . well, a little more about me," I said, "Why doesn't it bother you?"

His fingers tiptoed up my arm. "Bother me? Why would it? I knew when I met you that there was something wild about you. In fact, I find it immensely attractive."

How he could find my propensity for sprouting fangs, a natural fur coat, and a tail attractive I didn't know, but even with my neck torn half open, I was enjoying the shivers his touch sent through my body. "Really?" I asked.

"Why do you think I requested you personally on the account?"

I winced, remembering how badly the pitch meeting had gone. I had overdosed on wolfsbane tea to avoid transforming in the middle of my PowerPoint presentation; unfortunately, the side effects had included heavy drooling, lisping, and hallucinations. The event had culminated in me dashing from the room just before my sideburns sprouted.

Needless to say, I'd been shocked when we got the account. "So it wasn't just my excellent presentation skills?" I said wryly.

"I don't know how you held out so long, actually," he said. "I couldn't keep my eyes off you that day."

Waiting for my tail to sprout, no doubt. I cringed, then decided to change the subject. "So, you seem to know everything about me, but I know next to nothing about you."

"I'm your client, and a man who finds you very attractive," he said, squeezing my knee under the wool coat. Despite the pain in my throat from where I'd been mauled, I was very aware I was almost naked, and my body surged in response.

"But you haven't told me *your* secret. It must be

something amazing, if you managed to scare off those—"
I still couldn't say werewolves. "—thugs."

He massaged my thigh under the coat, and I felt my
body pulse with desire. As if reading my mind, he
slipped his hand under the wool; the contact with my
bare skin was like a spark.

His hand traveled up my thigh. "If I told you that, it
wouldn't be a secret, now, would it?"

"Not fair," I said, panting.

"But you never told me," he said. "I just found out."
His fingers massaged my inner thighs, and his lips
brushed my earlobe. "Does your boyfriend know about
you?" he whispered.

"Know what?"

"About your double nature," he murmured, his teeth
grazing my skin.

"Uh . . . no." Speaking of boyfriends, shouldn't Heath
be the one doing this right now? But then it was almost
as if someone pushed the thought away, and I was only
aware of Mark's lips, tracing my earlobe, traveling
down the undamaged side of my neck. . . .

Before I knew it, his fingers had deftly opened the buttons of my coat, and his lips were on my collarbone. His
tongue traced the curve of the bone, then dipped down
lower, slowly, until his mouth grazed my nipple. I gasped,
aching with desire, and pushed my hands up under his
shirt.

His abdomen was taut and muscular, and I let my
hands slide up then, savoring the feel of his smooth skin
beneath my fingertips. His tongue lazily circled first one,
then the other nipple, and when he took one into his
mouth, it was like liquid heat. My hand slid up toward
his chest and stopped at a little rough spot.

It was the shape of the crescent moon.

Twenty-seven

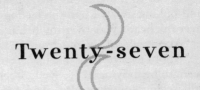

I jerked away.

His eyes devoured me. "What's wrong?"

"There's something on your chest."

"This?" he asked, unbuttoning his crisp white dress shirt to expose a pale, crescent-shaped mark.

The same little moon I'd seen when I dreamed of Mark last week. "I . . ."

"You what?" he asked, leaning forward to kiss my ear.

Despite the ripple of desire that passed through me at his touch, I pushed him away. "I . . . dreamed about it. But I couldn't have."

"Ah," he said. "Is it okay that I have it?"

"Yes," I said. "I mean, no. How could that show up in my dream? It's just not possible."

"Isn't your mother a strong psychic?" he asked.

"What does that have to do with anything?" I narrowed my eyes at him. "And how do you know my mother's a psychic?"

"I know lots of things," he said vaguely, then shrugged. "Maybe you inherited some of that, along with your . . . other talents." He leaned forward again, evidently hoping to pick up where we had left off, but the shock of finding that . . . that scar, or whatever it was . . . had dampened my desire rather abruptly.

"I need to think about this," I said, crossing my arms and pulling away. I had the feeling that I was getting in over my head. Way over my head.

"About what?" he murmured.

"About everything," I said. "You're my client, but we seem to be moving in . . . well, other directions. And I'm still seeing someone else. And I don't know anything about you, really." I raised my hands and massaged my temples. "And now I'm dreaming things about you . . ."

"What kind of dream was it?" Mark asked huskily, reaching over to touch my knee.

"I, um . . . don't remember," I lied.

His fingers tiptoed up my thigh, sending a shiver through me. "What exactly were you doing when you discovered my little . . . birthmark?"

"Like I said, I don't remember," I repeated.

"Then let me remind you," he whispered, and lowered his mouth to cover mine.

Before I could respond, his hands had pushed my coat away, and I didn't resist. His hands felt warm as coals as they stroked my body, his mouth hot and wet as he suckled first one breast, then the other. His fingers slid to the slippery cleft between my legs, and all of a sudden I wanted him more than anything else in the world.

What about Heath? my mind supplied feebly, but one flash of the utter humiliation I'd experienced in the lobby of his building was enough for me to overcome any qualms I might have had over cheating on my boyfriend. Not that they had much chance of stopping me, anyway.

I pulled Mark toward me, and he crushed his warm body against mine, pulsing with desire. I could feel the urgency in him—quite literally, since he was bulging at the seams—and fumbled at the buttons. In moments, we were both naked, his hot skin pressed up against the entire length of my body. His mouth teased my nipples, circling them and then licking the very tips of them, his hand stroking the wet warmth between my legs, until I couldn't stand it anymore. Just when I thought I was going to burst, he pushed my legs apart and positioned himself just over me.

Which is when I used the last tiny little bit of my self-restraint to stop him.

"You're kidding me," he gasped, voice ragged. "What's wrong?"

"Condom," I murmured, intoxicated by his smoky smell, the need to have him inside me. But safety first . . . "Need a condom," I repeated.

He swore in a language I didn't understand, then reached for his pants and tugged his wallet from a pocket.

I sat up a little. "You carry condoms?"

"I'm like the Boy Scouts," he whispered. "Always prepared."

Then he tore the little package with one hand and reached out to roll my left nipple with the other, which was enough to derail any further protests I might have had.

And then he was inside me, just like he was in the dream, and tendrils of heat snaked through my body as he thrust, deeper and harder, his mouth moving from one breast to the other, until I couldn't hold on another second longer.

He came a moment later and collapsed against me, smelling more like a bonfire than ever. "That was amazing," he murmured into my neck.

"Yes," I said. Then all of a sudden I realized where I was. And what I was doing. And with whom. I rolled over, dislodging Mark, and grabbed my coat. "I shouldn't be here."

"Why not?"

"This is just . . . not right. You're my client, I'm not officially broken up with Heath. . . ."

He smoothed my hair back. "I'm sorry if I pushed you too far. You're just so . . . irresistible." Mark leaned forward to kiss me, and I felt myself heating up all over again. "No," I said, marshalling enough self-discipline to push him away. "I think I need to go home now. It's been . . . an interesting night."

"Yes," he said. "It has." He stooped to retrieve his shirt. "I've got a great Jacuzzi tub, if you're interested."

"No thanks," I said. "I just want to go home."

"I understand," he said, and reached for the phone and called his driver.

Fifteen minutes later, we were in the back of the limousine again, Mark's arm slung protectively over my shoulders. As the limo turned on 4th Street, approaching my building, Mark squeezed me, then reached into his pocket and pulled out a little velvet box.

Uh-oh. "Mark . . ." I said.

"Don't worry," he said. "This is just a little . . . token. Consider it protection."

"From what?"

"What happened tonight is likely to happen again," he said. I assumed he was talking about the werewolf attack, and the little episode that had just taken place in the Driskill, although I was guessing both were highly likely. "If you're wearing this, it will help me find you. In case you need my assistance again." I leaned forward for a closer look. The band was silver, unfortunately—not my favorite metal—widening to a flat top, like a signet ring. Only instead of initials, the center of the ring was inlaid with a black, shimmery substance, in the center of which was a circle that looked like pearl. Maybe opal.

"Try it on," he said, removing the ring from the box and handing it to me.

"Um, sorry, but I only wear gold." Because silver, as

much as I loved the look of it, gave me third-degree burns if I touched it for more than about forty-five seconds. Which had seriously limited my jewelry options over the years.

He grinned. "Don't worry. It's not silver."

"Well, then. If you're sure . . ." I touched it gingerly, but didn't feel the hallmark burning sensation; it was definitely not silver. It was cool and slick and fit perfectly on the ring finger of my right hand. "It's beautiful," I said, admiring the gleam of the metal against my skin. What a treat—silver jewelry that wasn't silver! "But what is it?"

"It's an old metal."

"Not titanium, then?"

He shook his head.

"What is this?" I said, pointing to the opalescent orb.

"I thought you of all people would recognize it."

When I gave him a puzzled look, he smiled, and his dark blue eyes flickered. "It's the moon."

What were you thinking? I asked myself a few minutes later as I let myself into my loft. I'd sniffed the door first, of course—but either my allergies were acting up or no one had been there in my absence. Of course, according to Frank, no one had come by to visit, but he was hardly a reliable source of information lately.

As I closed the door behind me and slid the deadbolt home, I had the sensation that I was shaking off an enchantment of some sort. An enchantment that made me feel like a wanton woman. Was I starting to go into heat? Or was it just because Heath and I hadn't had any time together recently? Whatever the reason, I had behaved scandalously tonight.

After checking to make sure the blinds were closed, I shucked off my coat, headed for the bathroom, and turned on the shower. I needed to clean the wounds on my neck—which hopefully didn't look as bad as I was guessing. I also needed to wash the reek of werewolf off of me—not to mention the scents left by my recent encounter with Mark. Once the water was spraying, I braced myself, turned to look in the mirror—and gasped.

Except for four faint dimples, my neck was completely smooth.

I stared at myself from every angle. How had this happened? Werewolves healed fast, but not *that* fast. Had Mark done something to me? And how *had* he gotten rid of those werewolves?

Something was seriously out of whack here. What was Mark that he was able to face down two nasty werewolves? *And* heal the huge puncture wounds in my neck in under an hour? Without me knowing it? A tendril of fear snaked through me as I glanced down at the ring he had given me; the moon seemed to glow slightly, and the band felt warm. Warmer than my body temperature, actually. I grabbed the metal band and tried to slip it off, but it wouldn't budge. I tugged and tugged, but it didn't move a millimeter.

Maybe a little soap would help, I thought as I climbed into the tub. But nothing worked—not even a hefty squirt of lavender bath oil. After half an hour of struggling, I had nothing to show for it but a very sore finger. So I gave up and climbed out of the tub, wrapping myself in a big fluffy bathrobe and trying not to freak out too much.

A year ago, I'd been a nice, ordinary person—well, as ordinary as a person with irrevocable transformation tendencies can be, anyway—with a great job and a great boyfriend. No big nasty werewolves were stalking me, no mysterious clients with supernatural powers were giving me weird, perma-stick jewelry, and the Houston pack and I had been blissfully ignorant of each other.

Now, however, my life was a mess. And my mother's

"protection" spell sure didn't seem to be doing me any favors.

Unless, it occurred to me, that was what drew Mark to come to my rescue. . . .

I dismissed that thought and examined the ring again. The little moon gleamed in the light. If I was going to be stuck with permanent, potentially magical jewelry, I thought, it could be a lot worse; it could be ugly. As I heaved a self-pitying sigh and turned the kettle on for a cup of wolfsbane tea, something niggled at the back of my mind. Something important.

I was halfway through my cup of tea before I suddenly remembered what it was.

"Lourdes," I said into my office phone the next morning. "It's Sophie." After my brain flash last night, I'd done some Googling that only bolstered my suspicion. I knew where I needed to go. The problem was, I had no idea what I would find once I got there.

"Sophie! How are you?"

My fingers smoothed the top of the ring as I spoke; I just couldn't stop playing with it. "I'm sorry to keep calling, but I need your help again."

"No problem. I'm happy to help out. What is it?"

I told her what I had in mind, and she was quiet for a moment. "Weird. What do you need me to do?"

"I don't know what we'll find," I said. "And it might be dangerous; I hate to ask you, really. But I'm afraid I may need help translating again."

"No problem. I'm off today," she said. "Want me to come up now?"

"Unfortunately, it'll have to keep until this evening," I said. "I've got to work." Besides, I'd rather attempt what I had in mind after dark, when at least we had a bit of cover. I touched the ring again and said, "How about we meet at my place at six?" I gave her directions, and a moment later, hung up the phone and attempted to focus on work again.

I had just opened a file when Lindsey appeared in the doorway, her gray eyes ringed with dark circles. "What's wrong?" I asked.

"Tom hasn't called," she said, collapsing onto one of my chairs.

"Have you tried calling him?"

"No answer." She looked over at me, face drawn. "Usually I'd just blow him off—I have no time for men who can't bring themselves to pick up a phone—but I have a bad feeling about this. I think something's wrong."

Unfortunately, so did I. "Do you know where he's staying?"

Lindsey shook her head. "No. I know it's a hotel, but I don't know which one." She looked up at me. "Do you think we could ask your mother?"

"How would my mother know where he is?"

"Maybe she could do a reading or something. Consult her spirit guide, or whatever she calls it. I don't know."

I leaned back in my chair. "I guess it couldn't hurt," I said, although to be honest, I wasn't quite sure that was true. My mother's spells—first the invisibility spell that resulted in the loss of my favorite shoes, and then the "protection" spell that had landed me with two homicidal werewolves on my tail—hadn't been batting a thousand lately. "I'll call her; maybe we can head over there at lunch."

"Thanks, Sophie. You're a good friend."

I wasn't so sure I agreed with her—after all, I'd not only kissed Tom, but I had rather important information about him that I hadn't gotten around to sharing— but I just nodded and tried to squelch the guilt.

As she got up to leave, she turned back to me. "How are things going with Heath, by the way?"

"Not so hot, actually."

"Uh-oh. He still hanging out with Miranda?"

"I don't know." I shrugged. "We haven't spoken."

She cocked an eyebrow. "And Mark? How did your date go?"

I could feel the blood rising to my cheeks. "It was . . . unusual," I admitted, hoping she wouldn't ask for details.

"At least you're admitting that it's a date. So did you have fun?"

"Sort of," I said.

" 'Sort of?' Sounds kind of lukewarm," Lindsey said. That evening had been many things, I thought to myself, but lukewarm was not one of them. "Are you going to go out with him again?" Lindsey asked.

I shrugged, trying to look nonchalant—and to quell the stirring of lust I felt remembering Mark's dark blue eyes. "We'll see."

"My two favorite girls! I thought I might be seeing you today," my mother said as I opened the door to the 1910 bungalow that housed Sit A Spell. The door jingled as it shut behind Lindsey and me, and the familiar scents of herbs, incense, and old wood catapulted me back to my childhood. Every afternoon, after school, I'd come home to this store and the apartment above it; despite the intervening years, almost nothing had changed. I eyed the tables in the front room, which were festooned with love charms. Just in time for Valentine's Day, I thought with a sinking feeling. My mind turned to the little bag Heath had been carrying from the jewelry store a few weeks ago. Would I ever receive its contents?

Or had they been destined for Miranda from the beginning?

The ring on my finger tingled a little as my mother hugged me. I breathed in her patchouli scent and tucked my hand behind my back; I didn't feel like fielding twenty questions about Mark's little gift right now. As I covered the ring's smooth face with my thumb, my mother murmured, "Any more presents on your doorstep?"

"No," I whispered back so that Lindsey wouldn't hear. I decided not to tell her about last night's attack; I didn't want her to worry. Or cast any more spells on me. "Any more hexes?" I asked.

"A few," she said, "but nothing I can't handle. It's so good to see you, sweetheart." She gave me a last squeeze, then adjusted her velvet tunic and peered at Lindsey. "What's wrong, sweetheart?"

It could have been my mother's psychic ability that told her Lindsey was in trouble. Then again, it could have been because my friend looked like she hadn't slept in a week.

"It's Tom," I supplied. "The . . . guy Lindsey's seeing."

"The *guy*," my mother repeated, looking at me with a hint of accusation. Because I hadn't yet told Lindsey about the whole werewolf thing, probably. But what did she expect me to do?

"That's right," I said, ignoring the look. "He appears to be missing; Lindsey thought maybe you could help us figure out what's going on."

"It's worth a shot, I suppose. But I warn you, the spirit guides can be a bit vague." *A bit vague?* In my admittedly limited experience, they could be a whole lot more than "a bit vague"; they could be dead wrong. Six months ago my mother had called a murder victim back from the dead, and the information he gave us was not

only less than helpful, but out-and-out incorrect. Then again, since he was poisoned, perhaps it was expecting a bit much to ask him to figure out who killed him. "Let me get my cards, then, dearies," my mother said. "I've got to teach a spell class in about an hour, but this shouldn't take too long. Emily," she called to a young woman dusting herb jars. "Can you take the cash register for a while?"

She smiled, and her lip stud gleamed in the light. "Sure, Carmen."

"Thanks. I don't know what I'd do without that girl," my mother said to me. "Now, why don't we head to the kitchen?"

We followed my mom's comforting velvet-clad bulk toward the kitchen, which was at the back of the shop. I glanced out the rippled glass window at the yard outside; even though it was February, my mother's garden brimmed with herbs and cool-season flowers, including a lush bed of purple pansies. Her green thumb was yet another thing I hadn't inherited; the only type of plant able to survive my ministrations for more than two months was silk.

"Why don't you two sit down while I find my cards?" my mom said. As she bustled around, collecting what she needed, Lindsey and I pulled up chairs at the antique farm table where I'd done my homework as a kid—and where my mom did all her readings and spell preparations. As we sat down, my mom shook out a length of blue silk, letting it float down over the scarred wood surface. A moment later, she unwrapped and handed Lindsey a faded, dog-eared deck of Tarot cards. Her brown eyes crinkled at the edges as she smiled and patted Lindsey gently on the back. "Shuffle this a few times, my dear, and think about your problem."

Lindsey closed her long-lashed eyes and shuffled the deck as my mother settled herself across from her. After a few minutes with the worn cards, she gave them back to my mother, who pressed them together quickly before laying them out in what I knew was the Celtic Cross. I sincerely hoped the spirit world was feeling specific today; Lindsey wasn't the only one worried about Tom. "This is what covers you," my mother murmured, putting down a card with two lovers on it (which was not what I wanted to see, frankly), "and this is what crosses you."

The second card, unfortunately, was intimately familiar to me, as it involved two wolflike things baying at a yellow dinner plate in the dark sky. As I stared at the card, I touched the ring almost involuntarily.

It was the goddamned moon again.

Twenty-eight

"You were right to come to me," she said in a low voice. "Your friend is in danger . . . definite danger."

My heart dropped into my stomach.

"Look at all those swords! And I don't like this at all," she said, pointing to the Devil card, which was prominently displayed in the "situation" section of the spread. I wasn't too crazy about the card either, I realized; in fact, it creeped me out.

"I don't know if this is a person or a situation," my mom continued, "but either way, it's not good," she said. My skin crawled as I looked at the card. I had a feeling there was more to it than my mother realized, which was strange—usually she was the one who picked up the weird vibes. As I continued to stare at the horned creature wrapped with chains, my mother continued talking. "On the other hand," she said, tapping a card with the Star emblazoned on it, "he's got help coming from where he doesn't expect it. And the outcome is definitely decisive," she said. "Whatever the issue is, somebody powerful—potentially your friend, or potentially this person"—she tapped on a card labeled the High Priestess—"will prevail. The problem is, it's not clear."

To say that the reading was "vague" was an understatement, I thought, my stomach clenching at the picture of the shackled devil. And that stupid moon card. Was that referring to the San Antonio pack? Or was Tom's own werewolf nature causing him trouble? Again, not enough information. If the spirits were so darned powerful, I thought for the zillionth time, why couldn't they figure out how to use a word processor? Or at least a pen? I looked up at Lindsey, whose brow was furrowed in puzzlement.

My mother then took my friend's hand and said, "I must warn you, my dear. There's another theme in this spread."

"What's that?" she asked.

"Deception," my mother said, her eyes flicking to me. I smiled a tight smile.

"Do you think he's seeing someone else?" Lindsey asked, looking pale. "Is that why he hasn't called?"

"It's unclear," my mother said, and I squirmed, remembering the hot kisses Tom and I had shared. "But I don't think that's it." For a moment, Lindsey looked relieved; then the worried look returned.

I sighed. "The problem is, if Tom's in danger, how do we find him?" And what would we do if we did? I mean, Tom was pretty formidable in his own right. If he was in trouble, did I really think *I* was going to be able to help him?

"I don't know that we *can* find him," my mother said.

I stared down at the Devil card again, touching the corner with my finger. Suddenly, I had a feeling I knew exactly where Tom was.

"What's that?" my mother asked suddenly.

I looked up, startled. "What?"

"The ring on your finger," she said. "I've never seen it before."

I pulled my hand back. "Oh, it's just a piece of costume jewelry."

At least the mention of jewelry temporarily pulled

Lindsey from her funk. "I've never seen that before," she said, grabbing my hand. "It's pretty. Kind of looks like the moon. Did Heath give that to you?"

"Ah, no."

Lindsey's gray eyes widened. "It was Mark, wasn't it?"

"Maybe," I said. It was bad enough having a psychic mother; did I have a psychic best friend, too?

"Who is Mark?" my mother asked, her dark eyes sharp. "And why did he choose a moon ring for you?"

"Just . . . a client," I stuttered.

"Your clients buy you jewelry? Let me see it," she said, and I reluctantly extended my hand.

My mother's finger grazed the inset moon, then jerked back as if it burned. "Holy Hell," my mother said slowly. "That's not just a ring."

"What is it?" Lindsey asked.

"Whatever it is," she said, "it's got magic that's stronger than anything I've ever been able to conjure. Sophie, I want you to take that off right now."

"I can't," I said.

My mom blinked at me. "What do you mean, you can't?"

"It's stuck. It won't come off."

She closed her eyes, and her almond skin turned a shade paler. "Did you put it on, or did he?"

"I did. Why?"

Her dark eyes snapped open. "We need to get that thing off of you. I've got some wire cutters in the shed . . ."

"Wouldn't it be better to have a jeweler do it?"

"Sophie, I don't want to wait any longer than I have to. Hang on . . . I'll be right back," she said, and hurried out the back door into her garden, letting in a gust of cold air.

"So the CEO of Southeast Airlines gave you a magic

ring?" Lindsey said incredulously as the door banged shut behind my mother.

"It appears so," I said.

"Too bad it can't help find Tom. What do you think he got mixed up in?"

I suspected that he'd tangled with a pack of Mexican werewolves, but decided against sharing my intuition. "I don't know," I said. "Did he mention anything about what he was doing in town?"

"He said he was here on business. Sophie," she said, grabbing my hand. "Do you think he's in real trouble?"

"I don't know," I said. "But even if he is, my mom said there's a good chance he'll come out okay, so don't worry too much. Okay?"

She squeezed my hand so hard it hurt. "It's just . . . I haven't felt this way about anyone in a long time. If something happened to him . . ."

My stomach clenched. I really did need to tell her about Tom's true nature before she got in too deep. Then again, if something had happened to him, telling Lindsey he was a werewolf would be worthless.

Before I could make a decision on what to do, the door opened and my mother bustled back into the kitchen, brandishing a pair of hedge clippers. "I couldn't find the wire cutters, but this should do."

"You've got to be kidding me," I said, rising from the chair and backing toward the doorway, my hand behind my back.

"It's got to go, Sophie. Now come on, let me see your hand." She advanced toward me, clippers at the ready.

"No way," I said, backing up farther.

"I'm clipping the ring, silly. Not you!"

"It would be a shame to ruin such a pretty ring," Lindsey said, coming to my defense. "And since her client gave it to her . . . do you think it's a good idea to destroy it?"

"And wouldn't a professional jeweler be a better idea?" I added. "Besides, before we start hacking away at it, couldn't we could at least try some oil again, or soap and warm water? I'm sure you've got better stuff here than I do at home."

My mother grabbed my left hand and pulled me toward the table. "We'll try oil one more time, but if that doesn't work, I'm using the clippers. That ring gives me the heebie-jeebies, and I want it off you. Who is this Mark guy, anyway?"

"I told you. He's the CEO of Southeast Airlines."

"That's not all he is," she muttered.

"What is he, then?" I asked. I'll admit, I was deeply curious.

"I wish I knew," she said, rummaging through the cabinets over the sink and pulling out a vial of oil. "But I don't think I like him. Let's see your hand."

I surrendered it reluctantly, hoping my mom could come up with something I hadn't already thought of. But again, nothing worked—the ring refused to budge—and after twenty minutes of yanking unsuccessfully at my now-swollen finger, my mother picked up the clippers again.

"Mom . . ."

"I promise I won't hurt you. Now, give me your hand."

I reluctantly laid it on the table, palm up, and bit my lip as she held the clippers over me and placed the sharp points on either side of the ring. "Ouch," I said as one of them jabbed my skin. "Are you sure you don't have wire cutters?"

"This is all I've got. But don't worry. I just sharpened them."

"I can tell," I said as she dug the points in a bit deeper.

"Sorry about that," she said. "Lindsey, hold her arm."

As Lindsey gripped my wrist, I closed my eyes, unable to watch as my mother potentially removed my right ring finger. The urge to change rippled through me, and it occurred to me that that was an approach I hadn't tried. If I turned into a wolf, wouldn't the ring slide off? I opened my eyes and was about to tell her to stop when she squeezed the handles of the clippers together quickly. A sharp crack sounded, and the smell of smoke filled the room.

My eyes snapped open. My mother stood staring at my finger, hedge clippers dangling from her right hand, and Lindsey, who had released my arm at some point, was waving at a cloud of bluish smoke.

"What happened?"

"I was right; this is no ordinary ring," my mother said, peering at my hand. The silvery band was unscathed. "It doesn't want to come off."

"Evidently not," I said, rubbing the sore spots where the clippers had dug into me.

"I'm going to have to do some research on this," she said.

"So we're not going to try the clippers again?" I asked, cradling my abused hand.

"No," she said. "Not today. But I'm not done with that ring yet," she said, shaking the clippers. "I just have to research it a bit. For now, though, I'm casting another protection spell on you, young lady."

"They don't seem to be working too well lately," I said, thinking of last night's mauling. I was about to tell my mother about it, but then I remembered Lindsey was there and bit my tongue.

"Nonsense," my mother said. "You need it now more than ever. And I want you to lie low and stay out of trouble until we get this thing off."

Easy for her to say. She didn't have the Houston pack after her, baying for blood.

As she walked us out the front door, I caught a whiff of a familiar smell and froze. "Someone's just been here."

Lindsey squinted at me. "What do you mean?" she asked, but my mother knew what I was talking about. She scanned the front doorstep, reached down, and picked up something small and dark.

"Just a feeling," I said to Lindsey, and turned to my mother, who had taken whatever it was and shoved it into a pocket. "What is it?" I asked.

"Oh, it's nothing," she said, but from the paleness of her face, I wasn't buying it. "You two run along now," she said, hurrying us toward our car. As we were about to close the doors, my mother said to Lindsey, "Can you stick with her as much as possible?"

"Of course," Lindsey said. "But what do we do about Tom?"

"Lindsey, my dear, there's more to Tom than meets the eye." That was certainly true, I thought. "He can take care of himself."

As we drove away, I tried to dispel the feeling of dread that was closing in on me. Because the woman I had sniffed outside my mother's store was the same one who had approached me outside the ballet. And I was pretty sure whatever she left on my mom's doorstep wasn't exactly friendly.

At four-thirty that afternoon, I had just closed up my laptop and was getting ready to go home when Lindsey appeared at my doorway. I swore under my breath and summoned something like a smile.

"Leaving early?" she asked.

"Uh, no," I said, nudging my briefcase under my desk. "Actually, I think I'm going to stay a little late."

"That's why it's not even five, and your computer's packed up."

"I was just rebooting it," I lied.

Lindsey wagged a finger at me. "Don't lie. You were trying to leave without me."

"Lindsey . . ."

"Your mom told me to stick with you," she reminded me. "And that's what I plan to do."

I took a deep breath. "I really have something I need to do alone tonight."

"No dice."

"I can't take you with me, Lindsey."

"That's what you think," she said, settling into one of my chairs. "What's the big secret?"

Might as well be honest. At least partially, anyway. "I think I may know where Tom is."

Her face lit up for a moment; then she tilted her head to one side and eyed me suspiciously. "How?"

"It's just . . . I have a feeling."

She was still giving me that doubtful look. "I thought your mom was the psychic."

I shrugged. "Maybe it's hereditary."

"First I've heard of it," she said. "You pick stocks worse than anyone I know. Remember that Schlotzky's stock you were sure was going to skyrocket?"

I grimaced; she was right, and I had the portfolio to show for it. "This is different," I said. Because even though it was a hunch, I *did* have a little bit of physical evidence to back it up. Nothing I could tell Lindsey, of course, but still.

"Well, if you think you know where he is . . ."

"I think I do," I said, even though I really wasn't sure.

"Is he in Austin?"

I shook my head. "If I'm correct, then no."

"Well, wherever he is, I'm going with you," she said.

I shook my head. "Lindsey, you can't. I need to do this alone."

"Why?"

"It'll be . . . dangerous." *And probably crawling with werewolves.*

She shrugged. "So what? I deal with danger every day just crossing Sixth Street."

"This is different," I said. "Trust me. I just can't take you with me."

"Try to stop me," she said, steely-eyed.

I sighed, realizing—belatedly—that I should have just feigned sickness. Although in the wake of the whole Dude Ranch fiasco, odds were good she wouldn't have bought it anyway. "Okay," I said, with a sigh of resignation. "Meet me at my loft at six."

"What should I wear?"

"Something dark," I said. "We're going to have to be sneaky."

"I'm assuming we're talking tennis shoes, and not stilettos?"

"Exactly."

"Anything else?"

What else should I tell her to bring? "Maybe some bottled water. And your can of pepper spray, if you still have it."

"Do you think we'll need it?"

"I hope not, but better safe than sorry."

Her eyes flashed with excitement. "Maybe I could borrow my cousin's twenty-two."

"But you don't know how to use it," I pointed out.

"I'm a quick study."

I didn't argue. "Fine. Get the gun," I said. "Just don't point it at me."

Lindsey had perked up at the prospect of our proposed adventure, even though she had no idea what it might be. Come to think of it, I didn't have much of an idea what it might be, either. But I was sure about one thing: There was no way Lindsey was going along.

"I'll go ask her if I can borrow it. See you at six," she

said, and turned to leave. She paused at the doorway and glared at me from sharp gray eyes. "Sophie, if you stand me up, I'll never forgive you."

"I know," I said. We locked eyes for a long moment before she turned and swept through the door.

I had to protect my friend. But I wasn't sure our friendship would survive.

Twenty-nine

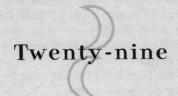

At 5:35, I was pacing back and forth across my loft and staring at the phone. I had told Lourdes to meet me at 5:30, and she was already five minutes late. If she didn't get here soon, Lindsey would be here, and there was no way I was taking her with me tonight. Belatedly, I realized I should have told her I was leaving at seven.

I was changing positions to avoid wearing a track in my Kashan rug and checking my watch for the fortieth time—5:38—when the phone rang.

I snatched up the receiver. "Hello?"

"Miss Sophie?"

"Frank?" It was the doorman.

"There are three young ladies here to see you."

I swallowed. "Three?"

"Yes, ma'am. Brissa, Teena, and . . . Lord, is it?"

"Lourdes," I said tersely. Why had she brought the other two along? It was bad enough having to take Lourdes with me. "Tell them I'll be right down."

"Will do."

I grabbed my bag and hurried out the door, glancing at my watch again—5:40—as I punched the down button on the elevator.

When I stepped out into the lobby a minute later, the grrls were standing near the front door, rather conspicuously decked out in camouflage. I took a quick sniff; the gear had muted most of their scent. They might stand out a bit visually—at least here in the lobby of my building—but least they hadn't layered on perfume or anything.

"Hi, Sophie!" Lourdes said, giving me a little wave as I marched over to them.

"What are Brissa and Teena doing here?" I hissed.

Lourdes ignored my bitchy tone. "They want to help."

"If anything happens, you'll need backup," Teena said with a toothy smile. The olive-drab camo actually suited her—either that or it was just an improvement over charcoal polyester.

"These are dangerous people we're dealing with," I said.

"You mean werewolves," Brissa said loudly.

"Shh." I glanced around toward Frank, hoping he hadn't been listening. As if. *Design on a Dime* was on, which meant I could have escorted an entire herd of mastodons through the lobby without him glancing up from the screen. I turned back to the grrls. "I need to get out of here—I've got to talk to Frank for a moment, then we'll head to the garage."

"Does that mean we're all going?"

"We'll talk about it in a moment," I replied, stalking toward the front desk and wondering how I could cut Lourdes out of the herd. Or the pack, in this case. So far, this evening was not going at all as I'd planned.

"Frank," I said, waving in an attempt to get his attention.

His eyes didn't swerve from the screen, but at least he grunted, which I took to mean he'd noticed me. I held a note out. "This is for my friend Lindsey."

"Right," he said, still staring at the TV behind the desk, where a perky blonde was stapling about ten yards of garish orange fabric to a piece of plywood. I resisted the urge to rip the cable out of the wall.

"Lindsey Mitchell," I said loudly. "She's expecting to meet me here, but I had to leave early. Please make sure she gets this."

"Uh-huh," Frank said absently.

I glanced at my watch: 5:45. Time to go. "You know, I would feel a bit more comfortable if you actually took the note," I said.

"Oh." He took the envelope from my hand and placed it absently on the corner of the desk, and for a brief moment, his watery eyes actually focused on me. "Sorry about that. Who's it for again?"

"It's on the envelope." I pointed out to him. "Her name is Lindsey," I repeated. "She'll be here at six. Make sure she gets it."

"Got it," he said.

Yeah, right. Thank goodness the envelope was labeled in block print and sitting on the corner of the desk. At least when Frank forgot about it, there was a chance she'd spot it herself.

I grabbed my big bag of gear and headed over to the grrls, who looked like they were auditioning for a *Charlie's Angels* episode set on an army base. A moment later, I hurried toward the elevator; the three werewolves trundled after me, rubber boots squeaking. I held the door and hit the button for the third parking level as they filed in behind me. Would we make it out of the garage before Lindsey got here? I glanced at my watch— 5:48—then shook my head at Teena and Brissa, whose eyes were gleaming with excitement. "It's too dangerous for you to come along. I'd offer you my loft, but it's not . . . well, it's not a good place to be tonight." Honestly, I wasn't sure which would be worse—braving a showdown with a pack of angry werewolves or facing Lindsey when she discovered I'd deserted her.

"We got gear," Teena said.

"Yes, I noticed. Very nice."

"Got another bottle of that scentproof spray, too. And we even brought a weapon. Just in case." Brissa fumbled in her bag for a moment. Then she pulled out a big honking gun and pointed it straight at my head.

Thank God I'd visited the little girls' room a few minutes earlier, or I might have been headed back upstairs for a change of underwear.

"Not at her!" Teena hissed at Brissa, pushing the muzzle down with her palm. My knees felt like Jell-O; I sucked in a deep breath and grabbed the wall of the elevator. Even if the bullets weren't silver, a point-blank shot to the head still wasn't something I wanted to experience personally.

"Sorry," Brissa said sheepishly.

When I'd recovered what was left of my sangfroid, I asked her, "What kind of bullets?"

Brissa tilted her chin up proudly. "Silver."

Gah! It was a very, very good thing she didn't have a twitchy trigger finger. The silver bullets might come in handy, though—provided one of them didn't end up embedded in my skull. "Ever shot it before?" I asked, hoping that maybe she had a marksmanship hobby, or worked part-time as a sniper or something.

"No," she said, dashing my admittedly optimistic hopes. Then she added brightly, "But my brother says it's not hard."

Great.

I mustered what I hoped was a kindly smile. "Ladies . . ."

"Grrls," Teena interjected.

"Right. Grrls. The thing is, you see, as much as I appreciate your support, I'm not sure this is the best idea."

"We're a pack," Teena said stolidly, her mouth a straight line.

"Technically, I don't think we ever really made that official," I reminded her.

"Not with you, maybe," Teena said. "At least not yet." She eyed me, looking for a positive sign. "But Lourdes is one of us. If she goes, we go. We heard what happened last time; we're not going to let her go without backup."

The elevator door slid open, and I glanced at Lourdes. She shrugged.

I looked at my watch one last time. There was no way I could take them back to the loft and get downstairs without running into Lindsey.

"Okay," I said reluctantly. "But once we get there, you'll have to wait in the car."

Teena gave me a mock salute. "Aye aye, captain."

"I'm not your captain."

"Alpha?" she asked hopefully.

I rolled my eyes and hit the unlock button on my keychain. The more the merrier, I told myself. And if nothing else, at least I'd managed to get out without Lindsey.

The sun was sinking toward the horizon as my overloaded—and very werewolf-scented—M3 pulled out of the parking garage a few minutes later.

"So what's our game plan?" Teena asked from the backseat, where she was wedged in with Brissa and my bag of camo gear.

As I pointed the car east, I said, "We're going to what I think is a werewolf compound that belongs to one of the Mexican packs. All we need to do is get in and find out what's going on in it."

"How are we going to do that?"

"By smell, partly. I'm looking for two . . . people."

"You mean werewolves," Teena corrected me.

"Werewolves, people. Whatever. You know what I mean."

"What if they're not there?"

"Well, then, I'm hoping we'll be able to look around, maybe overhear something." I glanced up at the rearview mirror; Teena was looking at me intently.

"That's why you need Lourdes," she said. "Because they're Mexican werewolves, and she speaks Spanish."

I sighed. "Exactly."

"How did you find out about this place?" Brissa asked.

"I was in the area recently, and I came across it."

"But why do you think they're there?"

What, was this twenty questions or something? "One of the werewolves who was in San Antonio the other day was there; I recognized his scent. He also attacked me in Austin." And was wearing a leather medallion that matched the one I'd found in the Greenbelt. And smelled like Tom.

"They attacked you?" Brissa asked, her face pale.

I nodded. Good. Maybe this conversation would encourage them to take cover in the M3. They'd better not mess up the upholstery, though. "Yup. Like I said, this is dangerous stuff."

Teena ignored me, and said, "So that's all you've got to go on? A smell?"

I glanced over at Lourdes. "That's not the only thing. Remember Clumpers?"

Her delicate brow furrowed. "Clumpers?"

"The restaurant those werewolves were talking about, down in San Antonio. The one they went to a lot. They liked the steak."

"Oh, yeah. What about it?"

"I found it," I said. "On Google. It's called Klaemper's, actually—it's a little German-American restaurant. And it's five miles away from the ranch we're going to."

"So we *did* hear something useful," Lourdes said.

"I think it's their base of operations. Or at least one of

them." And I didn't know why—call it a hunch—I was almost sure that Tom was there now—or would be there soon. I wasn't sure about Hubert, but I was hoping I'd at least get a line on him. Enough to toss a bone—so to speak—to the Houston pack.

As I gripped the steering wheel and passed a huge pickup truck with the Confederate flag on the back window, a little voice in my head—one that sounded remarkably like Teena's—started voicing some doubts. So what if I recognized the smell of one of my attackers from the ranch out in Roundtop? That didn't mean anyone would be there when I got there. And hunch or no hunch, even though I'd caught a faint whiff of Tom, that didn't mean he was out at the ranch. Even if he was—and was being held hostage, or something—did I expect the grrls and I would be able to help him? Besides, the whole point of this assignment was to track down Hubert, but there was absolutely nothing to connect him to Roundtop. Was I just going off half-cocked?

Unfortunately, I concluded privately as I turned onto 71, the answer was probably *yes*. And I was dragging three innocent young women—well, young werewolves, anyway—into it with me.

On the other hand, if I didn't do *something*, I was going to be run out of town. And if Tom was out there—and in trouble—I owed it to him to at least try to help. I gripped the steering wheel harder and hoped I wasn't totally off base.

"Won't they have lots of werewolves there, guarding the place?" Brissa asked.

"I don't know, but there might be," I said, trying to banish the little voices inside my head—you know, the ones that kept telling me I was nuts to be doing this—and looking up at Brissa's worried face in the rearview mirror. "Are you sure you want to go? I could drop you off somewhere."

I could see Brissa swallow—she was wavering—but before she could respond, Teena answered for her. "I told you, Miss Sophie. We're a pack. We go together, or not at all."

Oh, well. At least I'd tried.

As the sun dipped below the horizon and the scrubby oaks of Austin were replaced by the taller pines that grew east of town, conversation dwindled. I'd like to think it was because everyone was worried about our little venture, but I think it had more to do with the fact that it was hard to carry on a conversation when three out of four of us were busy belting out "Walk Like an Egyptian" and "I'm Your Venus." Loudly. In separate and unrelated keys.

As Madonna's "Material Girl"—which until that moment, had been one of my favorite songs—came on the radio, which was doing an eighties flashback night, I found myself fervently wishing we were already at our destination. Because it couldn't be worse than this.

Finally, I turned down the highway that had led to the Dude Ranch—and to the unmarked gate where I'd smelled the werewolves. I turned down the radio—the current track was "Careless Whisper"—and was met with howls of dismay from my passengers.

"It's not over yet!" Teena complained.

"We're almost there," I said.

"There's Clumpers," Lourdes said, pointing out the window at a barnlike structure with a blue-and-white checked flag and a parking lot full of pickups and large American cars. *Klaemper's,* read the white-painted sign.

"Great," I said. "Maybe if we're not dead in an hour, we can stop for steak."

"With backup like us, what could go wrong?" Teena said.

I didn't bother answering.

About fifteen minutes later, I slowed the M3 and opened the window, letting in a burst of cold air; a front had come through earlier that day, and the moonlit evening was turning frosty.

"What are you doing?" Lourdes asked.

"Sniffing the place out," I said. The headlights that had been behind me since we turned off 71 came closer; I pulled toward the side of the road to let the car pass, but it just slowed down, too. After I hit a pothole, I gave up and pulled back into the driving lane.

About five miles down the road, I caught the first whiff. I wasn't the only one; beside me, Lourdes looked like a hunting dog on the scent.

"We're here," she said. And a moment later, my headlights caught the reflective numbers of the entrance.

"Where should we park?" Teena asked.

"Probably a little ways down," I said. "We don't want to go too far, though, in case we need to get back fast."

"How about next to that clump of bushes?" Lourdes suggested, pointing to a scrubby area to our right.

"Looks good," I said, and eased the M3 onto the shoulder, wincing as gravel pinged against the undercarriage. My poor baby.

I had just put the car in park when there was a crunching sound, and light flooded the interior of the M3.

The car that had been following us had just pulled in behind us.

Thirty

"What do we do?" Teena asked.

"I don't know. Maybe they just think we need help," I said hopefully.

The headlights went dark, and the car door opened. "Got the gun?" I asked Brissa.

"Right here," she said, brandishing it at me again.

Teena grabbed it and pointed it at the window. "Not at Sophie, you goof! Now, give me that!"

As the two of them wrangled over the gun, I peered out the window, heart thudding in my chest. The driver's side door slammed shut, and I heard the crunch of gravel as whoever it was approached the car. I swallowed, my mouth dry, as the dark figure came closer. Who was it? Was it one of the werewolves?

I sniffed at the cold breeze and caught the scent just as a voice cut through the night air. "Sophie Garou!"

I closed my eyes and swore silently. It wasn't one of the werewolves.

It was Lindsey.

I glanced back at Teena, who was training the gun on the figure approaching the car. "Don't point it at her!" I said. When she looked confused, I reached out and pushed the muzzle down. "It's all right," I said, which really wasn't at all true, because (a) I wasn't sure how I was going to explain all this to my best friend, and (b) I wasn't sure I would get a chance. "She's a friend."

"Oh," Teena said. "What's she doing here?"

"I'm afraid we're about to find out," I said, and then Lindsey was yanking open my door.

"You stood me up!" she said, gray eyes flashing in the moonlight. She had dressed for subterfuge in jeans and a dark-colored jacket, her hair pulled back in a smooth ponytail. I hoped that if she brought the pepper spray—or the .22—she didn't feel inclined to try them out.

"Why did you follow me?" I countered.

"Because you tried to leave without me, you idiot! I saw you pull out just as I pulled in."

"Oh. Well, there was a change of plans," I said lamely. "I had to leave early."

"Who are these people?" she asked, gesturing toward the grrls.

"They're . . . friends."

"So you can bring them along, but you can't bring me?" Lindsey said coldly.

"I didn't want to," I said. "I needed Lourdes—she translates for me—but the other two wouldn't let her go alone."

"Hmmph," Lindsey said, crossing her arms.

"Look," I said brightly, as if everything was hunky dory and I wasn't sitting on the side of a back road with three werewolves and a pissed-off best friend. "Teena and Brissa are going to stay and . . . guard the M3," I said. "It'll be like the getaway car, in case we need it. Why don't you stay with your car, and if we come out with Tom, we'll have room for all of us?"

"We're going with you," Teena piped up from the backseat. I could have killed her.

"If they're going, I'm going," Lindsey said stubbornly. "And what the heck is Tom doing out in BFE?"

"How do you know Tom?" Brissa asked.

Lindsey's eyes swerved to the younger woman. "How do *you* know Tom?"

"I met him at Sophie's loft," Brissa said, and if I could have melted into the gravel right then I would have done it.

Lindsey rounded on me, and I swear the temperature dropped another twenty degrees. "In *your* loft?"

"It's not what you think," I said, raising my hands.

"Oh, no? Then what *is* it, Sophie? How do you know where Tom is when he won't even call me? What was he doing at your place when I wasn't there?"

"I can explain everything," I mumbled, and there was what I guess you'd call a pregnant pause as I tried to come up with something.

"I'm listening," Lindsey said in a voice that was dangerously low.

Teena blinked at me. "She doesn't know?"

Lindsey's eyes darted to Teena. "Know what?"

"Oh," Teena said. "Sorry."

Which didn't help at all.

"What's going on here?" Lindsey demanded, hands on her hips.

"It's . . . hard to explain," I said.

"You've been seeing Tom on the side, from what I can see. What's hard to explain about that?"

"No," I said, trying not to think about that one kiss. Okay, those two kisses.

My best friend stared at me. "Then start talking."

A cold wind swept over us. I sniffed reflexively and could sense the other three testing the air with me. *Werewolves.* My hackles rose as I detected the cumin scent of the werewolf who had attacked me at the ballet, along with what I thought was probably Mr. Big and Hairy. And another scent, too. Familiar, but elusive. Tom? I took another breath, closing my eyes to focus on the scent. He had been here, I was sure of it. Was he here now?

"Can you smell him?" Teena asked me.

"Smell who?" Lindsey asked.

I opened my eyes and dragged them back to my friend, who was glaring at me. "You're still not talking," she reminded me.

"There's something you don't know about me," I said slowly.

"I'm all ears," she said.

"If I tell you, you have to promise not to tell anyone."

She crossed her arms. "What, you're a nymphomaniac who can't keep her hands off other people's boyfriends?"

"I'm a werewolf," I muttered.

Lindsey blinked. "What?"

"A werewolf."

"You're kidding me, right?"

"I wish I were. So's Tom. And Brissa, and Lourdes, and Teena," I said, waving at the women in the car.

Lindsey was silent for a moment. Then she snorted. "You? And Tom? You get into that weird kind of subculture?"

"No, Lindsey. I'm serious. It's a real condition. Remember that hair problem I told you about? The one I take the tea for?"

She stared at me.

"And the meeting with Southeast Airlines? When I had to leave in the middle?"

"Oh, my God. You're serious, aren't you?"

"Dead serious," I said. "That's why Tom was at my loft the other day. Because the Houston pack knows about me, and they want me to leave Austin, and I needed his advice. And when I got sick at the Dude Ranch, it was because someone had poisoned me. Tom's just trying to help me."

She blinked, looking pale in the wash of the head-lights. Was she going to faint? I almost started toward her. "So you and Tom aren't . . ."

"No," I said, shaking my head.

She breathed a big sigh of relief. "Thank God."

I couldn't believe it. Here I was, baring my deepest, darkest secret, and all Lindsey cared about was whether I was snogging her boyfriend. "No," I said, banishing my distinctly unplatonic thoughts regarding Lindsey's sizzling hot beau. And our last kiss . . . "We're just friends."

Now that she was convinced I wasn't sleeping with Tom, Lindsey actually started to think about what I'd told her. I could tell by the look on her face; the last time I'd seen it she was facing down a client who kept insisting a missing million dollars was the result of a math error. "How can you be a werewolf?" she asked. "How is that possible? I mean, you can't be serious. So you grow a little hairy sometimes. That doesn't mean you actually turn into an animal." She narrowed her eyes at me. "Do you?"

I nodded.

"Wow. Are you sure this isn't just some kinky Goth thing you're into?"

"God, no," I said. "Do you really think I'd choose to be a freak?"

She shrugged. "You never know. Some people think it's a turn-on."

Hardly. "It wasn't a choice. I was born this way." It kind of sounded like I was coming out of the closet. In a way, I suppose, I was. "So was Tom," I added.

Lindsey turned to look at the grrls. "What about you three?"

"We weren't born," Teena said. "We were made."

"Made," Lindsey repeated. "How the hell do you 'make' a werewolf?"

"It's sort of disgusting," I said. "Evidently it's a contagious condition; it passes through blood. That's how they got it," I said, pointing at the grrls. "A blood transfusion."

"In a hospital?" Lindsey asked, looking horrified.

"No," Teena said. "With a syringe. We chose to do it."

Lindsey turned to me. "So if I wanted to be one, I could?"

"I guess so," I said, "but I wouldn't recommend it." Headlights appeared on the horizon; I turned and squinted into them. "You know, we probably shouldn't keep standing here. Someone's going to notice us." The car whizzed by without slowing, fortunately, and then we were alone again, back in the light of the moon—and Lindsey's headlights, which were still on.

"Why *are* you here?" Lindsey asked.

"I told you. I think Tom's here. In fact, I'm almost sure of it."

"How?"

"We can smell him," Brissa said through the car window.

"Smell him."

I nodded.

"Show me," Lindsey demanded.

"Show you what?"

"How you change," she said. "I want to see."

"Are you sure?"

She nodded.

I stepped out of the car and checked to make sure there were no headlights in the distance.

"Ready?"

Lindsey nodded once, her hair gleaming in the moonlight. Then I took a deep breath, closed my eyes, and let go.

The urge passed through me like water breaking over

a dam, rushing through every cell of my body. I could feel the tickle of fur sprouting up from my skin as the world took on extra dimensions. The whisper of each stalk of dried grass was amplified, and the cold breeze eddied with the smell of asphalt, dried leaves, a jackrabbit . . . and, in the distance, the musk of werewolves. Lots of them. The urge to let the change run its course was almost irresistible—kind of like trying not to eat a hot fudge sundae when you've been doing Atkins for three weeks—but I pulled back anyway. Partly to spare Lindsey, and partly because I didn't want to pop all the buttons on my blouse.

When I opened my eyes, Lindsey was staring at me, mouth hanging open, with a mix of fascination and something I hoped wasn't revulsion.

When she found her voice, she breathed, "Holy crap."

"That's only the sneak preview," I said when I had completed my return to fully human mode.

"You mean you . . ."

"Remember the German shepherd with the shaved legs?"

"The one in the paper last fall? Who mauled the guy when he was out for a walk?"

The newspaper's version of that incident—which had happened last September—still annoyed me. The report said I'd attacked an innocent pedestrian, but that was hogwash. It was self-defense.

"He was a car burglar, Lindsey. He'd just broken into my M3—remember when the window was broken?—and I was trying to get my purse back. My new Kate Spade bag. Less than a week old," I added to drive the point home.

"Oh, my God." Her hand strayed to her throat. "That was you?"

I nodded.

"No wonder you felt bad for the dog."

"Exactly."

Lindsey leaned against my M3. "Jesus. This is too much. I think I need a drink."

"You could head back to Austin," I suggested.

Lindsey's head whipped around, sending her ponytail swinging. "And leave you here by yourself? No way."

"I'm not exactly by myself," I reminded her, nodding toward the three werewolves in my M3. "Lindsey, what we're about to do is dangerous. I don't know exactly who's in this compound, but I've had a few run-ins with some of them, and they're nasty."

She lifted her chin. "If Tom's in there, I'm staying."

"And what exactly do you plan to do?"

"I don't know," she said. "Tag along with you and figure it out, I guess." She eyed the grrls and murmured, "So, does the liquid black eyeliner transfer along with the werewolf blood? Because that could be a pretty major deterrent."

"Don't even think about it," I growled.

"Who, me? You know I hate excess body hair," she said, although I could tell by the speculative look in her eye that she was already figuring out how much the extra waxing appointments would run her. Maybe I should have told her that liquid eyeliner was compulsory, and that you could only wear waders. "But what else do werewolves do? I mean, there's the smelling, and the whole fur and teeth thing. But do you have any special powers?"

"Not that I know of," I said. Except for the super sense of smell, the extra strength, and the semi-immortality thing, of course. But my goal was to *dis*courage her, not have her following me around with a syringe in hand, waiting for a chance to jab me.

She gave me an appraising look. "You're just being modest, aren't you?"

"No," I said. "Really, I'm not. But are you sure you wouldn't rather go home and have a glass of wine?" I asked, just in case she'd changed her mind.

She shook her head. "Just tell me what I need to do."

I would have loved to. The problem was, I had no idea.

It took about fifteen minutes for me to change into my gear and get everyone assembled and carbon-blasted—including Lindsey, even though she wasn't a werewolf. She wasn't wearing any gear, either, but I was hoping it wouldn't be too much of a problem.

When everyone was fully outfitted, the five of us crossed the highway and examined the fence, which—inconveniently—was about six feet tall.

"Barbed wire," Teena said, reaching out to touch one of the wires. A second later, she jerked her hand back. "Ouch!"

"Electric?"

"And how. Man," she said, shaking her arm and peering at the fence, which on closer inspection was constructed of nasty-looking barbed wire alternating every few inches with smooth, presumably high-voltage wires. Whoever put it up obviously meant business. "Aren't there voltage limits or something?"

"I guess that means we're not climbing it," I said lightly. But I was starting to worry a bit. I don't know why—call it wishful thinking, or maybe an excess of optimism—but I hadn't counted on major security measures. What would we do if we couldn't get through the gate? I would have dragged everyone out here for nothing. Correction: I would have dragged Lourdes out here for nothing. Everyone else came of their own volition.

And now Lindsey knew about me, I thought, glancing over at her. She seemed okay with it now, but how would she be tomorrow? And could I trust her to keep it quiet? A cold wind bit through my carbon-blasted jacket as we padded up the shoulder toward the gate, and the moon hung over our heads like a malevolent, half-lidded eye. Or maybe that's just because I'm not a big fan of the moon in general.

"What do we do if the gate's locked?" Lindsey asked.

"I don't know," I said.

"How many werewolves are here?" Brissa asked.

"I don't know."

"What if we can't get through the gate?" Teena asked.

We were back to twenty questions again. "I don't know," I repeated.

"What if there are like, a billion werewolves in there?" Lourdes asked.

God. Was this what traveling with small children was like? If so, perhaps remaining kid-free wasn't such a bad deal. My breath hissed through my teeth as I turned to face everyone. "Look. I don't have any answers. And I didn't ask you to come with me. My plan is to look at the gate and see if there's any way past it. Once we're in, I'll go from there. If you've got a better idea, I'm all ears. But if you need a schedule and a detailed map, I recommend you book a tour somewhere."

"Sorry," Teena said, and from then on we trekked on in silence—except for the squeak of our rubber boots and the sound of Lindsey humming. The song sounded suspiciously like "Werewolves of London."

"Shh," I said, nudging her in the ribs. "They've got great hearing."

"Oops. Sorry about that." And that, thankfully, was the end of Warren Zevon for the evening. Although I suspected I'd be hearing a lot more of it in the future. Provided we survived the next few hours, anyway.

As we marched down the gravelly shoulder toward the gate, the smell of werewolves got stronger. I took a deep whiff, trying to gauge how well our scent was masked. It seemed faint to me, but that could be because I was used to it. Which wasn't a comforting thought, so I decided not to dwell on it.

And then, before I knew it, we were there.

It was a tall, imposing-looking gate—kind of an "Abandon Hope All Ye Who Enter Here" affair—criss-crossed with what looked like a couple thousand wires. A heavy, rusted chain was looped through the door twice, terminating in an industrial-sized padlock.

It wasn't exactly a welcome mat. In fact, unless one of the grrls knew how to levitate, it looked like we had reached the end of the road.

Thirty-one

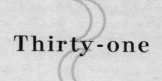

Lindsey crossed her arms and gazed up at the gigantic gate. "So," she said, "do your super-werewolf powers include leaping over tall fences in a single bound?"

"Unfortunately not," I admitted. "Doesn't look too welcoming, does it?"

Lindsey eyed the thick chain that held the gate closed. "A bolt cutter would be a good thing to have. Or maybe even your mom's hedge clippers." I shuddered, remembering my mother's failed jewelry-removal attempt. At least she hadn't accidentally removed my finger. I touched the ring Mark had given me; despite the near-freezing temperatures, it was warm. Hot, almost.

Just like Mark.

Who had said he'd come if I was in trouble again, I now recalled. Did this qualify? And if it did, did I really want him turning up on the scene like my own personal knight in shining armor? I wasn't quite sure. Besides, unless he could tame gates like he tamed werewolves, he wouldn't be much help with our current predicament. Once we got past the gate, though, he might be pretty handy to have around. . . .

No, Sophie. It was bad enough dragging Lindsey and the Texarkana trio into this; I wasn't about to call my top client out to help me trespass on a rural ranch. A rural werewolf ranch. So I banished thoughts of the mysterious and smoldering Mark and forced myself to focus on the gate. Which unfortunately hadn't done anything convenient like fall over or rust into pieces while I was noodling on about my client.

"I've got nail clippers," Brissa said, digging in the little purse she had strapped to her camo. "Do you think if we used gloves—kind of like potholders—I could snip the wires without electrocuting myself?"

"We could always drive through the fence," Teena suggested.

"In Sophie's BMW?" Lindsey said, snorting. "Fat chance."

"Just a thought," Teena said. "But your car—wouldn't insurance cover it, anyway?"

"Ain't gonna happen," Lindsey said.

"Besides," I pointed out, "it would probably set off an alarm or something."

Teena heaved a big sigh, and we all stood there in silence, staring at the gate. I was mulling over Brissa's nail-clipper suggestion when I noticed something that looked like an electrical box attached to the inside of one of the posts.

"Look," I said, pointing to the big black box. "I think that's the power source."

"And there's the cord," Lindsey said, pointing to a white cord that snaked away into the bushes. "If we could somehow unplug it . . ."

Unfortunately, there was no way to reach it from this side of the fence. "It's too far," I said. "Plus, I bet it would set off an alarm."

As we lapsed into silence again, a chilly wind swept through the fence, smelling like a mixed werewolf assortment.

"He's there," Teena said in a low voice.

"Tom?" Lindsey asked.

"Yes," I said; I could smell him, too. His primeval scent sent a shiver through me. But that could be because it was accompanied by the scent of several other werewolves, including Mr. Big and Hairy. And a few other choice aromas; that piney smell from the cave, and something else. Something unpleasant. "Problem is, so are a bunch of other werewolves."

"Well, if we can't get through, we might as well go home," Lindsey said peevishly. "Are you sure you don't want to try the M3?"

"Your Miata's here, too," I pointed out.

"Cheap Japanese tin can," she said dismissively. "Doesn't have the heft of those solid German cars."

"Wait a moment," Teena said, glancing down the road at our cars and back at the fence. "We might not be able to drive through, but if we drove up and parked beside the fence, maybe we could jump over it from the roof of the car."

I glanced at Teena in surprise. Maybe it wasn't such a bad idea for her to come along after all. "That just might work," I said, trying to estimate the distance. The car was about four feet tall, which would leave only two feet of fence to get over. Of course it was still a six-foot drop to the ground on the other side, but since none of us was wearing stilettos, it shouldn't be too bad. As long as we were careful not to scratch the finish.

"You know I'd offer the Miata," Lindsey said consolingly—she knew how I felt about the M3—"but it's a convertible. The soft top just wouldn't support us."

"Too bad I didn't know about the fence," Lourdes said, "or I would have borrowed my cousin's F-one-fifty."

"Anyone got another idea?" I asked hopefully.

As they shook their heads no, a sharp wind swept over us—from the wrong direction. "Wind's changing," Teena said in a low voice.

As if in response, a low howl sounded in the distance. The hairs stood up on the back of my neck, and I could sense Lindsey shiver beside me.

"Do you think they know we're here?" Brissa asked, eyes wide.

"I hope not," I said. "But we'd better get over that fence before they do." As I hurried over to my gleaming red M3, I tried to shrug off the feeling of foreboding that was creeping over me. Instead, I unlocked the car doors and ran a loving hand over my darling's candy-apple-red finish, silently promising to take her in for a deluxe detailing when all of this was over.

As Lindsey and the werewolf grrls waited, I U-turned and pulled the M3 up as close as I could to the fence, wincing as bushes scraped against the side of the car. When I was about six inches away from the fence, I cut the engine and opened the door.

"Who's first?" Lindsey asked as she and the grrls approached the car.

"I'll go," Teena said, and before anyone else could volunteer, she had clambered up to the top of the car—I winced as her foot slid on the hood—and launched herself over the fence. A moment later, there was a big "Ooof."

Brissa peered into the darkness after her. "Teena!"

"What's wrong?"

"Cactus," she groaned, and I winced in sympathy.

"How bad?" I asked.

"Just a few stickers in my left arm; it could have been a lot worse."

"I guess I'll go next," Lindsey said, climbing up the hood to the roof of the car. "Where should I aim?" she called to Teena.

"Over here," she answered, and Lindsey leaped.

I followed Lindsey, glad I was wearing rubber-soled boots, but cringing as I felt the metal of the roof buckle under my feet. The little car held up remarkably well, though—like Lindsey said, that solid, German engineering—and within five minutes, all of us were over the fence. It was only when Brissa stood up and was brushing herself off that Teena said, "Huh. I didn't think about that."

"Didn't think about what?"

She stared up at the fence. "We used the car to get in. But how do we get out?"

I was still trying to come up with a convenient way out of the compound as we skirted a giant stand of prickly pear cactus twenty minutes later. After a brief discussion, we'd decided to follow the perimeter of the fence until the wind was in our favor again. Which meant walking for what felt like six miles. I hoped we wouldn't have to make a quick getaway.

"We could always shoot the box, then climb over the fence," Lindsey whispered to me. Evidently she was still thinking about our little dilemma, too.

"This is supposed to be a stealth mission, remember?" I asked.

"I mean, if we get caught or something," she said.

"It's a good idea, but I'm not sure I could find the gate again if I tried." Which wasn't a comforting thought either, actually. I mean, what good is a getaway car if you don't know where it is?

We squeaked along for a few more minutes; then, suddenly, a chilly breeze swept over us, smelling rather strongly of werewolves. A lot of them. And not far away. Adrenaline pulsed through me, and I had to resist the impulse to transform.

"Ready?" I asked.

No one answered for a moment. Then Teena said slowly, "Are you sure we should be going *toward* the werewolves?"

"No," I replied in a whisper. "But I'm out of other ideas."

"Would it be better to transform first?" Brissa asked.

"We'd be faster that way," Teena pointed out.

"But they would smell us without the special clothing," Lourdes said. "Besides, Lindsey can't change."

"If they figure out we're here, we can transform to make a quick getaway," I reasoned.

"What about me?" Lindsey's gray eyes were wide with fear.

"Whatever happens, I won't abandon you," I said, glancing at my friend.

"Promise?"

I reached over to squeeze her hand with my gloved one. "Promise. Are you sure you don't want to stay out of the way, though?"

"If I've come this far, I might as well go all the way," she said.

"Positive?"

"I'm sure."

"Okay." I gave her hand another squeeze, then turned to the grrls and said, "Let's go."

As I headed in the direction of the scent, the grrls and Lindsey trailing behind me, I wondered exactly what we would find when we got wherever it was we were going. Would it just be a bunch of werewolves hanging out? Was Hubert at the ranch? I sniffed the air again; I thought I detected a scent that was something like Wolfgang's, but I could be wrong. Tom was here, though; his primal scent became stronger with every step I took. But was he here of his own accord—or had somebody captured him?

I was imagining Tom bound up in silver chains, surrounded by gnawed bones and a water dish, when a light appeared through the silvery mesquite trees in front of me.

I stopped, and Teena plowed into me. I bit off a curse and grabbed a tree to keep from falling over.

"What is it?" she whispered when we both regained our balance.

"It looks like it's a building of some sort," I said, squinting. "A window, maybe. Let's get closer."

Creeping as quietly as possible in our rubber boots (except Lindsey, whose tennis shoes I would have killed for just then), the five of us shuffled closer. The light was indeed a window, which glowed from the white-painted boards of a farmhouse, ghostly in the moonlight. There was no way to hide our approach; the scrubby trees ended about fifty yards away from the building. A bit beyond it was a larger, dark building that looked like a barn.

"Smells weird," Teena whispered.

She was right, I realized, taking another deep breath. Tom was close by—so close I could feel myself tingling in response. And there were werewolves there, including a few who from the smell of them, weren't overly familiar with the basics of personal hygiene. But there was that piney scent, and something pungent.

Not to mention a strong, rather disquieting smell of fear.

"I have a bad feeling about this," Lourdes murmured into my ear. She, Lindsey, and Brissa had moved up to join Teena and me.

"What now?" Lindsey asked.

I motioned everybody to back away from the house. When we had retreated a little ways back into the brush, I whispered, "I think we need to get close enough to see inside."

"But there's nowhere to hide," Teena protested.

I swallowed hard. "I'll go alone. You guys stay under cover; if there's trouble, just get out of here."

"By yourself?" Lindsey asked. "You're nuts."

"Take this," Brissa said, fumbling in her pockets. A second later, I was facing the barrel of a gun for the second time that evening.

As I stood rooted to the ground, fighting the impulse to drop down on all fours and run howling, Teena reached out and pushed the gun down. "Not *at* her, Brissa! Geez, Louise! How many times do I have to tell you?"

"Sorry," she said in a small voice as Teena grabbed the gun and handed it to me. "At least the safety was on, though."

I smiled weakly at the young Texarkana werewolf, who was looking at me from raccoon-ringed eyes. "Thanks, Brissa."

"I'll go with her," Lourdes piped up unexpectedly.

"Lourdes . . ." I protested.

"You don't speak Spanish, Sophie. And most gringos don't eat *carne guisada* at home."

Now that she mentioned it, there was an undertone of spiced meat in the air. Despite my—well, let's call it apprehension—my salivary glands kicked in.

"You can smell that?" Lindsey asked.

"Uh-huh," I said.

"There are an awful lot of werewolves here somewhere," Teena said.

"And there are only four of us," Brissa pointed out.

"And me," Lindsey piped up. As if I needed to be reminded.

"Well," I said, "the longer we wait, the higher the chances we'll get caught." I looked at Lourdes. "Are you sure you want to come with me?"

The moonlight glanced off her shiny black hair as she nodded.

"Okay, then." I fingered the ring Mark had given me. If worse came to worst, I told myself, I could always call him for help. Although it occurred to me suddenly that

Mark had never told me exactly how the whole ring thing worked. Would it just know when I was in trouble? Did I have to talk to it or something?

Well, it was too late now; I'd just have to trust my luck. And the protection spell my mother had cast for me, which admittedly was cold comfort. I loved my mother, but she wasn't hitting too many home runs in the magic department lately.

I flexed my fingers under the gloves, wishing I'd pushed the whole free tax work thing a little harder when I was visiting the Houston pack. Then I squared my shoulders and said, "Let's go."

Thirty-two

Lourdes and I left the little group hidden in a tangle of mesquite, then advanced slowly across the open yard. Despite the twenty pounds of hunting gear Lourdes was bundled into, a stray breeze still brought me a whiff of her scent—which at the moment was metallic with fear. Not a good sign: if I could smell her, so could everybody else. Fortunately, the mouthwatering aroma of *carne guisada* was growing stronger with each step, so at least it would be masked a little bit. I slowed down about ten feet from the farmhouse, struck by the almost overwhelming urge to transform. And then turn tail and run.

But I couldn't do either. I was sure Tom was here; his intoxicating scent grew stronger with each step I took. If he was in trouble, I owed it to him to try to help. And if I left now, I wasn't sure I'd have it in me to come back.

My eyes fixed on the lit window, I marshaled what was left of my resolve and motioned for Lourdes to follow me. We scuttled across the expanse of dead grass, trying to minimize the squeak of our boots, and as a cold breeze eddied past us, crouched under the wood-framed window.

I huddled next to Lourdes for a few moments, trying to get myself under control—fear was making the urge to change almost unstoppable. With a last look at Lourdes, whose dark eyes were rimmed with white, I eased myself up high enough to peer into the window, which smelled—even though it was closed—of chiles, stewed beef, and hard liquor.

The room was a spare kitchen; peeled-paint wood walls, rust-stained sink, a pot bubbling on a gas stove. The *carne guisada,* probably. But I didn't spend a lot of time analyzing the décor, because in the middle of the room, four werewolves sat around a worn wooden table. They were staring at the cards in their hands, playing what looked like poker. Two of them were unfamiliar to me. But I recognized Mr. Big and Hairy.

And Tom.

My breath caught in my throat as my eyes lit on him, and I felt an answering tug deep inside me. Mark was gorgeous, and incredibly seductive, but Tom had a pull on me that was different. Deeper, somehow. I studied him, forgetting for a moment that I was ostensibly here to rescue him. His golden eyes gleamed in the light of the bare bulb hanging from the ceiling; his blond hair was pulled back into a sleek ponytail, and a shot glass lay cradled in his right hand.

Hugin perched on the chair at his right shoulder, his dark eyes shining in the harsh light. He turned his head, one black eye fixed on me, and uttered a soft caw.

Tom's head jerked up, and our eyes locked for an instant. A look of utter surprise—I might even go so far as to call it shock—flashed across his face.

Unfortunately, however, Tom wasn't the only one Hugin had alerted with his little squawk. In the same instant, Mr. Big and Hairy's eyes flashed from the cards in his hand to Tom.

And then to me.

All four of them shot up from their chairs. I grabbed Lourdes by the arm, turned, and started running—instinctively, at first, toward our little pack of friends. A split second later, I swerved away from them, toward the barn; the last thing I needed to do was to take Mr. Big and Hairy straight to my friends.

As we tore past the barn and plunged into the undergrowth, a stray thought flitted into my head.

What the hell was Tom doing playing poker with Mr. Big and Hairy?

Further speculation was curtailed, unfortunately, when my left foot made contact with a rather large hole. I went down like a sack of potatoes—only less gracefully. Lourdes, who had been behind me, stopped to grab my hand and yank me to my feet. A moment later, we were running again, my hurt ankle—why was it always the left one?—twanging with each pounding step.

But it was too late. The first werewolf was on top of us, smelling of cumin and sweat and animal . . . and something else. A sharp smell I recognized.

But a funny thing happened then. As his greasy hand closed on the back of my neck, anger blazed out from somewhere deep inside me, and the change tore through me like a hurricane. I wrenched from his hairy grasp and whirled around to face him, shaking off the camo gear, a low growl ripping from my throat.

He quailed a little—I got a good look at his skinny face, a gold tooth gleaming from between thin lips—and then his features grew plastic, almost like melted wax, as the change rippled through him.

Within seconds, a skinny black wolf slunk out from the remains of his jeans and tattered T-shirt. Still cumin-scented, still sporting a gold tooth, still wearing a pair of dingy tighty-whities, which hung on his hindquarters like a loose diaper. But that's all I had time to notice before I was on him.

I don't remember what happened next, but something came unleashed in me. Something primal, and evidently something pretty scary—because a moment later, the

cumin-scented black wolf was running from me, tail between his legs, Fruit-of-the-Looms glowing in the moonlight. I could smell the coppery scent of blood. And as
disgusting as it sounds, it was satisfying. A brief thought
flashed into my head—was my mother part-vampire?—
as I licked droplets of blood from my chops and turned
to face the others.

Mr. Big and Hairy and his unfamiliar friend were behind me—in full wolf form, but without the underwear.
They were advancing on Lourdes, who was quaking in
her camouflage gear, but for some reason hadn't transformed. My lips curled back from my teeth and another
growl welled up in my throat as I hurled myself at them,
burying my teeth into the sour-tasting fur of the smaller
wolf.

I clamped down, tasting blood and grease, and a
whine sounded from beneath me. I released for a moment, to get a better grip, which was a bad idea, because
the smaller wolf slipped from my grasp. As I lunged to
retrieve him, something barreled into me from the right,
knocking the wind out of me.

I rolled across the grass and was back on my feet in an
instant, gasping for breath and seeking my opponent.
He was there—large, black, and coming straight for me.
I squared my shoulders and faced him, teeth bared as he
hurtled toward me. At the last moment, I feinted to the
left and whipped my head around, ripping open his
right flank.

A howl of anguish sounded as the big wolf wheeled
around for another pass. But there was someone else behind him.

Tom.

My focus wavered for a moment as our eyes met. Tom
was in wolf form again, looking huge and regal, his
black raven perched on his back. *Why are you just
standing there?* I thought. Then a grunt snapped my at-

tention back to my opponent. I jerked my eyes back toward the black wolf; Mr. Big and Hairy was inches away from me, long white teeth bared.

I lunged to the right at the very last moment.

Which was unfortunate, because Mr. Big and Hairy lurched to his left at the same instant. We slammed into each other, rolling across the dead grass, each of us scrabbling to get a death grip on the other.

Suddenly there was a sound like an explosion. My head swiveled to see Brissa, aiming her huge gun in the vicinity of my head. She raised the gun to shoot a second time, but before she could pull the trigger, a wolf slammed into her, knocking the gun from her hand. I wanted to help, but I had problems of my own to deal with.

After letting up a bit at the sound of the gun, Mr. Big and Hairy was on top of me again, his teeth on my neck; I bucked, throwing him off of me, but not before his canines raked my throat. We squared off again, eyes glued to each other, each watching for a moment of weakness. I did a quick scan of my surroundings with my peripheral vision; Lourdes was cowering against a tree, still in human form, but still in one piece, thankfully. I couldn't see Brissa—or Tom—at all.

Mr. Big and Hairy was tensing up for another assault when there was a crackling sound. We both froze, our eyes glued to something that looked like a ripple in the air. A familiar scent blasted through the little clearing, and suddenly a woman appeared, eyes flashing gold in the moonlight.

"You," she said, and smiled in a way that made my hackles rise. I glanced over at my opponent; he appeared to have forgotten about me, and was busy groveling, his nose pushed into the dirt. As I tried to figure out what to do next—attack Mr. Big and Hairy? Try to save Lourdes? Hurl myself at this magically appearing woman and ask her why she'd been in my loft?—she said something in a language I didn't understand, and the air crackled again.

I'm not sure quite what happened next. The world seemed to bend, somehow; the trees receded, and the earth opened up like a yawning cavern at my feet. Then the night sky tore open and a huge black shape hurled into me, plunging both of us into the void. I heard a yelp—was it from me? Then there was a blast of foul breath on my face, the rake of claws down my side . . . and darkness.

Thirty-three

"Sophie."

I was swimming, deep in darkness, the smell of pine and blood, the sound of drums and chanting somewhere in the distance, coming for me. . . .

"Sophie!"

The drums faded, drifting into a howl, and my eyes flew open. No drums, no howl; only Lourdes bent over me, her shimmery eyes wide in the dim light. I took a deep breath and smelled werewolves; dozens of them. And dankness, like stagnant water. "That woman . . . the drums. Mr. Big and Hairy . . . what happened?" I croaked. And what had happened to my friends? My heart squeezed. "Teena and Brissa. And Lindsey. Did they make it out?"

"They're all here," Lourdes said.

My stomach sank. I knew I shouldn't have let them come with me. "Where?" I asked, struggling to sit up. Which turned out to be a futile gesture, since my hands and feet were chained.

"Over there," Lourdes said, pointing with a shackled wrist toward a dark corner. It finally registered that we were in a cave of some sort, with the only light coming from a shaft high above us. I could hear the drip of water somewhere and smelled an aroma that could only be described as ripe outhouse. From buckets scattered around the floor, I realized. Ick.

I squinted my eyes and spotted Lindsey, lying on the floor. *Oh, my God.* "Is she okay?" I asked, heart in my throat.

"She's fine," Lourdes said. "Only sleeping. She tried to stay awake until you came around, but she didn't make it."

"And the grrls?" I shifted in my shackles, which were cinched tight around my wrists and ankles. The movement reminded me that whatever had attacked me had had claws and had made a good bit of contact with my ribcage. Someone had put my camo gear back on me—which I was thankful for, since the cave wasn't exactly toasty—but it was shredded and sticky with blood. I hoped the others had fared better.

"The grrls are fine, too—they're across the cave from us," Lourdes said, pointing to a shadowy area. Now that she mentioned it, I could smell them—and as I squinted into the dim light, I thought I could make out Teena's dark, glossy hair. "Teena found Brett," Lourdes continued. "He's here, along with the other missing Texarkana werewolves."

Well, that was something, at least. I shook my head again, trying to eliminate the fog that seemed to have seeped in through my ears. "Where the hell is *here?*" I asked.

"We're guests of the *Norteños,*" answered a sardonic voice from somewhere behind Lourdes. I struggled to sit up and find the source of the words, but I was pretty sure I knew whose it was; the clipped consonants sounded almost exactly like Wolfgang's.

"Hubert," I said. My eyes located him; he looked like his portrait, only much thinner, and unkempt. Even in the dim light, I could see his gold eyes blaze above a thin-lipped mouth that reminded me of Wolfgang's. Although he obviously hadn't had access to running water for a while, his smell was reminiscent of Wolfgang's. Like me—and Lourdes, and everyone else in the cave, he was in shackles.

"At least we found him," Lourdes said. "So we did what we set out to do."

"Except for the whole being chained up in a cave thing," I said. "Lindsey!" I called.

"She's asleep," Lourdes said.

"Are you sure she's okay?"

"She's fine, Sophie. I promise."

"For now, that is," Hubert said.

"What do you mean?" I asked, even though it seemed to me that being chained up in a cave was a bad sign.

"Your friend tells me you were sent to find me," he said. "Anita must have organized that."

"Actually," I said, "It was Anita and Wolfgang who asked me to find you. I think Anita would have been just as happy to stick me in a kennel."

"Which is exactly what she's done," Hubert said, jingling his chains.

"What?"

"Who do you think put you here?" he asked.

"Mr. Big and Hairy. And that woman," I said, not sounding too coherent, in retrospect.

He shook his head. "No. We're both here because of Anita."

"But Anita's with the Houston pack," I said, my brain feeling even foggier. I remembered those hard, dark eyes, and the scars on her face.

"He says she really isn't," Lourdes said. "That she double-crossed them. And that she's known all along that Hubert was here, because she arranged it."

"Anita knew where you were?" I asked.

"She's working for the *Norteños*," he said. "She lost her bid to rule them a few years back, and then allied herself with Wolfgang. Evidently the arrangement with my brother wasn't satisfactory, however, because she appears to have brokered a deal with her former rival."

"Who is her rival?"

"Xochitl. She is the one who left her with the white scars on her face. I believe you and Lourdes met her briefly."

"Is that the woman I saw the other night? The one with the big dark scary thing, who just appeared out of thin air?"

"Obviously I wasn't there," Hubert said, "but yes, it sounds like you had an encounter with Xochitl, queen of the *Norteños,* priestess of Tezcatlipoca."

"Weird name," I said, repeating it; it sounded like "So-cheet." The whole priestess thing was a bit beyond me, so I stuck with the facts that made sense. "So she's the one who's running the north Mexican pack."

"Yes," Hubert said. "And if Xochitl is successful in her bid to move north, Anita's reward will be all of Texas."

That made sense. But about the whole priestess thing . . . "So who's this Tezcatli . . . whatever you called it?"

"Tezcatlipoca," Hubert said slowly. "An ancient god. Originally of the Toltecs, then the Aztecs. A very nasty god, with rather unpleasant worship requirements."

"Such as?" I asked, although I wasn't sure I wanted to know.

"You'll find out soon enough," he said vaguely.

That didn't sound good. "What does Tezcatli . . . this Toltec god, or Aztec, or whatever it is, have to do with the *Norteños*?" I asked.

"Everything," he said. "Xochitl is the *Norteños'* leader. But she is also his priestess. Tezcatlipoca has a long association with the *naguales.*"

"The *naguales,*" I said.

"Yes. Shamans, shapeshifters . . . sorcerors. *Brujos.*"

I thought of the vanishing werewolf in my loft. Had that been a *nagual*? And the obsidian knife stuck in my door . . .

"There were originally several lineages," Hubert continued. "No one knows exactly how many; they all went underground in the seventeen hundreds. But they did not die. To our knowledge, which may be incorrect, Xochitl's is the only line that retains all of the old powers."

"What powers?"

"Like us, she is a shape shifter: a werewolf. Whether that power came from the god or from the European werewolves is unclear and has been hotly debated over the last hundred years. But Xochitl and her acolytes have other powers as well."

"Like being able to teleport into my loft?"

"Teleport?"

"Like *Star Trek*," I said, but evidently Hubert wasn't a big late-night TV fan, because he just stared at me. "Kind of appear and disappear," I said.

He nodded, finally getting what I was talking about. "Under the right conditions, yes."

"Cool," Lourdes said.

And I guess it kind of was. As long as you weren't the one whose loft was being broken into by magical werewolves. "How do you know all of this?"

"I have always been fascinated with the different strains of werewolves and with the Mexican lineage in particular. It has long been a subject of study for me; I have been trying to determine whether the lineages sprang up independently, or if they can be traced to a single source."

"Ah," I said. "So you were spying for the Houston pack because you know the history so well?"

"Speaking Spanish helps, too."

I had to agree with him there. "So what's her big plan? Why is she going after the Houston pack?"

"She plans to use those powers to regain her ancestral land," he said.

"Her ancestral land," I said. "Texas."

"Among other territories. Yes."

A chill ran down my back. "So the dark thing that attacked me . . . was that Tez . . . Tezcatli-whatever?"

"No; that was probably one of the spirit allies."

"Allies?" I glanced at Lourdes, who shrugged. Then I turned back to Hubert.

"The spirit allies are drawn to Xochitl's power; they are something like what we would call demons, or demigods. I don't know if she has a special relationship with one ally, or if she has multiple entities at her command."

This whole conversation, frankly, was more than a little weird. But then the incident with the woman flashed through my mind, and I had to admit it made sense. I knew whatever had attacked me after my bout with Mr. Big and Hairy wasn't your garden-variety werewolf, but something stranger. I shuddered, remembering the darkness engulfing me, the foul smell, the claws raking down my ribcage. And Tom, watching it all happen. *Tom.* Why hadn't he helped me? Had he gone over to the *Norteños,* too? "What about Tom?" I asked.

"Tom Fenris?"

"He was there, when I was being attacked. He just . . . watched," I said, feeling hollow inside. I hadn't been the only one he'd watched being hauled away, I realized, glancing over at Lindsey, who thankfully was still sleeping.

"I do not know," he said. "I thought he and Wolfgang were allied; they have a long history together. But Xochitl is powerful; she turned Anita. Perhaps she has turned Tom as well."

I swallowed the lump that had recently taken up residence in my throat. If Tom had turned, what was I going to do? I fingered the magic moon ring. Mark had said he'd turn up if I needed him, but he'd been conspicuously absent during the little encounter that landed me chained up in a cave, so I couldn't count on any assistance from that quarter. It looked like I was on my own. Along with a couple of dozen other werewolves, several of whom, if the stench was anything to go on, had been here a rather long time. "So there's an ancient god whose followers—including Xochitl the werewolf-priestess and her allies—are planning to retake their ancestral lands," I said to Hubert. "How did you end up here?"

"That was Anita's doing," he said bitterly. "I reported to her, because Wolfgang was out of town. She sent me home to rest, and her cronies were waiting for me."

"So it's because of Anita that we're stuck in a cave somewhere in Texas."

"Exactly."

I turned to Lourdes. "Did Brett say how he got here?"

"He told me they were forcing him to run drugs from Mexico up to the States. They would transform into wolves and slip across with the drugs belted to them. Remember when they were talking about *lobos,* and I thought they were talking about wolves? *Lobos?* I forgot that that's also a word for marijuana."

"Why did they kidnap Brett?"

"He refused to take a shipment," Brissa said from across the cave. "So they brought him here."

"Why?"

"The same reason you're here," Hubert said. "He's expendable."

I chose to ignore the expendable comment. "But that doesn't make sense. Why not just kill him on the spot? And you?" *And me,* I thought with a shiver.

He was quiet for a moment. "Because they need us."

"For what?"

"For the New Fire ceremony."

The New Fire ceremony. I thought of the bloody obsidian knife in my door and started coming up with all kinds of unpleasant associations. Then I asked the question I wasn't sure I wanted to know the answer to: "What exactly *is* the New Fire ceremony?"

"How much do you know about Aztec culture?" he asked softly.

"A little," I said.

"Then you will recall that their worship is rather active—particularly where Tezcatlipoca is concerned."

"Um . . . exactly what do you mean by active?"

"He is an old god, and a greedy one. He demands to be fed."

I swallowed hard. "You're not talking about cheeseburgers and fries, are you?"

"I'm afraid not."

An unpleasant thought occurred to me. "So that makes us . . ."

"The sacrifice," he finished for me.

Thirty-four

The drums seemed to swell in my head, along with a howl. I shook my head. I was going to be a human sacrifice. It was the twenty-first century, for God's sake. How was that even possible?

"They're going to kill all of us?" I asked.

"Unfortunately, yes. I believe that is the plan. I think we'll have at least a few days' warning, though; theoretically, there is a period of fasting and silence preceding the event." He gave me another twisted grin. "Oh—and ritual bloodletting, too, of course."

Lourdes drew in her breath, and a murmur rippled through the cave, along with the sharp scent of fear.

"What's the point of it?"

"Traditionally, it was a way of staving off what the Aztecs thought was the risk of the earth being destroyed. I think Xochitl has a different take on it, though."

"Which is?"

"I think for her it signifies the rise of Tezcatlipoca. The rise of the *naguales*—the Mexican werewolves. And the reclaiming of Texas."

The hairs stood up on my back at the tone of his voice.

"What exactly do they do during the ceremony?" Lourdes asked.

"Very little is known, because the tradition is shrouded

in secrecy. The archeologists believe the ceremony called for the extinction of all lights, followed by a sacrifice and a rekindling. I know the *Norteños* are planning one—I've heard several references to *xiuhmolpilli*, which is the old Nahuatl word for the ceremony. The original calendars have been lost for centuries—but the *Norteños* seem to have been waiting for something to signal the time was right. A particular event, perhaps, or a time of year."

Like Valentine's Day? I thought. That's the right time of year to rip your heart out. Although the way things were going, my romantic life was the least of my problems.

"I think the time is close, though," Hubert said. "Activity has been picking up these last few months."

I looked at Hubert. "There were some werewolves killed on the Greenbelt in Austin; I found a cave nearby, with some blood and burned incense that smelled like pine trees."

"It is highly likely. The incense was probably copal, and the blood was likely a ritual bloodletting. The worship of Tezcatlipoca often takes place in caves," Hubert said. Kind of like the one we were in now, I thought uncomfortably. "They were probably 'consecrating' Austin for the god," he said.

This whole thing was getting weirder and weirder by the moment. And not in a good way. "What about the murders?" I asked. "Wolfgang suggested that the Houston pack was responsible."

"Perhaps. By the time that occurred I must have already taken up residence here."

"One of them left behind a medallion—it looked like it had been torn off—with a wolf on it."

"It's a mark of the pack. All the *Norteños* wear them," he said.

"I got an amulet with the same thing on it from a *yer-*

beria in East Austin." My mind reeled back to the yerbe-ria, and the woman who had sold the amulet to me, and I sat up with a start. "I know her."

"Who?" Hubert asked.

"The woman who sold me the amulet. I saw her the other day, outside the ballet. And she was outside my mother's shop, too. What do you know about her? Yolanda Jimenez."

He shrugged, and the chains jingled. "I'm sorry," Hubert said formally, in his scholarly German accent, as if we were at a Kaffeeklatsch in Vienna, rather than chained up in a Texas cave. "I am not acquainted with her."

"Sophie." It was Teena, who was huddled across the cave from us, next to a young man I assumed was Brett. "If what Hubert says is right, they're planning to kill us. What are we going to do?"

"I don't know," I said.

Hubert raised his head. "They're coming."

He was right; I could smell them too. Three were-wolves. Mr. Big and Hairy. And Anita.

And Tom.

I must have been pretty desperate, because hope flared in me. Had Tom and Anita had a change of heart? Were they coming to rescue me?

A moment later, a door creaked open, and light pierced the darkness. "Lunchtime!" Mr. Big and Hairy announced. Anita watched as he set a pot of what smelled like over-the-hill beef stew on the floor. Several of the werewolves—made ones, it looked to me—scrabbled toward the source of the smell. From the gaunt look of them, they'd been here for quite some time. I wrinkled my nose at the pot. I was hungry, but I wasn't that hungry.

Anita stared at me, looking smug. "I told Wolfgang

you were worthless. But maybe we'll find some use for you yet." Her lips tugged up into an evil grin.

I ignored her and stared at Tom. His gaze glanced over me, and I thought his right eyebrow flickered upward in acknowledgment. But then his eyes moved on, leaving me to wonder if I'd only imagined it. Hugin the traitor sat on his shoulder, looking pleased with himself.

So much for my dreams of rescue. But what was going on with Tom? Had they brainwashed him?

"Good to see you, Tom," Hubert called out, his voice dripping with sarcasm. "And Anita, of course. I'm sure Wolfgang will be pleased to discover you've been here."

Anita ignored him, but Tom smiled politely, and said, "Likewise, Hubert," as if Hubert weren't half-starved and shackled to the floor of a cave.

"Lindsey's here, you know," I said to Tom.

He nodded. "Yes. I noticed."

I glanced at Anita and Mr. Big and Hairy, who were watching this exchange with interest, and then turned back to Tom. "Don't you even care?"

"It is not my concern," he said coolly.

"Better chow down," Mr. Big and Hairy said. "You've got a big night ahead of you." Anita laughed, deep and throaty.

The smell of fear grew stronger in the cave; even the werewolves who were fighting for the contents of the pot quieted for a moment. Then Mr. Big and Hairy turned on his heel and left the cave, with Tom a few steps behind him. I tried to catch his eye again, but he didn't turn around.

Darkness fell again, punctuated by growls and wet noises that did nothing to stimulate my appetite. I glanced at Hubert, whose face was lost in the shadows. "Does that mean what I think it does?"

His thin lips twisted into a grim smile that did nothing to improve my mood. "I sincerely hope not."

* * *

The rest of the afternoon passed incredibly slowly. Lindsey woke up and was remarkably perky, considering she was chained along with dozens of unwashed werewolves in an underground cave. I was glad she was far from the gaunt made ones near the door; several of them were eyeing her as if she were dessert.

"So, how are we going to get out of here?" she asked.

"Still working on that," I said.

"Don't you have some superpowers that will get you through this stuff?" she asked, shaking the chains at her wrists.

"I'm afraid not." I'd tried the transformation thing, but the shackles seemed to change size right along with me.

"What happened by the barn, anyway? I mean, one moment, we were standing there in the bushes, and then all of a sudden there were werewolves everywhere. Lourdes said something about a werewolf witch or something."

"It was Tom's raven," I said. "Hugin. He gave us away."

"That's too bad," she said. "Still, I'm glad he's here," Lindsey said, "or I might really be worried. I'm sure he's working on a way to get us out of here."

Based on my recent exchange with Tom over the stew pot, I didn't share Lindsey's confidence, but I kept my mouth shut. Evidently she hadn't heard about the New Fire ceremony, and I didn't want to be the one to clue her in. Hubert and Lourdes didn't seem too keen on spreading the news, either, thankfully.

As the afternoon waned and the dim light dwindled, Brett filled us in on the rest of his experience with the *Norteños*. Apparently part of their "Take Back Texas" plan involved making lots of werewolves and using them to transport drugs over the border, the idea being that wolves could travel much more easily than people. The plan was turning out to be a huge success, and the money was going toward buying land in Texas to set up strongholds. Lately, the *Norteños* had been expanding operations. They'd started with marijuana, which Brett was okay with, but when they started shipping heroin, he'd balked.

"They were using the cash to buy property in Texas," he said. He was a bit scrawny, but was a very nice young man—and obviously attached to Teena, who hadn't stopped clutching his hand since I woke up. "They had a place up in Texarkana, and I think there were a few others I heard about, too—distribution points."

"Like the house in San Antonio. They were stuffing piñatas."

"Probably with heroin," he said. "I think they mentioned that. And then there's this place. Where are we, by the way?"

"I think we're about an hour east of Austin," I said. "Near Roundtop."

Hubert nodded. "This property is the heart of their Texas operation."

Before I could ask any more questions, the low, steady beat of a drum began in the distance, like an eerie echo of my earlier dream. A moment later it was joined by another; the two beat out a steady cadence that made my skin crawl. Then there was a howl, long and low. Hubert's eyes glowed slightly in the darkness as he whispered, "They're coming."

Thirty-five

"What's going on?" Lindsey hissed as the drum beats grew louder.

"I don't know," I said, and nobody else bothered answering. Probably because they were all busy transforming into wolves.

The smell of fear escalated as the sound of the drums swelled. Every hair on my body was bristling. I struggled to stay human—I don't know why, but it seemed important—but most of the werewolves had already changed and were whining pitifully. A breeze filtered down from the opening at the top of the cave, bringing the faint smell of piney incense. Copal, if what Hubert had told me was correct. The drums grew louder and louder, and the tension in the cave grew almost unbearable. Then the door burst open, and the woman from the night before stood in the doorway, wreathed in smoke.

Xochitl.

It was hard to say what she looked like, because her face was painted black with a yellow stripe across the bridge of her nose and her cheekbones. Her hair was long and loose and reminded me of Brissa's—the whole Pantene commercial thing—but despite the salon-fresh tresses, the whole effect was downright scary. Particularly when you added in the flickery golden eyes.

She was surrounded by werewolves wearing what

looked like animal-skin tunics, their faces painted black and carrying torches. The leaping shadows licked at their blackened faces and sent a shiver down my spine. There must have been fifty of them, and the whole effect was terrifying.

My eyes quickly returned to their leader—Xochitl. I thought I recognized her from last night—although with the weird face paint, it was tough to tell. Unlike her retinue, she had eschewed fur for a green gown that reminded me of a toga. Her eyes blazed gold as they searched the cave like a beacon, and I found myself trying to become small and inconspicuous as they swept over my mainly transformed compatriots. Unfortunately, they stopped when they got to me.

The thrum of the mallets on taut skin drums boomed through the cave, and I didn't need to be psychic to know that the look she was giving me wasn't good. *"Alli,"* she said, her low voice a command, as she pointed a slender finger in my direction. *"Ella."* A woman—at least I think it was a woman; it was hard to tell with the fur and the black face paint—scuttled out from behind her and headed toward me, stopping a few feet away, holding out an open thermos. Which seemed a little out of place, really, considering everyone was wearing animal skins and carrying torches.

"No thanks," I said, even though my throat was paper-dry. I didn't know what was in the thermos, but even from a few feet away the smell was revolting.

This was evidently not the right answer, because she simply stepped forward and wrenched my jaw open.

"Yolanda!" I barked in recognition—I knew her smell and those dark eyes—and then she thrust the thermos to my lips.

"Yes," she hissed at me. "And now you will pay for what you did to my daughter." Maria Jimenez. Who had framed my mother for a murder she committed—and now, thanks to me, was serving forty-to-life.

Things were definitely not looking up.

The stuff was incredibly foul, but she poured it all down my throat anyway. Just when I thought I was going to drown in the disgusting liquid, she let me go. I gasped for air and clutched my stomach, wondering if I'd just been poisoned. It certainly felt like it.

When the thermos was empty, Yolanda gave me a sharp jab in my injured ribs and hobbled back toward Xochitl, who was intoning words I didn't understand—because the words were in Spanish and because I was trying not to puke my guts out.

The drums pounded in my head as Xochitl proceeded through the cavern, flanked by her posse of skin-clad werewolves, all chanting strange words that echoed off the dank limestone walls. There must have been fifty of them—they seemed to be everywhere. As my stomach heaved, the room shuddered around me, and the gap in the ceiling seemed to expand, filling with something darker than the night outside. There was some chanting, and some more drums, and then a bloodcurdling howl rose from the back of the cave.

My eyes followed the sound to Xochitl, who stood behind a large, flat-topped limestone boulder, looking kind of like a female Aztec version of the Pope, while two of the skin-clad werewolves dragged a gaunt young werewolf up to her. They held him down on the rock as he snarled and whimpered, and something shone in Xochitl's hand. She swayed slightly, then the drums and chanting swelled and her arm flashed down. A darkness seemed to coalesce behind her, and there was a piercing scream. She looked up, and a low guttural growl ripped out of her throat. "Tezcatlipoca!"

The drums swelled again as she lifted something in her hand. *His heart,* a little voice inside me said; in seconds, the coppery smell of blood had filled the cave. My stomach lurched again, and the cave walls seemed to spin. Then, under the thick smell of blood, I caught a familiar scent: Tom. My eyes struggled to focus as they swept the cave. Where was he? Would he watch as they ripped my heart out, too? I looked at my friend, who was staring at the scene at the back of the cave, white-faced. *Oh, Lindsey.* And Brissa, and Teena, and Lourdes. What had I gotten them into?

"They killed one of them," Lourdes moaned beside me. "And now they're grabbing another one. Oh, Jesus . . ."

I tried to answer, but my stomach convulsed, and the contents of the thermos came back up, splattering all over the stone floor—and Lourdes' camo-clad leg. For some reason, she and the grrls hadn't changed. "Sorry," I gasped—as if there hadn't just been a werewolf with his heart ripped out a moment ago—but I had barely wiped my mouth when Yolanda was there again with a fresh thermos.

As she grabbed my chin, I had a flash of understanding. This woman was a witch—her specialty was plants—and she hated me. "You hexed my mother," I said. "You were at Sit A Spell that day, you left something on the doorstep. . . ."

Her face split into a grotesque smile, and she nodded.

"The knife in my door. And the tea. You put mistletoe in my tea," I gasped.

"No," she hissed through rotten teeth, her face a grotesque mask of black. "The tea was a gift from Xochitl. But you should have died—I made it strong. You didn't die then, but you will now."

Then she pressed the thermos to my lips.

"No!" I screamed, wrenching my head to the side and trying to writhe out of Yolanda's grasp, but she pried my jaw open and poured a fresh batch of the nasty stuff down my throat. Although it sure beat having my heart torn out of my body. When the thermos was empty, she released me, and I fell to the rocky floor in what felt like slow motion, staring through half-lidded eyes at the smoke that twisted through the dark air.

The cave spun around me, stretching and contracting; I couldn't get it to stop. I focused on the woman at the back of the cave—Xochitl. Her green dress writhed like snakes around her, and her eyes were like knives above the yellow band that bisected her face. The shadow behind her had grown; just looking at it made my skin cold. It was angry and hungry. And unless I was hallucinating—which was entirely likely—whatever it was had eyes.

The incense smell grew stronger, and the smoke seemed to gain strength, wrapping around me like tendrils. There was another scream from the end of the cave. "It has begun," said Hubert from somewhere nearby. I opened my eyes and forced myself to look at Xochitl. She stared back, her eyes boring into me like daggers. I knew she held a bloody knife in her hand. I knew about the god, and how greedy it was, and that I would be brought up to feed it, just as I knew that Xochitl was the one who had been in my loft, and that she hated me. Beside her stood Yolanda, grinning, and the tongue that slipped out of the corner of her mouth was long, and thin, and forked.

I opened my mouth and raised my hand to point, but her mouth split into another toothless grin, and then Xochitl's voice was in my head, commanding my attention, and my eyes were pulled to hers. She was speaking to me, speaking a language I almost understood, but not quite, and the dark thing prowled behind her, growing larger, almost formed, and closer. My stomach seized up, and the walls of the cave seemed to ripple like oil as the dark thing behind her grew, and grew, and grew. Its foul breath was on my face again, and the ring on my finger blazed to life, burning my skin.

Then she spoke, a booming voice that made the cave walls shudder and the torchlight flicker. It wasn't English, or even Spanish—it was in a language I'd never heard before—but I understood every word. "The time of the white ones is over," she bellowed, her voice echoing on the inside of my skull. I closed my eyes to shut out her eyes, and the eyes of the thing behind her, but I could feel them pressing down on me, pushing the breath out of me. "For centuries we have waited, waited for the time to come. But it has finally arrived; Tezcatlipoca will rise again. With the blood of the chosen one, the cycle will begin again, and the white ones will be devoured."

The pressure was unbearable; I could feel the thing behind her growing, feeding on me, pushing at me so I could barely breathe. The thick copal smoke snatched the air from my lungs. She barked a command; then two hands gripped me. I heard the clank of the shackles falling away, and then I was moving, toward the blood-stained rock, toward her, toward the darkness that pulsed like a living thing behind her. My eyes locked with hers for a moment, and then the hands pushed me down onto the sticky limestone, my cheek against the rough wet surface. I could smell her now. She smelled of wolf, and woman, and the liquid in the jug . . . and something else.

I struggled against the hands that held me, waiting for the pain. But instead, Xochitl said, "No," again in that other language. How was it I understood the words? "Not yet." Her voice was low, like a cat's, and when I looked up at her, her eyes were full of greed—and something else. Fear? The blackness behind her pulsed hungrily; she raised a hand, and it stilled. "First, the others."

Hands lifted me, holding me up; there was a deep

thrum beneath the drums, like the purring of some large animals, and then they were leading Teena up to take my place. Her eyes were white-rimmed and her hair shone in the torchlight as they held her down on the bloody rock, the discarded body of the young werewolf crumpled beside her.

The woman in green held my eyes with hers as she raised the bloody knife in her hand. "NO," I gasped, lunging forward, away from the grasping hands. The metal band Mark had given me pulsed again, and as I slammed into the woman in green, the thing behind her grew and roared; I could feel it surround me, cold, dark, hopeless. *I'm dying,* I thought, feeling my consciousness recede to a small bright point in an endless night. Suddenly there was a crackling sound, and fire ripped through the air.

"She is not yours!" The words roared through the cave, ricocheting off the stone walls. The drumbeat faltered, then stopped. "She belongs to me," the voice boomed. Some part of my mind registered that the werewolves holding Teena backed away; she slid off the rock, huddling next to the dead werewolf. The crackle of fire filled the space, and there was a hum of worry— of doubt—among the black-painted werewolves.

The flames blazed up, and the cave seemed to grow bigger around me, painted with shadows. The darkness was there, writhing, almost animal-like; and before it blazed a burning figure, opening and closing a pair of fiery wings. It had eyes, too. Blue eyes. *Blue eyes?* The ring pulsed again, and I suddenly realized what the creature was.

It was Mark.

The hands that held me had slipped away in the excitement, and I backed away from the pair of creatures facing off in the middle of the cave. The walls kept pulsing, and the blackened faces around me seemed to shift—one moment wolf, the next human. My knees loosened beneath me as a wave of nausea swept through me, and I dropped to the floor, retching. The fire roared, searing me with its heat, and the cave was filled with the stench of burning hair. I heaved again, and there was a flutter by my ear. I wiped my mouth and looked up into the dark bright eye of a bird. *Hugin.*

"Tom!" I croaked.

He was right behind me; I could smell him, even over the fire and the blood and the burning hair and the reek of the stuff in the thermos. I looked up into his strong Nordic features, his iridescent eyes. Even in the flickering shadows I could see that his face was drawn, and there was urgency in his voice as he gripped my arm. "We have to get you out of here."

I blinked at his familiar face, and the cloudiness that had invaded my mind receded for a moment. What the hell did he think he was doing? He'd stood by while I was attacked by Mr. Big and Hairy, he'd let them chain me and my friends up in a cave, and had done nothing while they poisoned me and tried to rip Teena's heart out. "It's a little late for that," I said.

"There was a reason for my inaction. I promise I wouldn't have let harm come to you." He looked over my shoulder, and a shadow passed over his face. "We've got to go now; we can talk later."

"Yeah, right." I glanced over my shoulder at Mark, the CEO of Southeast Airlines, who was currently sporting wings of flame and brandishing something sword-like at Xochitl's dark, amorphous, creature-thing. Then I scanned the huddled werewolves, searching for my friends. "Lindsey," I said with sudden clarity. "And Teena and the grrls. We have to get them out of here."

"You're the one she wants, Sophie. You're the reason for the ceremony. They've been waiting for you."

"I need to save them," I said, turning to scan the cave.

I heard Lindsey before I saw her. Xochitl had transformed—I recognized the yellow paint on her black fur—and she was crouched, ready to lunge at my friend.

"No!" I roared, and the transformation ripped through me. The drums, the crackle of fire, the smell of blood and sour vomit vanished; there was only Xochitl and Lindsey and me. I bounded across the cave and slammed into Xochitl just before she leaped.

She growled, a low, violent sound that set my fur on end. Then Tom was there between us.

Lindsey cowered by the cave wall, whimpering with fear. I heard Xochitl's voice in my mind. *Step away from her, Tomas Fenris.* It was a command, not a request.

He growled his response, gold eyes blazing.

I stepped forward to challenge her, knowing that whatever was to happen was between the priestess and me. Tom seemed to understand; after a glance from me, he dipped his head and stood to guard Lindsey. Xochitl's eyes flared, and I could feel the power coiled in her long, lean body. From behind her, I heard a long, keening wail as the thing that I thought was Mark battled with the dark cloud.

And then it was only Xochitl and me, her low voice echoing in my skull.

It is time.

Thirty-six

With those words, the world spun away. I could hear the distant howl of a wolf and the crackle of flames; then all sound faded, and Xochitl and I were alone, cloaked in dark fog and silence.

She was black and sleek, teeth glistening, an aura of power crackling around her, a slash of yellow paint framing her blazing eyes. She growled—a low, menacing growl—and I felt an answering sound rip from my own throat. I crouched down, ready to attack; and then she was a dark streak, flying at me like an arrow.

I hurled myself back at her; there was a crack as we met, almost like an electric shock, and then I was tumbling onto hard packed earth, alone. She was gone. I had barely regained my feet before something barreled into me from behind. Her teeth tore at my neck, and the air was drenched with the smell of my blood.

I shook her off of me, pain searing me as her teeth ripped my flesh. Then I whirled to meet her, fangs bared. But she had vanished again. A coldness settled over me as my eyes searched the darkness; what was this place? The cave had disappeared, replaced by shifting mists, veiling things that were moving, but impossible to see. The piney smell of copal was strong here—and there was something else, too. Something big, and fetid, and utterly malevolent. Fear seeped into me, along with the overpowering urge to run. But where could I go?

All is lost. It was her voice, speaking in a language at once foreign and familiar. The words echoed in my head; or was the sound coming from the mists? *It has been foretold. Your time is over. The time of Tezcatlipoca is come. You are sacrifice.*

I took a few tentative steps forward, eyes scanning the mists, a heaviness infecting my limbs. She was right; I was lost, everything was hopeless. I saw Lindsey's face in my mind, and sorrow washed over me; I had gotten her into this, and she was going to die. And Teena and Brissa, and Lourdes, and my mother, too—I knew the crone would find her and kill her, that she was the one who had hexed her. Because of what I had done to her daughter. And Tom would pay for his betrayal . . .

No. I shook off the thoughts—it was like someone was feeding them to me, making me give in to despair— and lifted my head, trying to scent Xochitl. She was everywhere, and nowhere. And then there was a huge weight bearing down on me, crushing the breath out of me. I struggled to escape, but my limbs were paralyzed, barely moving.

Something curled around my legs—crawling up my body, caressing me, squeezing me. . . . I couldn't move, couldn't think, couldn't breathe. Then the fog dissipated, and Xochitl was there—not a werewolf anymore, but a woman again, her green dress writhing around her like snakes. Next to her was the hag—Yolanda. A twin of the amulet I had lost hung from her neck.

Yolanda's mouth curved into a gaping smile. *Now you pay for what you did to my daughter,* she said, and then Xochitl was above me, and the smoky knife flashed in her hands, and her mouth was forming words I couldn't understand, words of power, and for a moment, just a moment, a big cat padded beside her—it was the thing I had seen in the cave, with eyes bottomless and dark—and was gone, and the knife was flashing down, driving into me. . . .

No.

As the knife plunged down, something inside me tore free. A roar escaped me; the knife hesitated, then clattered to the hard ground. I caught a flash of uncertainty in Xochitl's golden eyes. Then there was another crackle, and she was gone.

The snakes binding me disappeared like mist as I leaped to my feet, rage burning in me. I breathed deep, trying to pinpoint her scent; maddening, that she was everywhere, yet nowhere. A flash of green caught my eye, among the shifting mists, and I hurled myself at it, intent on destroying the woman who would kill my friend—and kill me.

I had found her; my jaws closed on flesh, and I heard a low growl of pain; then my teeth clacked shut, empty. A scrap of green fabric hung from my jaw, but she was gone again.

I howled in fury; where was my prey? Then something inside me—something low and deep and old—rose up through the depths, almost like another creature that had been sleeping inside me and recently awoken, and I understood what to do.

My eyes closed, and the creature inside me extended outward, probing the mists. There was silence, and gray, and things half-felt, slipping away before my touch. There was the hag, limping away, cursing to herself—and then I found her. Xochitl, a little ways away, watching me, back in wolf form again, preparing to pounce. I could see the black hairs bristling on her shoulders, hear her panting, watch the twitch of her ears. I slipped through the air, like mist myself, and then I was behind her, watching the muscles bunch under her dark pelt. She paused, confused, and I leaped, feeling my teeth sink into her neck.

There was a howl, and then the cry of something not human, and a loud crash, as if someone had dropped a bowl on a concrete floor. Blood flooded my mouth, and the mist swirled around me, tearing at my fur. My teeth clamped down harder, and I felt Xochitl's life force slip out of her—I could taste it, almost, and smell it drifting by me. Then there was a cry from behind me, and the hag was there, hands open, hurling something at me. There was a weird swishing sound, and a jolt, and then I was hovering above the mist, watching as my body crumpled to the ground beside Xochitl, hearing the murmur of the half-seen shapes coalescing and fading into nothing.

The scene wavered for a moment; then I felt myself being sucked back into the body on the ground. I heard myself whine, a low, pitiful sound, and then there was darkness.

"Sophie."

The voice came from a distance—familiar, yet foreign. Why wouldn't it leave me alone? I just wanted to sleep. . . .

"Sophie."

I could feel something pull at me, dragging me up from the darkness, the warm, soft, comfortable darkness. I tried to go back to sleep, but whoever it was kept tugging at me until my eyes fluttered open.

It all flooded back to me. Lindsey, Xochitl, Tom, the thing Mark had become. I stared into Tom's eyes, and panic gripped me. "What happened? Lindsey . . ."

"She's okay," he said, "but we have to leave."

I sat up quickly, almost fainting as dizziness swept over me. I was back in the cave; the smell of blood and copal washed over me, and the walls echoed with the sounds of yelps and howling. Xochitl was nowhere to be seen, but the battle between Mark and the dark thing still raged.

"What is it?" I asked, staring at the amorphous thing that threatened to engulf my client—or whatever it was my client had become. He was shaped like a man, but his skin was pure fire—and the wings were a new feature. As were the horns. Maybe I had been right about the horns all along.

Tom's voice grabbed my attention than. "It's Xochitl's ally. Your friend seems to have it in check, but I don't know how long it will go on. And the *Norteños* are confused—their leader is missing."

"I think I killed her," I croaked.

"Looks like she almost got you, too," he said, helping me to my feet. "But you can tell me about it later; for now, we need to get you out of here."

"Where are the others?" I asked, feeling my brain click back into gear. I had attacked Xochitl to save Lindsey. Was she okay? Was she even alive?

Then I heard a familiar voice and sagged with relief. "Sophie!" It was Lindsey; with her were Hubert, Brett, and the grrls. Her eyes focused on my neck, which was pulsing with pain. "You're hurt!"

"I'll carry her," Tom said, and slung me over his back like a sack of potatoes. Which would have been offensive if it hadn't been such a relief not to have to walk.

"Give these to the others," he told Hubert, who was holding a ring of shiny keys. For the shackles, I realized. "I'd stay and help them myself, but we need to get out of here before they find Sophie." Hugin swept down from the opening in the top of the cave and perched on Tom's shoulder. The two of them stared at each other; then Tom said something guttural in a language I didn't understand. He looked defeated as he turned to Lindsey and the grrls. "All of the vehicles are guarded. I don't know how we're going to get out of here."

"I don't know if our cars are still there, but we parked by the gate," Teena said, gripping Brett's arm.

"But we don't have the car keys!" I said.

"I do," Lourdes said, jingling my keychain. "I hid them in one of these pockets when they caught us—just in case."

"But how do we get out? The gate is electrified," Lindsey said.

"We'll figure it out when we get there," Tom said. "Let's go." And then he led us out of the cave, into the relative quiet of the night; I could hear a screech owl somewhere, a haunting, neighing call, and the rustle of the wind through the trees. I kept thinking about that bizarre encounter . . . I still wasn't sure I hadn't imagined it all, even though I could still taste Xochitl's blood in my mouth. What had happened to me—had I really left my body and attacked her? I still wasn't sure how much was real and how much was a dream. Now, though, the night air was cold and clear, with not a hint of fog. Or of Xochitl, thankfully.

I don't know how long we traipsed through the woods; I kept drifting in and out of consciousness. Tom was gentle, and it was lovely having so much body-to-body contact, but the fact that I had a big rip in my ribs that sent shooting pains through me with every step he took made it less than delightful. Now that I was out of the cave, and whatever the hag had given me was wearing off, I had an opportunity to think about what had just happened—and to question my own sanity. I reached up to touch my wounded neck; the pain of the torn skin and the taste of blood in my mouth meant that I wasn't going *completely* insane.

And I was still worried about Mark—what exactly *was* he, and how had he gotten there, and what was the dark thing he was fighting? It was too much to get my mind around, so I finally gave up and let my thoughts drift away, breathing in the cold, clean air. After the awful reek of the cave, the scent of cedar and dead grass—and Tom—was comforting, even if we *were* running to escape a pack of angry Mexican werewolves.

Finally, someone said, "It's over there." I raised my head; sure enough, there was the gate, and my M3 was parked farther down, right where I'd left it.

"Too bad you don't still have your twenty-two," I managed to mutter to Lindsey.

"But I do," she said, pulling it out from under her waistband.

I stared at her. "You had the gun the whole time?"

"They didn't even check me. I think because I wasn't a werewolf, they kind of wrote me off."

"Why didn't you use it, then?" I asked.

"No silver bullets," she said, pulling back the safety and holding it up to the box. "But the lead should work just fine on circuitry."

There was a howl behind us, and the hairs rose on my back. "Better hurry up," Tom suggested dryly, and there was a loud crack and a sizzle.

"That's part one," Teena said, testing the now-inactive fence with a branch. "But what about the lock?"

"Coming right up," Lindsey said. She cocked the gun again; then there was another crack, and a moment later they were swinging the gates open. Before long I was sitting in the passenger seat of the M3, trying not to bleed on the leather, and Tom was pulling onto the highway, leaving Mark and Xochitl's spirit ally and Yolanda and the *Norteños* behind us.

Thirty-seven

It was almost two in the morning by the time Tom finished dressing my wounds and settled me into my couch with a cup of peppermint tea. We had made such a strange procession through the swanky lobby—me in Tom's arms, bleeding, trailed by a half-starved looking Hubert, Lindsey, and the disheveled, camo-clad grrls—that Frank had actually looked up from *Flip This House* and stared open-mouthed as we traipsed by. I'd waved as the elevator door shut behind us.

Brett, and the grrls had hung out for a while, but then decided to head home; after all, the *Norteños* didn't know where they lived, so if anything they were safer in San Antonio than they were at my loft in Austin. That left Lindsey, Hubert, Tom and me. Normally, that wouldn't have been an ideal arrangement, but tonight I was so tired and so glad to be alive that I just didn't care.

As Hubert and Lindsey wolfed down roast beef sandwiches in the kitchen, I clutched the warm mug between my hands and thanked God I wasn't still stuck in a stinky cave. Now that I was back in my loft, the whole experience seemed faintly ridiculous; if it weren't for the wounds on my neck and ribs, I would have thought I'd dreamed it. My head still felt fuzzy, like it was wrapped in cotton.

"The tea will help soothe your stomach," Tom said, arranging a blanket around me. "It'll take a few days for the effects of the peyote to wear off, though."

"Is that what that stuff was?" I asked.

He nodded. "Peyote, or mescal. Xochitl is very skilled in the use of it. She had someone give you enough to make it an 'even' fight—for some reason, she decided you were the sacrifice. It may be because you survived the poisoned tea."

"You know about the poisoned tea?"

"I first heard about it yesterday; she visited your loft when she found out about you, and to be safe, she added mistletoe to your tea to eliminate you. Or to see if you would survive. Apparently someone—a witch, she said—told her that you might be the sacrifice."

I remembered the crone from the cave. "Maria's mother. Yolanda. I saw her there tonight; she told me she was avenging her daughter."

"Her daughter was the woman who killed Ted Brewster?" Lindsey asked.

"Exactly. I'm guessing she decided to take her revenge by siccing the *Norteños* on me. I scented her at my mother's shop, too; I think she's been hexing her."

"Well, hex or no hex, it appears the witch was correct about the extent of your power. The sacrifice was the keystone of the New Fire ceremony; Xochitl planned it to access the god's power and help her in the takeover of Texas. But the sacrifice had to be a strong werewolf and preceded by a battle that was a fair match. That's why Xochitl had you drink the peyote along with her. Only it wasn't really fair. Because she had training—she'd even trained others—and you hadn't."

I stared at Tom, and some of the pieces fell into place. "When I was attacked outside of Bass Concert Hall, one of the werewolves seemed to disappear and then reappear. And he had that sharp smell—it was like the stuff they made me drink," I suddenly realized.

"Peyote," Tom said, staring at me. "But I still don't understand what happened back there in the cave. You told me to back off, and I did, although I wasn't entirely comfortable with it. I was going to stay and help out if you got into trouble. The two of you were there in front of me; and then there was some kind of cloud, and you vanished. A few minutes later, I found you lying on the cave floor."

"I'm not sure," I said, remembering how the weird smoke had almost smothered me. A shudder passed through me just thinking about it; I still wasn't sure exactly what had happened. Or if I'd dreamed it. I still felt dirty, as if a bit of Xochitl still clung to me. Even though I'd washed her blood off of me, I could still feel it; it burned a little bit. "Everything faded away," I said, "and then it was just us—Xochitl and Yolanda, Maria's mother. In this weird other place—it wasn't the cave, and it was foggy."

They all just stared at me.

"She's connected with the *Norteños* somehow," I continued. "But I don't think she's a werewolf. She's the one who gave me the wolf amulet at the *yerberia*—the one that went missing."

"Wolf amulet?"

I filled Tom in on my trip to the Greenbelt—including the torn-off medallion I'd found and the blood in the cave. "That was a dedication ceremony that was interrupted by a group from Houston," he said. "They were consecrating Austin—claiming it for their own. The *Norteños* lost two; Houston lost one."

"Who?" Hubert asked.

"Manfred," Tom said. When Hubert winced, Tom added, "I'm sorry. I know he was one of your protégés."

"So you and Wolfgang go way back," I said, reminded of Tom's connections with Wolfgang. "Back to Europe." I glanced at Hubert, who was finishing off a roast beef sandwich at the kitchen table, and suddenly remembered how Tom had ignored me—even when I was wrestling with Mr. Big and Hairy—whose name, Tom informed me, was Carlos, and who was third in command under Xochitl. "I don't understand. Why did you leave us in there? Why didn't you interfere when they attacked me?"

"I couldn't," he said. "I was deep under cover. If I'd gone to help you, they would have discovered me and killed us both. My best bet was to play it cool and help you escape later."

"Cutting it a bit close, weren't you?"

"I didn't know they were going to do the big ceremony so quickly. I knew they were waiting for a sign—for someone important to arrive—and that they were holding the others while they were waiting. It was only once they caught you that I figured out you were the one they were looking for."

"So you infiltrated the *Norteños*. How?"

"Why, by my charm and dashing good looks," he said dryly.

"No wonder they let you in," Lindsey said from a chair near the fireplace, and I felt a stab of jealousy. She was looking at him with big, moony eyes. Which was totally understandable.

I took a sip of my tea, and my stomach clenched as the hot liquid penetrated it. I still hadn't totally recovered from the stuff in the thermos. "So now what?" I asked. "I think Xochitl is dead—if she's not, she's in pretty bad shape. Now that Hubert's back, I'm hoping I'm clear with the Houston pack. The problem is, am I going to have the *Norteños* going after me for the rest of my life?"

"I don't know," Tom said quietly.

"And what happened to Mark?" I said. "What was that thing he was attacking?"

"Remember what I told you?" Hubert said. "It was an ally. One of its aspects appears to be a jaguar—a creature that is often linked with the god."

"Tezcatli . . ."

"Tezcatlipoca," he confirmed.

The pain in my side throbbed at the mention of the name. "That's what got me that night, when we snuck into the compound. The jaguar spirit thing."

Tom nodded, and I remembered how he'd just stood by and watched while Xochitl's spirit ally took me down. Not to mention Mr. Big and Hairy.

"I still don't understand why you just stood by and watched while that . . . *thing* attacked me."

His golden eyes flickered. "If I hadn't," he said quietly, "they would have killed me. And I wouldn't have been able to help you later."

"So you were spying on them?"

"Wolfgang called me when Hubert disappeared, to find out what had happened. I had met Xochitl before," he said vaguely, "so it wasn't too difficult to get into her good graces."

I felt my left eyebrow twitch upward, wondering exactly how he had managed it so quickly. "What exactly did *that* entail?" I asked.

"I have my ways," he said with a sexy grin that made me want to melt right there on the couch. Even if Lindsey was melting right next to him.

"If you were there, why would the Houston pack send me?"

He sighed. "I think Wolfgang figured the more information, the better. Besides, if they caught you, they wouldn't be able to get any information out of you; you don't know anything about the pack."

"Lovely," I said. "So you weren't just going to stand by while they killed me," I said, just to clarify things.

He shook his head slowly, and I shivered, remembering that dark, writhing thing behind Xochitl. I looked down at the bandaged place on my ribs, and an image flashed through my mind. "Anita's face. That's what scratched her, isn't it? Xochitl's ally. That's why she lost."

Hubert nodded. "I believe that was the deciding factor, yes."

I thought of the dark entity in the cave—and the fiery creature who had appeared out of thin air to battle it. "She belongs to me," Mark had said, unless my peyote-addled brain was entirely wrong. What exactly did that mean? I wondered. The ring Mark had given me was still hot on my finger; despite the whole "she belongs to me" thing, which was totally non-PC, I hoped he was okay. And not just because he was my star client. And excellent in the sack, too.

I looked up at the long-haired werewolf, who was staring at me with concern in his golden eyes, and felt a deep surge of desire that I struggled to quell. Now was definitely not the time; particularly with Lindsey five feet away. Although at least I no longer had to break the whole "he's a werewolf" news to her. "Tom," I said. "Do you have any idea what Mark is?"

He shook his head, and his eyes flickered. "No. How did he know to come?"

"I think the ring called him," I said, raising my hand. Tom and Hubert peered at the shining circle on its face.

"He's a pretty scary Most Eligible Bachelor," Lindsey said from her chair, "but not as scary as that thing he was attacking. All I can say is, let's just hope he won."

Somewhere, a phone was ringing. I climbed up through layers of darkness—women with golden eyes, dark jaguars, and fiery creatures—and opened my eyes to my living room.

Lindsey was sitting up in her chair, where she'd evidently fallen asleep, as I staggered across the room to the phone.

"Hello?" I said, my breathing ragged. My stomach felt better, but from the burning in my neck and ribs, I could use a good shot of Motrin. Or maybe something stronger.

"Happy Valentine's Day, Sophie."

I struggled to clear my head. Valentine's Day. Boyfriend. Jewelry bag. "Heath?"

"You don't sound so good. Is everything okay?"

"Um, fine," I said, surveying the two sleeping werewolves stretched out on the floor of my loft. "I was just sleeping, that's all. I've been . . . under the weather."

"I'm . . . I'm sorry about the other day. At my loft."

My mind reeled back to the episode he was referring to. The one where he left me and my Jimmy Choos stranded in the lobby. "You should be," I said.

He was quiet for a moment, then said, "I was just calling to see if I could take you out tonight."

"Umm . . . I guess so," I said muzzily.

"Great," he said. "I'll pick you up at seven."

"In the evening?"

"Since it's already nine in the morning, it's a pretty good bet. Why don't you get some rest so you're up for tonight? I'll come pick you up."

"Okay," I said, feeling totally disoriented. And furry, I realized, glancing down at my legs; I hadn't had wolfsbane tea—or access to a razor—in a couple of days, and it was becoming pretty obvious. I glanced back to make sure Lindsey hadn't noticed; then I remembered she now knew all about my little condition.

"Sophie?"

The voice from the receiver made me jump. Evidently

I was still recovering from the whole peyote incident; I'd almost forgotten I was still on the phone with my semi-estranged boyfriend. "Right. Tonight's fine," I said.

"See you at seven," he said.

"Seven," I repeated. "Got it."

"Heath?" Lindsey asked lazily as I hung up the phone. Tom and Hubert had woken up and were staring at me with shimmery golden eyes.

"Uh-huh," I said, lurching back to the couch. "He's picking me up at seven. It's Valentine's Day."

"It is?" Lindsey asked. She cut her eyes at Tom. "Got any plans tonight?"

"What did you have in mind?" he asked in a seductive voice that made me look away.

"We need to contact the pack," Hubert said, his mind on less romantic matters. "Warn them about Anita."

"I already did," Tom said. "I sent Hugin last night. I'm sure Wolfgang knows everything by now and has sent reinforcements."

As if on cue, there was a knock at the door. I started to get to my feet again, but Tom motioned for me to stay. "It's Wolfgang," he said, and a moment later the Alpha of the Houston pack was in my living room, and he and Hubert were pounding each other on the back and speaking in archaic-sounding German.

As the three of them caught up on old times, I hobbled to the kitchen to brew a pot of coffee. Something told me it was going to be another long day, and I was in need of a big shot of caffeine.

I had sucked down a cup of coffee and three Motrin and was feeling slightly more lucid by the time Wolfgang and Hubert remembered I was there. They briefed me on what I had missed. When he got the news bulletin from Hugin, Wolfgang had sent a small army out to Roundtop, where they found several dazed werewolves from both packs, but no sign of Xochitl—or any of the other folks in the upper ranks, including the traitorous Anita.

No one was clear on the outcome of the big battle between Mark and the shadowy thing—they had exploded out of the top of the cave and headed off for parts unknown—and nobody had any idea what had happened to Tezcatlipoca's high priestess, either. When he had briefed me on the news, Wolfgang fixed me with his penetrating eyes, and I gave him a weak smile in return. "I thank you for using what appear to be your extraordinary powers to assist us in containing the *Norteños,* and I apologize for the mistreatment at the hands of my former companion," he said in a formal tone. "I also want to thank you for your efforts in recovering my brother."

"You're welcome," I said modestly.

"As a reward for your services, we would like to offer you amnesty."

"Amnesty. Does that mean I don't have to move to Houston?" I asked.

"No. You may remain in Austin . . . for now."

"For now?"

He inclined his head. "For the foreseeable future," he amended.

"Thanks, I guess."

"So you're a pack member now?" Lindsey asked.

"Not exactly," Wolfgang said. Which was fine, actually, but still a bit annoying. Amnesty was fine, but after everything I'd done for them, you'd think they'd at least *offer.*

"So I don't have to learn the secret handshake," I said coolly, looking at Wolfgang, who was acting like he'd just knighted me or something.

Tom laughed. "Or learn to scoop wolf poop."

I shot Tom a look that didn't faze him a bit and returned my focus to Wolfgang. "So I can stay in Austin.

There's only one problem," I said. "What do I do if the *Norteños* come back?" I asked.

"From what I saw in the cave, I think you'll be able to handle them," Hubert said.

"And the reports indicate that the pack has been fragmented," Wolfgang said. "Most of their leadership appears to have been in Roundtop for the ceremony. And now that we know where their power bases are, we will be doing a sweep of the state."

"I will guard you," Tom said. "At least until we determine whether the *Norteños* are still a threat."

Lindsey arched an eyebrow, but didn't say anything. Aside from the fact that my best friend was still dating a werewolf—and my client was still AWOL—all's well that ends well, I was thinking. I'd managed to deal with the whole Houston pack issue, pretty much all by myself. Provided the *Norteños* didn't pop up again, for the first time ever I could have a normal life without worrying about being discovered. Which meant going to work like a normal person . . . "Oh, shit!" I jumped up from the couch.

"What?"

"It's Saturday! We missed work yesterday!"

Lindsey leapt up from her chair, eyes wide. "We've got to call the office! We just disappeared without telling anyone. . . . I hope we still have jobs!"

"What do we tell Adele?"

"Good question," Lindsey said, pausing as she reached for the phone.

"We'll just say we were force-fed peyote and detained by Aztec werewolves," I said. "I'm sure she'll understand."

"And that your star client is actually some kind of supernatural freak who was last seen battling a big dark cloud?" Lindsey added, and I felt a twinge of worry. Was Mark okay? And if so, where was he?

Thirty-eight

Although I'm not sure Adele was completely convinced that Lindsey and I had both caught a freak flu, we managed to appease her by promising to work through the weekend. And by early afternoon, everyone had left my loft—including Tom, who departed only after I reminded him that it was Valentine's Day and that he'd probably have better luck facing down Tezcatlipoca himself than meeting Lindsey on Valentine's Day empty-handed.

He made me memorize his cell phone number, though. And to be honest, I was jumpy when he left—and relieved to know that Hugin was stationed on my balcony, just in case. Even if he had accidentally given me away at Roundtop.

Uncharacteristically, Frank rang right at seven to tell me that I had a visitor in the lobby. My stomach twisted into a pretzel as I took a last look in the mirror to make sure my mascara hadn't smeared—and that I hadn't bled through the bandage on my neck. Five minutes later, I stepped out of the elevator in a form-fitting red dress to meet my boyfriend.

He was dressed in a chocolate brown suit that looked tailor-made, and his dark hair shone in the light. His eyebrows rose when he noticed the large chunk of gauze taped to my neck. "What happened?"

"I had a problem with a hanger," I lied. "One of those metal ones."

"How . . ."

"Don't ask," I said, and before he could say another word, I kissed him, relieved to be able to put the world of werewolves behind me and return to my normal human life. But I couldn't help noticing he smelled smoky.

In fact, he smelled like Miranda.

Needless to say, the drive to Chez Nous was rather quiet. And even though the table for two was crowned with candles and a dozen red roses, I still had a bad feeling about the evening to come.

Which was confirmed even before we'd made it through the *foie gras.*

"Sophie," he said.

"Yes?"

"I've been thinking . . . about us."

I took a swallow of my Pouilly-Fuissé. This was it. He was going to break up with me and come clean about his wine-country getaway with Miranda. "Yes?" I managed to choke out.

"I know things have been busy lately, and things between us haven't been quite . . . right."

I couldn't think of anything to say, so I just smiled tightly and took another swallow of wine.

"I was thinking of taking you to the wine country for the weekend, actually. Sometime in March."

I almost dropped my glass. "But . . ." I was about to say, *I thought you were planning a trip there with Miranda,* but I stopped myself just in time.

"The trouble is," he continued, looking at me over the remains of the pâté, "I'm not sure you're interested."

Not sure I was interested? I was about to tell Heath there was nothing I'd rather do but head off to the wine country—and eventually the sunset—with him, but something stopped me. I thought about what Tom had said—that I would likely live centuries, relatively agelessly, whereas Heath would grow old like any other human being. And any children we had would likely carry at least some of the werewolf genes my father had passed to me.

I took a deep breath. I loved Heath. But was it fair to either of us for me to keep things going?

He sighed and fumbled under the table for something. "I was going to give you this tonight," he said, pulling a velvet box out of his pocket. I swallowed hard as he opened the lid; a diamond solitaire gleamed from a bed of dark velvet. The band was gold, not silver, I was relieved to see. "But I'm not sure if it's what you want."

I choked out a laugh. "And I thought you were going to tell me you were seeing Miranda," I said.

Something flickered over his face, and I knew my instinct hadn't been entirely wrong. "She's attractive," he admitted, "but she's not you."

I took a deep, shuddery breath. "I appreciate the ring—it's gorgeous—and the offer of a wine-country getaway." I raised my eyes to his. "I do love you. But things have been a bit . . . crazy lately, and I have a lot to think about."

His shoulders drooped a little, but he reached out to squeeze my hand. I squeezed back, then lowered the lid on the glinting diamond. "Can I let you know in a little bit?"

"Of course," he said. Then the waiter appeared, Heath whisked the box off the table, and we ate the rest of the meal making polite conversation and trying to avoid the awkward silence that kept stealing into the space between us.

Heath dropped me off by ten—neither of us had the heart to draw the evening out any longer—and as I arranged the roses he had given me in a vase on the table, Hugin let out a reassuring squawk from the balcony. I still hadn't forgiven Tom's raven for giving me away out at Roundtop, but it was a comfort to know he was keeping an eye on things now. Even if his companion was out wining and dining my best friend.

I had washed my face and was about to investigate the wounds on my neck when there was a light knock on my door.

The hairs stood up on my neck as I stepped out of the bathroom, checking to make sure Hugin was still standing guard. I grabbed the phone, ready to call Tom, and padded to the door. "Who is it?" I called.

"It's Mark." I opened the door a moment later, and his smoky smell filled my loft.

"You're okay," I breathed, and he pushed the door shut behind him and pulled me into his arms.

When he released me, I had to stop and catch my breath. Hugin, I couldn't help noticing, had observed the proceedings from his perch on the railing and was giving me a rather judgmental look. I walked over and pulled the curtains closed.

"What happened?" I asked as I returned to Mark's arms. "How did you know where to find me the other night? And what was up with the whole fiery wing thing? And the horns—I knew I'd seen horns on you that day. I knew it!"

"It just seemed appropriate for the moment," he said, grinning, and for a moment his smoky smell intensified.

"What was that . . . thing you were fighting? Someone told me it was an ally, but it didn't seem too friendly to me."

"It was an old spirit," he said. "A challenging one, really, but no match for me in the long run. I haven't had a battle like that in a long time, actually—it was fun getting the blood pumping again." He leaned down and kissed me again, letting his hands travel down to my throat; he paused when his fingers touched the gauze. "I hope you're not too badly hurt," he murmured.

"I'm fine," I said.

"I can heal that."

Before I could protest, he lifted the bandage and touched the gaping wound on my neck; I could feel my skin growing, knitting itself together. Then he slipped a hand under my robe to the gashes on my ribs, where the black thing had mauled me. When I raised my fingers to my neck, the skin was smooth.

"How did you do that?" I drew away from him. "I appreciate you coming to my aid . . . but what exactly are you? I need to know."

"Why?" he asked, stepping toward me. "Don't you like a man with a little mystery?"

"No," I said. "I really don't. And I make it a habit to identify supernatural creatures before I get involved with them."

"So you're thinking of getting involved with me?"

"I didn't say that," I protested.

"I think you did," he said, and before I could answer he had swept me into his arms and was heading for the bedroom.

I'd like to say I fought him off, but the truth was it felt so delicious I didn't do much of anything for a few minutes except moan. It wasn't until his finger was hooked around my bikini panties that I came to my senses.

"Stop," I said.

"But it was just getting interesting," he protested, his breath hot in my ear.

"Not until you tell me what you are."

"Do you really want to know?"

"I really want to know."

He sighed. "I have another name; it's Ash."

"Ash like ashes?"

"Yes," he said.

"So is that why you smell like smoke?"

"Sort of," he said, his teeth nibbling at my earlobe.

"But you still haven't said what you are," I reminded him.

"I've given you my name," he said. "Isn't that enough?"

Before I could answer, there was a shimmer in the room; Mark—or Ash—sprang away from me, and there was a low caw from the balcony.

It was Xochitl.

I gathered my bathrobe around me and shot to my feet as her peyote-laced scent filled the room. Her neck was bound like mine had been. But I still didn't want her popping up in my bedroom. "What are you doing here?" I asked.

She stared at me and spoke in heavily accented English. "You won for now. But I will be back."

Mark's smoky smell intensified, and Xochitl's gold eyes leaped to him.

"I told you she was mine," he growled. "I forbid you to return here. Ever. If you do, you know what fate awaits you."

Her gold eyes flared for a moment, and I wasn't sure what she was going to do, but something Mark—or Ash, or whatever his name was—said seemed to scare her, because she shimmered again and disappeared. When she was gone, I pushed my hair behind my ears and turned to Mark. "So what's the whole 'she's mine' thing? Didn't anyone tell you we were in the twenty-first century?"

"It doesn't turn you on?" he asked, his lips brushing my neck.

While his rather prefeminist words hadn't done much for me, his mouth certainly did, and before long, his fingers were hooked around my bikini panties again. And this time I didn't stop him.

I'd always enjoyed sex in the past, but today, I was starving for it. I tore at his shirt, hungry to touch his chest. His smoky smell made me want him even more, and as I ran my tongue across his chest, he shivered beneath me, hot to my touch. He tasted intensely male, with a hint of ashes. *Ash*, he'd said his name was.

"Ash," I murmured, and his eyes widened at the sound of it.

"Sophie Garou," he murmured in reply. His voice was ragged. "I want you so badly."

"Then hurry up and take me," I said.

"No condom?" he said.

"Safety first," I said. He tore off his clothes and plucked another condom from his wallet; then, properly equipped, he turned his attention back to me. He started by sucking eagerly at my erect nipples, teasing me until I was panting for more, running his finger around the edges of my panties, close, but not too close—then, when I thought I couldn't stand it anymore, he grabbed the band and tore them off in one swift movement, so that I was totally naked. Then he reached around and lifted me, his hands hot on my buttocks, and pulled me to him, lowering me onto him. He hesitated for a moment, the head of his cock pushing at the entrance of my now very wet folds; then I pulled him deep inside me, gasping as he withdrew, then plunged again.

"You're incredible," he moaned as he impaled me again and again, making me whimper. "I can't stay away from you." I ran my hands all over his skin, loving the feel of him, breathing in his smoky smell as he thrust deep into me. He thrust a hot tongue into my ear, then trailed down my chest, feeding hungrily at my nipples, sucking and tugging at them as he pumped into me. Just when I couldn't hold on anymore, he thrust deep into me a final time, and I dissolved.

We lay together on the bed a little while later, and I glanced down at my ribs, which had been torn open just twenty minutes earlier. My neck, too, was smooth.

"How did you do that?" I asked.

He bent down and kissed me lightly on the lips. "Magic."

Tom arrived a half hour after Mark left, looking good enough to eat in faded jeans and a black T-shirt. His eyes were wild, though, and he gripped my arms like he wanted to make sure I wasn't going to disappear. "Are you okay?" he asked.

"Fine," I said, not entirely truthfully. It had been a rough couple of days—and the evening hadn't exactly been a fairy tale, either.

"Hugin told me that Xochitl was here. Why didn't you call me?"

"I took care of it," I said, not entirely truthfully.

His eyes drifted lower, and he touched my neck, eyes dilating with surprise. "Your neck. It's healed."

"Yeah," I said. "I guess it is."

"It seems you've had an interesting evening," he said, and I wondered how much Hugin had told him about my activities. I'd closed the curtains and taken a shower, but still . . . I could feel the blood rise to my cheeks and decided to change the subject. "So, how was your Valentine's dinner?"

"It was fine," he said with a sigh. "Unfortunately, however, Lindsey is very interested in becoming a werewolf. She seems to think it's very glamorous."

"I hope you told her no."

"Of course," he said. "And how was yours?"

"My dinner?"

"That's what we were discussing, wasn't it?"

I let out a long breath. "Heath asked me to marry him."

There was a long pause before Tom responded. "And what did you say?"

"I told him I'd think about it," I said. And had proceeded to sleep with my client, come to think of it, which kind of indicated that wedding bells weren't in the offing.

"I see."

We sat there for a few minutes longer, and despite my recent romp with Mark, I found myself increasingly aware of Tom. Heath was an attractive man, and Mark was incredibly sexy. But there was something about Tom that stirred something deep within me. His masculine, animal aroma intensified as we sat across from each other; when I looked up at him, there was a flash of something like longing in his iridescent eyes. Who was he really? I wondered. Was he hundreds of years old, like Wolfgang? Why had he left Norway? Why was he not in a pack? And I was pretty sure there was an old bond between Wolfgang and Tom . . . but would I ever know that history?

And perhaps more important: exactly what was his relationship with my best friend? "I've been meaning to ask," I said. "What's going on with you and Lindsey?"

He leaned back and crossed his arms. "What do you want to know?"

"Are you . . . well, you know. Serious?"

"Lindsey is a woman," he said.

"I'm aware of that."

"She is a beautiful woman. I enjoy spending time with her, and I care for her." He took a deep breath. "But she is not one of us."

"I know," I said, swallowing hard. He was inches away from me; I could feel the warmth of his body. God, I wanted him. But even if he and Lindsey broke up, she would never forgive me if I started dating Tom. And to be honest, I wasn't sure what his feelings toward me were. "What are you going to do?" I asked.

"It depends," he said.

"On what?"

"On lots of things." He grimaced. "I may have to go back to Norway soon."

"Why?"

"On business," he said shortly.

"What's your history with Wolfgang?" I asked suddenly.

"Why do you ask?"

"I just want to know," I said. "I'm curious, I guess."

He seemed to weigh the question for a moment. Then he looked out the window, toward Hugin. "He loved my sister once," he said quietly. "Many years ago."

"What happened?"

"She died," he said shortly.

"Oh, God. I'm so sorry." We stood in silence for a moment—and then something clicked. "Her name was Astrid."

His eyes flashed to me. "How did you know?"

"I saw her portrait. In Houston." I took a deep breath. "She has your eyes."

He was silent for a moment, and I could see the pain in his chiseled face. "She did, yes."

"What happened to her?"

"That is a story for another day," he said, and stood up abruptly. "If everything is fine here, I should let you sleep." He strode toward the door, and I followed him.

"I'm sorry I asked," I said. "I didn't mean to stir up painful memories."

He turned and touched my chin with his finger. I caught my breath.

"I'll tell you the story someday," he said. His finger

traced my jawline. "I am sorry about what happened in Roundtop. I meant to protect you, not to harm you."

"It's okay," I murmured, feeling the room swirl around me. I was close enough to see the flecks of green in his golden eyes; and before I could help myself, I reached up to push a strand of hair off his forehead.

"No," he said. "It's not okay at all. I put you in harm's way."

"It wasn't your fault."

He stared down at me, black pupils huge in those iridescent eyes. For a moment I thought he was going to say something; but instead, he leaned down and kissed me with such hunger I thought my legs would give way.

The room receded around me, until there was nothing but Tom and me. I pulled back for a moment to study his face, as if I could brand it on my brain; the tilt of his wide cheekbones, the fullness of his lower lip, the chin, sharp like a knife—but he pulled me to him again, as if he were devouring me.

His hands traveled down my throat to my robe, tugging at it, and then his hands were on my breasts, and all I could think was *yes, yes, yes.* My hands moved down his muscular back, fitting into the hollow. I felt a low growl in my throat as his mouth traveled down between my breasts and felt an answering growl from deep inside him—a growl that made me want him even more. Then his lips grazed my nipple, and I gasped.

Lindsey.

I pulled away. "We can't," I said, my voice thick with desire.

He sucked in his breath.

"Lindsey," I explained.

He closed his eyes. "I know. I have to end it."

"She'll never forgive me," I said.

He pulled me to him again. "What do we do?"

I didn't know what to say. His breath was warm on

my hair, and just the smell of him had my body yammering to forget about everyone and everything but Tom, and how right it felt just being with him. *And what about Mark?* my mind whispered.

"I don't know," I said, thinking of Lindsey and Heath and Mark and everything that had happened the last few days. "I wish I knew. But I don't."

Tom sighed; then he leaned down and kissed me one last time, lingeringly, sending tendrils of desire surging through me. He cradled my face in his hands, his eyes dark with longing. "Happy Valentine's Day," he murmured, and released me. Then, with a last golden look that almost sent me to my knees, he opened the front door and let himself out.

Hugin cawed quietly from the balcony as I slid the door open and slipped into the February night. A cold breeze ruffled Hugin's feathers as Tom stepped out onto the street; after a few steps, he glanced back up at me and nodded. I waved, watching as he shoved his hands in his pockets and walked down the street, his stride the slow, sure gait of a born predator. The white light of the waning moon gleamed in his blond hair; he looked ageless for a moment, like something out of a fairy tale. My heart called to him, and part of me wished he would turn around and come back to my building, and that we could forget about everything but us.

But instead he kept on walking. And a moment later, he turned the corner and was gone.

Acknowledgments

Thank yous, as always, go first to my family—Eric, Abby, and Ian—for all their love and support; also to Dave and Carol Swartz and Ed and Dorothy MacInerney—I'm very blessed to have such wonderful parents so close! Thanks too to Bethann, Beau, Mara, and Sam Eccles, my adopted family; my wonderful nieces and nephews on both sides; to my sister, Lisa, and her family; to my fabulous grandmother, Marian Quinton (and Nora Bestwick); to Merrie MacInerney, whose humor is always welcome in my inbox; and to Hal and Jane Quinton.

Many thanks to Jessica Faust, who is there for me at every plot turn, and to Kate Collins and Signe Pike at Ballantine for all their work bringing Sophie's second book to life. And to Thea Eaton, for helping with my online presence.

Finally, a big thank you to all those supportive friends out there—particularly Dana Lehman, Lindsey Schram, Susan Wittig Albert, Michele Scott, Debbie Pacitti, Leslie Suez, Njambi Wanguhu, Martha Winters, Mary Flanagan, Melanie Williams, Jo Virgil, and all my friends at the Westbank Library and my local coffee shop and bookstore. Thanks also to Austin Mystery Writers: Mark Bentsen, Janet Christian, Dave Ciambrone, Judy Egner, Mary Jo Powell, Manfred Reimann, and Kimberly

Sandman—and, of course, to my friends and fabulous fellow authors at the Cozy Chicks (www.cozychicks.com). And to all of the folks who have taken the time to e-mail me about the books, thank you so very much. Your kind words always brighten my day, and keep me going at the keyboard.

If you enjoyed *On the Prowl*
get ready to sink your fangs into this excerpt
from Karen MacInerney's next book

LEADER OF THE PACK

featuring the hilariously lovable werewolf
Sophie Garou.

Most of the time, I'm not too crazy about being a werewolf. For so many reasons: the compulsory and inconvenient transformations, the excessive reliance on Lady Bic razors, not to mention the difficulty explaining to potential mates that our children would probably grow a natural fur coat and tail every twenty-eight days or so. Maintaining a normal relationship—much less a career—is a hairy proposition when you tend to sprout fangs every time someone pops *Moonstruck* into the DVD player.

But there are compensations. The lightning-fast reflexes, for example. The ability to scare the pants off of would-be muggers and rapists. The deep, almost carnal enjoyment of a rare prime rib at Ruth's Chris. And, as is currently the case, the ability to smell every nuance of a gorgeous spring day.

It was a warm mid-March afternoon in Central Texas, and I was on my way back to Austin from a meeting with my favorite client in San Antonio. The radio was on, and windows in my M3 were wide open, letting in the mingled scents of fresh earth, new grass, cows—and a complete and total absence of werewolves, which was fine by me. The cows, however, were making me hungry. Lunch had been a long time ago, I realized as I gulped back a mouthful of saliva and reached for my tumbler of wolfsbane tea.

I was mentally reviewing the more intimate details of my meeting with Mark Sydney, CEO of Southeast Airlines. He was my client, to be sure—and landing the Southeast Airlines account had recently netted me partnership—but most of the afternoon had been spent at a romantic River Walk restaurant staring over a giant margarita at my client's deep blue eyes. I was reviewing our good-bye kiss when my cell phone rang.

I flipped it open as the M3 rolled past another tasty-smelling herd of cows. "Sophie Garou."

"So, how did your 'meeting' go?" It was my best friend, Lindsey.

"Fine," I said. "Everything's great."

"Are you dating yet?"

"Not officially. We're kind of keeping things quiet; I'd rather Adele didn't know." I didn't want to know what my boss thought of my mixing business with pleasure. And boy, was it a pleasure.

"Mark's a good match for you. I liked Heath, but he just didn't have the same . . . I don't know. Zing?"

Lindsey was right about Mark—he was all about zing—but my heart still wrenched a little at the mention of my ex-boyfriend. Heath had asked me to marry him on Valentine's Day, just over a month ago, and I'd had to decline. Partly because I wasn't sure how he'd take the whole "I'm a werewolf" announcement, of course. And partly because I suspected he was sleeping with his gorgeous associate Miranda. But even without those rather significant mitigating factors, things just hadn't been right between us for a long time. It was a hard decision, but I was pretty sure it was the right one.

"For the record, Mark and I are not dating," I repeated. Even if we had enjoyed a few—okay, more than a few—steamy episodes together. "He's my client," I reminded her. But Mark was also something else, something even stranger than I was. About a month ago, when I'd gotten into trouble with a pack of deranged Mexican werewolves, he'd appeared out of nowhere wearing wings and what looked like a full-body coat of liquid napalm. Which was convenient—as was the fact that he knew I was a werewolf—but enough to give me pause when I thought of becoming involved with him long-term. It was bad enough that my children would have intermittent episodes involving a full coat of fur and a tail. A full coat of fur doused in napalm would be a bit much. Particularly if it occurred while I was giving birth.

Still, I had to admit Mark was absolutely fabulous in bed. I squeezed my legs together just thinking about our last episode, which had taken place between acts at the Zachary Scott Theater.

"Is he up for this weekend?" Lindsey asked.

"What?" I asked, pulling my mind up out of the gutter. Or, in this case, the coat room at Zach Scott.

"The Howl. Aren't you going?"

I'd blocked it out of my mind so thoroughly I'd almost forgotten about the upcoming inter-pack meeting, which was scheduled to start Friday in Fredericksburg, an hour or two west of Austin. Since I wasn't affiliated with any pack, I didn't feel too inclined to attend, even though Wolfgang, the leader of the Houston pack, had asked me to poke my nose in. To which I'd said a polite no-thank-you. As far as I was concerned, the less I had to do with the werewolf world, the better. "God, no," I said to Lindsey.

"Since you're not officially *dating*, why don't you go and leave Mark behind? You might meet a cute single werewolf."

Like Tom? I thought before I could stifle it. Tom was perhaps the most intoxicatingly handsome werewolf I had ever met. Granted, I hadn't met a whole lot of were-wolves over the last twenty-eight years—I'd been "under cover" for most of that time—but I'd seen enough to know that Tom was something pretty special. He had long blond hair, chiseled Nordic features, shimmery gold werewolf eyes, and a tanned body I just couldn't stop staring at. And then there was his smell, which was enough to reduce me to a quivering puddle of lust.

But Tom was dating Lindsey, which meant he was strictly off-limits—even if we had, in a weak moment, acknowledged a rather powerful mutual attraction. Still, his unavailability wasn't necessarily such a bad thing; if my father was any indication of werewolf quality on the mating front, a werewolf was the last thing I needed on my dating resume.

Twenty-nine years ago, my mother had had the bad fortune to fall—quite literally, since she tripped stepping off a *bateau-mouche*—for a werewolf in Paris. According to my mom, it was Romeo and Juliet all over again, only with gypsies and werewolves instead of Capulets and Montagues. Despite extreme family disapproval, my mother and her lover continued to see each other in secret—at least until I came around.

Romance or no romance, the arrival of a bouncing baby werewolf was too much for Luc Garou: so he sent my mother and me out of the country. My mother still claimed it was "for our protection"—the story had always been that the pack would kill us both if they found us there—but since we hadn't seen hide nor hair of him for almost twenty-eight years, I suspected my wellbeing wasn't my father's primary motive in shipping us overseas. I still carried his surname, Garou, but that was all that I had to do with him. Other than the whole were-wolf thing, of course.

"No, I think I'll just kick back this weekend. Maybe

use my Lake Austin Spa Resort gift certificate. It's been a busy couple of weeks; I could use some R&R."

"Do you think I could talk Tom into letting me go to the Howl?" Lindsey asked.

I closed my eyes for a second. Then I remembered I was driving and jerked them back open, swerving a split second before the BMW slammed into the trunk of an Intrepid. "No."

"Why not?"

"It's a bad idea." In fact, Lindsey having anything to do with Tom at all was a bad idea, but I'd given up trying to convince her of that.

She hmmphed, and said something else besides, but I missed it because my phone started beeping.

"I've got to go," I said. "My phone's dying."

"Come see me when you get back to the office," she said. Since she worked right down the hall from me at Withers and Young, it wouldn't be much of an effort.

"I will," I promised, and hung up a moment later. Lindsey's fascination with werewolves—werewolves in general, not just Tom Fenris—was worrisome. Ever since she'd discovered my lupine identity last month, she'd been badgering me to "share my magic" with her. Personally, I didn't understand why anyone in their right mind would want the burden of compulsory transformations, excessive hair growth, and a need to drink gallons of wolfsbane tea, which was anything but a taste sensation. True, there were some benefits—a few extra centuries of life, for example—but in my opinion, the cons definitely outweighed the pros. Lindsey kept hounding me, though, and it wouldn't shock me if she showed up with a hypodermic needle and attempted to do an impromptu blood transfusion in the coffee nook one morning.

I was considering calling Tom to ask him to dissuade

her when the phone rang again. The battery light flashed as I picked it up: it was my mother.

"Sophie, darling, I have some big news." She sounded breathless.

"You finished getting your tax paperwork together?" As a CPA, and auditor, I did the taxes for Sit A Spell, my mom's magic shop, every year. It wasn't my favorite job—my mother is not the most organized witch on the planet—but I soldiered through it anyway, because I loved her.

"Oh, nothing like that," she said. Then she said something else, but I lost it because of the beep.

"What?" I asked.

". . . coming to see you. It's amazing."

"What's amazing?"

"Your . . ." Her bright voice trailed off.

"What?"

The phone was dead.

I folded up the phone and whatever it was would have to wait until I could call her from the office. Or till I swung by tonight for another package of wolfsbane tea. Thanks to my thrice-daily infusions, I'd managed to minimize the compulsory transformations to full moons that fell near solstices and equinoxes, which came only four times a year. But the spring equinox was coming up, which meant it was time to up the dosage and to plan my quarterly trip out of town.

I set cruise control, played with the radio until I found a Red Hot Chili Peppers song, and took another deep breath of spring air, enjoying that rare feeling that all was right in the world, even if the pollen did make my nose run.

Of course, if I'd had any idea what was waiting for me at my office, I would have turned around and driven straight to Mexico.

*   *   *

"There's someone to see you," my assistant Sally said as I walked past her desk. In lieu of her traditional spandex, she was dressed in a flattering blue suit that actually covered her midriff all the way around. Sometime in the last few weeks, her wardrobe had undergone a major change. I wasn't sure why, but I liked it. She was even wearing fewer layers of eyeliner.

"Who is it?"

"He told me it was a surprise . . . said he's an old friend."

"No business card?"

She shook her head, and I sighed. She might look more professional from a sartorial standpoint, but she was still less than ideal as an assistant.

I straightened my jacket and headed for my office, wondering what "old friend" had turned up. I took a deep breath as my hand touched the knob and froze.

"Something wrong?" Sally asked.

Yes, something was wrong. Very wrong. Unless my nose was deceiving me, Sally had let a werewolf into my office. But I wasn't about to tell Sally that.

"Next time somebody comes to visit me," I said, "would you please have them wait outside my office?"

She shrugged, and I resisted the impulse to snarl at her. Instead, I turned and opened the office door.

He was sitting at my desk.

Adrenaline pumped through me as I closed the door firmly behind me. The mystery werewolf stood up and smiled at me, exposing a line of pointy teeth. He was tall—well over six feet—with red hair and the golden shimmery eyes of a born werewolf.

"Who are you?" I asked. "And what are you doing in my office?"

"Sophie," he said in a strange accent. "You're beautiful."

I backed toward the door as he rounded the desk in

one fluid move. His smell was strong, overpowering, almost, even under the heavy cologne, and somehow, familiar.

"Who are you?" I repeated.

"Don't you know me?"

"I have never laid eyes on you in my life."

"Oh, but you have," he said, moving closer. "How about a hug?"

"I think you must be deranged," I said, pressing myself against the wall. Adrenaline pulsed through me, and it was a struggle to keep from transforming. "I don't know who you are, but I want you out of my office." When he continued to stand there looking at me, I clarified my position. "Out. Now. Before I have to call security."

He paused, arms extended, and looked a little bit hurt. He was a handsome man, probably in his late thirties, with a smile that was charming, even with the pointy teeth. "As if security could do a thing to stop me." He had a point, but I wasn't about to concede it. He didn't give me a chance, anyway. "You really don't know me, do you?" he asked.

"Nope." I shook my head. "Now please leave."

"But Sophie," he said, hands extended. "I'm your father."